JAKE

In the Company of Snipers

Book 16

IRISH WINTERS

COPYRIGHT

Jake; In the Company of Snipers, 16

Cover design and author photo: Kelli Ann Morgan, Inspire Creative Services

Interior book design: Bob Houston, eBook Formatting

Editor: Linda Clarkson, Black Opal Editing and Proofreading

ISBN Paperback: 978-1-942895-51-0
ISBN eBook: 978-1-942895-52-7
Library of Congress Control Number: 2017953890

Irish Winter's websites: http://www.irishwinters.com
and irishwinters.blogspot.com

In the Company of Snipers

You can find Irish Winters on Facebook:
https://www.facebook.com/author.irishwinters

On Twitter: https://twitter.com/irishwinters1

For news on upcoming releases, sign up for Irish Winters' Newsletter at IrishWinters.com.

For more information about all my books, visit IrishWinters.com.

IN THE COMPANY OF SNIPERS

This series revolves around ex-Marine scout sniper, Alex Stewart, and his covert surveillance company, The TEAM, home-based out of Alexandria, Virginia. An obsessive patriot and workaholic, he created the company to give ex-military snipers like him a chance at returning to civilian life with a decent job.

This is not a serial with each book ending at a cliffhanger. I wouldn't do that to you. *In the Company of Snipers* is a collection of passionate love stories involving women and men who are tough enough to take on the world alone. Each is a stand-alone read, where in the course of an active TEAM operation, one agent comes face to face with his or her demons. The men and women I write about are all patriots and warriors, dealing with what they've lived through or the mistakes they've made

Spoiler alert: Every novel contains adult scenes including sexual situations (some explicit), language, and violence. I don't write sweet romance, so be forewarned.

At the end of each story, it's my hope that you, along with my heroes, will come to realize...

Love changes everything.

Dear Readers,

Every once in a while, a character comes along who begs for the chance to tell his story. Jake is that character. Since he first appeared in Zack's story, book #3, Jake has haunted me in all the best ways. I couldn't just leave him singing his heart out in the shower at Zack's place, could I?

This isn't your regular TEAM fare, and Jake isn't one of Alex Stewart's finest, not by a long shot. He's broken and skittish. He's smelly and grubby. When you first meet him on the streets of Anacostia, he's the kind of bum most people would avoid.

But don't. Not this time. Take a chance on Jake. Let him tell his story.

Thank you for being the best fans ever.

Irish Winters

Prologue

Three Years Earlier

"For gawd sakes! Can't you walk no faster?"

Jake Weylin silently accepted the whining rant of his good buddy, Jamaal McCune, and picked up the pace. Both ex-Marines and down on their luck, Jamaal made the difficult street life he'd chosen worse by drinking his troubles away. This afternoon's rant evolved from his hangover from the night before. It hadn't lessened with the stubborn guy's application of more alcohol. By ten he was long past inebriated. By noon he should've been flat on his back and snoring like the banshees of Jake's ancestral homeland.

No such luck.

At two in the afternoon, Jamaal was falling-down-sloppy-drunk and crying because he missed his mama. When the big guy decided to put one away, there was no keeping up with him. Jake didn't blame him. He'd drowned his sorrows almost as often as Jamaal did his, but the bigger problem at the moment was the two-inch gash on Jamaal's right butt cheek, proving once again that even the smallest flask of cheap red-eye didn't belong in a man's back pocket. Why Jamaal had a mini-bottle stashed there was another story not worth telling.

"The place'll be closed by the time we git there if'n we don't hurry," he grumbled while shuffling along, one big palm holding the wad of blue paper towels from the service station at the last corner to his bleeding backside. The Good Samaritan Free Clinic on Good Hope Road was five blocks away from their basement hangout in what used to be an IGA store.

With only two blocks to go, Jake knew every step of them would be painful. "The clinic never closes," he offered meekly.

He didn't fight or argue anymore. There was no sense in it. The wars in the Mideast had taken the last of his aggression and most of his self-confidence. He didn't look people in the eye anymore, and the only reason he'd come to Anacostia was to find Jamaal. He'd never intended to stay, only to look up his buddy, talk about the could-have-beens, the what-ifs, and the whatcha-gonna-do-nows. Maybe see if Jamaal had a spare room to offer a buddy for a night or two.

Everything changed the day Jamaal opened his front door, blubbering his eyes out. He'd been evicted. Jake almost hadn't recognized the once proud black man he'd deployed with. Jamaal had sunk into serious depression after his mother passed away, but numbing his pain with booze didn't pay the bills.

They'd been on the streets ever since because the bond between brothers-in-arms ran strong. It all came down to the fact that Jamaal refused to leave his childhood neighborhood and Jake refused to leave Jamaal. It was an odd pairing at best: two bedraggled has-beens who'd once belonged in the company of 'the few and the proud'. But there they were, one average-sized white guy and one bigger-than-life black guy, hanging out together in one of America's toughest neighborhoods and drowning their sorrows every chance they got.

At first, Jake stood out like a sore thumb on the mostly African American side of the Anacostia River, directly south of the nation's Oh-Say-Can-You-See capitol. But Jamaal set the local gangbangers and riffraff straight when he'd told them Jake was a trained USMC scout sniper who'd gone crazy during a firefight in Kabul, Afghanistan. He'd bragged that Jake could shoot a man's head off at two thousand yards, that he'd killed four men with his bare hands in a sneak attack. That he was stark-raving crazy and could snap at any moment. *Best watch your backs and be careful.*

At least Jamaal got one thing right. Maybe not the stark-raving part, but Jake was pretty sure he was leaning on the down side of crazy. Wasn't everybody who'd been in the sandbox?

Jamaal jerked to a stop and pointed his index finger on the hand not holding his big butt, at a gray Subaru parked alongside the clinic. "Who dat?"

Jake cringed. After a binge, Jamaal's grasp of the English language deteriorated along with his good sense. But who indeed was that slender woman standing at the open door of the parked Subaru, clutching the car's doorframe like a shield to ward him off? Or maybe she was afraid of Jamaal.

The chilly December breeze shifting through the alley alongside the clinic pulled a loose strand of her hair out from the big black clip on the top of her head. He saw the problem clearly. The clip was too small for the bounteous mounds of brownish, reddish, goldish curls she'd tried to restrain. *Good glory in the morning!* She was a sight to behold. His heart damned near forgot to beat.

She seemed frozen in place, so he stopped dead in his tracks, too. The stupid thing in his chest did a funny kind of sucker punch, shutting off his windpipe and wiping his mental whiteboard clear of intelligent words like *'hello'* or *'good evening'* or *'hey there'*.

Instead "huh" was what fell off his lips. Jake swallowed hard, certain that he was making a fool of himself. Like that was news.

She'd parked in one of the parking stalls marked Employees Only. Did that mean she worked at the clinic? He hadn't seen her here before, and with all the trouble Jamaal got into, he was here plenty. Was she new? Just visiting? A man could hope.

Another puff of the breeze set the rest of her hair loose to billowing like a cloud behind her head. A halo shimmered around her delicate face at the same time her right brow spiked like the devil. Capturing her unruly locks with a quick handful at the back of her neck, her nostrils flared. Her shoulders squared and her chin stuck out with defiance. Was she making a stand? *Against me?* It sure felt like it. *Damn. What a sight.*

Just who was she, another mean volunteer nurse at the clinic or some fiery warrior goddess from Valhalla? The sun at her back added to the illusion of fierce, feminine power, the kind that could back a man up as fast as if she'd stuck an M40, bolt-action, USMC scout sniper special up his nose.

Without thinking, Jake took a step away, yielding the alley to this alpha female. She could have the street if she wanted it, too. He didn't. Then he took another step back in case she didn't believe his first gesture.

"Hell, Jake, I'm gonna bleed to death if we keep walking backwards like we is," Jamaal complained, shifting his weight from one big flat foot to the other.

"Shut it," Jake whispered, his hand on his buddy's thick bicep to prevent any further altercation. "You ain't going to bleed out. It's just a scratch."

This Amazon warrior already had Jake by the balls, and she hadn't so much as said hello yet. *Or go to hell and get out of my way, but hey. A guy could dream about that too. Right now he'd take a slap in the face if she offered it to him.* "'Sides, you got plenty of blood. Let her get inside the clinic first where she'll feel safe." *Nice and easy. Don't scare her. I'm liking the view...*

Jamaal huffed and grumbled but held his position.

The woman pulled a backpack out of the squat vehicle and shut the door without taking her eyes off them. Then, very deliberately, she tossed her head and came straight to them—like a torpedo. Jake stopped breathing for sure then, like he had a choice. The closer she came, the more certain he was that he might pass out. Hunter green eyes scrolled over him like he was actually visible to the naked eye, making him acutely aware that he needed a shave and a trim. A month ago.

He smelled like every other guy who lived in abandoned buildings. Bad. Real bad. Nonetheless, his spine straightened, and he didn't break eye contact with his target. Dread itched up the back of his neck, warning him. *Exactly who's the target, you or her?*

"Who are you?" she asked, looking at him as she broke the spell. "And what do you need?"

His gaze fell to where that simple question had come from. Had sincere concern just passed through those delectable, kissable lips that looked good enough to eat like the red roses on wedding cakes? The closer she came, the more breathtaking she looked.

It wasn't merely hair on her head; it was some kind of exotic silk that refused to be ignored or controlled. Strands of it caressed the pink blush on her high cheekbone, twisting under her chin like tendrils of some loving red vine until she captured it and made it behave. The longest, darkest eyelashes fringed pretty green eyes, but it wasn't welcome he saw glowing there. More like, *'Who the hell are you and what do you want?'*

He expelled the breath he hadn't realized he'd been holding. "Ah... ah... Sergeant Jake Weylin, ma'am," his dumb mouth declared to diffuse the situation.

Jamaal grunted and groaned. He was such a baby when he got hurt.

"You're ex-Marines," she guessed correctly, stuffing her hair back into its clip, her sharp eyes cast to the street behind them. "Do you guys live around here?"

Jake nodded, not sure where she was going with that question. Would a woman like her ever deign to pay a guy like him a visit?

Of all things, the tragic love song from *West Side Story* showed up in his head with joyous exclamations of, *'Maria! Maria! Maria!'* That tender refrain couldn't compete with the boisterous USMC men's choir belting out a raucous, *'We are proud to claim the title of United States Marine!'* that showed up next.

His brain worked like that, forever lost in timeless ballads he couldn't forget. That was the problem with a lot of guys who came back from the sandbox. They couldn't remember, yet they couldn't forget… stuff.

"We, umm, live over there," he said, motioning vaguely toward the east behind him, where the broken down IGA grocery store stood like a skeleton in a graveyard of broken neighborhoods.

"Well, why are you waiting out here?" she asked bluntly. "Get inside. The last I heard Dr. Anderson doesn't perform surgery in the alley."

He would've snapped to at her brusque order, but a shadowy current of—something—shimmered between them. The woman gulped one very noisy gulp, giving herself away. Oh. Now he got it. All that bluff and bluster was more worry than challenge. *She's scared of me?* That didn't make sense. A has-been wasn't anybody to think twice about, much less fear.

"My buddy here's Jamaal McCune," Jake offered quietly, making tentative eye contact so he didn't come across as threatening. Small talk had always worked in delicate situations before. "He sat on some broken glass, and he might need stitches in his, umm, on his..."

The woman peered around Jamaal's considerable rear end, her fingers nervously working at the straps of the backpack she'd kept between her and Jake. Back and forth. Back and forth. Yeah, he'd called it right. She was scared, probably because she'd been outnumbered by two halfwits.

Jake tried once more. "You're new here."

Her brows went up, but she extended a hand. "Yes, I'm the new CNA. Lacy Wright."

Lacy, huh? That's a pretty name. I like it.

"What's a… C-NNNNN-A?" Jamaal slurred.

"It's a Certified Nursing Assistant," Lacy explained, the edge to her voice replaced with the pleasing lilt of professional patience. She almost looked friendly and it was obvious she'd worked with idiots before. *What a difference a couple of minutes makes, huh?*

Jake wiped his hand on his dirty jeans, ashamed that was the best he had to offer a lady. "Nice to make your acquaintance, Miss Wright," he said very politely as he extended his hand, so damned thankful he wasn't drunk. Come to think of it, he hadn't had a drink for more than a week. That ought to count for something.

Her fingers felt small and breakable, a china doll's hand caught in the callused confines of his. Her handshake was seriously firm and determined, though. She might be scared of him, but she meant to be taken seriously.

I can do that.

Loosening her grip, she nodded toward the clinic's rear entrance and the flashing red sign that clearly said: EXIT when it should've said: EMERGENCY ENTRANCE, or something profound like that. "Let's get your buddy inside where Dr. Anderson can treat him, shall we?"

We shall. Jake let go of her, instantly aware of how cold the wintery afternoon had grown. How lonely. His index finger rubbed the pad of his thumb, missing the satiny feel of her skin. The warmth.

But a man like him couldn't resist the smile that tugged at the corner of his mouth. It had finally happened. A beautiful woman smiled. *At me.*

Chapter One

"Lacy!" Dr. Marlee Presley's authoritative voice rang out stronger and louder than usual. "Exam Room One. Now!"

"On my way," Lacy Wright answered from the opposite end of the hall where she'd been restocking the latest shipment of latex gloves. What the free clinic really needed was a few boxes of smalls and mediums, not the large and extra-large sizes do-gooders seemed to donate. Still, beggars couldn't be choosers. Shoving the half-empty box under the bottom shelf, she scrambled up off her knees to do the physician-on-staff's bidding.

"Gloves," Dr. Presley ordered, not bothering to look up from her blood-spattered patient. "Take hold of his right bicep. I'm not seeing a knife wound, but I need you to logroll him just enough for me to get a backboard under him."

Lacy gulped. This was Jamaal, one of the two USMC veterans living on the streets of gritty Anacostia, the southwest section of Washington D.C. Judging by his face and hands, he'd lost a fight. A bad one. Blood dripped from an open gash over his left eyebrow and from both sets of knuckles. Good. He'd fought back. Air wheezed between his swollen, split lips. Not good. Broken ribs meant a possible punctured lung. Maybe worse. Marlee was obviously worried about a possible spinal injury.

Obediently, Lacy pushed her fingers into latex protection before she clasped the unconscious man's upper arm, easing his chest toward her. All Marlee needed was inches, but moving dead weight required a firmer grip. Lacy counterbalanced his slack muscles by gripping his hipbone. He felt hot to the touch.

"Take it easy, Jamaal. I've got you, buddy," she soothed, just in case he could hear her at some deep dark level.

Jamaal McCune was a regular visitor to the Good Samaritan Free Clinic on Good Hope Road, Anacostia. He wasn't a bad guy, but his big mouth got him into plenty of trouble. It was worse when he talked someone dumber than he was into buying a bottle of hooch for him. The crazy muscle-bound jarhead. What'd he think? That people would take his crap just because he'd served?

Lacy knew better. She'd served too and was damned proud of it, but most folks didn't care, and they sure didn't want to hear about God, flag, and country from some belligerent lowlife on the street. Civilians were like that. The war didn't touch them, so the warriors were just another set of welfare applicants as far as most of them were concerned. The whole mindset of the average American was so wrong, but especially when it came to remembering who'd served.

Scarred and bedraggled, Jamaal was a lot worse than the first time she'd seen him. That was three years earlier, the day she'd run away and off the grid. After all, who'd think to look for the fair-skinned, strawberry-blond daughter of East Coast royalty at a free-clinic in down and out Anacostia? Apparently, no one.

It might have been a drastic decision, but a Marine did what needed to be done to survive. Besides, she'd had no choice, and all that helpless-little-white-girl persona was bullshit. She had a license to carry, and she damned well knew how to use the nine-millimeter hardware in her backpack.

Rowdy Stokes found that out the hard way. A local tavern owner, he'd no more than put his hand on her knee when she'd had the business end of her weapon pointed nice and low, right at the bottom end of his zipper. Rowdy wasn't bad. He just thought he'd seen an opportunity and took it. Well, he'd thought wrong.

One look down at his family jewels and all he'd stood to lose, and he had moved his hand into a smirky salute and a quick, "Yes, ma'am." They'd gotten along fine since, and oddly enough, he was one of her silent protectors. Like Jamaal and his buddy Jake. Speaking of which, *where the hell is Jake?*

The man was a mystery and as noticeable a standout as she was in ninety-nine percent African American Anacostia. He and Jamaal made quite the odd couple: one white guy and one black; one ripped enough to look like he worked out, the other not so much. According to Marlee, Jamaal's clinic visits had noticeably dropped since Jake came to town.

When Jamaal did come in, it was for stitches or maybe a fever, and he didn't come alone anymore. Jake brought him these days. And flu shots. Who would've thought two bums would show up for something as ordinary as flu shots in the fall? But they did. Every October. As regular as clockwork. Judging by the belly on the guy, Jamaal was eating better, too. That also had to be due to Jake. Jamaal certainly wouldn't think about it. He was too busy planning on his next bottle.

Street life was tough. The scruffy beard covering Jamal's plump lower face also covered scars, blemishes, and boils. His breath smelled of tooth decay, maybe something else. She wasn't a doctor, but Lacy knew enough about smells. The sickly scent of infection mingled with alcohol wafted up from his wide-open mouth to her nostrils. Strep maybe?

Where's Jake? He should be standing with his buddy, shifting in his boots like he had somewhere else to be. That was Jake for you, uncomfortable in close spaces and around people.

Marlee positioned the board quickly. "Let him down," she said brusquely as she peeled out of her gloves and grabbed another pair. Her pinkie finger bled even as she rolled the fresh pair on. "I should've known better, damn it. The big oaf had a broken bottle in his back pocket again. When's he going to learn to set his booze aside before he brawls? Sliced me a good one when I transferred him from the cab to the gurney. Where is his twin? I thought he and Jake were joined at the hip?"

They are. That raised Lacy's brows. "Who brought him in then?"

"Believe it or not, a cabbie. That doesn't happen very often, does it?" Marlee's spiked eyebrow belied her shock. Good Samaritans were few and far between on these rough streets.

"Jamaal has got to learn to stay away from the bottle," Lacy said to no one in particular, her mind on Jake. Had he been in the same fight as Jamaal? Was he too hurt to take care of his friend? That would be like him, defend Jamaal even if it cost him dearly.

Marlee was already inserting a trach tube down Jamaal's windpipe, intubating him to help him breathe easier while Lacy cut his shirt and pants away, instantly revealing the rest of the story. He'd been beaten all right. A mass of black and purple bruises started at the top of his breastbone and covered his ribcage all the way to his right side. She let the dirty clothes drop to the floor. The clinic kept a supply of new sweatshirts and pants for just this kind of occasion. There'd better be a triple X pair in that closet, maybe some men's underwear. Socks and new boots would be nice, too.

"I don't like what I'm seeing," Marlee murmured, peering down his semi-illuminated windpipe with her scope. "This man's a walking contagion. Hand me a swab. Let's see what we come up with."

Lacy reached for the requested sterile cotton swab, unwrapping it from its plastic wrap before she handed it over. Grimacing, Marlee stuck the swab into the back of Jamaal's throat, collected the sample and returned it to Lacy, who swabbed the culture plate, sealed and labeled it.

"This man can't wait for the results. I'm starting him on a strong antibiotic now. Do we know if he has any allergies?"

Lacy scanned the chart resting on the counter. Jamaal McCune. Six feet, four inches. Two hundred and eighty-one pounds. Blood Pressure. Temp. Wow. One hundred and three? No wonder he felt warm. No allergies were listed.

"He's good," she answered. "Let him have it."

"Look at that bruising," Marlee said quietly, her angst under control now that her patient was breathing easier. She administered one hypo into Jamaal's thick bicep, covering the tiny puncture hole with a plastic Mickey Mouse bandage. He'd like that when he came to. Her skilled fingers proceeded over his throat and along his neck and collarbone, then down over his ribs and abdomen as she diagnosed and discovered. "It almost looks like a car hit him."

"No, ma'am," Lacy replied while she fastened the straps, immobilizing his legs, waist, and shoulders to the backboard. He might not like it when he woke up, but it would save his life if he'd suffered neck or spinal damage. "Look at his hands. Jamaal's been in a fistfight. Looks like he gave as good as he got, too." *Way to go, buddy.*

Another spiked brow. "What did I tell you about all that *'ma'am'* crap, *Miss Wright*?"

"Sorry. Force of habit."

"Well, stop it, Lacy. I'm no better than you are. Besides, it makes me feel old." Marlee pressed three fingers into his side. "His spleen is swollen. I'll suture first, but prep him for an x-ray. When Hershel comes in, I want an MRI to check brain and abdominal."

"You're thinking head injury?"

"Anything's possible, but yes. He's got a hematoma the size of a grapefruit back here. I want to check for bleeding in his brain," Marlee said, her fingers gently skimming her patient's hard head. "What's wrong with these guys? Do they think they have to fight the world?"

"Yes," Lacy answered quickly. "They do. They're Marines."

"No, they're not," Marlee said gently. "They're veterans, Lacy. Their war is over. They need to let it go and get on with their lives."

Lacy bit her lip. Civilians didn't understand. She knew from personal experience that every guy and gal who'd survived twenty-four-seven combat still thought they were fighting the world. The war didn't end just because a guy came home. Jake and Jamaal would never again fit into mainstream America, not if they tried for a million years. She hadn't, at least not until she'd left her parent's home, got her CNA certificate, and joined the clinic. Of all the hideouts in the world, it was another kind of warzone that had finally given her a sense of security, as well as purpose. Yes, she might just be as crazy as some people thought she was. Once a Marine always a Marine. But what she did mattered.

"Take it easy, Lacy," Marlee said softly. "I know these guys are your buddies, but you also know they're on self-destruct, don't you? Make no mistake about it, at the rate they're going, it's a matter of *when* they show up dead on our doorstep, not *if*."

Lacy nodded. She disagreed with Marlee's opinion of Jake. Of the two vagrants, he seemed the most stable, but one of these days, she knew she wouldn't be calling the ambulance to run Jamaal across the bridge for treatment or emergency surgery at the nearest hospital. She'd be calling the police. And they'd be calling the District's Medical Examiner.

"Set up a surgical tray for me?" Marlee asked, her voice softened with understanding. "Let's get him cleaned up and stitched while we're waiting for Hershel. We can do an EKG while we wait, too."

"Yes. Okay," Lacy answered, holding back the perfunctory salutation of respect. At least Marlee was the physician on duty instead of dickhead, Dr. Anderson. He handled the free clinic patients like they were vermin instead of people down on their luck. His nose tended to flare when he was forced to touch the mostly impoverished clientele, more so if they were bleeding or vomiting. Even the babies. *The jerk.*

Too many times, Lacy had watched his brusque detachment send a frightened sick child into screaming fits. Kids were smart—like dogs. They instinctively knew when someone didn't like them, or didn't care to touch them. Karma needed to pay Anderson a visit, big time. She only wished she'd be there to see the day his snooty butt got its comeuppance.

With Jamaal out cold like he was, it was easy for Marlee to stitch him up, run an EKG, and take x-rays. Lacy assisted every step of the way, thankful when the x-ray panels showed nothing broken. Hershel only worked part-time, but when he finally showed, the MRI prognosis was as good as the EKG. Jamaal's skull was fine, or at least as fine as a Marine's hard head could be. No bleeding in the cranial cavity. Not clots or hydrocephaly either.

Marlee was right in saying that these two guys were Lacy's buddies. She'd never served with them, but she'd recognized exactly who they were the very first day on staff. Jake had dragged Jamaal in for stitches. That time, he'd sliced his backside on another broken bottle in his rear pocket, and he was roaring drunk, but she'd recognize that cocky Devil Dog swagger anywhere. Even down on their luck, Jake and Jamaal were Marines. Who could've missed the super polite posture and promptly provided answers from Jake? Somewhere beneath all that scruff and shaggy hair, an honorable jarhead still served.

Of the two, Jake was probably better off because he still had friends who kept track of him. She'd seen him with another big guy in a Porsche, but Jamaal didn't seem to have anyone but Jake. Lacy shuddered to think what could happen to a man stuck in the downward spiral Jamaal seemed to be on. He needed a break. *Don't we all?*

"He can't stay here," Marlee interrupted Lacy's thinking. "Call the ambulance. Let's get him into a clean hospital bed for a change."

Lacy didn't answer. Marlee meant well, but she was one of those follow-the-rules people. She went by the book, followed procedure, and just plain didn't always see the real person under her professional care. For her, life was one big emergency room of curtained cubicles where a busy doctor dealt with difficult problems, made snappy judgments because she didn't have time for anything else, peeled her soiled surgical gloves off, and moved onto the next cubicle without a backward glance.

Lacy didn't blame her. Work at the free clinic never slowed down. It was a tough place to work most days, more so when folks received their welfare or social security debit cards and decided to spend it on booze or drugs. The problem? Jamaal would freak when he opened his eyes and found himself in a clean hospital bed in a strange hospital without his buddy. He was a round kind of problem that didn't fit a square hole. Still, where else could he go?

She paused with her hand on the phone with every intention of fulfilling at least two of Marlee's directives. Jamaal couldn't stay there at the clinic, but he did need a clean bed.

"I'll take care of it," she answered promptly, leaving the handset in its cradle.

Dr. Presley would never know. She'd never check. Once her critical patients were sent off to the county hospital, she moved on. Just like now. She'd already turned her expert attention to poor Mother Washington, the seventy-three-year old grandmother of little Dwight Digman.

Twisted and stooped with rheumatoid arthritis, Dwight's grandmother was a study in sheer perseverance. Not only did she take especially good care of her grandson and ensured he was headed to West Point instead of Folsom, but she did it on a widow's mite and never once complained.

"Elizabeth," Dr. Presley exclaimed kindly as she entered Exam Room Two. "How is that strapping young grandson of yours these days?"

Mother Washington's dark eyes lit up in her wrinkled face. Dr. Presley pulled the examination room door closed behind her, and Lacy moved fast. She rolled Jamaal's gurney to the back exit where an actual ambulance would park to transfer a patient. Except for today.

Chapter Two

Stars. Blinding white stars zapped from temple to temple, bouncing inside Jake Weylin's skull. Like a psychedelic pinball machine, they pinged, and everywhere they landed, pain followed. He dropped to his knees and sucked in a lung full of air, shaking the blinding hit off.

Sure enough, Rocky Rabbit followed through with a kick to Jake's side, knocking his hands out from under him. "You need to butt out," the guy bellowed.

Well, yeah… Jake caught himself on one elbow before his chin hit the asphalt. He had never liked Poindexter's right-hand man, even less today. A helluva lot less.

Rafael Poindexter, the slick snake-oil real estate chump from the West Coast, hired local muscle to do his dirty work for him. Jake had had run-ins with Rocky Rabbit and Ferret Face before. The two toughs swaggered everywhere they went and thought they could bully anyone who got in their way. Jake thought otherwise.

The last time ended in a shoving match that Jamaal got caught in the middle of. One look at Jake's buddy and Poindexter's men turned tail. At six-foot-four and nearly three-hundred pounds, Jamaal did have a way of blocking the sun and making an opponent think twice.

But Rocky Rabbit? The guy was nothing but a hitman from the flat soles of his high-priced leather loafers to the top of his greased back, blond hair. He needed dental work. If Jake hadn't been outnumbered two-to-one and face down on the pavement, he could fix those buckteeth for him. Once and for all.

Only right now he was ground level and about to eat those sissy leather loafers.

"Your buddy better back off, Weylin. Make sure he gits the message. You guys mighta been in the Army, but you need to mind yer damned business." Ferret Face followed through with a kick to Jake's kidneys. "Now you been told. 'Bout time you listened."

Jake groaned, rolled to his side, and spit. *What are these assholes talking about? Butt out of what?* He'd never been Army. *Oh hell, no.*

"The boss catches you sticking your face in his business again, he ain't gonna be so polite," Rocky Rabbit declared, his index finger pointed sternly in Jake's face like he expected to be obeyed.

"Yeah," Ferret Face agreed like the dumb ass he was. He clenched his meaty fist and shook it at Jake. "Next time, you get the hammer." The two thugs stomped away, grunting to each other like the lowland gorillas they were.

Jake rolled to his back, lifted one hand to his sweaty forehead, and blew out a big huff into the frosty air. Damn, it was cold, a bitter East Coast kind of December cold. Staring at the bright sky overhead, he should've been thankful he was still alive. He should've been thankful he wasn't hurt worse. He should've been thankful for a lot of things. But he wasn't.

He'd just gotten his ass handed to him. Shrugging off the pain and embarrassment of the encounter, he pushed up from the grimy ground. His swollen bottom lip tingled. Maybe tingled wasn't the best word. More like buzzed. His jaw and ears, too. That didn't happen often.

At least the beat-down happened behind what used to be a busy grocery store. Now it was just another vacant building in the neighborhood, where vagrants camped and troublemakers jacked up with their drugs, needles, and shit. The important thing was that no one had seen him, not that it would've mattered if they had. Folks didn't often come to a stupid white guy's aid any quicker than a stupid black man's, not in this part of town.

But still. He had his pride. It was a rare event when two jack-holes got the best of an ex-Marine. Jake shook that stupid notion out of his head. God knew there was no such thing as an ex-Marine. Only civilians used the term. Jake wasn't ex-anything. Not yet.

Right on cue, a mighty *'Oo-rah'* from the good old days roared to life within. He rolled his shoulder and stretched both arms over his head to ease the kink of that last kick out of his lower back. And his neck. And his butt. Damn. He should've seen Rocky Rabbit and his sidekick coming. Wished he had. Also wished he knew what he'd done to merit a warning from a creep the likes of Poindexter.

It was still early. Jake hadn't made his early morning rounds of Sector 18 yet. Jamaal was over at the Flying Angel Tavern turning in a week's worth of recycle. Rowdy Stokes owned the place. Ex-military and understanding of other vets down on their luck, he paid a half dollar a pound for recyclable aluminum trash. It wasn't much, but it put some GWs in their pockets and bought a decent sandwich and a Coke once in a while. Maybe a cold beer. Conversation.

Jake had planned to meet Jamaal over at Lamont's Pool Hall. He'd wanted to chat the owner, Lamont Adams, up for a job, but he didn't get the chance. The old fart wasn't there. The door was still locked and Jake chalked it up to his wife. She had an awful wasting kind of cancer, so Jake always cut the grouchy guy a little slack. God knew he had his hands full. There wasn't anything worse than standing by and watching the woman you loved die a slow death. Yeah. He cut Adams a lot of slack. Looked out for him, too, because that was what Sector 18 was all about.

Jake arched his back and stretched. Litter patrol wasn't much of a life, and picking up other people's garbage might look like a waste of time, but it kept him and Jamaal close to the folks they cared about, the folks who might not know someone was sneaking around their business with a crowbar. Or breaking into their car. Or bullying their kid on the way home from school and forcing them to run drugs across the bridge to high-end folks in fancy cars who wouldn't be caught dead in poor, rundown Anacostia.

Dusting his scraped palms down his dirty jeans, he called it one helluva hard lesson learned. Poindexter's message was clear. He was on his way to fame and fortune. The have-nots were in his way. But if Poindexter thought he could send his henchmen into Sector 18 and expect Jake to turn tail and run, he had another thing coming. Jake Weylin didn't desert his post, not ever, and this piece of Washington D.C. wasn't just Ward 8 anymore. No sir. It was his and Jamaal's prime real estate. It was Sector 18, and they were the self-proclaimed guardians of it, not Poindexter.

Acid pooled in the pit of Jake's gut. If Rocky Rabbit and Ferret Face were on the prowl, where the hell was Jamaal?

And what'd Ferret Face mean by *'your buddy better back off'*?

It took Jake less than ten minutes to hightail it over to the Flying Angel, but Rowdy hadn't seen Jamaal yet. Only one place remained to check for his buddy. Well, make that two. He could very well be floating in the Anacostia River or he could be down at the free clinic. Jake opted for the clinic. He jogged, scared of what he might find. Jamaal was the only family he had. He couldn't afford to lose him, too.

Approaching the clinic, he caught sight of Miss Wright pulling out of the rear alley, and who should be in the passenger seat next to her with his head lolled back like he was taking a nap? Jamaal. The slacker! But damn, it looked like he'd been in a fight.

Jake kept his distance, not like that was hard to do. Lacy was, after all, on wheels. Once he'd seen her look both ways before she pulled into traffic, he knew where she was going. He'd followed her plenty before, mostly just to make sure she'd gotten home in one piece.

Ever since that first day in the alley behind the clinic, Lacy was on his safe list, one of the many innocent and kind people he kept track of. It was damned unusual, though, for a pretty white gal like her to live in shabby, low income Anacostia. She was no cast off like he was, not even down on her luck, either. She had a good job. So why was she here? He hadn't figured that one out yet, but, oh well. There were lots of things he couldn't figure out these days, like why she'd put on such a tough act that first day.

It was a good thing he liked to walk, so he followed her. How else would he get to his buddy Zack's place over in Maryland? Or the hospital in D.C. the few times Jamaal had been incarcerated under the guise of needing medical care? Besides, physical exercise worked wonders. It cleared a man's head, a damned good thing in Jake's book. Working up a good sweat also worked the kinks out of a man's back and exorcised the mental demons out of his head a helluva lot better than the shit Jamaal chose to put in his mouth. No way was that crap going into Jake. It all ended up in a guy's head, and he had enough crap in there to last a lifetime as it was. Maybe two lifetimes. He didn't need more.

Their continual trips to the clinic were all Jamaal's fault. Like the first one. If Jamaal hadn't been playing drink-and-cry, *'let-me-tell-ya-another-sad-story'* that day, he wouldn't have fallen on his butt and broken the bottle of cheap liquor that cut him. Of course, he didn't need many stitches, not like that ornery Dr. Anderson would've wasted more time or catgut on him than he had to.

Aggravation skittered across Jake's shoulders just thinking of the prick. Anderson couldn't sew a straight line. Didn't look like he'd even tried to make his stitches even, not like the kind Dr. Marlee did. Of the two, she was the real doctor. He'd left Jamaal with an oozing wound that healed into an ugly scar on the left cheek of his ass, not like anyone else would see it, but still. Jamaal might get lucky. Some woman might want to see his big backside. It could happen.

Jake spread his fingers on his right hand wide, flexed them a few times, and let the aggravation roll away. He wasn't about to hit a doctor over a few lousy stitches. Besides, it was Jamaal's fault he'd gotten cut. It was also Jamaal's fault that Jake came face-to-face with Lacy. Now there was another story.

She'd literally taken his breath when she'd looked up from her car like a trapped animal, and Jake had all but suffocated on the spot. *No shit.* His heart kind of stopped pumping. His lungs quit processing oxygen, and he, a big tough Marine with one too many forward deployments under his belt, wanted to tuck tail and run away. From a woman. How crazy was that?

When Anderson had asked Jake that day what happened to Jamaal in his sarcastic way, Jake had stuttered like a dimwit, not able to take his eyes off Lacy. She'd looked down at the instrument tray like she didn't want him to know she'd seen his moment of total stupidity, her dark lashes fanned over a sprinkle of freckles on blushing pink cheeks.

Lacy had that redhead complexion thing going for her, the creamiest skin beneath a clipped up tangle of burnished red hair, all of it intent on escaping said clip. The knowledge that he'd put that glow on her face had excited Jake at some primal level. That's what made the blush all the more noticeable. It declared he was still a man; that this particular woman noticed him and couldn't control her body's response to him.

He hadn't missed that just the tip of her tongue peeked out briefly between moist lips already glistening with a hint of pink gloss, either. Like a fifteen-year old boy with raging hormones, his eyes had drifted to the front of her scrubs, hoping for a hint of hardened nipples beneath the fabric. Instead, pockets covered the swell of her breasts, nice plump pockets that created a rigid hard-on in his pants. He'd been glad he was sitting that day. He'd dropped his hands in front of his lap to camouflage his reaction.

But Lacy had secrets, too. He could tell. She might not trust him enough to share, but that was okay. He wasn't much for sharing, either.

For some crazy reason, that single meeting sparked emotions he hadn't admitted to in years. Out of the blue, his feelings for her ran as deep as hot-blooded Rodolfo's did for the fair Mimi in Puccini's tragic opera, *La Bohème*. It didn't help when Jake's dysfunctional brain immediately set his vocal cords to humming, '*O soave fanciulla*,' the duet between the love-struck couple that translated meant, '*Oh lovely girl.*'

Didn't it figure? His gray matter could instantly pull up the musical score from any opera in the world, but he couldn't form a coherent answer to Dr. Anderson with Lacy watching. Yeah. Puccini's Rodolfo turned into a blithering idiot the moment he'd met Mimi, too.

The opera played in the back of Jake's mind while his feet followed her car, not like he worried he'd lose her. He knew where she was going. But with every step, Jake's mood plunged headlong to regret. There would be no tenderness between him and the lovely Lacy, especially not enough to make a happy ending. He had a job to do. She was an unsuspecting client, but his responsibility nonetheless and nothing more. Besides Rodolfo's and Mimi's story hadn't ended happy. Why would Jake and Lacy's?

He'd put the frivolity of unnecessary things like romance aside the day his men died at that other Sector 18, the front gate of Camp Eggers in Kabul, Afghanistan. He honestly couldn't remember how the nickname came to be for that gate. It might've started as a joke. For all he knew, it was some make-believe battlefield in a video game that one of his USMC brothers or sisters had played.

He might not be able to remember that, but he knew he was damned proud of his men and women that day. On an assist to the Army, his USMC squad had fallen in like the topnotch troops they were. Not once did they complain, and there was plenty to piss and moan about in Afghanistan. They should have, but helping their Army brethren was part of the deal. It was what jarheads did. They manned up, marched on, kept on keeping on, and all that bullshit.

Two of his best corporals brought up the rear that day, Aiden Scott and Emile Blum. Trained and ready, they'd recognized the danger at Egger's main gate before anyone else knew what was coming at them. Jake had jerked around when he'd heard Emile bark at the driver of that ratty mini-truck to, 'Halt!'

The tough little blonde didn't ask twice. There wasn't time. With calm integrity, she'd lifted her M16A4, took careful aim, and sealed the deal, taking her shot and killing the driver. Aiden backed her up with a steady hack-hack-hack of his rifle. The two stepped forward instead of running away like they probably should have, and Jake was even prouder of them for that. Prouder and sadder.

They took the war to the jihad-screaming driver all right. They did their job and stopped him cold at the gate rather than let him in to spread his son-of-a-bitchin' holy war inside Eggers. Only the truck was full of explosives, and the Army got a hell of an assist from the Corps that day. Jake's squad took the brunt of the hit, lost two damned good Marines, and there wasn't a thing he could've done about it but scream for the rest of his guys to get down while a shitload of fire and brimstone took out everything in its path. The explosion knocked everyone not in the immediate kill zone off their feet. Everyone but Aiden and Emile.

When Jake got to where they'd been standing, the guard shack was obliterated. What was left of the truck steamed in the middle of a blackened crater like a smoking carcass. Aiden and Emile's charred bodies, or what was left of them, had still smoldered where they'd landed. In pieces. *Bit and pieces...*

Jake cocked his head and looked up, hoping to see stars instead of the dismal wintry sky overhead. For some reason he couldn't understand, stars helped him forget. They were so far away, they couldn't get hurt by assholes with guns and bombs and—death.

The day Aiden and Emile went to their eternal rest as true heroes still haunted Jake. Their remains were shipped home via Dover AFB in Delaware. Their mothers cried; one in Winnemucca, Nevada; the other in Detroit, Michigan. Like the true heroes they were, both Aiden and Emile were interred at Arlington National Cemetery amongst the other men and women who had given all.

But sometimes, Jake could swear he was still there at Egger's front gate. To this day, he detested the smell of summer barbeques on the wind. Chargrilled hamburgers. Bonfires. Just the hint of burning autumn leaves could time warp him overseas and back to hell. Back to that day.

Fireworks were the worst. The Fourth of July might be a day of celebration for most, but it was a day of hiding out in Zack's basement and watching noisy movies in his home theater to block the noise. Yeah. Independence came at too high a cost, and coming home sucked.

Jake growled off the mantel of despair settling over his shoulders. He had work to do. This wedge-shaped neighborhood between Eighteenth Street, Good Hope Road, and the Anacostia River had become his alternate universe, a second chance where he could make everything right again. He'd even named it the same corny name as what all the guys called the gate at Egger's: Sector 18. It felt the same.

Jake kept walking, his mind edging closer to that numb zone between then and now. Jamaal was there that day, too. He knew the fallen. The dirty streets of Kabul didn't seem so far away some days. Jake knew he couldn't bring Aiden or Emile back, but if he could keep Jamaal alive, maybe Aiden and Emile would forgive him for ordering them to bring up the rear. He could still hear Emile's cocky, "Yes, Sarge."

He just wished he couldn't.

Chapter Three

"Come on, tough guy," Lacy muttered beneath the weight of one damned big man. Mostly slack muscle at the moment, Jamaal woke up just enough to help her transition him from the gurney at the backdoor of the clinic into the passenger seat of her very economical, but not very big, four-door sedan. But getting him to shuffle those extra-wide feet of his up the two flights of stairs to her third floor apartment proved the more daunting challenge.

With each step, she and Jamaal had become more intimately acquainted. It didn't help that he was only dressed in a couple of skimpy hospital gowns, one turned backwards to keep the winter chill off the big guy's butt. She'd topped that scant outfit with a thin robe from the clinic's small stash of luxury items, but it was too small for a man with the girth of Jamaal. He belonged on Saturday morning television in the wrestling ring, not tucked into hospital duds.

His big hairy arm angled around her neck, his open palm slapping against her breasts like a loose sweatshirt sleeve in the wind. More than once, she'd used his butt cheek as a rudder. Mostly unconscious, he still seemed to grasp that one good five-fingered clench on his rear meant *move your ass, Marine.*

Finally at her door, she was sweaty from the load she'd half-carried, half-dragged, and afraid of being caught. Her neighbors didn't need to know her business, but Mrs. Brown just two doors down, did have a nose on her. Ha. Mrs. Brown should've been named Mrs. Buttinsky. That nose of hers could pick up the slightest hint of anything happening in the third floor hall. The woman had radar ears, too, and she'd have no trouble minding Lacy's business either.

Lacy could almost hear the inquisition now. "What you doin' child? Why you taking a man into your place? You sleeping around? Is he sick? What's he got? He drunk? Lordy me, you don't want to be hauling no drunk man home to be taking care of him. Next thing you know..."

Lacy allowed a tight grin as her imagination provided a very realistic scenario of all Mrs. Brown would say if she *just happened* to step into the hall right now. But that would be the day Lacy had a man in her apartment, a cold day in hell. Jamaal didn't count. He might be a man, but he was more of a soldier in need, and not that kind of need, either. The only reason he was here was because she couldn't stomach the thought of him being restrained over at Country General. Heck, they'd dope him up, send him to the state mental health facility, or worse, maybe shock him.

Nope. Not going to happen. Not to Jamaal.

Fumbling to pull her keys out of the rear pocket of her too tight jeans where she shouldn't have put them in the first place, Lacy heard the squeak of the front door to the apartment complex. Like always, it banged when it slammed shut.

Damn it. Someone's coming. Get your butt inside and out of sight.

Jamaal blew out a big nasty breath into her face. Propped up against her like he was, only made pulling her keys out of her rear pocket more difficult, but then he started leaning. If she didn't hurry, he was going down, and she was going down with him. Mrs. Brown would have plenty to talk about then.

At last! The keys were clear of her fat ass and in her fingers. Trembling more from panic at the neighborhood gossip than over-exertion, she rammed the key into the door lock and inside the apartment she and Jamaal went. Kicking the door closed behind her, Lacy blew out a puff of satisfaction for a job well done. Nobody, but nobody, knew she had Jamaal in her place, and she intended to keep it that way.

"Over here," she said as she directed the semi-conscious Bradley tank at her side over to her sofa. It creaked when she tried unsuccessfully to ease him down, but no matter. He'd landed with a thump in the corner of it, but at least he was mostly sitting up. His head tilted limply to the side. Good enough. He was down and she could straighten him up. Maybe.

Lacy stepped back, stretched the muscle strain out of her back, and sucked in a deep breath. This might just be the craziest thing she'd ever done, but damn. Jamaal was a helluva big guy to move all by herself. Every muscle in her back declared that loudly and clearly, but regret never entered her mind. He needed a unique brand of help that only another Marine would understand. Maybe she couldn't provide all the technical side of medical care, but what she had to give was his for the taking. What he needed most was a warm place to hide out, lick his wounds, and do it without being judged, poked, and prodded. Or restrained.

"You want a drink?" she offered in one out of breath sigh, just in case he was more awake than he looked. No such luck. Jamaal was out for the count, and she was lucky he'd made it this far. "Never mind," she told him. "If you don't, I sure do."

Turning one quick about-face landed her smack dab in her kitchen and at her old-fashioned refrigerator. Ewww. Whoever thought yellow was any kind of a color for kitchen appliances had to have been on drugs, and the idiot who'd tried to re-paint it that same color? Dumb and dumber.

Her apartment was small, and small meant simple and mostly furnished with second-hand furniture, but good enough for now. The open kitchen faced the back of the couch, which itself faced the only window in the place, where Lacy could contemplate the brick wall of the neighboring building. She considered herself lucky for that much of a view. She could've been facing another set of peeping tom windows and some perv with a zoom lens and a camcorder. *No, thank you very much.* Some apartment complexes were built with just that much lack of foresight and privacy. Hers was one of the good ones. She faced a wall.

Off to the right of her couch was the typical closet style bathroom where a person could brush their teeth and spit in the sink while they sat on the toilet and finished their business. A desk lined the wall outside the bathroom. An easy chair took up the opposite corner. Her window to nowhere stretched between.

To the left of her couch was her bedroom, a lonely place with a closet full of dreams long forgotten. Or nightmares. It depended on the day as to how she thought of them. Bad days made them all living nightmares. Good days made them— useful.

Throughout the entire cozy place was what once had been beige carpet, but now looked just plain ugly. The day she became rich and famous, all that stained beige would change to mellow sapphire blue. A white couch. Maybe one of those tiny little apricot-colored teacup poodles with a glitzy red collar. A maid would be nice. It might not come true for a few years, but hey. She could dream.

Pulling the refrigerator door open, she snagged a can of Coke instead of the Bud-Lite she would've preferred. Her lunch break was long over, and instead of a cuddly dog on her couch, she had Jamaal. He snored like a water buffalo, his lips flapping with the vibrations coming up from his throat, and his big feet taking up most of the living room floor. Damn, he was a mighty big man.

Lacy took a deep breath, slugged back half the soda, and contemplated her next move. Even sprawled half-on and half-off the couch like he was, Jamaal should be okay until she returned. Heck, it beat lying in the gutter or wherever he called home. He needed more than just the one hypo of antibiotics that Dr. Presley had administered during the course of his examination, so Lacy had also filched antibiotics before she left the clinic. The 5-day wonder drug ought to do the trick for whatever infection roamed at the back of his throat.

"You need mouthwash," she said firmly as she returned to his side with the drugs, a bottle of water, and a kitchen towel. She tucked the towel beneath his chin. Popping one tiny pill out of its foil bubble, she held his nose. Right on cue, his mouth opened. The pill went in, and before he knew it, he'd swallowed a gulp of water and the pill with it. He never even coughed or sputtered, but then swallowing was one thing he was good at.

"Good job. That was easy," she told him confidentially. "Let's see how much you'll take." Following the same drill, she got half of the water down, some on his chest and some on her couch before he stiffened his back and pulled away.

"You're going to live, Jamaal," she murmured, wiping his mouth first, then the couch. "I'll be back at six," she told the now snoring black man as she covered him with her best and only knitted afghan. It was red, her favorite color of deep, burgundy red. "Do me a favor, big guy. Don't tear my place apart when you come to. Just take it easy, okay?"

He didn't even grunt.

"I'll leave the kitchen light on. It'll be dark by the time I get back, but don't go all crazy on me when you hear someone at the door. It'll just be me." She kept chatting and he kept snoring. "You like Chinese?"

Lacy stalled leaving. Safe and clean or not, when Jamaal woke up, he wouldn't know where he was. He might panic. Did she dare take the risk? *Do I have a choice?*

Chapter Four

Jogging, Jake turned two more corners before the red brick building where Lacy lived came into view. Tucked between an abandoned textile warehouse and an all-night fast food drive-in, her apartment complex was as lackluster as everything else this time of year. Winter brought nothing but dismally bleak days and bitter cold to the East Coast.

Flipping up the collar of his ragged denim jacket against the chilly breeze, he lowered his head, hoping he looked less like a vagrant and more like a rent-paying resident. The cheap lock at the glass-paneled security doors of Lacy's apartment didn't latch securely most of the time. Like today. So in he went. The damned door squeaked like a banshee behind him, though. It slammed shut with a loud crack of aluminum against steel, another nerve-grating sound that didn't need to be.

Most landlords were non-existent when it came to maintenance on their properties. If he had the time and the tools, Jake would re-attach the loose end of the pneumatic spring back onto the door jam. That was all that was wrong with it, and it wouldn't take more than a couple screws and a screwdriver to fix it. A few drops of household oil on those hinges would solve the squeak. If he had time.

Up the stairs he went, two at a time. One more flight and he stepped out of the stair well on level three. Lacy's door?

Three doors to the right on the east side of the hall. He headed south, intent on making this visit quick and staying out of sight until he knew what was going on with Jamaal. It would've worked, except she opened her door and stepped into the hall at that precise same moment.

Jake froze. There was nowhere to run and nothing to hide behind, not that a Marine would hide, for hell's sake. But still. The thought did cross his mind. She hadn't seen him yet, intent on closing her door extra quietly like she was. The doorknob didn't even click, she'd pulled it shut so gently.

He cringed, his shoulders half-turned in retreat. Sometimes, the better part of valor was to turn tail and run. Too late. Lacy pivoted with a sigh of relief. The second her forest green eyes met his, they lit up with that same glow of a thousand lost wishes. The tiniest smile tugged at the right corner of her mouth, like she might want to smile, but didn't think she should. Just like that first day at the clinic with Jamaal. *Damn.*

His chest hurt in a 'crazy good' way. He couldn't swallow, though, and his knees locked up. Who turned the heat up in this two-bit rental? He loosened the fake collar of his already loose sweatshirt beneath his denim jacket, like that was hard to do. And he, Jake Weylin, the guardian of Sector 18, was Puccini's *Rodolfo*, just another helpless man caught in the orbit of a beautiful woman.

"Jake?" Lacy asked, and the sound of his name on her lips felt more like a prayer than a question. He licked his lips at the notion that hers and his might meet some day. His nostrils flared with the powdery scent of her. Damn. He was losing ground, and the conversation hadn't even really started yet.

"Well, yeah," he muttered hoarsely for lack of enough blood supply to fuel his oxygen-deprived brain. Shit. Why'd she have this effect on him?

"You're here," she said, her eyes pulling him into more than he was ready to admit to or allow.

He nodded. At last the reason he was there in her hallway—like a stalker—came back to his mind. "Umm, I saw Jamaal in your car. Is he okay?"

That was another thing he liked about this particular redhead. She turned crimson at the drop of a hat. The warmest, rosy glow spread up her neck, and he liked watching it come in waves like the sunset tide on a warm Malibu beach. Against all odds, that simple feminine response of hers declared him to be the masculine side of the equation. He could make her blood move. It almost made him a real man once more.

She made a funny face, ducked her head into her shoulders and looked so damned cute. "Don't tell anyone," she whispered, casting a furtive glance over her shoulder toward nosy Mrs. Brown's door. "He came into the clinic today needing stitches, but he's real sick. I couldn't let them send him to the hospital."

"What happened?" Jake pulled himself together enough to act less like a love-struck puppy and more like the tough guy he was. He'd tangled with Mrs. Brown before. If anyone had to worry about her, it was him, but he wasn't going to take her guff today. No way was she going to scold him for standing on the sidewalk on the other side of the street to make sure Lacy got out the door okay in the morning or made it home safely at night.

"Do you want to come in so I can explain without anyone hearing?" Lacy whispered, the smile gone as she took a step closer and got a better look at him. The delicate arch of her light brown brows furrowed. "Oh, my hell, Jake. What happened to you?"

Even the cuss words out of her pretty mouth were perfect. Pretty and tough. Sweet and salty. Yeah, he was in over his head and going down. He should run before he sank, but no. He wasn't thinking fast enough, not with his blood supply pooled in his nether regions like it was. Neither could he duck fast enough to avoid her touch when she stretched her slender hand up to cup his jaw. "You're hurt," she told him like he didn't know. "Who did this to you?"

An involuntary bolt of lightning shuddered down his spine at the gentleness of her touch. He couldn't speak. This little woman was a good foot shorter than him and maybe a hundred pounds soaking wet, yet he was lost, damn it. Lost in the warm touch of soft clean fingers that meant him no harm. Only they did. Just in a different way. The kind of harm he might not survive.

He cupped the hand that was cupping him, holding it still before he came undone. No woman had touched him in years, and he couldn't allow it. He had work to do. Important work. A good covert operator never got involved with their clients. Didn't she know that? Oh wait. No, she didn't. No one knew. Only he and Jamaal knew.

"Were you in the same fight as Jamaal?" she asked, the light within her still at the stone gate he kept locked.

"No," he whispered, struggling against what sure as hell felt like a losing battle. Lacy had some kind of magical power over him. How could a battle-scarred man withstand such gentleness? Such grace?

She eyed him suspiciously, her sweet glance skating over his face and down to his open collar. "You're bleeding. Come in and I'll get you cleaned up."

He shook his head, not wanting to admit personal defeat, but speechless at the depth of compassion in her eyes. Darker flecks of green shimmered within the green forest around the black iris. If he didn't know better, he'd say he was falling into them. Maybe diving. Head first. Would it hurt? Diving into green trees? They looked soft. And pretty.

"I ran into a couple of Poindexter's men," his dry mouth finally said. "That's all. I'm good."

"What's going on?" she asked, her hand still in place beneath his. "Why'd they hit you?"

He shrugged. "Not sure. Rocky Rabbit and Ferret Face—"

"Who?" she asked, her brows knitted together into an adorable crinkle.

He had to get away from her. That fiery red gold halo of hair made her look too much like an angel who had no business consorting with the likes of him.

"Umm, shit. I mean, darn. Sorry, ma'am. I don't know their names, but they're Poindexter's men. I know that much. The one guy's got big old pointy buckteeth. I think he sharpened them to make himself look meaner. Anyway, he looks like a rabbit when he opens his trap and—"

"So you call him Rocky Rabbit? That's funny." Her eyes lit up, and the whole damned hallway filled with the most glorious light from heaven. Jake blinked, not wanting to miss one single beam of her smile. Damned if she didn't glow.

He dropped his hand and took a full step back. Guys like him had no business with messengers from heaven. That was just plain—wrong.

A shadow cruised over her freckles. The light was gone, and he felt like shit. He'd done it again, spoiled the perfect moment. Made her worry if he was crazy or not. Well, she should worry because he was. *Sometimes*.

The hand that had been holding hers just seconds before raked over his hard head, tangling in the knots and rats of too many nights on the street until he wanted to pull his hair and beard out, hair by hair. But he couldn't. He didn't want to scare her.

Jake shifted his boots, uncomfortable in his own skin. It always ended this way. Tongue-tied. Dumb sounding. Worthless. Jamaal would have to fend for himself, not like that'd be tough with someone like Lacy looking out for him. "I gotta go."

"No, wait." She snagged that same hand back again and intertwined her fingers through his. "Stay."

The sensation stopped him cold. People didn't touch guys like him, not like this. Turning their joined hands over, he looked at the puzzle box she'd just created out of two very different pieces. The interlocking mechanism of his four fingers of graduating sizes linked with hers of coordinating sizes. It seemed an unlikely match, but they seemed to fit. His were longer, the fingernails dirty. Hers were slender, the nails pink and capped with a pure white edge of icy cleanliness. Only her thumb moved in a gentle circle at the heel of his thumb, calming the shit out of him.

Jake turned their conjoined hands over, flexing both of their fingers as he did. Damn. They did fit. Warmth seemed to be running like water in his veins, upward to his elbow and into his bicep. It kept on going past his collarbone until it invaded his ribcage, but gently, like a babbling stream tumbling over bones and sinew, until it blessed the barren desert deep inside of him with a life-giving trickle. Somehow it seemed to know that the wasteland he was inside couldn't quite handle more than a trickle of something so sweet. So pure. Anything more would sweep the parched desert that was Jake Weylin's soul off the face of the earth. Never to be seen again.

He couldn't stop looking. Those tiny fingers of hers were strong, but that thumb. That kind, little thumb with the perfectly clean nail... He gave her hand a soft squeeze in return, not wanting her to let him go.

"Jake. Are you busy right now? Do you have time to help me?" she asked, tugging on that ten-fingered link between them.

"Sure," he readily agreed despite the dry lump in his throat. "What do you need?" *What on earth do I have that she could possibly need?*

He tore his eyes off her thumb and fell back into her eyes. He couldn't seem to catch his balance around this gal, but he'd always help her. That was his way. His code. *Help the helpless. Protect the innocent. Stand between good and evil.*

"Someone has to stay with Jamaal while I go back to work. I'm afraid he'll be upset when he wakes up and doesn't know where he is. I don't want him to freak and tear my apartment up. Would you mind?" Lacy slipped her fingers out of his and reached into her pocket. At first, he thought she wanted to wipe the cooties off from having touched him, but a key popped into her fingers, and, oh yeah. She had to unlock her door. *Duh.*

He swallowed hard. He should've thought of that. Of course he'd stay with Jamaal. There was only one problem. He'd have to be indoors. Inside. And her apartment only had one door. Jake knew because he knew everything about this building and some of its occupants.

"Umm, in *your* place?" he asked hoarsely. "All the way, like inside with the door shut? Is that what you w-w-want?" His right boot started tapping. Kind of sounded like it was sending out an S.O.S.

"Well, of course. That's the whole idea." She'd already unlocked her door and stood waiting for an answer. "Hangout with Jamaal until I get back. Come on in. I've got heat."

Heat was good. Inside was not. Stall tactic. "Can't I just hang around out here in the hall and listen for him? He's noisy when he wakes up. I'll be sure to hear that big mouth of his."

Lacy shook her head, her smile filled with gentle humor. "No, silly. You need to be inside where he can see you if he wakes up. Please?"

Silly? Me? The word almost sounded like an endearment the way she said it.

Hmmmmm.

"You got windows in there?" *Big windows?* He already knew the answer to that, too. Heat wasn't the problem. A fast getaway was. He didn't like being trapped inside four walls, not any more. The cloying grasp of claustrophobia always wound its slimy, creeping tentacles around his throat when he stayed indoors for too long. The damned stuff never stopped trying to kill him. He'd already been inside too long as it was, but the thought of crossing that threshold of hers and entering a smaller room induced a suffocating sort of panic. His throat would close off next. Then he'd be in real trouble. So would she. His S.O.S. was louder now, but—seeing would confirm, and after all was said and done, she had called him silly. Somehow that—helped.

Lacy pushed her door all the way open and took his hand again, but not pulling. Just holding. That was kind of nice. "I've got one big window with the most awesome brick art for a view. You want to see it?" she said with another funny face. For a second there, she was a little girl, and he was just a kid. It was summertime, and they were playing hooky.

Oh wait. Kids don't play hooky in summer unless they're going to summer school and... Whatever.

Without taking one step, he tilted his body forward enough to peer through her open door. She hadn't lied. There was a good-sized window on the opposite wall. The curtain was open. It was easy to see clear through the entire place where she lived, where she might walk around in her pajamas after work. Where she might want to watch a football game and eat caramel corn and maybe drink a cold beer. His toe tapping slowed.

Hmmmmm. A man could get out through that window if he needed to. Even Jamaal would fit if push came to shove. Jake's discomfort faded. The claustrophobia let up. The S.O.S. faded to nothing. But what did she mean by brick art? Looked like a damned wall to him, but then, what did he know? Only that... *She called me silly.*

With the cutest smile and a gentle tug, Jake was lured over her threshold, past a dingy yellow refrigerator, and, shezam. He was all the way inside of her four walls. Damned if the door wasn't still open, and here he was—still breathing.

She didn't seem to have a problem with him being here, didn't even think twice when she broke the magical connection between their hands to gesture toward her kitchen. "Eat what you need. Drink what you want. I'll be home between six and seven. Can you stay until then or do you have someplace else to be?"

He stood his ground and nodded emphatically. No Marine ever admitted he couldn't handle easy duty. Jamaal seemed to be dealing with it okay. He did look a little worse for wear, all sprawled out on her couch like he was, his head tipped back and his big mouth wide open. The oaf had a few bruises, some stitches, and the prettiest red blanket snuggled under his chin. One might say he looked like a little boy, an ugly little boy with a hairy face and bad teeth.

"Okay, then, thanks. I was worried about leaving Jamaal alone, but now that you'll be here, I feel better. Do you like Chinese?" she asked, her cheery smile restored. That magic thumb of hers hooked a strand of silky red hair behind her right ear.

"I like most people," he answered, though where that odd question came from he had no clue. "'Cept most of them Taliban assholes. Maybe a few Muslim clerics. A couple congressmen. Terrorists." *Okay, so maybe I don't like most people, now that I think about it.*

Another mega-watt smile lit up his world. "I meant do you like Chinese food, silly," she corrected, her face aglow with pure sunshine. "I'm bringing rice noodles and honey walnut shrimp home for dinner. Would you like a couple egg rolls and dipping sauce to go with it? Maybe an order or two of Chow Mien?"

"No," he said firmly. No Marine worth his salt accepted charity. "Don't worry about us. Me and Jamaal will be fine. Once he comes to, we'll be on our way."

Her left brow lifted, and he had to look away before he got sucked back into that incredible vortex spinning around her. It had been a long time since he'd wanted to kiss a woman like he wanted to kiss Lacy now. Hadn't even thought about it in years, well, not much anyway. She did kind of make him think about it, but just the hint of being this close to a pretty woman cranked his anxiety into the red zone. She'd lit a fire deep in the pit of his belly, and if she didn't leave soon, he'd burst all over her. And it wouldn't be pretty. There'd be blood. Gore. Other stuff.

"Okay then, but lock the door while I'm gone," she said evenly. "Don't forget. I'll be back between six and seven, Sarge. Bye. See you later."

Like a warm spring breeze, she blew out of her apartment, closed the door behind her and was gone. Jake stood there staring. *Sarge?*

His heart stuttered. Who just left? Emile? It took a full minute to get his brain to reboot. Not Emile. Lacy. *Are you sure?* He nodded to himself. "Yes. Lacy," he said out loud to confirm what his mind was telling him. "Lacy lives here. This is her place."

She hadn't even argued, and he honestly didn't recall how she'd persuaded him to enter her apartment in the first place. Her home. The place she would be coming back to. But calling him Sarge? She shouldn't have done that. It made him feel responsible and important, but it made him remember things, and, *oh hell.* Once he got things sorted out in his head, it made him feel good.

Chapter Five

"You're late." Marlee's gaze scrolled over Lacy before it dropped back to the chart in her hand.

"I know and I'm sorry, but guess what?" Lacy asked the moment she spied her supervisor leaning against the customer service counter with her brows angled into a stern V. "I ran into Jake at lunch, and he needed medical attention, too. I couldn't just leave him."

She hated lying, but it wasn't a total untruth. She had run into Jake. He did need medical attention, and she did plan to treat him when she got back home—if he'd let her. Jake always had that force field of his on high alert, like he was afraid to breathe around her. Mental note to self: *Buy a couple shaving kits on the way home. No. Make that one. Two will overwhelm Jake. He'll have a hard enough time accepting one, but buy two toothbrushes. They don't need to share dental hygiene.*

"I guess we all do what we have to do," Marlee replied.

Lacy glanced at the attending physician out of the corner of her eye. Marlee almost sounded like she knew what happened, but by then she had her face buried in another chart. Lacy couldn't tell for sure what was going on.

The flu season was in full swing, as well as all the usual ailments that came with cold December weather. The clinic walls were thin. It was hard not to know everyone's business.

Myra Miller brought her mother in with another UTI, urinary tract infection. Stanley Bernstein needed a different blood pressure medication, and shy little Deloris Wasserman came in under the pretense of needing a flu shot when she'd actually wanted contraceptives. She was thirteen, going on thirty, also going behind her mother's back, but the law was the law. Deloris went home with a six-month supply of birth control and a gentle admonition from Marlee that boys who wanted you to prove you loved them weren't the right kind of boys to hang around with. Deloris hurried by Lacy with her head lowered and the small brown paper bag tucked under her arm.

All in a day's work.

The Good Samaritan didn't close its doors to anyone for any reason or at any time. The night shift was due at six pm. Until then, Lacy went back to restocking the supply cabinet.

The next emergency came through the front doors with two firemen and Mr. Lamont Adams, the elderly owner of Lamont's Pool Hall, an established hangout on Sixteenth Street. The aroma of smoke and ash came with the threesome, only Lamont was on a stretcher with an oxygen mask strapped to his face, and he was fighting mad.

"He insisted," the taller fireman with the crooked smile, said. The name on his chest said Cruz. Hispanic, she guessed. Sexy, her brain noticed. "Besides, we couldn't wait for the paramedics to show up. Chief said to transport so we brought him here ourselves."

"What burned?" Marlee asked as she took over the gurney, her hand on Mr. Adams' shoulder to calm him.

"They torched my pool hall, Doc Presley," Lamont growled beneath the mask. He was in his late seventies and as feisty as ever, but angry tears stained the sides of his sooty black face, dripping through the wiry hair of his gray sideburns.

"And I'll bet you tried to put it out all by yourself, didn't you?" Lacy asked, relieved it was just his pool hall and not his home. Mrs. Adams was sickly. She might not have made it out alive.

He nodded, choking with emotion. "'Course I did. Only way they could get me to move was to burn me out. I been there fifty-five years. I wasn't going easy."

"Who?" Lacy asked. "Who wanted you out?"

"That sissy from California, that Poindexter punk. He's been by my place a couple times with his highfaluting offers that ain't worth crap. He's got another thing coming. I ain't giving him squat."

"Were you there when the fire started? Did you see anything?" the other fireman asked. He was as rare as Lacy and Dr. Presley, another white person in all dark Anacostia. They did tend to stand out.

"'Course I was there, sonny," Mr. Adams snapped. "I'm always there. You can't trust anyone these days. Don't you know nuthin'?"

The guy winked at Lacy for the chewing out he was taking. Her gaze shifted over his name. Smyth. Even with soot on his face, he cut a handsome profile. Tall, dark and extra hot. Crap. After six years in the military, she was still attracted to a guy in uniform, even the dirty yellow turnout jacket and pants this guy wore. Designed to repel heat, they weren't working on her. Damn, he made his protective gear look good.

"I just need to ask a few questions, Mr. Adams," he said, his attention back on their cantankerous patient. "Tell me exactly what you saw."

"I seen them two sneaking bastards of Poindexter's driving away in a dark blue SUV just before I unlocked my front door and smelled the gasoline. There was smoke everywhere by then. The basement must've already been burning. Soon as I opened the door, the whole place..." He choked, dashing his tears away angrily. "The whole place went up like they'd planted a bomb in my pool hall." His thumb hit the center of his chest. "My pool hall, goddammit. They blew me off my own front step and twenty feet into the street. Damn punks."

"Don't you worry," the tall fireman said, thumping poor Mr. Adams' ankle. "I'll check what's left of your business once it stops smoking. I think you're right. It looked like arson to me too, but we need to make sure."

"You're damned right it was arson," Mr. Adams barked, coughing and sputtering, his anger getting the best of him. "That snot-nosed punk made me an offer two days ago. Said I couldn't refuse, well I showed him. I told him where he could stick his twenty K."

"He offered you twenty thousand for your pool hall?" Lacy asked in shock.

"That's all?" Marlee asked right on the heels of her question.

Mr. Adams nodded, lifting the oxygen cannula out of the way so he could talk. "It's winter. I got no insurance," he muttered. "I got nothing. And Martha's sick. What's an old man supposed to do now? I can't start over. I can't rebuild. How am I supposed to take care of my wife? I can't even buy her a Christmas present now. Damn him. He got what he wanted after all, didn't he?"

Poor Mr. Adams fell apart and no one spoke. Marlee took over, soothing him with medical chatter while she rolled him into Exam Room One. The firemen retrieved their gurney and went out the door and back to work. Smoke inhalation wasn't a two-woman emergency, but Lacy hovered within earshot anyway. Mr. Adams refused to go to the hospital for further treatment, said he still had work to do at his pool hall. Marlee said no, he didn't, and that she'd prefer to keep him for observation the rest of the afternoon just to be safe. He relented, but only because Mrs. Norton was staying with his wife. Lacy added his name to the list of people in special need of Christmas assistance.

She and Marlee had spent one glorious evening last December delivering surprise packages to folks who had nothing. Some of the donations came from local merchants and grocery stores. Some came from other doctors and nurses, but some were from her own pocket. The thrill of hiding behind bushes to watch what those random acts of kindness meant once they were received? Priceless.

But something was definitely going on in already troubled Anacostia and all fingers pointed to Poindexter.

The mighty Anacostia River used to divide the haves on the north side from the have-nots on the south side. There was a day not too long ago, when just the thought of making a wrong turn and ending up across the Pennsylvania Street Bridge was enough to send a visiting tourist into cardiac arrest. After all, certain sections of the district were known for their high murder rates, drug use, and lots of other unsavory stuff. Nice tidy tourists didn't care to see squalor, poverty, and the rundown side of the nation's capital while on their vacation.

Even Rafael Poindexter never showed up in this lowly part of D.C. without his stretch limousine and bodyguards. You'd think a real estate chump in a three-piece suit would stay on the safe side of the river where he belonged, but no. Intent on what he called, '*The abundant opportunities for gentrification of downtrodden Anacostia,*' Poindexter had rammed one new business development after another down the throats of the beleaguered whether they wanted it or not.

First came the artsy-fartsy cafes, the upper-scale smoke and espresso joints, the one-of-a-kind museums that sold off the wall crap they called art. Those kinds of businesses were designed to intrigue the free thinkers and hippies with low rent and the slim possibility of getting rich quick. But then came the clever franchise stores with their familiar names and the implied trust it brought with them. It wasn't like their presence didn't lure a few brave entrepreneurs and customers across the bridge, but they pushed a lot of the artists out, and despite all, business remained slow and lackluster. This was Anacostia after all.

Poindexter didn't seem to understand that a bad rep was a hard thing to turn around and Anacostia had one of the worst. Hell, the town had always had double-digit unemployment, even when the rest of D.C. prospered. What'd Poindexter expect? It would be easy?

So why didn't he just pack up and go back to the West Coast where he belonged? Was beating up a couple bums the likes of Jake and Jamaal going to change anything? And who needed the one-eighth acre lot where Lamont's Pool Hall now lay burned to the ground?

Lacy put in another half hour of work to make up for being late. She couldn't afford to have her paycheck docked. While Marlee was busy with a patient, she requisitioned an extra-extra-large sweatshirt and matching pants for Jamaal. He needed more than a skimpy hospital robe to wear when he came to. But just in case, she guessed wrong, she snagged another size. Who knew? Maybe he liked his clothing loose? Stashing the sweats, a couple packs of men's briefs and socks into her backpack, she breathed a sigh of relief. At least Jamaal would be warm until she could find a way to replace the clothes she'd cut off him earlier.

For her last duty of the day, she dusted off the cardboard carton from the farthest back corner of the supply closet. She'd meant to decorate the clinic counter before Thanksgiving, but the flu and cold season had been busier and earlier than usual. After rinsing the cheery red and green garland, she shook the excess water off and taped it to the edge of the customer service counter. A small tabletop Christmas tree with white twinkling lights took up its normal post to the side of the counter while a box of tissues and a bowl of peppermint candies sat beneath it. If nothing else, the patients who came and went during the holidays would have fresh breaths when they left.

With her backpack securely over her shoulder, and finally on her way home for the day, Lacy turned and ran smack into Dr. Presley.

"We need to talk," she said sternly.

Crap. Lacy gulped. She'd been caught. To make it worse, Marlee's toe was tapping on the linoleum. She must've found out that Jamaal wasn't at the hospital where she'd sent him. Maybe she knew what was in the backpack, too? *Crap.*

Dropping her gaze to the floor, Lacy followed Marlee to the end of the hall and her office opposite the supply cabinet.

"Have a seat," Marlee directed as she closed the door behind them.

Lacy took the chair in front of Marlee's desk. *Crap. I'll be fired for sure. Damn it. Who'll hire me now?*

"As you may or may not know, we've had some thefts lately," Marlee said as she took her seat opposite Lacy, too serious to be anything less than a stern administrator and her brown eyes intent on the pen in her hand.

Lacy gulped past the dry knot lodged at the back of her throat. She'd done wrong with the best intentions and gotten caught anyway. Marlee must know about the Z-pak, too. *Crap.* All Lacy could do was apologize for not following orders and hope Marlee gave her another chance. And if not? *Crap.* Giving Jamaal back wasn't in the cards. *Crap and double damn.* She'd be back in the unemployment line by morning. How could she help Jamaal then?

She bit her lip and faced Marlee, prepared to face her consequences head on, if she'd ever look up from that stupid blue pen she kept rolling between her index finger and thumb. Lacy held her breath. She'd learned damned early in the Corps. Never volunteer anything.

Finally, after what felt like ten minutes but was probably only sixty seconds of sheer hell, Marlee lifted her chin and stared Lacy down. "I want to trust you."

You can—most of the time. Swallowing with a gut full of guilt was impossible, so Lacy gave Marlee more time to expand on that very duplicitous statement that didn't tell her a damned thing. *You can trust me all right. To do what's right even when it gets me in a pile of steaming crap. I am a*

Marine, remember? I don't follow bullshit rules, and I don't give up on my men.

"Something is going on in this clinic," Marlee said quietly.

Okay, go on. That could mean you're still going to stick it to me. Spit it out. Why am I here?

"Oh?" Lacy offered nothing up and went fishing instead. Her jarhead swagger began to emerge. Instinctively her chin cocked and her already stubborn back stiffened. If Marlee wanted to make accusations, she'd better be ready for a fight. "Like what?"

"Like Mr. Adams for one thing," Marlee said quietly. "Mrs. McCallister for another. Did you know someone burned a cross on her back porch two nights ago?"

Anger replaced Lacy's defensiveness. Sweet Emma Shirleen McCallister? The elderly widow who showed up every Christmas Eve with homemade cookies and hand-crocheted doilies for everyone who worked at the clinic? The thoughtful grandmother who called everyone doll or honey? "Was she hurt?"

Marlee shook her head. "No, but she left town the next day to move in with her sister in Rhode Island. The poor thing walked away from everything she owned, even left her door unlocked. Lamont told me Rafe's men paid her a visit before she left, too. Her place is across the alley from his pool hall. Now it's empty, but that's not all."

Lacy held her breath. What could be worse than bullying a poor widow out of her home and all her earthly possessions?

"I want you to take something home with you tonight," Marlee said, pivoting her knees to her right while opening her side desk drawer. Out came a black cash box with a silver handle on the lid. It measured no bigger than a shoebox. She set it in the center of the desk. "I'd take it, but I already take all the narcotics home every night. I could get fired, but I don't care. I'd never ask you to do this if I didn't trust you implicitly."

Whew. Lacy swallowed. Implicit trust was good. Out went the fear of reprisal and in came cold hard dread. What was so bad that Marlee took the narcotics home every night?

"I used to live in Sacramento," she confided. "I've seen Rafael at work."

"Mr. Poindexter?" Lacy had to ask, just to make sure she'd heard right. What did he have to do with the drugs or what was in that lock box?

Marlee nodded. "He's a driven man, Lacy, and he *will* turn Anacostia around. It will prosper by the time he's finished if he has to drive everyone out to do it." She gulped, and for the first time, Lacy's eyes were drawn to the tight lines in Marlee's slender neck. Her fingers trembled on the lid of that black box between them.

"What's in it?" Lacy nodded her chin toward the box.

Marlee's eyes brimmed. The tremors of her hands had moved to her head. This poor woman was falling apart. "Evidence," she whispered.

Chapter Six

Jake helped himself to a single glass of tap water from Lacy's kitchen faucet, washed the glass after he'd taken a full drink, dried it with the towel draped at the edge of the sink, and replaced it on the lowest shelf of her side cabinet exactly where he'd found it. After double-checking that the apartment door was still secure, he made himself comfortable on the floor where he could keep an eye on everything—the window, the door, Jamaal. With his back to Lacy's bedroom wall and sitting cross-legged, he prepared for a long watch.

He knew it was Lacy's bedroom behind him because the only other door in the place opened to her bathroom. Unless she slept on the couch every night, that made the room behind him a bedroom, and he wouldn't betray her trust in him by opening the door and looking around. No way. A woman's bedroom was a damned scary place.

Jamaal had grown more and more restless. It wouldn't be much longer before he jumped up and commenced to swearing and screaming, but until then, Jake planned to take it slow and easy. Maybe Jamal would overreact. Maybe he wouldn't.

The place seemed okay, especially since it had a good-sized window. Lacy kept the glass cleaned and polished. A man could actually see outside. Craning his neck, he looked upward to the brick masterpiece. It did have some fancy artwork along the wall, done with recessed bricks, cutouts and carvings. What'd they call guys who laid bricks like that—brick masons? Brick artists? It didn't matter. Whoever'd created that wall had done a good job. It made for a nice view. A safe view.

The solid reddish, dirty canvas soothed some of his panic away. The wall gave him one less point of entry to have to watch. No way could anyone get up high enough to get in through there.

Easing out of his denim jacket, he folded it once and laid it across his thighs. He was warm enough for a change. He used to carry a heavy pistol on his hip and enough ammo to always be prepared, but now all he had was a plastic case of peppermint breath mints in his pocket and a pocketknife. His shooting days were behind him.

The bathroom door was wide open and the damned commode sparkled like a porcelain throne. His nose detecting a pleasant flowery fragrance mingled with a twitch of pine cleaner. She must like to clean things. Clean was a good thing, but here he was sitting in her place with a dried up, bloody nose and filthy hands. He lifted his palms off her carpet, half-afraid he'd already left a dirty mark. Oh, good. He hadn't.

The bathroom beckoned. If he was careful, he could grab a warm shower and be half-presentable by the time she got off work and came back. She did smell clean. The thought translated to Jake's tapping nervous fingers. Bathrooms were small places with only one exit. Showers were smaller, and a woman's shower was a minefield full of fancy things he might break if he turned around too fast or if he had to run. Still....

If he was quick about it...

Jamaal arched his back, let out a belch and went back to snoring. It might be hours before he woke up.

Jake's eyeballs strayed back to the immaculate tiled bathroom floor. His fingers tapped another hundred rounds of *should I, or shouldn't I?* At last, he lifted his butt off the floor and ventured forth. He owed it to Lacy to man up, clean up, and remove some of the grit from his grubby body before she returned, especially since she was probably bringing food even though he said he didn't need any.

He didn't guess she'd listen to him, but she *was* a lady and she most certainly deserved a respectable guest. She wouldn't mind if he cleaned up. He'd be quick. If he could find one of them little fingernail scissors, he might even hack a few inches off his beard.

With one last analytical glance at the kitchen/living room, he licked his chapped lips and jumped to. The bathroom door didn't even squeak when he closed it behind him, but the second he turned around, Jake caught a glimpse of himself in the mirror. *Holy shit.* He looked worse than he'd thought.

One eye was black and puffy. That would be where Rocky Rabbit had landed a punch, but the dried blood in his moustache and beard looked just plain disgusting. *Lacy invited me in looking like this?* He shook his head. *That woman.* She shouldn't have, but he was glad she had. He was, after all, an honorable man. Maybe a little forgetful sometimes, and maybe a little bit grubby most of the time, but he'd never hurt her, not in a million years.

Very carefully Jake slipped out of his clothes, folded them neatly and set them on the top of her white wicker hamper. They were scroungy, but they were all he had.

Turning the shower faucet to warm, he took one last look around the feminine bathroom.

She liked red. There was no clutter of make-up and fancy bottles on the vanity, only a red glass bottle in the shape of a Christmas tree with a gold star on top that was a bottle cap in disguise. Probably hand lotion or soap. A single red plush rug lay at the foot of the cabinet. Two folded bath towels hung off the rack behind the door. Both red. It contrasted nicely with the white walls and counter top. But wow. Lacy really liked red.

He lifted one of the towels off the rack and came face to face with a red nightie. A nightgown. A pretty, silky, red nightgown with black lace trim at the hem and neckline, and skinny little black straps. Spaghetti straps. Very carefully Jake avoided touching her gown. Lacy was clean and pure. He wouldn't defile her, not even her pajamas by laying one grubby finger on them.

What a sight though. She must look beautiful every night if that was what she wore to bed. His mind wandered to her body beneath the covers. Lacy. Red gown. Maybe red panties. On. Or off. Warm and soft. And—

ARGH! He scrubbed a quick hand over his scruffy face to banish the image. *Nope, nope, nope. Not going there. I'm here to lose a pound of dirt. That's all.*

Resolutely, he took two steps to the tub, stepped inside and pulled the shower curtain closed. And everything went from bad to worse. There were intimates hanging on a metal rack inside the tiled enclosure just below the showerhead. Only now they were soaking wet and his heart was a throbbing beast in his chest. It had been so damned long since he'd had anything to do with a pretty woman's pretty underwear, much less an underwire padded bra, a thong, and both of them in hot-damned red.

They're just clothes, his brain told him loud and clear.

Yeah, but they're underwear and they're hers and they go over her naked body and...

Politely, he lifted the rack off the showerhead and set it outside the tub enclosure. A man could only take so much, and by hell, he needed a bare minimum of five minutes of uninterrupted scrub time. He'd wring those items out later and reinstall the rack, and Lacy would never know.

The water was hot. The liquid soap smelled good, but his mind was lost in the heady world of desire. As much as he cleaned and lathered, his body perked up, ready for another activity all together because of those red under-thingees. His pulse quickened. He concentrated on diversionary tactics like litter patrol while he shampooed with some kind of flowery smelling shampoo that smelled like her.

Lacy. Lacy. Lacy.

He focused on Jamaal.

His heart rate chanted, *Lacy. Lacy. Lacy.*

Every touch of his fingers became hers, the slippery feel of soap more than just a shower. *I'm a Marine, damn it.*

Lacy. Lacy. Lacy!

Jake stopped scrubbing. Clean was one thing, but this was more like foreplay, and foreplay alone was just plain sad. As sexually frustrated as he hadn't allowed himself to become in a long time, he was now. He leaned one forearm to the tile below the shower spray and buried his face in the crook of his arm. It happened again. He wasn't in Anacostia. He was in the dirty streets of Paris looking down. *Look down. Look down. Look down...* The beggars' chorus filled his head with anguish from another time, anguish that fit the tenuous state of his mind.

But that would make Lacy, Fantine, and me... Jean Valjean? Not hardly.

Swallowing his own peculiar brand of angst, Jake doused the water, slapped the shower curtain open, and lifted the red towel from the counter where he'd left it.

He dried quickly, but stalled getting back into his dirty clothes. Wrapping the towel around his waist, he wiped a clear path through the steamy mirror. It was nice to be clean for a change, but the same heathen stared back at him. Shaggy. Disheveled. Clean or not, he still looked like the devil. *Lacy should've never let me in. She should've never touched me. Jamaal either. What am I going to do with that girl?*

Swallowing hard, he inspected his face, scrunching his lips to one side and then the other. He needed a shave and a few stitches, but thoughts of what he *could* do for that girl—*with* that girl— danced through his head.

I could fix dinner for her. Oh wait, she's bringing take-out back.

A couple stitches wouldn't hurt, either. His eyes were both on their way to black and blue. He'd look like a raccoon by morning.

I could fix the front apartment door, maybe the front door lock. At least she'd be safe.

Rocky Rabbit had landed a lucky punch. The one-inch cut across Jake's left orbital bone still oozed, but at least his nose had stopped bleeding. It hurt, but he was used to living with a crooked nose. It wasn't the first. He tapped his swollen lip and his mind went straight to Lacy's perfect mouth. Her lips.

I could kiss her. Jake froze. Would she entertain the notion of swapping spit with a bum like him? A has been? A wannabe? A man who looked just plain ugly and was rough as a board? He ran his fingers over the coarse growth of two long months on his face. It had been early October since he'd been clean shaven, the last time he'd been over to Maryland visiting his buddy Zack if he remembered right.

Zack had a family now. Three little girls. Two dogs. A wife who thought Zack walked on water. But the guy was solid, always had enough beer in the house to get a man sleepy and comfortable, and always offered a change of clothes to send Jake home in. That little cutie-pie, daughter, LiLi, had made him a peanut butter and jelly sandwich the last time he was there. It was kind of gooey. She'd used too much peanut butter and extra raspberry jam.

His tongue slipped over his bottom lip as if still tasting the best sandwich ever. That was why he'd shaved that day. He hadn't wanted to scare Zack's baby girls, LiLi, Song, and MiKi. Wouldn't think of it. Yet here he was with another pretty little girl, in her apartment, and he was as scary looking as all get out.

I'd like to kiss her.

A pretty pink razor rested in the shower soap dish, but he needed a pair of scissors first, and he wasn't about to rummage through her drawers looking for anything. No, sir. Who knew what he'd find? With a deep breath followed by a laboriously slow exhalation, he let the foolish notion of being clean shaven go. It was better this way. His beard could be his last line of defense to keep his mind where it belonged and off Lacy.

Jake doffed the towel and hung it to dry on the shower curtain rack so she'd know he'd used it, that it was dirty. Stifling the foolish wish for cleaner clothes, he donned his smelly attire once more. With nerves of steel, he lifted her soaking wet bra and panties to the sink, wrung them out, and put them back on the rack where they belonged. Out of sight and out of mind.

When that tidy little chore was done, Jake swallowed his pride and the truth along with it.

What am I dreaming about? I'll never kiss her.

Chapter Seven

Lacy stomped on her brakes harder than she meant to, but her heart was more of a banging drum than a cardiac muscle at the moment. Across from her front door, the apartments boasted—not loudly—a long line of semi-covered parking stalls for long-term residents. They charged a one hundred dollar deposit to rent each stall, which Lacy had signed up for the moment she'd moved in. Parking anywhere near D.C. was a nightmare, even in Anacostia.

Only a single gray SUV had parked on the opposite side of her assigned stall, making it a tight squeeze for her to manage. The car was running, but the windows were too dark to see who was watching her. If anyone was. Panic had her thoughts pinging in all the wrong directions as she cranked the wheel and slid into number 622. Her assigned parking stall didn't match her apartment number, mostly because nothing matched on this side of town. Like her.

With her backpack tucked tightly under one arm, she took one more look at the strange SUV. *Damn, those windows are dark. Here goes.* Taking a deep breath, she kept her head down and made like she wasn't coming undone when she opened the door and set one foot to the pavement. Only she was rattled. Her feet led her to her sidewalk, but if that guy in the SUV had her in his crosshairs, she could be down on the pavement with a bullet in her head and never know what hit her. Had to be one of Poindexter's men. Who else knew she lived here?

All but running up the two flights of stairs to her apartment, the backpack she carried felt extra heavy with Marlee's secret evidence hidden at the bottom of it. Fear shivered up the back of Lacy's calves, straight up to her butt, urging her to, *'Run!'* She did. Footsteps sounded one flight behind her. It might be no one, but it could be—them. The guys from the SUV. Poindexter's killers. *'Hurry!'*

She couldn't go fast enough. Fumbling, she rammed her key into the lock at her door. Before she had the chance to turn the key, her door swung inward.

"I've been waiting for you," Jake muttered in that quiet rumbling voice of his. "You're late."

Out of breath and not wanting to look any more foolish or scared than she already did, Lacy bolted into her apartment, slammed the door behind her, and cranked the deadbolt until it clicked loud and clear. The safety chain went next. The simple lock on the doorknob after that. Finally—*whew!* She slid the metal bar home on yet another lock below the others. Swallowing hard, she stepped back and cocked her head to detect whether those footsteps had passed her door and kept going, or if they'd stopped. If those guys from the SUV intended to kick her door in.

Too much adrenaline flooded her petite five-foot four-inch body. Rubbing her arms enough to warm her fingers, she dropped her backpack to the floor. Maybe it was nothing. She might have just scared herself. There might not have been anyone behind her at all. She gulped. Or it might have been Rafe Poindexter in person come to give her the same message he'd given poor Mr. Adams.

Not until Jake clutched her biceps and turned her to face him did she realize how close he was. His hair was still wet and that poor black eye looked tender. He'd showered while she was gone, but he hadn't shaved. *Cool.*

Stormy gray peered from beneath a shock of dark brown curls and tangles. "What wrong? Who's out there?"

"I, I thought I heard someone behind me on the stairs," she answered truthfully, out of breath and beginning to feel stupid

"Who? Did you see who it was?"

She blew out another big breath between pursed lips. The nurse who taught Lamaze at the clinic would've been proud. If only Lacy could slow her heartbeat and stop shaking enough to be sensible. It had to have been her over-active imagination. Why would anyone follow her? How could anyone even know that she had Marlee's secret with her? For that matter, did anyone even know Marlee had a secret?

"It was probably nothing." She swallowed past the dry lump at the back of her throat. Glancing over Jake's shoulder to the prone Marine sprawled all over her couch, Jamaal looked like he was in a more comfortable position than how she'd left him. Jake must've put his feet on the couch. His feet hung over the armrest, but he snored, so his position must not have bothered him.

"Can we talk?"

Jake made a funny, puzzled face. "I thought we were?"

"I mean, in the other room? I don't want anyone else to hear what I have to tell you."

Another puzzled shadow shifted through those gorgeous gray eyes. Honestly, the man was a little dense. He blinked extra-long eyelashes like he was trying to figure her out.

Couldn't he see that she was scared out of her wits and needed emotional support?

He peered over her shoulder to the open bathroom door on the other side of the living room. The sincerest glint of determination flitted across his face. His brows furrowed. "Not there."

Fine. Whatever that meant. Anxiety got the best of her. She didn't have all day for him to decide if he was coming or not. Grabbing his hand and the backpack, she tugged him to her bedroom and closed the door behind them. Flipping the light switch up, she caught the most amusing combination of wonder, worry, and delight when his eyes scrolled over her bed to the pile of dirty laundry in the corner. A pair of black panties lay on top. Of all the times to be embarrassed for being a slob, this was definitely it.

Cutting to the chase, she ordered him to focus. "Jake. Look at me."

He pulled his eyes away from her laundry, and, darn it anyway. A tender smile twitched at the left side of his mouth. "Okay, so tell me. What's so important that you ran up two flights of stairs? You don't usually do that."

She should've asked how he knew that, but instead she blurted, "Poindexter's men burned Lamont's Pool Hall this afternoon. It's gone."

Anger flared to life in his face. "They hurt him?"

She shook her head. "Not really, at least not directly. Two firemen brought him into the clinic. He thought he could put the fire out by himself. You know how he is. He's got some smoke inhalation, but that's all. Marlee sent him home with oxygen. He'll be okay."

"What else could he do? That place was his life, damned near his everything."

"I know. Isn't that terrible? At least he and his wife are safe."

"Sons of bitches." Jake glanced at the door behind her. "I'll bet that's who beat up Jamaal. What going on in this town?"

"Did they beat you too, Jake? Poindexter's men?"

He stiffened. "Maybe."

Oh, you stubborn man. Why can't you just tell me?

"There's more." Lacy lowered her voice, lifting the box between them. "Marlee asked me to keep something for her. It's in this lockbox. That's why I ran up the stairs like I did. I kind of scared myself. I thought I heard footsteps behind me. I thought someone was following me."

He eyed the box. "What's in it?"

Setting it on the edge of her bed, she knelt in front of it, wishing she'd had time to ask more questions before Marlee hurriedly left. The only place she could think to hide it was under her bed. "I'm not sure. All she said was it was evidence. She had to meet someone. There wasn't enough time to talk."

"Where's the key to unlock it?" He knelt beside her. "What kind of evidence? On who?"

"I don't know about a key. She didn't give me one, but she was scared, Jake. She said she had information on Rafe Poindexter." An involuntary shudder shivered up Lacy's spine. She wiggled with the attack of goose bumps, jostling into Jake's very solid right bicep. That momentary contact was all she needed to fall apart. She took advantage of him right there and then, leaning her full weight into him until he had no choice but to wrap one timid, big, strong arm around her shoulder or let her fall. Turning her face into his shirt, she took a deep breath of body odor and another scent, too. Her shampoo. Her body wash. It smelled good on him.

"You okay?" he asked gruffly, his body coiled tighter than the springs in her mattress.

"I don't know," she whispered, afraid of being overheard. "First you and Jamaal get beat up. Then poor Mr. Adams. For a minute there, I thought I was next."

"'S okay," he soothed, his deep voice unexpectedly deep and comforting and his beard soft on her forehead.

She let him hold her while she caught her breath. Maybe she hadn't really heard footsteps.

"I didn't stop for Chinese," she admitted. "I'm sorry, but I forgot all about it when Marlee told me to take this home. She made me take a full emergency first-aid pack, too. I've got drugs, antibiotics, painkillers, and a defibrillator in the backpack in my car. I've never seen her so scared. She knows Poindexter from when she lived in California. She didn't exactly say how she knew him, but she seemed to know how dangerous he is. She said he'd make Anacostia prosper if it was the last thing he did."

What would Poindexter's men have done if they'd caught up with her? Slapped her around? Burned her out? Worse? A full body cringe coursed over her at the scary possibilities. Women alone were so damned defenseless, no matter how tough they thought they were. All it took was the law of the jungle, two against one, and she might have become a victim. Again.

Jake grunted. "Don't worry. He's nothing but a flaming bully. I've seen his type before."

He seemed taller suddenly even though they were both kneeling like a couple of kids at prayer next to her bed. All timidity was gone. There was an inner strength to Jake that he didn't seem able to admit to. Maybe he couldn't see it, but she could. It proved itself in the way he gripped her more firmly as if he meant to protect her.

"I'm glad you're here," she said, her heart finally calmer. "I don't want to be alone."

His grip tightened in response. "You won't be."

Chapter Eight

Well, this was a strange turn of events. Here he was holding Lacy and talking like he had an army to back up the big talk coming out of his big mouth. Hell, Jake didn't even have Jamaal at the moment, not like his buddy was much help when it came to a fight anyway. Mostly he just caused trouble. Jamaal tended to talk a good story, but he usually went down with the first punch when it came to fists. But still. A man didn't let a woman go unprotected, especially not one shivering up against him like Lacy was doing. If she needed help, by hell, Jake would stay by her side and fight to the last drop of his blood.

"What do you want to do with it?" he asked, nodding at the lock box. He'd seen Dr. Presley plenty. She wasn't the type to get rattled very easily, but the box didn't look strong enough for the kind of secret Lacy thought was in there.

"For tonight, I'm putting it under my bed," Lacy answered as she crouched over to shove the box far beneath her bed. "It's not like I have a safe to hide it in. I think Marlee just wanted it out of her office anyway. It should be safe here until she wants it back."

Lacy shouldn't have done that, not stuck her butt up in the air while she watched where the box went under the bed. Like she didn't know what that position did to a guy? A woman should never bend over in front of a hungry man, not with her butt clad in tight stonewashed denim like Lacy's was.

He licked his lips and pulled his mind out of the gutter. At least, he tried. Real hard. "You'd think she'd give the evidence to a lawyer or someone instead of to her nurse," he said hoarsely.

"I know, huh?" Lacy agreed as she came back to his eye-level. "That's what I was thinking. Why me? I'm just her assistant. Why didn't she give it to her buddy, Dr. Anderson?"

"She must trust you more than her lawyer or Anderson."

"Maybe, but it's scary having something in my house that could convict someone like Rafe Poindexter."

He nodded. Conversation stalled. All he could think of was the tight curve of her ass in those jeans. The seam between the cheeks of her ass. The heat that was sure to be there. Her scent.

"What's next?" she asked, her voice a pitch lower than he'd ever heard it before.

He had a few ideas, but she probably meant something besides what was going on in his head. "I know how to cook," he admitted weakly, like that solved a damned thing. Thoughts of her plump round backside still enticed. He took hold of her arm ready to pull her to her feet. "I could fix dinner since, you know, you worked all day. You're probably tired."

She scrunched her shoulders, but didn't attempt to get on her feet. "I have a kielbasa in the fridge. I could slice it up and make spaghetti."

His stomach growled at the thought of sausage simmering in tomato sauce. A home-cooked meal was a rarity for a guy from the hard streets of Anacostia. "You got any garlic cloves? Oregano? Parmesan cheese?"

"I do," she whispered.

He heard her swallow, and that simple sound of her throat working hard against the lump of fear broke something open deep inside his hard jarhead heart. All she had on was a light blue, short-sleeved scrub top over those jeans, not even a winter jacket. Her bicep felt warm and vulnerable beneath his fingers. This woman wasn't made to fight the world, and she shouldn't have to.

"What's a nice girl like you doing in the middle of nowhere Anacostia?" he asked, the feel of his hand on her arm the perfect narcotic for the constant ache in his heart. Something was happening between them, and it wasn't the lure of his first decent dinner in a long time, although it did have something to do with appetite. Whatever it was, he didn't want it to end. Not yet.

"Same as you," she murmured. "I was a Marine. I got out and came home three years ago. My parents, they—" She gulped a noisy gulp again. "I might as well tell you because you're bound to find out. I, umm, had a nervous breakdown. I freaked one day. Funny. I don't even remember what set me off, but by the time I was through, I was... I was...."

He tipped her trembling chin up with the tip of his index finger so he could see into the depths of her eyes. Lacy had the softest green eye color, the color of the tips of pine tree branches in early spring when they were new and tender, but still not tough enough to face the world.

"I had one of them myself," he admitted to another human being for the first time ever. She needed to know she wasn't the only Marine who fell apart after they came home.

Hell. He had his good days, but he had plenty of bad ones, too. "'S why I live here, I mean, over on Fifteenth Street. It ain't perfect, but it's good enough." *Like me. I'm good enough for the ragged streets of Anacostia, and Anacostia's good enough for me.*

"You and Jamaal hang out in the old IGA store?" she asked, her lower lip trembling. And moist. And lush. Her eyes seemed to shine with an open invitation he didn't want to accept, but he couldn't make his eyeballs move out of those shimmering pools of mossy green comfort. The more he looked, the more he wanted to look. Hell, he wanted to touch. This woman was heating up under his fingertips.

How could she possibly look at him like that? Like he was worthy? He didn't deserve one taste of her bottom lip much less all the other body parts he was thinking of tasting. Taste nothing. He hadn't allowed this feeling in years. This appetite. This craving. He licked his lips. Lacy was sugar and cream with a hint of wild clover honey. Those succulent lips tempted. The uniquely feminine scent of her wafted up in the warm draft between their bodies. Pay dirt. If they didn't get out of this bedroom, he was in trouble. Big, hard trouble.

"They had me committed," she confessed, her eyes not blinking despite the tears streaming out of them. "They… they… put me in a straight-jacket, and they took me away, and they… they strapped me down. They did this shock treatment thing to my head."

His heart melted into one angry, sad blob at her feet. "Who did that to you, baby?" he asked, his hand suddenly cupping her jaw, his now clean thumb good enough for her, wiping those tears out of the forest in her eyes. *How could anyone do such a thing?*

"My mom. My dad. The doctor." She blinked then, her lashes full of tiny drops of pain and betrayal. Again with the noisy gulp. He kept soothing, but she kept crying, and now, damn it. Right here and now, he wanted her to let it all out so she'd never have to think about it again. Not the pain. Not the barbaric treatment she'd endured. *Not none of it!*

"Tell me about it," he begged.

"I hated them for a long time, but now..." She leaned more heavily into him, and he didn't think twice when he wrapped her up tight and safe in the circle of his arms. She snuggled in under his chin like a lost child. He wasn't much, but damn it, he was there, and she seemed to need what little he had to offer. "But now that I've had time to think about it, I know I probably just frightened Mom and Dad when I flipped out. I mean, it's not like we could talk about what happened over there. They didn't know what to do with me, and there are lots of treatments for hysteria, and it could've been worse, and—"

"How could it have been worse?" He begged to differ. Her parents did something like *that* to her? She must've been out of control for them to resort to such drastic measures, but restraints? Shock treatments? What flaming morons!

"They could've drugged me," she said softly, her breath moist against his Adam's apple. "They could've made me forget. You know how it is, Jake. As bad as it was over there, I don't ever want to forget what happened, not any of my friends, either. They're who made me what I am today. They brought me here."

To me.

She sighed as if she agreed, the most perfect music to his ears. He dared lower his nose into her hair and warmth suffused his heart and soul. Heaven couldn't compare. He'd used her shampoo, but it smelled so much better on her. Jake closed his eyes and wished with all his heart they didn't have to get up off their knees and leave her bedroom. That he didn't have to let her go.

"I might not be rich like my parents," she said as she glanced over her shoulder and above her brass headboard. He followed her gaze to the wooden crucifix on the wall. "But I know who I am, and I make a difference in this world. I help people. They might not know it, but the people of Anacostia need me."

"You're just like me," he murmured. Maybe it was the guy hanging on that crucifix or maybe it was the fact they were still kneeling, but a reverent feeling joined them right then and there. Or maybe it was just—her.

The day he'd finally caught up with his drunken buddy, Jamaal, was the day Jake had decided that if he could help one guy in need, he could help a couple others, too. Jamaal wasn't much work. Mostly he just needed a friend to steer him out of the line of fire when his mouth got him into trouble. Jamaal picked fights for nothing when he got drunk, but he seemed to listen to Jake. That was how Sector 18 happened into existence. It wasn't a whole lot different than that other Sector 18. Only no one was going to die this time.

Jake had watched out for Lacy since the day he'd seen her at the clinic. So what if her apartment wasn't within the self-assigned boundaries of Sector 18? He'd made an exception.

Built just southwest of Barry Farms, so named after the flamboyant and controversial former mayor of D.C., her place was as rundown as the rest of Anacostia. But Lacy wasn't.

She'd had a bounce to her step that day, like she'd just moved into the up-scale Hilton across the river instead of a two-bit dive. Like she hadn't gone to war at all.

When her arms circled his waist and her cold fingers drifted under the back of his shirt, he knew better. He should've jerked away from her, but he didn't. The lure of her rounded, heaving breasts stole what common sense he had left. This woman was different. He'd wanted to get closer to her from the first day he'd seen her.

As if she could read his mind, she stretched up and placed one gentle warm kiss into the hollow of his neck. Just his neck. She was short after all, but she might as well have set it directly on his heart. It burned. A million gigawatts of need tripped his last circuit breaker, melting the eternal damper of his negativity. Jamaal could wait. The world could wait. Jake lowered his chin, never more certain of anything than the woman in his arms. He was good enough, damn it. He was.

His fingers daring to explore the curve of her slender back. Her graceful neck. The way her skull fit perfectly in the palm of his hands. The feel of her head in his big rough hands set his heart to trembling. As a fellow Marine, she knew damned well what a man could do with a neck as dainty as hers, and yet she'd willingly let him hold her life in his hands. This woman trusted him.

"Lacy," he growled, wanting so much to believe he belonged here in this perfect place and time. With her.

She met his gaze, her eyes swimming with soft emotions. "Yes," she said clearly, only it wasn't a question. It was an answer, the perfect answer to the question he hadn't asked yet.

Pushing off the floor, he gathered her up with him and slowly lowered her onto her bed. The time was finally right. The woman was perfect. There would never, could never be another. Only Lacy. Only now.

He'd no more than pressed his lips to her lips, when out of the deep dark pit of despair in his soul, Fantine's soul-rending plea for mercy from *Les Misérables* burst forth, drenching him in bone-chilling waves of regret. The melancholy spirit of her song lapped at his core. Life had killed his dreams as sure as it had killed sweet Fantine's. God wasn't forgiving, and Lacy was truly as pure, if not purer than Fantine.

What the hell am I doing?

The reality of his ugly, smelly male body doing what it was doing to her very delicate and exquisitely feminine self, stalled every good intention, every impulse. Even her skin was clean and white, not marred by the sun. But Jake wasn't pure, nor could he ever be again. And he knew it. He was scarred in so many ways. His face. His hands. His soul. There wasn't one part of him that had not sinned. *I haven't even shaved.*

Her bedroom walls closed in like a trap, his throat along with them, and this was wrong. He couldn't draw a breath, so he pulled away before he ruined Lacy like all those evil men had done to poor Fantine so long ago. *She's too good for me.*

He could've sworn Fantine argued, "Don't, Jake. Please, don't."

"Don't?" he asked, afraid he'd gotten lost in Victor Hugo's tragic love story, that he'd already committed the unforgiveable sin of humiliating this woman. Afraid he was on the verge of losing his mind.

"Jake. Look at me." Two hands came into his dream and pulled him back through the swirling vortex between nineteenth century France and into the reality of modern day Anacostia. It was Lacy beneath his body, not poor broken Fantine. It was Lacy's slender fingers knotted into the sides of his shaggy head, pulling him back until they faced each other, nose to nose. It hurt. She wasn't gentle, but up he came, face to face with her depths of emerald wonder, instead of lingering in Fantine's bleak grays. The pristine truth shining in Lacy's eyes stopped his heart. *I'm not the noble Valjean, but neither am I the devious Thénardier.*

"Stop thinking so damned hard," she growled, holding him fast. "Don't you dare quit on me, Jake Weylin. Not now. Not here. I know you probably think I'm ugly and crazy, but—"

"I do not," he cried out, suffering to his core that she could ever mistake his repulsion of himself for rejection of her. "It's not you. You're not ugly. You're the most beautiful creature in the world, and you're not crazy. It's me. I'm the beast. I never should have—"

"No, you aren't!" Her eyes brimmed with tears that couldn't fall because she was flat on her back. They welled up like soft green pools in her amazing eyes, and he was looking through a shimmering mirror into the soul of the most perfect creature he'd ever seen. Lacy was a well of mercy, and he was on the verge of falling into her. Of believing.

"But I've done things," he murmured, trying to understand what it was she saw in him, why she'd looked twice at him that first day in the alley, much less how she could allow him to touch her now.

"So have I," she growled, her chin up in a Devil-dog dare. "I'm a Marine just like you. I've been there, only I…" She hiccupped, her body shaking with emotion. "I need you so damned much, Jake. Don't you get it? I can't live the rest of my life being sorry for what happened yesterday. I can't stand coming home to nothing while you watch me from the shadows across the street. Let the past go. Push it away. Kick it off. Stay with me."

He couldn't bear that she, a woman so rare and sweet, was begging him, of all the men on the planet, to stay.

"I'm sorry," she said softly, the tender pads of her thumbs wiping away the trickle of moisture leaking out of his eyes.

"For what?" Jake ground out through too much regret. He blinked hard, not wanting to ever stop watching her or basking in the glow of her acceptance.

"For making you cry," she whispered. "It's just that—"

"I can't do this." With one last shudder he pulled his hands off her and lifted to his knees. Then to his feet. He was already falling for this woman, and he had to leave before it happened all over again. The last time, she'd died. Fantine was Emile and Emile was Lacy and…

Where am I going with this?

It didn't matter. They were all the same story, the same beginning and ending, and if Fantine and Emile died…

It had to stop. Lacy had to live.

Jake closed her bedroom door behind him.

Chapter Nine

She couldn't bear to look at him, afraid the moment they made eye contact he'd know her heart was broken. Her dinner lay cold on her plate mostly untouched but for a few brave forkfuls that tasted more like glue than spaghetti.

Jake wasn't like most homeless men on the streets. Yes, he was spooky tense, but he also had manners and couth. He hadn't eaten much, but the way he handled his fork spoke volumes. Instead of clenching it like a baseball bat, he held it between his thumb and first two fingers, as if he were holding a pen instead of a weapon. His fingers, though calloused, were elegant and long. Warmth flushed up from her chest at the thought of where those fingers had been. Lacy brushed a hand over her heated cheeks. They weren't the only parts of him she adored.

Despite Jake's rugged, unkempt exterior, a gentleman and a damned sexy lover lingered beneath all that overgrown hair and whiskers. Her lips and chin would know. He could've ground his face into hers during their very brief and unexpected encounter in her bedroom, but he'd seemed intent on pleasing her. For a moment.

Her thighs clenched at what could have happened. What should have happened.

Jamaal was finally awake and groggy, and eating like a starving man. He slurped the spaghetti, burped, itched, and didn't lift his eyes up from his plate once she'd brought it to him. But Jake? He sat erect with his back to the wall outside her bedroom, his plate of spaghetti on his knees as untouched as hers.

At least he and Jamaal were now clothed in the clean gray sweats she'd brought home, the sweats that declared they were the property of the Good Samaritan on Good Hope Road. Jake had balked, the stubborn ass, but Jamaal was thrilled to get into clothes that covered his entire body. Once he'd changed, Jake had begrudgingly done the same. The sweats were probably a size too large for Jake and a size too small for Jamaal, but they were clean. She'd tossed Jake's clothing into her washer after he'd emptied his pockets. His jeans and three shirts were now on the cotton cycle in her hand-me-down dryer. The minute it stopped spinning, Jake and Jamaal would be gone.

Jamaal had been strong enough to take a shower unaided while she and Jake fixed dinner. Jake moved efficiently in the kitchen and took over heating the sauce while she boiled angel hair pasta and chopped spinach, apples, and carrots for a salad.

It almost felt intimate to be working alongside this ex-Marine, doing the mundane chores of a couple. Except he didn't want her. She wasn't good enough, not even for a guy who lived on the streets. His rejection still stung. For the first time in forever, she'd offered her body up to a man who felt like he just might be the right one. What a fool she was.

The phone jangled on her kitchen wall. Thankful for the reprieve from the awkward silence in her small living room, she jumped up from the couch to answer. "Hello?"

"Lacy?" a deep male voice asked. "This is Fire Chief Balthazar. I'm sorry to bother you so late, kiddo. My guys told me they saw you at the clinic today when they brought Mr. Adams in. Listen, there's been some trouble at the clinic. Can you come down?"

Fear spiraled up her spine at the shriek of sirens and heavy engines nearly drowning out his rich baritone. "Ernie? What's going on? Who's hurt?"

"I'm sorry, but someone set the clinic on fire. Can you get away?"

Jake was at her side, his palm cupping her elbow. "What's going on?"

"Sorry, Lacy," Ernie Balthazar continued. "You might as well know. The M.E. needs you to identify a body we pulled out of the fire. If this is inconvenient, you can come to the morgue in the morning."

"A body?" She stilled. "A woman's body?"

"Maybe," he said grimly. "Check with me when you get here. We need to talk."

"I'll be right there," she said as she hung up the phone and turned to face Jake and Jamaal. "I have to go. There's been another fire. At the clinic."

Jake dropped to the couch to put his boots on. "I'm going with you."

"No," she resisted. He needed to stay with Jamaal, and she needed time away from him to think. It wasn't everyday she threw herself at a guy. "It's okay. I'll only be an hour or so, and besides, someone needs to stay with Jamaal, and—"

"Like hell," Jamaal declared from his corner of the couch. "Jake don't need to be babysitting me while you go traipsing around town in the middle of the night all by yourself. Git your coat, Weylin. See the lady to the clinic. You got a car, Miss Lacy?"

Jake was already sliding into his jacket at the door. "You know she's got wheels. Come on, Lacy. I'll drive."

His eyes glowed with all that tenderness, but Lacy pulled her gaze from his, not wanting to see any hint that he cared. What difference did it make? She stuck her hand into the side pocket of her backpack for her car keys. "Fine then. Let's go."

"Where's your coat?" Jamaal asked. "You need a coat, young lady. Don't you even be catching no cold while you're on the Lord's errand."

"It's okay," she argued. "I'm just going to my car. It's got a good heater. I'll be fine."

Jake's gray stare caught her short. "You don't have a coat, do you? How about a sweater?"

"I'm okay," she insisted, and just that fast, his jacket was around her shoulders, and she was lost in the smells and the warmth of him. It should've made her sick with the confused emotions roiling around in her heart, but it didn't. Her nose automatically filled itself with the best scent ever. Him.

"It might not be as clean as you'd like, but it will keep you warm," he apologized while he ushered her out the door. "Keep the home fires burning," he called over his shoulder to Jamaal. "We'll be back soon as we can."

"Don't you worry about me none. Just keep that pretty lady of yours safe," Jamaal retorted with a cheesy grin and one of those winks that guys give each other when they think they know something.

Jake grunted, but Lacy didn't hear much of a rebuttal. All she heard was, *pretty lady of yours*. Jamaal had picked up on that quickly, but he was dead wrong. Jake didn't want her. He liked his memories better.

She handed over both of her keys, the one for her apartment, the other for her car. "Darn it, I forgot to bring the first-aid kit in. It's still in my trunk. I hope nobody stole it."

Jake escorted her through the hall to the stairwell, his hand pleasantly on the small of her back. "Don't worry. I'm not sure why Dr. Presley wanted you to take it, but I'll run it back up to your apartment after I get you situated and start the car. That way you'll be out of the cold while the engine's warming."

"Where do you think you're going?"

Mrs. Brown. Dang. She must've heard the door close. Lacy closed her eyes and counted to ten.

"Just walking Miss Lacy to her car," Jake muttered without missing a step. "Good evening, ma'am."

"That right?" Mrs. Brown asked sharply. "Turn around and look at me, Miss Lacy. This man bothering you?"

Lacy shot her nosey neighbor a quick glance over her shoulder. Conversation with the woman was like talking with a used car salesman. As long as you listened, she kept talking and prying, asking and gossiping.

"I'm fine," she said as brightly as she could muster, not up to Mrs. Brown's brand of neighborly concern tonight. "I need to go back to the clinic. Jake offered to drive. That's all. Goodnight."

"But what's he been doing in your apartment? You been drinking? That ain't like you." Mrs. Brown took a step into the hallway and along with her came Tootsie, her snorting pug.

As Jake opened the stairwell door, his palm still on her back, Lacy turned and waved. "Bye now!" She nearly giggled. Mrs. Brown was probably just doing what she thought was best, but she seriously needed to back off sometimes. Thank goodness she didn't follow them down the stairs. Tootsie didn't either.

Lacy's world seemed to have changed. Despite the emergency they were running to, she felt safe. The damaged warrior walking beside her walked like a fellow Marine, wary maybe, but ever the gentleman.

Jake held the door for her at ground level, his hand cupping her elbow through his coat sleeve. It had started to snow. Lazy snowflakes twirled down from a dark gray sky, itself glowing from too many city lights. He smiled down at her, his eyes aglow, his hand and the key fob pointed at her car, and just that fast, her heart filled with hope. He leaned in closer. She tilted her chin up as he hit the remote unlock. His gray eyes were fixed on her lips like he might kiss her again. Her foolish romantic heart skipped a beat, and—

BOOM!

Her car blew up.

"Holy shit!" he cursed, his arms and legs encompassing Lacy, shielding her as shrapnel blasted sideways and whistled overhead. He didn't remember falling on her, but here he was, on all fours over his woman and fighting mad. Instead of sassing him, she clung to him this time, her face buried in his chest and crying, "My car! Oh, my God, my car!"

"It's not a car, it's an MRAP!" As in a Mine-Resistant Ambush Protected military vehicle. Why couldn't she see that? "We're in the middle of fucking Sector 18! They mean to kill us and everyone else if they get through that gate! Move it!"

Wrapping one arm possessively around her waist, he pushed up from the sidewalk and took off running, dragging her along with him. Paralyzing fear ratcheted up every vertebra of his spine, higher and higher until it flooded his brain with the overwhelming need to fight back and hit hard. But fight with who? He hadn't seen anyone. All he knew was that he had to get Emile to safety first. It couldn't happen again!

"Move your ass, Marine," he growled, his fingertips digging into her bicep. She had no choice but to comply. He wasn't taking no for an answer. There'd be no sassy, *'See you later, Sarge,'* this time either. Frantic for her safety, he swept her off her feet and dropped her ass into a corner where someone's stairs met the foundation of some building he didn't recognize. Fellow Marine or not, it was his job to save her life, and this time he would, by hell! She wasn't dying again!

The scenery rippled and shifted. The swirling black that thought it could win, that tried every damned day to choke the life out of him, was back. He pushed her deeper into the corner behind him before he turned to face the bastards who'd just tried to kill her.

Full of fight or flight, his body throbbed. Jake scrubbed a quick hand over his eyes, sure that crater in the street was the same damned crater from years ago. But it couldn't be, could it? No way. The smells of gasoline burning and plastic car parts melting morphed into the suffocating stench of diesel fuel, cordite, and burning flesh. He could've sworn someone yelled in Pashto, the dialect of death and war. That he now saw shemaghs around arrogant Afghan necks and the pajama-like trousers on the dangerous Taliban in a crowd that wasn't actually there proved that his nightmare had come back to life.

Once more, ghostly women drifted by in darkly colored burqas and long gray veils that hid grenades and C4 within their folds. The prevalent stink of every day Afghanistan—sewage—filled his nostrils. The distinct metallic scent of sweat and blood came with it. And death.

Sirens screamed, confusing the nightmare of Afghanistan with the reality of America.

Shit. I'm not really over there, Logic told him.

But the Taliban is here! They're everywhere! Panic interrupted with its pushy demanding need to speak too damned loud, always trying to drown out Logic. To be heard. To be believed.

Jake shook from head to toe, struggling to decide which warning was right this time and which to listen to. Pushing Emile into the corner where she'd be safe from any sniper, he shook his head, wishing he could see better through the smoke and frosty vapor billowing off the wreck. Who the hell was out there? Taliban or Poindexter? Police cruisers or MPs in Humvees? Foreign terrorist or homegrown assholes?

"Jake." Emile's fingers pinched the beard on his chin, drawing him out of the desert, back through time and space to the cold streets of nighttime Anacostia. Why was she doing that? He needed to stay right where he was so he could focus. He shrugged her off.

"Jake. Look at me," she demanded. "Are you hurt?"

"Yeah, I mean no." He turned to his right, facing away from her, needing to be one hundred percent sure they weren't being stalked and targeted. No place was safe, and this wasn't the time for small talk. Crammed into the corner with Emile like he was, he could see everything coming at them within this ninety-degree angle of visibility. No one was getting past him.

Chapter Ten

Wait a minute. A good old American, bright red fire engine had just roared up to the curb. The ground shook from its massive weight and engine power, and Jake calmed. *Good glory in the morning. Red was good.* The USA flag painted on its side proclaimed something every school kid in the United States knew. The good guys were here, and they were smart, too. The extra-long emergency vehicle blocked a good percentage of any sniper's view of Jake's hidey-hole. Several black and white police cruisers screamed to the scene. The front tire of one of them bounced onto the curb in its haste. Officers in heroic blue scrambled to the pavement.

Jake swallowed past the hard knot in his throat. *I'm in America. Not over there. I'm home.* His lungs opened wide to drink in the cold night air. *Red, white, and blue. My favorite colors.*

Panic taunted. *Are you sure this isn't Kabul?*

He nodded to himself. All that mattered was that Emile was safe this time. She wouldn't have to die tonight. He'd no more than thought that thought, when his heart shuddered to a stop at the flawed deduction his scrambled brain had just declared. Emile couldn't die *again* because she was already planted at Arlington with Aiden Scott. Asleep. Forever. There were no do-overs. There'd never be another *again.*

Jake blew a deep breath of the here and now, shaken to his core at the quandary he was caught in. He hadn't had an attack like this in a long time. The illusions always seemed so real when they hit. So damned real. Summoning up the last of his shaken courage, he turned to look closer at the woman behind him, the one he had pinned in the corner with his palm in the middle of her chest so she'd stay put.

It wasn't Emile's pretty blue eyes smiling back at him with that cocky attitude. It was Lacy's ever greens. Worry crinkled her brow. Both of her tiny hands circled the wrist holding her in the only safe place he'd found.

Jake swallowed hard. That thumb of hers was fast at work on his wrist, rubbing a small circle of comfort while her forest green eyes pulled him out of the insanity of the hallucination and back into reality. She hadn't let go of him. Better yet, she was all in one piece. No blood. No charred flesh. She had all her hair.

"I thought... I thought...." He shut up then, and scratched his fingernails down the side of his beard. It didn't matter what he'd thought. None of it was real, and he'd done it again. Time warped. Made a flaming jackass of himself.

Lowering his hard and sweaty forehead to Lacy's, he bumped it harder than he intended to. No matter how much he wanted it to be true, he hadn't saved Emile. That chance was past. That time was over. But he had saved Lacy.

"Weylin!" Jamaal screamed from the steps just above where Jake huddled with Lacy, his big voice booming over the railing. "Where you at, buddy? Weylin! Say something to me! Where's Miss Lacy?"

"Here," Jake called out, raising his right hand to signal his position. His left hand hadn't moved from Lacy's waist. It was kind of wedged in between her and the building now, not that he minded the bricks scraping his skin away. The feel of her grounded him to this moment in time. *This Sector 18. This war. Not that other one.*

It was like living in a crazy time warp, caught between that other one where Emile had died and this one where Lacy lived. Jake didn't know if he could keep bouncing back and forth between the two. Fear that he'd get stuck back in time haunted him. It could happen.

Jamaal ran down the stairs to them and instantly joined the huddle, kneeling on the sidewalk. "You okay?" he asked, his eyes wide and his big paws all over Lacy like he was checking for an injury. Funny. He didn't seem to care if Jake was hurt, just brushed right by him and headed straight for the woman in the corner.

"Let her be," Jake growled, brushing Jamaal's overly solicitous attention off her face and head. "For hell's sake, stop mauling her."

"I ain't mauling. I'm making sure is all." Jamaal always was a hands-on kind of a guy, and it was beginning to piss Jake off.

"I said let her be," he snapped.

"It's okay, Jake," Lacy murmured, her hand now soft and gentle on his tense jaw. "Let me up. You and Jamaal will keep me safe. I'll be okay from now on. I know I will."

She said the right words, but it didn't always work that way, did it? Jake looked down into the purest emerald treasures. He'd just found her. What if he lost her before he ever got the chance to tell her how he felt? Like the last time? How could he live if anything happened to Lacy? He'd done it once before, but he wasn't strong enough to go through that again. NO man was.

Finally, he had no choice. Jamaal pulled him to his feet and Lacy came along with him. "You kids sure you're not hurt?" he asked, his big mitts brushing the snow off Lacy's butt and down her legs.

"We're good," Jake said as he tucked her protectively under his arm where Jamaal couldn't help her so much. She had more to fear from his buddy at the moment than anyone else. Jake dusted the snowflakes out of her hair. Good didn't begin to describe the knot in his throat with her tight up against him like she was. Her warm palm in the middle of his pounding chest felt perfect.

The funny shine on Jamaal's face caught Jake's eye. The big guy had tears streaming down his face. Well, hell, yeah. Jamaal was there the day Aiden and Emile were killed, too. Maybe he was time warping? Jake had never thought of that before. He grabbed Jamaal's wrist before the big guy manhandled Lacy anymore. "You okay, buddy?"

Jamaal ducked his head, avoiding direct eye contact, but he wiped his face with the back of his hand as he looked into the street and muttered, "Yeah, I'm always good after I damned near lose my best buddy and his girl to some crazy-assed bomber. Hell, no, I ain't good! I'm mad is what I am!"

"It's okay. No one was shooting and we didn't get hit by any shrapnel," Jake reminded him.

"Yeah, well…" Jamaal shrugged his grip off. "You two scared the crap out of me. I dropped my damned plate of spaghetti when I heard the explosion, and I come running."

"I'll make more the minute I get back," Lacy assured him.

Jamaal shuffled his big bare feet on the icy sidewalk. Damn. The guy hadn't even put his shoes on.

"You need to get back inside," Jake said as his heart settled down to a manageable pace.

Jamaal leaned against the side of the stairs. "Not going anywhere 'til I know you're safe."

"My car," Lacy said softly. "It's gone. Guess I'll be walking from now on."

"No, you won't," Jake declared. "I'll find a way. I'll... I'll…." *I'll call Zack. He'll help me.*

Lacy didn't argue, just snuggled into his side like she belonged there. Damn, her pulse throbbed through her whole body. She might not look it, but she was plenty scared. "I've still got to get to the clinic. Fire Chief Balthazar is waiting for me. I told him I'd be there."

"Ernie?" he asked, smoothing a hand over her head, needing to touch her, to feel her trust in him.

"You know him?"

"Sure. Everyone knows Ernie Balthazar. He's one of the good guys," Jamaal broke in. He waved at one of the boys in blue with one knee to the ground while taking crime scene photos with his camera. "Hey, Bro. Yeah, you! We got us a real important lady over here who needs to get to the Good Samaritan clinic" —he snapped his fingers— "right now. How about you jump up like a good boy, and give her a ride?"

Jake cringed. Jamaal's big mouth would be the death of him someday, but asking a police officer to provide taxi service was too much. Calling him *boy* was another offense all together. Disrespect never ended well, even between two black men.

Sure enough, the officer shot Jamaal an aggravated look, but he did climb to his feet. "Just cuz I'm black doesn't make me your brother, wise guy, and your lady friend's not going anywhere. The clinic's a crime scene. She needs to answer some questions."

"She ain't my lady friend. She belongs to him." Jamaal stabbed a thumb at Jake. "Besides, I know all about the fire at the clinic cuz Captain Balthazar called her to come help him, only now her car blew up, and you're standing there giving me a bunch of lip when you oughta be offering her a ride in your nice safe cruiser. Don't you guys know nothing about customer service?"

The officer ignored Jamaal's rant and strode over to Lacy, raking a suspicious eye over Jake. "Evening, Lacy. This is your car? Are you okay?"

"Yes, I am, Kevin. It's good to see you, but I'm sorry it had to be for something crazy like my car getting blown up. This is Jake Weylin," she nodded toward Jake, "and this is Jamaal McCune. They're staying with me for a while. Guys, this is Officer Kevin Madison. He's a good friend of mine and one of Anacostia's finest."

When Kevin shot Jamaal and Jake another disparaging glance, Jake shifted from one foot to the other with Lacy still in his arm. He was beginning to feel persecuted.

"Sorry, Lacy. I don't mean to pry, but we received an anonymous report right before the fire at the clinic. The caller said he'd seen two suspicious guys hanging around there tonight, and except for their clothes, these two fit the description. You mind telling me where they've been all day?"

"In my apartment," she answered quickly. "A cabbie brought Jamaal to the clinic early today with a near concussion. He couldn't stay there, so I brought him home with me at noon. He's been asleep most of the afternoon, and Jake came to watch over Jamaal so I could go back to work. That's why they're in gray sweats from the clinic. Look at them, Kevin. A couple of guys beat them up earlier today, probably the same ones who torched Lamont's Pool Hall, the clinic, and now my car."

The young officer peeled his penlight off its belt holster and shone a spotlight right into Jake's eyes. He squinted and lifted his hand to block the beam. "You always take your male patients home with you?"

"I do when my friends need help," Lacy replied, her fingers squeezing Jake's hand. She shot him a determined look. He winked automatically. She was certainly jumping out on a limb for him and Jamaal.

"Hmm. You do look like someone might've hit you a good one. You'd better get that eye looked at." Kevin gave Jamaal the same once over with that damned bright light. "Who's this guy to you?"

Jamaal shrugged, his hand in front of his face to block the light, too. "All I know is I was going to meet Jake for litter patrol this morning, only I ended up at Lacy's apartment, and she just fed me the best damned spaghetti I ever tasted, and my head feels like it's going to explode through the top of my head if you keep sticking that light in my face. You ever had spaghetti with kielbasa sausage?" He rolled his eyes. "Man, that's some good stuff, brother."

"I'm not your brother," Officer Kevin hissed, a definite warning in his voice. "And what's litter patrol? Some kind of community outreach program you two hooked up with?"

"No," Jamaal declared, rubbing two fingers together. "It's just something me and Jake do to make a little cashola. You know, coinage? We collect aluminum cans and Rowdy down at the Flying Angels buys it. It's what gets us by."

Kevin grunted. "What you mean is that it gets you a bottle. Listen, I'm going to let the two of you go, but only because I know Miss Wright, and her, I believe. You guys I'm not so sure about."

"They're Marines," Lacy said proudly, and Jake could've kissed her. "They're every bit as honorable as you are, Kevin. The only difference is they served, and you're still serving."

"Former Marines," Kevin bit out.

"Ain't no such thing as a former Marine. Can you give Lacy a ride to the clinic or not?" Jake asked before Jamaal ruined the trust Kevin had in Lacy by shooting his big mouth off again.

"I will as soon as I finish my report. You going with her?"

"I'd like t—"

"Yes. He is," Lacy interrupted, her hand clenching his tightly once more. "We're together."

Officer Kevin looked as surprised as Jake felt. Once again, threatening brown eyes scrolled over him like a razor with a mission to get to the bottom of all things, but Jake didn't shuffle his feet this time under Kevin's intense scrutiny. Lacy's quiet declaration might have come out of the blue, but it stirred that same protective feeling deep in his gut. She didn't care what anyone thought of her hanging out with a shabby looking guy like him. He lifted her hand to his lips and kissed the back of it, his eyes pinned to Kevin's to prove her point.

Kevin's upper left lip lifted. He took a menacing step into Jake's comfort zone. "You'd better take damned good care of Miss Wright," he said, his voice laden with threatening promise. "Do you hear me? Lacy is one in a million, and I'm not convinced you deserve her."

Neither am I. "Yes, sir," Jake answered automatically. Hell, any fool could see he didn't deserve her.

The police report didn't take as long as Jake feared it might. Within the half hour, Officer Kevin, Jake, and Lacy were at the Good Samaritan crime scene. By the looks of the clinic, the fire had done only minor damage, most of it contained in the lobby. The front glass doors were shattered, but none of the staff was around, not even the swing shift crew. With Chief Balthazar standing at their heels, the medical examiner unzipped the body bag, and the time warp commenced sucking at his limbs and eyeballs, his stomach and his soul all over again. As much as he didn't want to be there any more, Jake forced himself to breathe in slow and steady breaths. Lacy needed him in the here and now, not time warping to who knew where.

She gathered her hair over her right shoulder and peered down at the corpse. Whoever it was, the decedent's wrists were wrapped behind its back with wire. Its ankles were restrained the same way. There was every possibility this guy had been burned alive while seated, possibly tied to a chair, only the chair had burned completely away. The flesh was burned off the blackened skull, leaving no hair, no eyeballs in the sockets, and a twisted, wide-open jaw that still seemed to be screaming for help.

It's her. It's Emile. That's what she looked like, Panic stated emphatically.

But you're holding onto Lacy, wise Logic intervened. *It's not Emile because she's asleep at Arlington. She's at peace, Jake. Let her be.*

Logic always did have a euphemistic way about it. Jake nodded that he understood precisely where Emile now was even as he cringed at the gruesome sight. Letting his fingers clench Lacy's shoulders, he wished he could identify the remains so she wouldn't have to. Burned flesh was never an easy sight to take in.

The odor of the place taunted him with pounding flashbacks. One moment he was holding onto Lacy in Anacostia, the next he was back in Kabul, pissed and angry and sick at heart because he hadn't saved Emile and Aiden. He loosened the fake collar on his sweatshirt and hung on tighter to Lacy, scared the moment he lost contact with her that he'd time warp for good. That he'd never find his way home.

Home. Funny. That was how he felt with Lacy. Safe and sound and—home.

"I don't know who it is, umm, was," she said in the quietest voice. "But he... he looks like he was scared when he died."

An odd buzzing sensation swept up from Jake's boots, all the way to the roof of his mouth. He clamped onto Lacy's trembling shoulders and turned her away from the grisly scene before he lost control and the buzzing took over. "Why'd she have to come all the way down just to look at that?" he growled, casting a dark look at the fire chief.

"There's no way to positively ID anyone who's been burned that badly." *And I would know.*

Balthazar nodded sadly. "Maybe not, but I had to be sure. I also needed her to see this." He led Lacy and Jake to the side of the building. Painted in red across the white concrete wall of the clinic was the threat: *Lacy Wright Dies Next!*

Chapter Eleven

"It's blood, isn't it?" Lacy asked, bile climbing up her throat at this awful night.

"Yes," Balthazar said. "We just don't know whose."

Lacy couldn't speak. Her pounding heart hadn't let up since she'd left her apartment. *Lacy is next?* What was that supposed to mean? *I'm nobody. All I wanted was to stay hidden and small and—invisible.*

Only Jake's extra tight hand at her elbow kept her knees from buckling. When an especially vicious shiver jerked up her spine, he pulled her into his side and led her back to the front of the building.

"Wait a minute. Where is everyone?" she asked, her head reeling. "This place should be jumping. There should be patients lined up and ornery because they have to wait their turn. It's the flu season, guys. Where are all the people? The staff?"

"The clinic was empty when we responded to the call, all except for the deceased," Balthazar explained while the M.E. rolled the body bag away from the scene on a gurney with squeaky wheels. "The police are canvassing the neighborhood to see if anyone saw or heard anything. The clinic was still working a twelve hour, twenty-four-seven shift rotation tonight, correct?"

"Yes, we were. Dr. Anderson, Roxy, and Jeanette should've been here, Carol and Bonnie too. Nights are always busy." She peered through the broken glass door to the demolished office. "Maybe Dr. Presley, too. Where are they?"

"Lacy, look at me. What aren't you telling me?"

Fire Chief Balthazar's tone caught her short. The kindest gaze reached out to her from the worry lines of his dark, handsome face. He always did have some kind of weird sixth sense where she was concerned. Maybe he was like that with everyone. The man just seemed to know when she was having a tough day, but there was no way she would betray Marlee's trust.

"I've told you everything I know," she replied evenly, *because I can't tell you what I don't know for certain, and I don't know what's in that black box. Yet.*

Ernie Balthazar's eyes were the kind of gentle, grandfatherly eyes that could see right through a person and make them feel like a sneaky kid. The kind that could make a girl confess to anything and everything she'd ever done wrong in her life. If she let him get to her.

She returned his gaze, determined he'd only see what she wanted him to see—a strong woman and a Marine, not some hysterical nutcase with bright red burn lines across her forehead, and a rubber plug in her mouth so she couldn't bite her tongue off. Or scream too loud.

Experimental treatment for hysteria, my ass. That jerk-off lied to my parents. He'd claimed he could cure me with one shock treatment. Then why'd he keep me locked up for seven days? Why'd he keep shocking me? Why'd I finally have to lie and tell him I was cured before he'd take the straps off? Why can't I ever go back home because I'm afraid of what my parents think of me? Because of what he might've told them? The sonofabitch!

Jake must have sensed she'd taken a mental detour down Hysteria Lane. He'd pulled her into his solid body, and her butt once more pressed tight against his thigh. She gulped despite the strength radiating from his touch.

"Are you going to be okay?' he asked, his lips nearly in her ear. "Do you need to sit down?"

"No, I'm good," she said. *I guess. But what moron wrote that creepy message? Why would anyone want to kill me? What could I possibly know? That my secrets are driving me nuts? That I can't walk this tightrope much longer before I start screaming again and prove I've lost my mind? And furthermore, whose freaking blood did that psycho paint this message with? Who's dead? Everyone, but me?*

"Are we done here?" Jake asked.

The steady and strangely calming physical contact with the other half-crazy person at the scene amused her in a verging-on-hysteria kind of way. After the day she'd just had, her nerves were shot, but not so bad that she couldn't see that she and Jake were at the same level of sane, which, if she guessed right, was mostly just barely. Maybe even borderline cuckoo. Her hands shook despite his arm circling her shoulder and neck to rein her in. Did he know how close she was to falling apart? Could he tell?

Working long shifts at the clinic had kept her moving forward, but some days were just damned hard to get through, and this was the worst. Her mind strayed to the secrets hidden in her closet, the things she'd never let anyone see.

Maybe it's time to pull them out, and declare to the world in one bright and bloody statement who and what I really am. Maybe it's time everyone knows.

Hysteria eked steadily up the back of her throat like water from a plugged drain that had nowhere else to go, pushing for release. She ground her butt harder against Jake, scared to death the maniac within her might make a break for it and start cackling any second now.

And how will that look, huh?

Jake circled her neck and shoulders with his arm, sticking his chin into the crook of her neck. He seemed intent on keeping her close to him, but he didn't seem to think she was crazy.

Ha! What does he know?

Chief Balthazar rubbed the back of his neck and sighed in the patient way of an honest man who'd worked too many long hours in a thankless job. "We're done here," he said wearily. "I'm sure the police will have more questions for you, Miss Wright. Call me if you think of anything else."

Oh, crap. Did he just call me Miss Wright? Not Lacy? Not kiddo?

"My car got blown up tonight, Ernie," she offered weakly, needing him to know she was in more trouble than she'd ever been in before. Needing him to care like he always seemed to when he'd visited the clinic. Crazy or not, Jake was right. Ernie Balthazar was one of the good guys, and she needed him to see her.

A soft smile tugged the corners of his weary brown eyes. "I know, Lacy. Heard it over dispatch on the way here. Wished I'd been on that call instead of this one."

Me too. Tears sprang to her eyes. Her heart stopped pumping too much blood for its own good. He still cared about her. *See? That's all I needed.*

"You do know I'm always here if you want to talk, don't you?" he asked. "About any of this? Anything? Anytime?"

"I do," she sighed. There were good men everywhere, even on the tough streets of Anacostia. "Thanks, Ernie. I'll be in touch." *There. That didn't sound crazy now, did it?*

"You can bet your next cup of coffee on it, little girl," he said, his grandfatherly kindness in place once more. "I'm buying. Maybe a piece of that chocolate silk pie you like so much, too."

Lacy could have cried. The simplest things were all that kept her going some days. How did people not get that? Kindness freaking mattered!

Kevin had stayed to give her and Jake a ride back to her own crime scene, but she knew he'd been watching and listening the whole time. He tucked his handy dandy little notepad into his shirt pocket, no doubt with every word she'd said recorded for his report. She expected more questioning, but he surprised her. "Are you ready to go home, Miss Lacy?" he asked kindly. "I've got a nice warm patrol car at your bidding."

"Yes," she said. This damned crazy day had to end. It just had to.

Chapter Twelve

He couldn't hold her tight enough, not in Kevin's patrol car, not walking up the stairs to her apartment, and not once he got her inside her apartment with the deadbolt and all those other nifty fasteners firmly locked behind them. It didn't matter that he'd come to his senses earlier during their brief encounter in her bedroom. Jake was a man and he was wrong about Lacy. He needed to prove it.

They didn't make it past the refrigerator before they devoured each other in one long physical connection that they both seemed to need more than oxygen. She clung to him, trembling with more than just fright. Even Jamaal turned his face out of respect for the hungry kiss Jake covered Lacy's mouth with.

Her breath became his breath, her pulse pounding in sync with his as if they shared the same fire in their blood. With one hand firmly rooted at the back of her neck, he deepened the kiss, wanting every last thing she had to give him right there and then. She returned the offer, her tongue tangled with his and tasting, her teeth nipping at his lips while both arms hooked around his neck and held him tight. Like he needed to be held, too. Like she couldn't bear to let him go.

Such lovely restraint only made him more certain. Jamaal was on his own tonight. He'd better keep his big black ass inside the apartment where it belonged, and he'd better not screw this one good thing up because Jake was bedding down with Lacy, no ifs, ands or buts.

"Ahem," Jamaal coughed politely, which meant he either wanted more spaghetti or they were embarrassing him. Jake broke the kiss, but didn't release Lacy. No way. With his fingers still in her hair and around her ear, he pressed her head under his chin while he turned to face his buddy.

"You good?" Jamaal asked.

Jake nodded. *I am now.* "We need to talk," he said decisively. The time had come to strike a better offense against Poindexter, and who better to fight that war than three Marines who just happened to be in the same place at the same time? "I'm not waiting for Poindexter's henchmen to come back and finish what they started. It's time we strike back."

Jamaal's eyes lit up, but those weren't the eyes Jake needed to see. He peered down at the soft and warm woman in his arms. Forest green glittered up at him with determination and maybe a little bit of *Oo-rah* and a dash of *hell, yeah.*

"When?" she asked, her chin tilted in defiance like the good Marine she was.

Suddenly Jake was front and center of his squad again, and all eyes were on him. His inner sergeant stepped up and cocked his head. Right on cue his shoulders squared. "We have something Poindexter wants. Lacy, you're up. Tell Jamaal what you brought home with you. It's time he knows."

She took a deep breath, squared her shoulders, and faced Jamaal. "Marlee gave me evidence that might convict Poindexter. At least that's what she said."

"Why don't y'all come in here and sit down so I can see you better?" Jamaal asked, his big bruiser body half-turned on the couch to face his buddies in crime still in the kitchen. "Hell, I been waiting for you half the night. I had to make my own fourth helpin' of spaghetti. Cleaned the kitchen, too. Did y'all notice?"

Jake took a minute to scan the spotless kitchen. His buddy had even dried the dishes. "Thanks. You're a lifesaver."

Jamaal shrugged, but the light in his sappy eyes said it all. Even a big drunk needed an 'atta-boy' once in a while.

Lacy pulled out of Jake's arms, headed for her bedroom. While she was gone, he hurriedly doffed the Good Samaritan duds and changed back into his jeans and T-shirt. Her apartment was warm enough that he left two layers of his shirts folded and sitting on her desk. Before she returned, he dropped to his butt alongside the couch, leaving room for Lacy. Wearing underwear after months without having any was a nice touch, a little confining in the crotch at times, but nothing he couldn't handle.

When she came back, Marlee's cash box rested at her fingertips by its silver handle. "I don't have a key, and I don't know what's in it, so don't ask," she said as she took her seat beside Jamaal.

Jamaal lifted the box out of Lacy's hands and studied the keyhole, his face scrunched up like it always did when his mind was actually working. "These things have a simple rotating lever the key flips up into a hole inside the frame of the lid. When the lever's up, it clamps onto the lid. When the lever's down, it releases. It's not like there's tumblers or anything complicated to work with. The key blade only turns the lever. I'm surprised she didn't use a stronger lockbox with a combination if her evidence is so important."

"Can you open it?" Jake asked, wanting to get to the point. Whatever Marlee had on Poindexter, he needed to see it.

"You bet your ass I can. Get me a screwdriver, and we'll be inside this baby in no time."

Lacy jumped off the couch and went to the cabinet below her kitchen sink. Pulling out a small plastic toolbox, she returned promptly with two screwdrivers. "I didn't know which you needed," she said, offering a Phillips and a standard, handles first to Jamaal.

He shot Jake a sly wink. "Now how's she think I'm going to pry the lid off with a Phillips?"

Jake had to readjust his position on the floor as the most adorable blush colored Lacy's neck and cheeks. He hated that Jamaal had put it there, but damn, her feminine response glowed all over her lithe body. She'd probably thought she was being efficient and saving herself another trip bringing both screwdrivers, but thank goodness she hadn't seen how the sight of her affected him. Or his jeans.

She punched Jamaal's bicep to bring her point home. "It's been a long day. I wasn't thinking, okay?"

He chuckled, stuck the flathead screwdriver under the edge of the lid and very gently turned it less than a quarter turn to the right. The top popped open as easy as if he'd used a key.

"Wow. That was quick," Lacy said.

"You see, Lace, it's all in the wrist," Jamaal demonstrated like anyone cared. "All a guy's got to do is—"

"Yeah, yeah," Jake muttered as he scrambled to see what was so important.

Jamaal handed the box over to Lacy. "It's all yours. Open it."

Her fingers trembled on the handle, but she lifted it without any fanfare. A thumb drive was taped to the bottom of the box. That was all.

"Talk about anti-climactic," Jamaal grumbled. "I was hoping to see a wad of cash, maybe the pistol Poindexter used to kill a senator or something."

"Do you own a computer?" Jake asked as Lacy peeled the drive out of the box.

"It's in my closet," she said, a funny look shadowing the usual light in her eyes as she handed the box back to Jamaal. "Hold this. I'll get it."

When she was out of earshot, Jamaal asked, "She keeps a computer in her closet? Don't you think that's a little weird?"

"No weirder than two guys hanging out in her apartment all day like a couple ghouls." *At least she owns a computer.* Jake pushed off the floor. "I'll go see if she needs any help."

"Yeah, you do that, why don't you." Jamaal snickered.

Jake ignored the taunt, but that was when he discovered what Lacy hid in her closet. Were they her secrets? Peering into her darkened bedroom about stopped his heart. She hadn't turned the light on. Only her trusty nightlight caught the show. But what a show.

Jake closed the door behind him. He had to. The place was filled with artwork. Of sorts.

One canvas after another now lined the closet side of her room. She stood half-inside her closet, pulling out another wood-framed oil painting. And another. He stopped dead in his tracks. The war in Afghanistan had come to life with all its ugly reality in oil painting after oil painting. One showed nothing but a box of bloody legs and arms. One particular arm reached out from the bloody mess, the fingers spread wide as if reaching for help.

Another canvas was filled with a close-up of half of a man's sweaty face, his angry eyes framed by tear-laden lashes. Jake looked closer. In the brimming reflection of his eyeball was the horrific view of a beheading. The sword was still raised in the fierce Taliban warrior's hand. The object of his wrath, another Marine, lay bound with his arms behind his back, his body bent over a tree stump. A chopping block. A very bloody chopping block.

Jake licked his lips, not realizing his mouth was open until he did. In yet another painting, a soldier knelt in globs of oil painted mud with his hands clenched uselessly at his sides, his head tipped back, his eyes squeezed shut, and tears rolling down his bearded face. Jake recognized the horrific angst of that stranger. His mouth wasn't opened. He wasn't screaming. That poor soldier was—coping. Coming to grips with Death in the only way he knew how. Cursing God.

"Lacy," Jake said hoarsely, not sure what he was looking at, torment or therapy. The lovely tragic paintings were everywhere.

She jerked upright with yet another canvas clutched in her hands. "Jake, I... Umm, I didn't hear you."

"What's all this?" he asked, gesturing toward the macabre gallery. "Did you paint these?" *Please tell me you didn't.*

A particularly sad one had just caught his eye, a depiction of a soldier's boot in the sand, only no leg was attached to the foot in it. Blood dripped from the severed veins as if a heart still pumped. The damned stream of red ended at the stem of a pink rose growing out of the desert sand. The leg had to have belonged to a woman to end up at that pink flower like it did.

Claustrophobia swept up from the bedroom floor, filling Jake with the need to leave in order to breathe.

"I paint," she answered quietly, her gaze riveted to his face. "Least I used to."

There were no words. Each painting was a beautiful work of the saddest art. She'd caught the light and darkness of each scene in such a way that she'd brought the soldiers, or what was left of them, to life. Or death. The one of the man on his knees looked vividly lifelike, his anguish palpable, so think Jake could taste it.

The reflection of the beheading looked eerily lifelike, too. Lacy certainly knew how to capture the face of terror. But how could one human being put all that raw heartache on canvas? The undeniable beauty of her work scared Jake, but it also pulled him in. There was a reason behind this—art. A scary reason.

Taking one slow step after another, he pushed the suffocation aside and entered the realm of a woman he didn't really know. The woman he thought he honestly already loved, but who just might be as bat-shit crazy as him.

"Why?" he asked, his throat as dry as an Afghanistan desert. "Why remember all this? All of them?"

"I don't," she whispered guiltily. "Once I paint them, I say a prayer, and I let them go. It's the only way I can help them—and me—move on."

He gulped, needing a helluva big open window and a lot more air than this tiny room offered. "Help them?" *God, woman, they're not the ones who need help. It's you.*

Lacy set the large canvas she'd just pulled out of her closet on the bed. "I can't help them if I can't paint them, Jake. They roam around in my head, and they keep dying until..." She gulped one of her noisy gulps. "It's like they're stuck in time like me. They can't go forward and they can't go back, so I put them on canvas, and I let them be real one last time. I breathe on them while I paint them, Jake. They get to be warm again."

She nodded at the portrait on her bed, a collage of blurred faces where only one stood out in horrible, dramatic detail. She'd painted an Army Ranger with his buddy cradled in his arms. *God, the pain in that haggard Ranger's eyes.* "I give them a part of my soul, and I talk to them, Jake. I let them feel the hairs of my paintbrushes and the soft, smooth glide of the oils. They get to smell the linseed and the turpentine. If it's a good day, they listen to my music with me. Sometimes I cry with them. Sometimes they do all the crying. None of them wanted to die, you know. But sometimes we laugh, too. They tell me their stories. I tell them mine. Then I tell them it's okay now, and then..." Her voice trailed into a whisper. "I let them go."

He couldn't stop staring. "Do they leave then?" *Christ, I hope so.*

Her pretty red head bobbed adamantly. "Oh, yes. At least the ones I've painted so far have left. I think they find peace in knowing they haven't been forgotten."

To anyone else, Lacy would've sounded fifty shades of stark raving crazy, but Jake got it. He knew right where she was coming from. She'd found a way to keep one foot in both worlds, one with her lost friends from Afghanistan and one in the sometimes scarier, civilized world called America. She'd found a way to self-medicate that didn't involve drugs or booze. Or suicide. In her mind, she'd found a way to help her buddies. Best of all, she'd found a way not to time warp out of control.

But the thought of all she'd seen during her deployments scared him. "How many f-friends did you lose?"

"You have to understand," she said. "I was part of the security detail attached to the foreign press corps. Because they needed to be where the action was, I travelled all over Iraq and Afghanistan. Wherever they went, I got to go."

There was pleading in her eyes, so Jake gave her what he could. "Tell me," he said as he lowered to the edge of her bed, wanting to better understand.

She blew out a deep breath between pursed lips and pointed to the canvas of the leg and the pink rose. "Okay. So for instance, this is Lance Corporal Terry Ash. Roadside bomb. IED. She bled out in Laghman Province before anyone could get to her. Her mother owned a floral shop in Oklahoma. I can't remember the name of the town, but I'm sure she told me. We talked a lot while I was painting her portrait. So okay, umm, I wanted Terry to let go of what happened to her over there and go home to her mom, so I painted her blood trickling into the rose. Nourishing it so that something beautiful would grow in the desert that took her life. Her mother likes pink roses. I sent Terry home in a rose, Jake."

Jake stilled and listened. It made sense to him, but then, it would. He was crazy, too.

"And this guy." Lacy tapped the canvas of the Marine on his knees. Her fingers grazed his muscular shoulder like a compassionate friend. She'd even caught the layer of dust on his anguished face and the prism in the teardrop in the corner of his eye. "This is my buddy, Guy Rodriguez. He and his K-9 were part of our detail. They were killed in Ghazni Province, Afghanistan. Taliban ambush. That's what he looked like right after his dog went down in a hail of automatic fire. Kiska. A silver German Shepherd with black tipped ears."

Lacy took a deep breath. "Guy got shot within seconds of Kiska because he ran to help her. It happened fast. I know because I was there. He loved that dog. I killed the bastards who killed him and his dog, and I'd do it again if I had to. He wanted me to use a palette knife instead of a soft brush. Guy said he needed to feel again."

Her voice had taken on an eerily calm tone, as if she were repeating lines she'd memorized from an old high school play. "It's funny though. I never thought to paint Kiska. Maybe because she's already home? Huh."

"Who's this?" Jake asked of another piece. It showed nothing but a rectangular piece of the stars and stripes, but he knew exactly what it was—the flag over a casket on its way home to someone's mom and dad. Or their wife or husband.

"Gerald." She stroked the flag tenderly. "Fire fight. Helmand Province. He wanted his dad to be proud of him, so I painted the flag he went home under. He said his dad would know he was beneath it because it was our flag and the reason he gave all," she explained as if she totally believed she had spoken with the dead man. "May I paint someone home for you?"

"No, umm," Jake paused. A once perky blond in scorched and bloody desert cammies sprang to mind. *Man, what if this crazy idea worked?* "Maybe..."

Lacy sat with him. "I don't blame you if you think I'm crazy, Jake. When I processed out, I came home to this huge void in my life where no one knew what I was talking about. It's like I was a walking zombie, only no one seemed to care that I was still dying, and they sure didn't want to hear what I needed to tell them. So I stopped trying, and I kept everything to myself."

She folded her hands in her lap. "Only I couldn't stop crying. I had this big ugly hole in my heart, and an ocean of tears inside of it that no one could see. I couldn't sleep, and my brain was on overload trying to remember what and who I was before I joined the Corps. It's like I was caught in a game of *Whack-A-Mole,* and someone kept hitting me in the face with a sledgehammer to make me fit into America like everyone else, only I couldn't. I still can't. I never will."

He grunted, knowing precisely what that sledgehammer did to a person.

Lacy kept going. "I don't understand the people in my country anymore, Jake. I don't think I want to. It's like they're too busy with stuff that doesn't matter. None of them care what's going on over there. None of them care about us, or what we have to live through once we come home. One day it hit me. I was so alone that all I could hear was the echo of my pain dripping in my soul like a drippy bathroom faucet nobody could fix. And do you want to know what it sounds like? It's the pebble you drop into a deep dark hole, only it never hits bottom. It just keeps falling and you keep waiting. I started screaming, and it kept dripping, and, well, you know how that turned out."

"Do your parents know you're in Anacostia?" Jake asked.

"No. Do yours?" she asked right back.

"No," he had to admit. He hadn't talked to them in a couple years. Didn't think he could. That was what had brought him to Jamaal. Only someone who'd been there understood.

She took his fingers in her hand, stroking them individually. Her fingertips smoothed over his nails and cuticles like she needed to commit them to memory. Or she was crazy.

"See. You're hiding, Jake, just like me. My mom and dad live in Baltimore. My sister and her husband own a nice home down south in Richmond. They're not far away, but I don't want to see them. Why do you think I don't have a cell phone with a bunch of stupid apps like every other person in the world? Cell phones have GPS cards, Jake. Somehow my parents would find me. I know they would. They'd want to fix me, and I'm sorry, but I don't want to be fixed. I'm not the one who's broken. They are."

He looked into her eyes, searching for a hint of crazy, but all he saw was trust. Everything Lacy had just said made perfect sense. Even the paintings. They were her brand of self-medication, her way of finding closure with the havoc war had left in her psyche. In her heart.

He lifted her slender, clean fingers to his lips and placed a kiss on the tips of them one by one. "You're amazing, Lacy Wright."

She grunted. "Ha. You're the one who's amazing the way you took charge before. I thought I was going to lose it at the clinic. That threat or whatever's painted on the side of the clinic freaked me out, and poor Ernie gave me a look like he didn't know who I was. I had the craziest urge to start painting again, only I don't know who that burned up corpse used to be. How could I help someone I don't know find their way home? That corpse looked like a banshee. All I could see was the scream coming out of its mouth and—" A full on body shiver attacked her. She pulled her hand away from Jake to rub it off her arms. "I can't get that picture out of my head until I know who it was. You don't think I'm too crazy, do you?"

Too crazy? Not just crazy? He retrieved her hand, needing to maintain the physical contact. Holding onto her gave him time to formulate an answer. It made him feel grounded for the first time in a long while. "You're no crazier than I am."

"Is that supposed to make me feel good?"

Jake had to smile. She was right. Either they were both crazy or they were both struggling like hell to adjust to time and space they'd never fit into. Either way, they were now in it together. "Maybe there is one person I want you to paint," he said, "but not until this thing with Poindexter is settled. Her name was Emily Blum, only she changed the spelling to Emile so her CO's would think she was a guy when they looked at the roster. I know I was looking for a guy the day she showed up."

"She was important to you?"

"Yes," he answered honestly. "Only I never told her. We served together." He stopped right there. Talking about the past never helped the present. Only mucked it up was what it did. Made it harder to focus. To not time warp.

Lacy's eyes lit up. "I'd love to do that for you. Anything. And you'll see. It helps to let them live one last time even if it's only to say goodbye. Thanks for believing me."

"Why wouldn't I? You're nothing but believable, Lacy Wright," he said with another kiss to her fingertips. That led to a taste of the tender pulse at her wrist. Another on the pulse at her neck, and she was as aroused as he was. He eased her down to the mattress, but the thought of her lying with those brutal paintings spoiled the mood. There were just too many people in the room and most of them were dead.

As if he'd been summoned, Jamaal pounded on the door. "You two fall asleep in there? I thought we were going to plan defense? If you're staying in bed, I'm going back to sleep."

Lacy burst into a giggle. "Oh, oh, we've been caught."

"Do you really have a computer in your closet?" Jake asked before she pulled away.

"Actually, I do. It's a laptop. I never use it because I thought maybe there was a GPS locator in it, too. I'll get it, but it might need a charge."

"Stop worrying about being found," he said, his fingers refusing to let go of hers even as her hand slid out of his. "I think you already are."

And there was that smile again, that breathtaking piece of heaven dropped straight as an arrow into an apartment in crappy Anacostia. She crashed on top of him, the warmth of her soft breasts mashed into his chest, her palms at his cheeks, and her lips temptingly close. Every muscle sprang to stiff attention. She had to know what she was doing to him. No way could she miss the proud salute his body was giving her.

"You know what that means, don't you?" she asked breathlessly while she planted a kiss on the end of his nose. Another on each shaggy cheek.

The sweetest breath brushed over his face, blessing him with the love of an amazingly tough and resilient woman. Now he knew how those guys and gals on the canvasses must've felt like when she painted them. Life seemed to flow from Lacy. The atoms of oxygen in her breath made him want to suck in a deep breath of her and start living.

"What?" he asked weakly, his hands on her taut little backside and his heart in his throat. If he kept tearing up every time she came close, he'd have to turn in his dog tags and his man card with them.

She landed one last whisper-kiss on his nose. "It means you're found, too."

Chapter Thirteen

"I don't understand," Lacy muttered. This was the big secret? The scary evidence? A video of Rafe's fiftieth birthday party?

The video on Marlee's thumb drive looked innocuous enough. And totally boring. Rafe Poindexter had shot some of the footage himself while Marlee shot the rest. They were at his California house in La Jolla with his family. Go figure that one out. Apparently, Marlee and Rafe weren't the lovers Lacy suspected at all. Either that or they were damned brazen to be at the same party with his wife and daughter.

Birthday banners and balloons decorated the huge outdoor deck overlooking the Pacific Ocean. His pretty wife, Kelly, waved in one scene and blew him a kiss. In another, a blond little girl named Kenzie called him daddy and asked him to pick her up, which he promptly did. Nothing looked out of the ordinary. Rafe mugged for the camera with Kelly, their cheeks pressed together while Marlee captured the seemingly happy couple. Marlee interacted with Kelly and Rafe's only child as if she were a close family friend.

"Boring," Jamaal said for the eighth or ninth time from the opposite end of the couch. Jake said nothing from where he sat on the floor at Lacy's knee. The three had watched it play all the way through without seeing anything suspicious or sinister.

"Play it again," Jake said. So they did. Jamaal yawned, and Lacy had to admit, it was the kind of family video that put everyone to sleep. Poindexter didn't swear in it. He didn't threaten or intimidate anyone, either. He fixed Kelly and Marlee an apple martini, and he played peek-a-boo with his daughter, Kenzie. He even snuggled his cute little white schnauzer, Pekoe.

"This video makes him look like father of the year," Jamaal muttered. "Turn it off."

"No," Jake said. "Let it play. We're missing something."

Jamaal rolled off his end of the couch and shuffled to the refrigerator. "You got any cold beer in here, Lace?"

"Bottom shelf. Don't drink them all."

"You don't need a beer," Jake said without looking up from the laptop screen.

"Who are you? My father all of a sudden?" Jamaal asked.

"No, I'm your friend. Remember me, the guy who drags your sorry ass to the clinic every time you drink too much? You know what will happen."

Jamaal giggled, the can already opened and at his lips. "Pretty soon I'll have to pee?"

Jake sighed. "Just one."

The beer disappeared in three swallows. Jamaal smacked his lips, burped a loud one, and opened the refrigerator. "I hear something calling my name. Oh, there you are."

The video ended. Lacy crossed her arms over her chest, frustrated. She hadn't expected a puzzle for evidence.

"Can we watch it in slow motion?" Jake asked, his elbows on his knees and his eyes still riveted to the blank screen. The man did have a powerful ability to focus.

"Can we stop watching it and go to sleep?" Jamaal whined, another beer in his big hand. "It's been a helluva day, and if I'm tired, Miss Lacy's got to be exhausted. She's the only one of us been working and runnin' her pretty backside off."

Lacy held her breath. Something felt wrong in that perfectly normal video, but she couldn't put her finger on it. "How about if we turn the lights off, close our eyes, and just listen to it while it runs?" she asked. "Maybe our ears will pick up what our eyes are missing."

"The minute you turn off the lights, I'm going to sleep," Jamaal grumbled, his fingers wrapped around his third beer. "Unless you two want to join me on the floor and we could have us a threesome?" He lifted his hefty arms and shook his backside like he meant to dance. Or something.

"Knock it off," Jake growled, finally moving his eyes from the screen to his buddy's bounteous jiggling butt. "Lacy's in trouble and you're not helping."

"Well, excuse me," Jamaal ground out, the comedian routine stowed. "Who put you in charge of me?"

"I'm not in charge, but you know how you get when you start drinking."

"I knows I gets loose, and I gets sexy, and if'n I'm lucky, I gets down," Jamaal purred as he shimmied across the floor behind the couch, only to moon-dance in reverse once he reached the bathroom door. "Chill out. I got my jive on, but you need to git yours on, too. Want a beer?"

"Are there any left?" Lacy asked. Jamaal seemed to swallow them whole.

"Turn off the lights, Lacy," Jake said quietly. "Let's try listening like you suggested. With our eyes closed and our other senses engaged."

"Don't do it, Lace," Jamaal declared, his finger in her face. "I ain't staying if you turn 'em off. After the day I've had, I gots to par-tay!"

She opted for camaraderie instead of confrontation. "If you're tired why don't you go sleep in my bed? I won't mind and—"

"I ain't really sleepy, Lace, if you catch my drift." Jamaal waggled his brows. "Will you come sleep with me?"

Jake's head came up with a snap. "Knock it off."

"It's okay. He's just—" Lacy started to answer, but Jamaal was having none of what Jake was giving him.

"You need to back off, bro," he growled as he leaned over the back of the couch, pointing an index finger in Jake's face.

Jake took a deep breath and rose to his feet. The difference between the two men was night and day. Jamaal was big-bellied, thick-necked, and just plain big all over. He easily made two of Jake, whereas Jake stood tall, his build lean and wiry. He looked more like the typical old west gunslinger with a slight bow-legged stance and his jeans riding low on his hips. All he needed was a six-shooter at his side on those hips and a Stetson to go with the glint in his eye. His palms were spread at his side, his right index finger flexing as if searching for a pistol grip.

Lacy climbed out of her corner of the couch. These guys were squaring off, and she didn't want it to be because of her. "I could make popcorn," she offered as a last resort.

Jake didn't back down, but Jamaal's nose twitched. He stood facing Jake for another long minute before he asked out of the corner of his mouth, "You got butter to go with that popcorn?"

"Butter and sea salt," she answered quickly, her heart pounding to beat the band. If these two giants decided to go at it…

Jamaal burped and immediately covered his mouth with his fingertips. A silly smile crept over his face. "Oops. I farted."

"Oh, for god's sake." Jake rolled his eyes and stabbed a finger in his buddy's big chest. Honestly. Jamaal had man-boobs all the way around to his back. "You're drunk. Listen up. If you disrespect my woman one more time, you and me are going to have trouble, you understand?"

Lacy's ears perked up. *My woman?*

"Sure, Jake, whatever you say, old buddy and friend," Jamaal answered, the problem seemingly out of his mind and the last of Lacy's beers in his mitt. "Miss Lacysure knows how to pick 'em."

Lacy turned to grin at Jake. He pushed his hair out of his eyes and winked slyly back at her. "Jamaal gets a little rowdy when he drinks. It only takes one. How about we take a break? I'll help you make popcorn."

"Sure." Lacy didn't need help making popcorn, but if it brought him into the kitchen with her, she was all for it. "I've got orange juice if you need something to drink."

"Nah. Water's fine," he said, looking into the cupboard over her sink. "I used to drink as bad as he does. Spent a lot of time being stupid before I figured out it only made me feel worse."

"Glasses are in the next cupboard over," she directed him while putting one bag of popcorn in the microwave and attempting to slow her pulse rate. Just having him in the same room was doing crazy things to her body. Crazy wonderful things. His words to Jamaal still burned. *My woman.*

He filled two glasses with ice from one of her ice trays and topped them off with water. "I expected he'd freak once he woke this afternoon," Jake confided, the glasses on the counter and his fingers comfortable on her shoulder. "He doesn't usually do this well in small spaces. At least he's not drinking whiskey. It's like poison to him. He can be a mean drunk, mostly because he starts telling everyone how bad it was in the Corps and how grateful everyone should be for guys like him."

"Well, let's eat and solve this damn puzzle. I'm ready for bed," she replied, the popcorn done popping, and who cared about food anymore? Sexual tension arced between her and this wild man from the streets. Every move he made, every seemingly innocuous contact between them sparked her need to be lying beneath him on that bed of hers.

Jake bumped her with his hip, glancing over his shoulder at Jamaal. "I'm sorry I panicked earlier. You wouldn't mind a little company tonight, would you?" His hand slid down her spine, over the waistband and straight down the seam of her jeans. She held her breath. When those fingers could go no farther, he cupped her ass, squeezing heat into her already overheated and clenching butt muscles, like she needed to be set on fire when she was going up in flames.

Lacy turned into his arms, her mind made up and feverish with need. "It is an awfully big bed."

Jake wrapped his arms around her, mischief welling up in those gray eyes. "Can you last just a little longer? I'd like another shot at that video, then we'll, you know."

Lacy didn't care what was on that stupid video anymore, but Jake made sense. They'd barely gathered the bowl of popcorn and the drinks when Jamaal declared, "Hey, you guys. Git in here. You gotta see this."

Lacy stood behind the couch with Jake peering over Jamaal's back.

"What are you watching?" she asked. An entirely different scene was on the screen, a still shot of some disgusting pornography or something. There weren't nearly enough sheets to cover that old man's saggy ass, not in the expose-all position he was in.

Jamaal shrugged. "I don't know. I just did this." He snagged the mouse and clicked the cursor twice to open the video file again. Only it didn't bring up the boring .wmv.file of the Poindexter home this time. The picture on the screen blinked off and a menu box displayed with the two headings: EVIDENCE and 911.

Eight bullets of what looked like surnames with jpg. extensions were displayed beneath the first heading. Wilson. Schwartz. Cummings. Delong. Croyhill. Middleton. O'Grady. Pine. There were no bullets beneath the 911 heading.

"Which one were you looking at?" Jake asked as he came around the couch and sat next to his buddy. Lacy took the cushion on the other side of Jamaal, the popcorn bowl in her lap.

Jamaal positioned the mouse over the first name and clicked the cursor to open the file. "This one right here. Wilson."

The same disgusting shot flashed back on screen. Whoever the old fart in that photo was, he had an anchor tattooed on his flabby right butt cheek. And he was busy screwing whoever he had in his grip.

"Keep going," Jake urged, and Jamaal complied. The second picture was full frontal and very recognizable.

"That's Dylan Schwartz, the governor of California," Lacy gasped. "Ewww. Gross. Turn it off."

"Who's the chick with him?" Jamaal leaned in closer. The naked governor had a naked woman in the crook of his arm while he planted a kiss on her cheek. Her eyes were squeezed shut. She looked too young to be with a man his age.

Each bullet revealed similar shots of naked older men with dark-skinned younger women of Asian heritage. None of the girls looked happy. Despite wearing too much make-up, their eyes were flat, devoid of the skanky come-on gleam of a happy pro on the job.

Jamaal skimmed through the photo shoots quickly until they were lined up in a disgusting matrix on the monitor screen. The final menu item titled 911 was a video clip of a very frightened Marlee Presley sitting on the edge of a bed in a lavish bedroom, facing the camera, and shaking from head to foot.

"In case I wake up dead, I want the world to know that Rafe Poindexter is black mailing all of the governors and politicians on this clip. That's why he's got so much clout all of a sudden. That's why he thinks he can do whatever he wants." She glanced to her right and then to her left before she continued. "I'm in his house in California right now. If you're watching this, then something's already happened to me. Don't waste time looking for me, because make no mistake. He will kill me if he catches on. Listen. There are more. He keeps all of his blackmail shots in the safe behind the desk in his home office."

Another fearful glance over her shoulder, another worried look, and Marlee licked her lips. "These little girls aren't hookers, and they aren't Americans, either. They're fresh out of Thailand and they're scared. They're part of the virgin trade from Cambodia. Most of them aren't even fourteen years old yet." Marlee leaned into the camera. "Please help them. He's got to be stopped."

Lacy held her breath. Why was Marlee in the middle of something so awful?

"There's only one problem," Marlee whispered, her face closer to the camera now and the sweat on her brow easy to see. "Rafe's got another file at his office in D.C. that documents where he's getting the girls and who's providing them. I've seen it. Some guy named Prentiss is behind all this. He runs a private airstrip on the East Coast and he flies back and forth from Thailand all the time. That's how he gets them into the country. I don't know who their contact is in Thailand. The only reason I know anything is because Rafe—"

Marlee glanced over her shoulder and called, "Just freshening up in the guest bathroom. Don't start without me."

Her last words were hurried. "He's got balls, I'll give him that. The dumb ass thinks I'll help him treat the girls when one of these jerk-offs he sells them to, hurts them. I will, because I care about the girls. You can't imagine what I've seen, but listen. He's bringing more into the country on December twenty-third. They're just babies and I don't know what he does when he's done with them. I'm afraid he's killing them. Please, please help! I gotta go." The video went black.

"Oh, my God, it's her," Lacy whispered. "That burned corpse. It's Marlee."

Chapter Fourteen

"I'm going in," Jake declared, his hands on his knees and his mind made up. Now that he knew what he was up against, the clock was ticking. Those little girls needed help, and he needed to move before Poindexter knew what hit him. A surprise attack was the only way, but it had to happen fast.

"In where?" Lacy asked, her eyes tearing up at what they all knew now to be true. Rafe had murdered Marlee Presley in the most gruesome fashion. The bastard had to pay.

"Into Poindexter's downtown office. Let's stop the bastard once and for all."

"Sex slaves," Jamaal hissed. His alcohol daze had faded. "It's bad the world over, but it's damned disgusting in Thailand and Cambodia. Parents there sell their little girls just so the rest of the family can survive. Damn it, I want to look at those pictures one more time."

Jake didn't need to. All they did was make him angry to the point of losing his self-control. They confirmed why his flesh crawled every time he'd seen Poindexter's arrogant face on the cover of some magazine or newspaper at the newsstands. The only way this takedown could be sweeter was if Marlee had gotten a shot of Poindexter with one of those girls.

"Guys. Talk to me," Lacy ordered, her voice quavering. "Tell me what's going on."

Jake took a deep breath. "Cambodia's a stinking poor country. There's no such thing as children's rights over there, and it's not uncommon for families to sell their daughter's virginity when times get bad. It's a sickening practice, but it's been going on for generations. It's one of those cultural beliefs where older men believe sex with a virgin will increase his virility."

"The younger the better," Jamaal growled, his finger tapping the mouse to click from file to file. "Look at this one. She look old enough to be doing something like this?"

Lacy peered closer. A young girl peered over the shoulder of the man named Croyden. Stark desperation showed on her face. "No. Someone's put a lot of makeup on her, but look at her eyes. She should be at home with a loving mother. She's just a little girl."

"I say we go to the police with this, Weylin," Jamaal declared. "Where's your phone, Miss Lacy?"

"And do what?" Jake jumped to his feet. "All we've got is pictures of everyone but Poindexter in compromising positions. These jokers will be in trouble, but he'll walk. No, Jamaal. I'm going into his office for that file in his safe. I want the smoking gun that ends this bullshit once and for all."

"That's why he's able to do whatever he wants," Lacy said thoughtfully. "He's blackmailing these guys."

"And some of them are damned powerful," Jake agreed. "All he has to do is snap his fingers and they make whatever he wants, happen. Zoning variances. Real estate deals. Land swaps."

"It's not working so good for him here in Anacostia," Lacy said.

"You don't think so?" Jake asked. "Look around. Is there a grocery store within miles that anyone who doesn't own a car can get to? I'll be honest. More guys than just Jamaal and me have been getting beat up. I just never put two and two together until now. Think about the increase in arson. Lamont Adams' place isn't the only one that's been torched in the last few months. It all makes sense now."

Lacy's eye color changed from forest green to nearly gray. "Marlee said the same thing, but you can't go looking like you do," she said quietly.

Jake stuck his fingers into the roots of his thick, messy hair. No, a wild man would tend to stand out in Poindexter's office. "You'll help me, won't you?"

"No," she answered quickly, shaking her head. "I won't. I'm not going to help you get killed. Like you said, look around. Where's Marlee? And where are the rest of my friends from the clinic? I'm scared they aren't alive anymore, Jake. I'm not going to lose you, too."

Her voice had grown higher with every word, and he got it. He really did, he just didn't have it in him to walk away from endangered children. Who else would save them if not him? Still, he couldn't hurt Lacy, either. Fantine's sweet words whispered a song of regret to him, of dreams dying and hope along with it. A familiar wave of helplessness surged up within his soul again. There had to be a way to reveal Poindexter's vile sex trade without destroying the beautiful thing he'd just found with Lacy.

He put it to her and let her decide. "What would you have me do? Tell me and I'll do it."

"Not fair," she murmured, her tears glimmering once more.

"I know." He fell to one knee in front of her, taking both of her hands in his. "It's not fair, but what if that was your daughter in one of those shots? You of all people know what it's like to be betrayed. Hell, Lacy, what if that was you? Should I call the police and stand around and wait for them to do something?"

She blinked, her eyes brimming with emotion, and he felt like an ass badgering her. "Their parents are the reason they're with those men in the first place," she said quietly. "You know that. If all you do is send them home, they'll just get sold again."

"You're right," he agreed, "and your parents are the ones who sold you out. You're just like those little girls."

"Not fair," she whispered once more, and he knew exactly what she was thinking. Between her worry for him and the goodness he knew was inside her, Lacy battled her conscience and her common sense. Hell, he was too. Could he get into the mighty Rafe Poindexter's office without raising suspicion, then get out with the incontrovertible evidence to bring him down? That remained to be seen. Would he try his damnedest? Could he bring Poindexter to his knees? You bet, but only with a lot of luck behind him, and— if he had Lacy stashed somewhere Poindexter couldn't reach her.

"Life isn't fair," he said softly, her fingers as cold as ice in his hands. He lifted them to his mouth and blew warmth on them, rubbing them to chase the chill away.

"You're just like me," she said, so quietly that he leaned in closer to hear her better. "I paint. You do stupid stuff like getting yourself killed."

He offered her the only argument he had left. "We're Marines. I guess we were born to do everything the hard way. Go figure."

She launched herself into his arms, nearly bowling him over. Jake caught her and settled back to the floor with her in his lap. Her tears wet his skin, and he choked. *What am I doing? Hurting her to save others? What is wrong with me?* He couldn't even speak. All of his bravado had fled, and once more, he was just a man holding onto the most precious thing in his life. Afraid he'd lose it.

"I'll help you," she murmured into the crook of his neck, "but only on one condition. Don't you dare die."

Chapter Fifteen

Lacy couldn't stop shaking. Her hands weren't all that was cold.

"I trust you," Jake reminded her, his eyes forward. "Make me look good."

Well, he'd better trust her. A woman with a pair of scissors in her fingers could be mighty scary, especially one who already painted ghosts for a hobby. Holding a strand of his hair above his head, she held her breath and took the first snip that would turn him from vagrant to civilized. The man had a gorgeous head of hair now that she'd brushed the tangles out and had her fingers sifting through it.

She hated cutting it, but he needed to fit the profile of a businessman, and he refused to wear it in a man bun or a ponytail. He said it made him look like a sissy and no Marine wanted that look.

For now, Jamaal had fallen asleep on the floor alongside the couch. He said he preferred the floor and she understood. She did too sometimes. It connected her to her old life. To her friends in the Corps.

It was past midnight and their plan to infiltrate Poindexter's office was in place. They'd pooled what little financial resources they had. Jamaal knew where he could pick up a second-hand suit and matching men's dress shoes for Jake at a local thrift shop in the morning—if someone hadn't already bought them. He'd pick up three burner phones on his way back. If Jake was as good as he thought, this nightmare could be over by noon tomorrow.

She'd Googled Poindexter's office address. It ended up being in Foggy Bottom, instead of in the District like Marlee had said. One of the oldest neighborhoods in D.C., its name derived from the industrial haze and fog off the Potomac River to its south. George Washington University took up most of Foggy Bottom's real estate, but Rafe Poindexter's recently built office building stood like a beacon of extreme wealth overlooking the river. Facing south, its mirrored glass windows by day were outlined by muted blue lights by night, making it look as if it belonged in Las Vegas instead of the nation's capital.

He owned the entire fifteen-story building and leased all but the ground floor where his real estate office was located. According to his on-line ad, thirty-three agents worked for him. They were listed along with their pictures. Jake had immediately recognized the two who'd beaten him up. Rocky Rabbit's real name was Bret Clayton. Ferret Face was Leo Shunck.

The plan was simple. Step one: Lacy would call Rafe first thing in the morning. She'd insist on speaking with him personally, because she had a blackmail offer he couldn't refuse. Only she had to meet him in person. That ought to get Rafe out of his office in a hurry. His henchmen, too.

Only Lacy and her cohorts wouldn't be at the meet-me address she was supposed to give him. They'd already be in Foggy Bottom and watching his office from a safe distance. Once Rafe and his thugs cleared out, step two would commence. Jake would enter the building on the pretext of being one of Rafe's fraternity brothers. The things a person could learn on the Internet.

Jake would pass himself off as Bernie Rothschild, the same college friend who'd trounced Rafe in a previous real estate venture that ended up costing him millions and a lot of pride. Jake's resemblance to Rothschild was uncanny. He figured he could schmooze his way into Rafe's office to wait for him, because while Rafe might be proud, he was also greedy. He'd want another chance at his old fraternity brother.

At that point Jake, aka, Bernie, would divulge his plan to publicly declare a merger with his Fortune 500 company, *East-Go-Tech*, and Rafe's real estate business that could make Rafe millions.

Crunch time started once Jake was inside Poindexter's office under the pretext of fraternal camaraderie. If Rafe fell for Lacy's threat of blackmail, he'd be on his way to Anacostia, a good drive from Foggy Bottom on a good day. Once there, Jake would make the second call as Rothschild, to bring Rafe running back. Another thirty minutes.

That gave Jake an hour to locate the information on the girls from Cambodia, and get his ass out of Dodge before Poindexter made it back to his office. The plan hinged on pride, greed, and on Jake keeping his cool.

Jamaal had said, *'Ain't nothing hard about it.'*

But Lacy thought, *'Sounds impossible to me.'*

Pinching another section of Jake's silky hair in her trembling fingers, she eyed the portion she'd already cut and snipped again to the same length. Jamaal snored like a banshee while section-by-section, Jake's shaggy hair fell to the floor. With every snip, a very handsome man emerged beneath her hands. By the time she'd taken the electric shaver to his neckline, Lacy was trembling for another reason all together. She'd always been attracted to the neckline of a strong man, but damn. This guy cleaned up nice.

"Wait," she said, needing to make a minor adjustment to the length over his left ear. "I can do better. Hold still."

She'd left his hair longer on top. Streaks of mahogany mingled with dark browns fell to his forehead, but it was a hack job at best. Raking her fingers through his hair to make sure all lengths were semi-even, she froze. The tips of her breasts were mere inches from his lips, and his hands were suddenly on her hips as if he needed to hold her in place. Like that helped. Every calloused fingertip of his burned through the thin fabric of her scrub top to her skin. Dark gray eyes peered up at her from beneath the thickest black eyelashes that no man had a right to own, and she knew damned well that her nipples were all but shouting for his attention, the treacherous, swollen little traitors.

"Could I talk you into giving me a shave while you're at it?" he asked innocently, his palms warming her thighs and other places he hadn't touched yet.

Uh-huh. Yeah. You can talk me into anything. Liquid heat spiraled to her core. She couldn't break eye contact, and she was melting at his feet.

"Lacy?" he asked as if she might not have heard. Did he have chapped lips or what? He kept running his tongue over the bottom, licking it like she wanted to lick him.

"Sure," she answered breathlessly. If one of them didn't blink pretty soon, she'd combust on the spot, right there. All over him. "But I only have the shaving cream I use, umm, for my legs."

"Legs. Face. I'm sure it all works the same."

Heat flamed up her neck at the thought of their faces and legs in close proximity. As quiet as this guy could be, Jake certainly knew how to tweak her libido. Easing away from him before she went up in flames, she set the dangerous scissors in her shaking fingers on the counter and went to retrieve something even more deadly. Her razor.

Determined to get her mind out of the gutter, Lacy marched to her bathroom and shut the door behind her before she flicked the light on. The woman smiling back from her bathroom mirror positively glowed.

Trembling, Lacy gathered her shaving supplies, another towel, and a washcloth for later. She changed the cartridge in her razor. That beard was tough. Stiffening her resolve, she opened the bathroom door.

The sound of her vacuum caught her by surprise. Lacy gulped, paralyzed from the neck down. Jamaal still snored from the floor. The noise of the vacuum didn't seem to faze him, but it was fazing her. At least the man using it was.

Jake's shirt now hung over the back of her couch. For a low-life transient, he was built. Pure muscle. Wiry muscle. Lean. Trim. Hard as a rock muscle. His neck and arms were tanned in the way of guys who worked for a living. His broad back was clean. No USMC tattoos marred him, at least not as far as she could see. Lat and traps, holy hell he was packed. Narrow at the waist but thick and solid from there on up. His biceps bunched, stretched, and contracted as he pushed and pulled her cheap little second-hand vacuum. Damn. He made it look like a toy.

To make it better, he was singing, his voice low and nearly overwhelmed by the noise of her vacuum, but not enough that she couldn't detect the tenderness in his deep baritone. The passion. He closed his eyes and his voice lifted into a heartrending, "Bring him home!"

Lacy's fingertips reached out to him. She wanted to touch. The guy was to-die-for gorgeous, a bit rough around the edges but one hundred and fifty percent male, and he was in her living room, singing his heart out and working it like a Chippendale stripper. All he needed was the black bowtie around his neck and—

How am I going to shave him now? My hands are shaking. I'll hurt him.

Jake looked up from his chore and turned the vacuum off. A puzzled smile shifted through his gaze. "Did you say something?"

"Umm, no," she said, embarrassed unto death because she might've blurted that last thought out loud. "You sing?"

His shoulders lifted. "Les Misérables. Sorry. Jean Valjean sings it much better than me. I don't do it justice."

She couldn't stop staring. "It was amazing."

He shrugged, wrapping the cord around the vacuum's handle. "Ready?"

Lacy nodded. "Yes, um, take your seat."

He obeyed instantly and resumed his position at the slaughter, umm, chair. But damn. How did a horny woman, one who could barely keep her hands steady, shave a half-naked man, when she'd rather hang on to those handsome body parts? Right on cue, she fumbled the scissors and they fell. He caught them neatly before they hit the carpet, turned the handles back to her, and it was all she could do to not meet his gaze. One look would do her in.

"Thanks," she offered a raspy appreciation and took the scissors without touching his fingers. Or looking into his eyes. "It's shaggy." *And thick and sexy.* "I'll need to trim the length first." *If my fingers will stop shaking.*

He gave her a quick nod of agreement, lifted his chin like an USMC enlistee about to be shaved jarhead style, high and tight. It was all Lacy could do to swallow. He might be sitting there with his hands politely flat to his thighs, but—those thighs. She wanted to be straddling those monsters, not leaning against them.

Once she made the first cut, it was easier to focus on what she was doing and how she had to do it. NOT. This was damned personal work on a gorgeous male, and she was touching his face, nose, and lips, not just the hair on his head. Her fingers refused to stop trembling.

By the time the beard on his sharp rugged chin was shorn to a manageable length, she was drenched and throbbing. Her toes kept curling. How could she continue revealing him, body part by sexy body part, and still give him a proper—and safe—shave?

This handsome face was all hard edges and angles from the jut of his brows over his sexy eyes to his squared-off, delectably clean-shaven jaw. And it was tough not to notice how his nostrils flared. The man seemed to be drawing in steady breaths of—*me.*

Arousal slammed into her at what he was smelling. Her body's desire. For him. Shaking her head to clear her mind, she traded the scissors for her razor. Her pink razor. Now the tricky part.

"Don't you want to apply shaving cream first?" he asked.

Duh! She cringed, stalked to her kitchen sink and ran hot water over the washcloth, sucking in enough air to clear her frazzled mind. "Yes. Sorry. I was—" What? Distracted as hell? Horny as all get out?

"Never mind," she said brusquely. "Tip your head back."

His obedience Did. Not. Help! The second he did as she'd ordered, every muscle south of her heaving ribcage clenched. The man was polite, considerate and just plain thoughtful. He'd be so-o-o-o good in bed. Covering his face with the hot wet cloth brought her a short reprieve, but *GAH!* How was he not affected by the steam rolling between them like waves off the desert? The quicker she finished, the better.

Peeling the cloth off his face, she tossed it into her sink, and lifted the can of shaving cream. If only she could've covered those gray 'portals-to-his-soul' with the foam. Gallantly she filled her left palm with the pink gel and stepped in close.

"I really do appreciate all you've done," he murmured in that hot sexy baritone that rumbled straight to her groin.

"'S okay," she said, her fingertips full of gel. With one sweep, she covered those full lips only to discover they were soft. His cheeks and chin went under the foam next. The pink gel turned to white lather when it hit his damp beard, and her knees turned to spaghetti. Leaning backward to the counter, she grasped the handle of her razor and steeled her frazzled nerves. As long as she didn't look into Jake's moody eyes, this shouldn't take long.

God, give me strength. I just need another minute or two.

"Chin up," she ordered.

His chin lifted, exposing his rugged neck. Carefully, she took long slow strokes up his neck, shorter ones around his lips and under his nose. Between rinsing the blade under the stream of the running hot water in her sink and twisting back to shave another clean path up his face, he'd transformed once more. Inadvertently she'd leaned against his thigh with her elbow at his upper arm to steady her hand to keep from nicking him. Her lower back ached with need.

A puff of heated air hit her arm. "You were right," he growled as his hands settled to her hips.

That came out of the blue. She paused. Lather streaked his face. She'd missed a few whiskers, but no more freaking foreplay! "I was? Right about what?"

His eyes darkened. With one hand still on her hip, he removed the razor from her fingers and set it on the edge of the counter. He pulled her down to his lap. "I don't want to live the rest of my life being sorry for what happened yesterday. I can't change it. I can't fix it. All I can fix is now and what happened between us today. I'm sorry I made an ass of myself before. I didn't know what I wanted then, but I know now."

"Whatever's haunting you, you can survive it," she whispered, finger-combing his thick, lush hair. "We can help each other. It's okay to be two instead of one."

He groaned, his eyes squeezed tight, against what she didn't know. Strong emotions radiated off him. "I thought finding Jamaal would make it stop," he ground out. "I thought saving him would make it go away."

"Make what go away?"

He took her left hand and placed it over his heart. "This hollow feeling right here," he said as he moved her palm to his cheek. "And this pain." He moved her hand to his forehead. "The nightmares."

She straddled him. Arousal coursed through every inch of her body. Jamaal was just feet away, but she was ready to comply with whatever Jake wanted regardless. Sex in the kitchen? *You got it?* On the floor? *Ready, set, go.* But he seemed sad.

She cupped his chin with both hands, her heart opened wide for this tender, battered warrior. "Kiss me," she whispered. "Let me in. Let me help."

He took her mouth slowly, tasting her lips and tongue carefully. He seemed almost tentative the way he tilted his head for better access. Breathing was over-rated so she inhaled nothing but him and the scent of shaving cream that came with him. This was all about being with him. When he breathed, so would she. Until then...

The warm hand at her hip slipped to the cheek of her ass. With one gentle clench of his fingers, she was on fire. If he hadn't tasted so good, she'd have pulled him to the floor and had her way with him, but she couldn't bring herself to break the connection with his mouth. Not yet. Hunger flamed to life, roaring for satisfaction. He deepened the kiss, and her soul responded in kind.

With both hands on her backside, he secured her legs around his hips and stood. He kept kissing. She kept on tasting. With a few long strides, he angled past the couch and through her bedroom door.

Only when he set her carefully on her bed did she open her eyes to drink him in. The light from the other room did him justice. Rakishly handsome, his hair flopped loose over his forehead, the rest of him trimmed and neat. Rubbing the back of her hand over her lips, she wiped his shaving cream off. She hadn't noticed his well-defined chest before or the smattering of hairs that delineated his pecs, but she noticed now.

His muscles didn't bulge like the juicers she'd seen at the clinic, though. His were massive squared-off hunks of granite suspended over a trim waistline, and they were as hard as the rest of him. Her tongue took a trip around the inside of her mouth, hungry for more.

But he was unsure. Hesitant. "Are you sure you want a guy like me?" he asked.

"Jake Weylin," she growled. How could she get through to him? "Look at me. What the hell do you think?"

Bouncing off the bed, she flipped her light switch on so there would be no doubt left in that hard head of his. Standing in front of him, she tilted her chin up so she could see into his eyes. So he'd know once and for all. Wordlessly, she unbuttoned her top and shrugged it off her shoulders.

He bumped the door shut with his butt, and those dark grays didn't miss a thing. His gaze softened to hazy when it landed on the tops of her breasts. He almost made her feel embarrassed, but the light in his eyes was nothing short of adoration.

When her fingers unsnapped her jeans and pulled the zipper down, the gray turned to black. His breathing shallowed. She shimmied her ass out of her pants and toed them away. There she stood in nothing but matching mint green bra and panties. The only reason she'd bought this set was the dark green satin bow between the cups of the bra, set off by a red glass bead. They looked Christmassy, like holly and a berry. She'd never intended to be doing a strip show, but for this man? *Whatever works.*

A smile tugged at the right corner of his mouth. He dropped his pants and underwear and....

Now it was her turn to groan. She gulped loudly, an annoying tell she had to get over one of these days. He had to have heard. The man was—blessed, and by the looks of him, damned sure of what would happen next.

He winked, a sexy smile tweaking his lips. "I like holly."

She offered her hand, inviting him to her bed. Instead, he gathered her up in one armful and tossed her onto her mattress. Placing both palms to the bottom of the bed, he stalked her. The prey instinct within her quivered when his sinuous shoulders moved like a jungle cat's. She wanted to run from him as much as to him. Wet with desire, she lifted onto her elbows, half afraid to take her eyes off him. The second she bent both knees and dug her heels in to scoot backwards to her pillows, he pounced. She squealed.

"Oh, no you don't," he growled playfully, his hand at her ankle. With one smooth jerk, she was beneath his naked body. Out of breath, heart pounding in her ears, and her legs spread. One hot and sexy man hunkered in between them.

Lacy was as wanton and as ready as hell. She wiggled against him until he snagged both her wrists and raised her arms over her head, pinning her beneath him with his hips. And his tongue. She whimpered at the meal he was making of—her. At the power he held over her, and the way it aroused her. If he didn't hurry, she'd detonate all over him

"Hi," she said weakly and totally enamored. Wow, he was a big guy.

Weighing her left breast in his right palm, the sexiest growl rumbled up from deep in his throat. "You're perfect," he muttered.

The deep baritone rumble shivered over every tightly strung chord in her body and soul. The panties had to go. She was already too close to the edge. Just one wrong word and she'd—

"Come," he said, his hand extended to pull her to her feet.

And she did, but not how he'd meant. His gentle foreplay was her undoing. Shockwave after shockwave of screaming heat consumed her while Jake knelt over her in awe, the dearest light in his eyes as he watched her unravel. Finally loved, there was nothing she could do but hold onto him and cry as wave after wave of exquisite pleasure tumbled over her.

"I'm sorry," he crooned, stretching his rugged body alongside hers. "I didn't know you were so responsive."

Yeah, me neither. She swallowed her tears, spent with the quickest climax she'd ever experienced and the rolling aftershocks that came with it. The rollercoaster ride continued with more fireworks at every crest, and barely enough dips on the track to catch her breath. She clung to him. *And I intended to seduce him?* She'd never gotten out of the gate. If this was what he could do with just his hands and mouth… Penetration would definitely be interesting.

"What you do to me," she whispered, her cheeks wet with emotion.

The man was pleased with himself. Male pride glittered in those sexy dark eyes. "What you do to me." Lowering his head, he covered her mouth with his, and the game was on.

Chapter Sixteen

"The light," Lacy whispered, pointing to the wall switch at the left of her bed, but Jake was past modesty. He wanted to see every last piece of her.

Kneeling over her in one of the Corps' best push-ups, with one elbow to support his weight, he slipped his fingers beneath the strap of her bra. Exposing one small but plump breast, the dark pink nipple had already peaked and pebbled, waiting for his mouth to work its magic. He used to know to work that kind of magic, but now it felt more like a miracle had unfolded over them both. Something bigger was happening, and with all his heart he wanted it to never stop.

He kept on going, taking her nipple between his lips, afraid he'd hurt her with the intensity of the storm building within him. But a man could only want for so long before nature took control and set loose a million years of animal instincts. When Lacy arched her hips upward into his cock and moaned, forcing more of her breast into his greedy mouth, he succumbed to the powerful magnetism of her body. He tasted, nibbled, sucked, and all out devoured the tender offering. Around and around his tongue went, pulling her nipple into the hot recesses of his mouth only to release the succulent nub so he could torture the other.

Nothing. Not one damned thing in his life had ever tasted sweeter. She growled from deep in her throat, her long bare legs wrapped around his waist, and her fingernails in his back, spurring him on. Like he needed encouragement. His hands seemed to know what they were doing, but he was operating purely on instinct, tasting, kissing, and all but inhaling every tender piece of flesh his lips touched. Her breasts. Her stomach. The twitching, ticklish band of muscle that stretched below her abdomen and between her hipbones.

Moving back up, he sealed her mouth with his unbridled desire for forgiveness and an insatiable need to live again in peace. To not be afraid to live. Into that kiss, he poured the things he never thought he could feel or would want to share again. Or need to give away so desperately that it hurt. The only things he owned. His honor. His heart. His love.

Please don't let me fail this woman, he begged the universe. *Help me love her best. Treasure her most. Never fail her. Never hurt her.*

Lacy took all that he gave, her delicate fingers laced through what was left of his untamed hair. She pulled him tighter, not offering any quarter, but forcing her tongue into his mouth and devouring him as much as he was devouring her. Panting for breath, she attacked him with a passion and a need so desperate and feral that only another warrior could understand where it came from.

It was the same for Jake, a hunger to belong to someone who truly cared, to not have to face the torment he'd dragged home with him alone. In filling Lacy's needs, the strangest sensation happened to the hollow thing barely living inside Jake's chest for years. It wasn't' an empty hole anymore. His heart warmed. It expanded. It throbbed and pulsed with—life.

He swallowed hard. The ugly black shadow that had taken over his soul and his sanity faded, and in its place came something better. Something real and pulsing and alive and… God, he wanted more.

"Love me, Jake. Please, just love me," she demanded as her fingers moved to his neck, holding him in place as if she needed to trap him. She didn't. His self-doubt had fled along with the shadow of regret. He was willing to love again. Her pretty panties went next and Lacy became his world. Poor desolate Fantine was forgotten, consigned to tragedy while he chose life and love and Lacy.

Well, yeah… His world had gone erotically tactile. The light in her eyes encouraged him to keep going. Her fingers hadn't released him. He wanted her to forget the dangers that lay beyond her apartment door. He wanted her to be one hundred percent focused on him. A fire raged between them.

"Jake, please," she begged. "I can't take any more."

Jake smiled. He was a man once more, able to pleasure his lady, to give her something no one else could give her. While he stoked her libido, he watched, his eyes wide open and filled with the sight of her coming undone. The sight of her body flushed with desire and needing his to make her whole, of her clutching the bedspread beneath her, urgently working to get him to enter her. Him. Sergeant Jake Weylin. That guy. To enter someone as sweet and pure as heaven itself.

He kissed and licked his way back to the satiny skin of her highly responsive neck and her kiss-swollen lips. She wanted more, and he had more to give. More than he'd realized. Once again in a push-up over her heaving, breathless body, he paused and let his heart fall into the forest of her sultry green eyes. A man could get lost in there. Somehow that didn't seem so bad any longer.

She licked her lips, her intentions pretty damned clear. There was no hesitation. For once, there was no mournful dirge in his head to distract him, either. There was only beautiful, pure Lacy. The time to let go was now. With her hand guiding him, he slipped into paradise with a shudder of unspeakable pleasure. Inside her. Inside the man he used to be. The man he still was.

"Oh, Jake," she purred, the sexy growl in his ear all the enticement he needed to push home. Clutching his back with all ten fingernails, she met him every inch of the way.

He set a rhythm, and by hell, she wasn't just along for the ride. He slammed into her and her hips lifted, welcoming him every time. It didn't take long before she stiffened beneath him. One more deep hard thrust sent her into her release and him along with it.

The night exploded around them and she came apart in glory with him. The sweetest muffled squeal announced to the world that she was claimed and claimed well. Together they unraveled, only to come back to earth together in shimmering waves of the damnedest ecstasy. Making love had never been like this before. Their separate worlds disappeared. Their separate futures, too. They were joined, and he had no clue how a simple physical act between two sweaty bodies could mean so much. But it did.

No more would she walk alone. Nor would he. The gift was given. Hope was bestowed and at long last, accepted. He just hadn't known he had any hope to give. His heart filled with a new truth, one he could live with. *Lacy Wright is mine. To serve and protect. To love. Forever.*

"I know it's too soon, but you need to know what's in my heart, and I'm saying it anyway," he declared with every intention of making sure she damned well knew who she was getting. "You are mine. All mine. Damn it, I love you, Lacy Wright. I think I've loved you since the first time I saw you in the alley behind the clinic." Brave words for a man with nothing to his name, but his name.

The crazy woman giggled beneath him, her breath moist and warm in the crook of his neck. "Funny guy, I love you, too."

He sank into her, the last of his strength spent, but the rest of his life beginning. The wonder of what they'd just done together stole his breath. He, a man so lost, so unworthy of anything good in his life, was suddenly as claimed as she.

Lacy lay in peace, hugged tightly against Jake's chest, his arms wrapped around her and his nose in the crook of her neck. Twice he placed a soft kiss behind her ear and whispered, "I love you, Lacy." And twice she clutched his arms to her, wanting him to stay in the safety of her bed.

But she couldn't sleep. The pleasant soreness of her body only reminded her that when the morning came, he'd be gone on a mission of his own choosing. The ugly things she'd seen on Marlee's video were reason enough for him to do what he felt he had to do, but Lacy was selfish. Why not just call the authorities and let them deal with Rafe Poindexter? Why did Jake have to be the one to put his life on the line again? Hadn't he done that enough already? Didn't he have enough scars?

The answer rang out loud and clear. More than anything, Jake Weylin was an honorable man. He would do all he could to rescue the girls on Marlee's thumb drive, and that was why Lacy loved him. Despite his own unresolved memories of the war, he'd come to war torn Anacostia to help his friend and now he wanted to help others. He had to. That was who he was.

Carefully untangling herself from the masculine fingers cupping her breast, she slipped out from under her sleeping man and shrugged into her bathrobe. Lacy went to her closet and pulled out a few art supplies and a clean canvas. This painting had been calling to her since her car exploded, and she'd found herself beneath the body of a man willing to die for her.

She turned a small desk lamp on, situated herself on the bed beside Jake with her easel, and began to paint. The strokes came easy as oil met canvas in sweeping strokes of Chromatic Black mingled with more ornate Titanium Whites of inspiration and the barest hint of Phthalo Turquoise for depth. Within the hour, her work was done. A single kiss of startling Alizarin Crimson completed the piece.

"Hey, Lacy," Jake murmured from his pillow. "What are you doing?"

She looked at the sexy smile of a man in love. The mussed up dark curls on his head gave him a jaw-dropping, just-had-incredible-sex look. Her heart flipped three backward somersaults before it nailed a perfect landing.

"Good morning," she answered, the painting done and needing a safe place to dry for a couple days. She turned it to face the corner, shrugged out of her robe, and climbed back into bed.

Instantly, his very capable hands found purchase on her body, pulling her to face him. "I like touching you," he admitted softly. "All of you."

There was no doubt. The man was aroused and ready for round two. She wrapped her arms around his neck, acutely aware at this early morning hour that round two might be all they had left.

Chapter Seventeen

At the first light of day, Jamaal knocked on Lacy's bedroom door. Jake rolled out of bed, pulled his jeans on, and opened the door, blocking the view of his lady in bed. Lacy stretched, still sore, still tired, and still wishing there was another way. She did what any woman would. She eavesdropped.

"What's up?" Jake asked.

"I'm, umm, gonna run over to Moe's, you know, and get that suit for you like I said I would," Jamaal whispered. "You got any bills on you?"

"It's okay, Jamaal," Lacy called out. "I'm awake." He might as well know she was with Jake now.

Jake tugged his wallet out of his back pocket and removed a few denominations. "This is all I've got. Don't spend it on booze."

"Would I do that to you?" Jamaal chided.

"You know damned well you would," Jake growled. "Just remember, the lives of those little girls depend on us. No one else knows what we know. It's got to happen today."

"I know, I know. You and your lady friend get ready while I'm gone. I'm buying three metro tickets for the trip on my way back."

"Thanks," Jake said earnestly. "We'll be ready to go. I'll make breakfast while you're gone."

"You'd do that for me?"

Lacy flung a wrist over her forehead. Jamaal was such a kid at heart.

Jake grunted. "Hurry back." When he closed the door, he flopped onto the bed beside Lacy. One look at his thoughtful face, and she knew he was thinking the same thing she was. The best laid plans and strategies of any military op they'd ever been on had never gone as planned. The unexpected always happened and things could still go horribly wrong today. Plus, they were grossly ill equipped for the task ahead. Poindexter had the world at his disposal. All they had was each other.

"I need to use your phone," he said quietly, his index finger tracing the line of her jaw. "I have a friend who might be able to help us today."

She pulled the blankets to her neck and sat against her headboard. "You do? Who?"

"Zack Lennox. He's a good guy. Always ready to lend a hand when I need him. I trust him more than I trust myself. The guy he works for owns a security company of ex-snipers. Name's Alex Stewart. Most of the work he does is for federal clients, but he's got a stellar rep. They're both Marines like us, and Zack does undercover work for Alex all the time. He's been inside China, North Korea, and just about everywhere American interests are at risk."

He sounded hopeful. For the first time, so did Lacy. She eased out of bed, embarrassed she'd left her robe at the end of the bed. "Don't look."

A glorious smile broke out over his face. "But I like to look at my woman. She's the only thing in this world worth looking at. Who else should I look at?"

His telltale wink stopped her short. She dropped the robe she'd just picked up off the floor. "Well, since it's you."

He grinned, his hand outstretched for hers. "How about I make the call and we grab a quick shower together before Jamaal gets back?"

Lacy fell into his open arms. "Works for me."

"Good morning. Lennox household. LiLi Lennox speaking," Zack's oldest daughter brightly proclaimed over the phone.

Jake's lips curled into a smile. Zack's three girls were the cutest little bugs on the planet, and Jake was convinced that LiLi was a nine-year old genius.

"Hi, LiLi. This is Jake. Is your dad there?"

"Uncle Jake!" she squealed. "Mommy, it's Uncle Jake! When are you coming back to see me? I'm doing chores so I can earn enough to buy a telescope. I want to see all the stars." Oh, yeah, she was pretty sure she was going to be an astronaut when she grew up too. Or a scientist. Or the President of the United States. Her vocation changed with the days.

He smiled at Lacy, wrapped in the blankets and still snug on the bed beside him. She'd get a kick out of meeting LiLi. Zack Lennox was family, the kind a guy chose for himself. Zack had been a little rowdy when he'd first gotten home from Iraq, but that was over now. He'd spent a lot of money on the high life back then, but he'd never quit on his buddies. "It's almost Christmas, LiLi-bug. How about I come visit the day after so you can show me what Santa brought?"

"Okay," she squealed again. *What was it with little girls?* Always loudly exuberant and right in his ear, too. "But Uncle Jake, Daddy's not here right now. He has important work to do. Do you want to talk to Mommy?"

"Sure, thanks LiLi."

"Love you, Uncle Jake. Bye!" she yelled as she handed the phone off to her mother.

"Hello, Uncle Jake." Mei's mellow voice was a little easier on his eardrums. "I'm glad you called. It's been too long. How are you? The girls are expecting you for Christmas Eve, you know."

Hearing the genuine concern from two of the women in Zack's family never failed to soothe Jake to his soul. Damn, he loved them. Lacy had just joined him. Pulling her into his side, he winked down at her. "I'm real good for a change, Mei." *Zack's wife,* he mouthed. "I can't make Christmas Eve, but I'll be sure to stop by the day after Christmas if it's okay with you. I'd like you to meet someone."

"Oh?" Mei asked a thousand questions with that one word. "As in a woman someone?"

"Yeah," he answered with a quick kiss to Lacy's forehead. "Lacy Wright is definitely a woman. But listen. Will Zack be home later tonight?"

"No. He's on a local stakeout of some kind. You know how it is. If he told me who he's watching, he'd have to kill me, but give me your number. He always calls in the evening to tell the girls goodnight. I'll have him get in touch with you then. Will that work?"

"You bet." Jake passed Lacy's phone number onto Mei and ended the call with a sigh. "Damn, Zack's working today. Looks like we're on our own."

Lacy pulled her knees up under the covers. "Are we sure Rafe will fall for the blackmail ploy?"

The feel of her silky legs against his thighs sparked the image of another go around, but his heart wasn't in it. The clock was ticking for all those frightened girls in those disgusting videos. "Pretty sure. Besides, it's the only leverage we've got."

"Then let's shower. I need some time with you before Jamaal comes back."

What should've been another magical encounter turned into gentle washing of each other's bodies, gentle kisses, and tender embraces. He couldn't tell if Lacy was crying or not, but the light in her eyes was tempered with the seriousness of the mission. They rinsed, toweled each other off, dressed, and were in the middle of making pancakes when Jamaal returned.

He'd done good. The three-piece pinstriped suit he'd brought with him fit the bill perfectly. A dapper hat came with the get up, but Jake opted out of that one. The fluffy black feather tucked in the band of that hat wasn't the look he was going for.

Jamaal plunked it on his head with a wicked leer. "Good. I'll keep it."

"You would," Jake muttered as he flipped the last pancake onto Jamaal's plate. "Anybody ask about the outfit you're wearing?"

Jamaal almost looked offended. He didn't seem to mind the Good Samaritan logo stamped across his chest. "What's a matter? You don't like 'em or something?"

Lacy lifted her eyebrows waiting for Jake to reply, but all he did was roll his eyes. If Jamaal was happy in sweats, who was he to argue? Food silenced any further chatter, but it didn't work with Lacy. She'd only taken one pancake, but didn't eat any of it. All she had was coffee.

Jake took his half-filled plate to the sink and hers along with it. "I'll do dishes when we get back," he promised, hoping that would project her thoughts past the dangerous mission they'd set their hands to.

Jamaal kept shoveling his pancakes into his mouth, but Lacy caught Jake's eye. Worry etched her face and her pretty eyes were subdued. This wasn't a day for smiles.

"Let's do this then," he said. Latching onto the suit hanger, he headed into her bedroom to change. "You did get the burner phones, didn't you?" he asked Jamaal over his shoulder.

The big guy thumped his new-used jacket pocket and kept on eating. He'd shopped well and he'd needed the jacket over his sweats. Their money was gone, but Jake didn't mind.

He dressed quickly and made Lacy's bed when he was done. After they returned tonight, he planned to mess that bed up good and ask her to marry him. It was early and he knew the chance she'd marry a guy like him was slim, but guys like him never knew what would happen next. He had to strike while the iron was hot.

Sitting on the edge of her bed, Jake sucked in a deep breath and blew it slowly out through his nostrils. There was a day not too long ago that he was the guy in charge, the sergeant, the baddest badass, and the go to guy. For good reason. He'd led his men into firefights that turned ugly real quick, but he'd also led them onto success and then back to base. He'd kept them alive. There'd been days he'd lost more ground in Afghanistan than he gained, but there were victories, too. Most of all, he'd honest to God loved every last one of his troops. Male or female didn't matter. They weren't much to look at, but damn it, while in that godforsaken country, they were his.

His eyes strayed to the wooden cross on Lacy's wall. "You know we're going into hell," he told the man hanging there. "If you love her as much as I do, you'd better ante up and send us one of your damned Christmas angels, and he'd better be packing."

As usual, the man on the cross promised no such thing. Not like that was a surprise.

Chapter Eighteen

The metro from Anacostia to Foggy Bottom didn't take long. They transferred from the Green Line to the Blue at L'Enfant Plaza, but when the McPherson Square stop came up, Lacy about lost her nerve. Only Farragut West remained. Then Foggy Bottom Station.

Her heart pounded at the audacity of their foolish plan, and for what? A bunch of girls none of them knew? A human trafficking ring that the whole damned federal government should be dealing with instead of three has-beens from the wrong side of the river? Yes, she felt bad for all of those girls, but why did Jake think he had to save them? Couldn't someone else?

The moment that pitiful rationalization hit her brainpan, she knew better. Good men would always stand up to be counted while the masses would forever stand behind their lame excuses. Lacy swallowed hard. This was the bitterest cost of war. The good and noble went off to battle, while those who would not, stayed behind and lived their safe little lives.

Jake seemed in tune with her melancholy. He dropped his hand to her knee and squeezed. His other arm already extended along the back of her bench, his hand firm on her shoulder.

"Have we lost our minds?" she whisper-growled, pulling her crocheted beret over her hair again. If anything would give her away, it was her flaming crown of red, for now encapsulated beneath her favorite winter hat. "I know crazy, but I'm pretty sure what we're doing makes us poster children for the funny farm with a capital C."

A tender smiled graced his lips. "I'm okay with crazy," he muttered, his lips pursed and instantly seeking her temple. She closed her eyes and absorbed his kiss into her soul for what might be the last time. Instantly, she repented for not wanting to rescue the girls she knew were in mortal danger. Of course, she would do whatever she could. She was a former Marine, too. Lacy just wished there was another way.

"You have pre-combat jitters. Don't worry so much," he whispered into her hair. "It'll be done before you know it. As soon as I get what I need in Poindexter's office, I'll take a shot of it with my phone, and I'll forward it to you and Jamaal. That way if one of us gets caught, the other two will have copies and can still go to the authorities and take Poindexter down."

"You can send it, but I'm not leaving without you," she declared stubbornly, her chin up and USMC pride in her glare.

"And I'm not leaving without you," he promised.

"I'm damned scared of Poindexter," she admitted tersely. "We still don't know what happened to Anderson and the staff at the clinic, to Marlee either, for that matter. I haven't had the nerve to call Ernie to see what he knows yet. For all we know, Anderson and everyone else at Good Samaritan could be at the bottom of the Potomac."

"True, but Poindexter's still human like us. It's not like we're fighting a superhuman ghost or some guy in a cape with super powers. He's a flesh and blood man, and I'll bet if you land a right hook on his chops, he'll bleed."

"We've both been fighting ghosts," she murmured. "For years."

Another warm kiss blessed the side of her head. "Then let's make this the last one, Lacy. Let's finish Poindexter once and for all. After today, we start fresh, okay?"

Starting fresh sounded promising. Foggy Bottom was just minutes away. Their time was running out. Lacy stowed her apprehension and soldiered up. Despite her doubts, these two men depended on her, and she wouldn't let them down. When the last passengers boarded and the train doors closed, Lacy leaned into Jake's side. With a deep breath she became Corporal Wright and steeled her soul for war once more.

Once they disembarked, she handed her backpack to Jake. Her pistol was in there. He'd need it more than she would. They'd allowed themselves one hour of prep time to *case* Poindexter's joint, as Jamaal called it. Prep time included a walk about the area while hopefully staying out of sight.

Jamaal wanted to stroll right into the building lobby for a closer look, but Jake vetoed the brash option. Jamaal had already taken a beating. He could be recognized. Hell, all of them were on Poindexter's radar, so they stayed discreet and clear of security cameras and guards.

At the end of the hour, they stood across the street and watched Rocky Rabbit and Ferret Face leave through the rear exit, and then return fifteen minutes later through the same door. They seemed to be in a hurry, but they'd parked in a parking garage behind the building.

"I'll bet Poindexter parks there, too," Jake said. "I've got a couple dollars left. Let's grab a Starbucks."

Lacy used her debit card to order three coffees. They took a seat near the window and watched the front door of the real estate mogul's building across the street. They'd done as much reconnoitering as they could. It was time.

"You're up, Lacy." Jake reached across the table to clutch her hand. "Make the call."

Her throat went dry, but she nodded and dialed Rafe's office number, her hands trembling as she placed the phone to her ear. Jake and Jamaal's eyes were on her.

A woman answered. "Good morning, Mr. Poindexter's office. How may I direct your call?"

"Put Rafe Poindexter on the phone," Lacy demanded.

"I'm sorry, but he's with a client at the moment," the woman purred. "May I take a message?"

"I told you to put Rafe on the line," Lacy snapped. "I've got something he wants. Tell him Lacy Wright doesn't have all day to wait for his sorry ass to return her call."

Jake winked. Jamaal gave her a solid thumbs-up, but for the life of her, she didn't know where she'd summoned this tough persona from all of a sudden. Her knees hadn't stopped shaking since she'd sat down.

"One moment please," the woman said as the soft sounds of Lawrence Welk's orchestra filled Lacy's ear with mind-numbing boredom.

"I'm on hold," she explained.

"You're doing good," Jake said. "Eyes on me, Lacy. You can do this. Trust me."

And then Mr. Poindexter himself was on the line and in her ear. "Lacy Wright?" he asked calmly. "It's about time. I've been waiting for you to call me."

I'll just bet you have, you pervert. She gulped an extra noisy gulp. "Well, wait no more. I've got something you want, and you know what it is. We need to meet. Now."

He had the nerve to chuckle. "Exactly what would someone like you have that I want? This is the same Lacy Wright who used to work at the free clinic on Good Hope Road, isn't it? I understand that it caught fire yesterday afternoon. Tsk, tsk, tsk. Don't you live in the Rochester apartments on Manley Drive? Didn't you drive a Subaru Forester before someone put it out of its misery?"

The sinister edge to his voice caught Lacy cold. He knew everything about her, so she returned the favor. "Very good, jerk-off. You've done your homework, well so have I. Don't you have a pretty blond wife named Kelly and a daughter named Kenzie who likes her son-of-a-bitchin' daddy to lift her up and carry her? Do you or do you not own a pathetic white mutt named Pekoe? Shit, what kind of an asshat names their dog after a teabag?" Lacy dragged the back of her trembling hand over her lying mouth. Not once in her life had she threatened a man like this, much less his innocent wife, child, and a cute little dog.

A moment of silence filled her ear, all except for the sound of her pounding heart, and she was pretty sure Poindexter couldn't hear that. Her audacity surprised her, but she had to make this guy believe she meant what she said. Jake's wink calmed her, so she doubled down and went all in.

"Yes, Poindexter. Trust me. I've seen the pictures and the videos. I know where you and your cute little family live. You almost looked like a decent human being there for a minute, but don't think for one second I believe that shit or that I'm playing." She held her breath and waited for an answer.

"Where?" Poindexter snapped.

"Where are you now?" she snapped right back. "I want to know exactly how long it will take you to get here. I don't intend to be the next rotisseried corpse on Good Hope, you asshole."

"Foggy Bottom," he bit out. "I'm at my office, where are you? I know you're not home."

Lacy blinked at Jake. *He knows I'm not home*, she mouthed.

Jake lifted his fingers to his throat and made a slicing motion for her to shut up. He gestured her to get on with it.

She cleared her throat. "It doesn't matter where I am. I'm the one calling the shots, remember? Meet me outside the front gate of Joint Base Anacostia-Bolling in one hour. Bring five million in small bills, and come alone. This is between you and me. If I see anyone with you, I'm inside the gate and you're screwed. I'll tell those guards every last thing I know. You've got thirty minutes before I take everything to the press. Don't be late." She hit the end call button and blew out a huge breath, her poor heart climbing up her throat. "Shit. That guy sounds like Jack Nicholson in *The Shining*."

"And you sound like you've done this before," Jake said, his eyes lit with adrenaline and admiration. "Who are you anyway?"

"I'm USMC issue, remember?" she muttered, swallowing past the knot of terror stuck in her throat. Pissing off a grizzly bear didn't seem like a smart thing now that she'd done it. "I had to make him mad enough to do something crazy."

"That should do it," Jamaal said quietly. "If we guessed right, our boy'll be shooting out the rear door of his building in a couple minutes."

Lacy sipped her hot coffee, trembling so hard she barely tasted it before Jamaal's prediction came true. Out the rear exit of his East Coast headquarters strode a very intense looking man in a long black trench coat and a silver briefcase. Rafe Poindexter. A black SUV with darkened windows pulled to the curb. The driver exited. Poindexter climbed behind the wheel and slammed the door behind him. With a sharp jerk of the wheel, he pulled away from the curb, and without yielding to oncoming traffic, he turned right onto the busy main street. Tires screeched and Lacy's mouth went dry. *God, what have I done?*

"Whew," she said weakly, feigning courage she didn't feel. "It worked. He's gone."

"Shhhhh," Jamaal cautioned, his face lowered to his paper coffee cup. "Don't look now. You got a rabbit and a ferret on your six."

Lacy lowered her head. Rocky Rabbit and Ferret Face here? Now?

Jake had another idea. He pulled her in close and laid the most glorious kiss on her mouth, his hands clutching her cap to her head and his back blocking Rocky Rabbit's and Ferret Face's views.

She forgot about Poindexter. She forgot about his henchmen. Hell, she very nearly forgot her name. Sparks filled the inside of her head, pushing the fear away and bouncing like firecrackers. Jake took her tongue by storm and the Starbucks vanished. All she could taste was Jake. His mouth. His lips. The smooth, freshly shaved chin that she herself had run a razor over just hours earlier.

Lacy sighed, pulling him into the cellar of her soul where all of her hopes lived and waited. Damn, he smelled so good and he tasted better. She wanted every last bit of him.

When at last he disengaged, Poindexter's men were gone, and she was breathless and dizzy.

"You good?" Jake asked her, his forehead pressed to hers and the most devilish smile on his handsome clean-shaven face.

"Umm, yes," she muttered, touching her fingertips to her swollen lips. What he did to her. "Thanks, umm, I needed that."

He smiled. "Good. You stay here. Stay out of sight. Jamaal? Let's roll."

That was how he left her. Dazed. Kissed. And scared to death she'd never see him alive again.

Chapter Nineteen

"Comm check," Jamaal's disembodied voice ordered through the burner phone at Jake's ear while he walked with long quick strides toward the front door of Poindexter's building and right into his lobby. The thick glass opened silently. An information desk stood at the center. Two hallways branched behind the desk, one to the right, one to the left. Eight elevator doors lined the wall between the entrances to those hallways.

"Copy that," Jake replied smoothly. He'd donned a pair of dark glasses for added anonymity, and to conceal his black eyes. The glasses were cheap knock offs, similar to the Oakleys he'd once owned in the Corps, but they'd do. With his phone in his ear, he hoped he looked like any other arrogant, too-busy-to-be-bothered yuppie owner of a high-tech empire.

"Copy that," Lacy's sweet voice answered calmly. Her backpack hung off his right shoulder with the concealed pistol tucked in an inside pocket. He wished he'd taken the time to handle it, but the honest truth was, he plain didn't want to. He'd used others just like it to take a few lives in his dismal past. It was only there as a last resort.

If there was ever a time to be one hundred percent focused, it was now. Jamaal had taken up position outside

Poindexter's building, while Lacy remained glued to the window inside the Starbucks across the street.

Jake grinned to himself. Beneath that innocent demeanor of hers was one damned tough woman. Lacy might look like strawberries and cream, but there was a definite shot of Jack Daniels splashed over her sweetness. *Make her mad enough, and, whoosh, stand back and watch her burn, baby. Then promise you'll never do it again.*

"May I help you?" the young male security guard at the desk asked. Busy people walked by on their way in and out of the lobby.

"Just point me to Rafe Poindexter's office, kid," Jake answered smoothly.

"Is he expecting you?"

Jake offered his biggest smile, shifting the phone at his ear up enough to speak to the guard. "Probably not, but I'm an old frat buddy. Name's Bernie Rothschild. Bet you've heard that name before." He cocked a brash eyebrow. "Yeah, I'm the guy who got one over on Rafe on the Williamsburg deal. Let me guess. Top floor? Penthouse? The dog. He's made a killing since then, hasn't he?"

The guard cocked his head. "I have no idea who you are and I wouldn't know. Mr. Poindexter runs a professional office. His office in on the first floor, not in the penthouse. Go past the elevators, take the left hall, and keep walking. You can't miss it."

Jake nodded his thanks, hitched the backpack up higher, and off he went with his cell phone still at his ear. "You guys copy that?" he asked his team.

"Sure did," Jamaal came back to him. "Anyone we know?"

"No, and thank you for asking," Jake replied cheerily as he sauntered past three women in stacked heels and tight skirts. The blonde in the middle shot him a brilliant smile, which earned her a quick smile and a nod.

"Thank me for asking what?" Jamaal asked.

"Nothing. I had company. Had to make it sound good."

"Would it have been those three hot chicks who just exited the building?" Was there a little snark in Lacy's voice?

"Why yes, it's about time," Jake had no choice but to keep up the routine as a bevy of male agents stormed out of one of the office doors at his left and nearly ran him over. "Excuse me for being in your way," he shot over his shoulder, but not a one bothered with an apology. Guess the real estate market had taken a dip or something. None of those guys looked happy.

"Keep talking, pretty boy," Jamaal muttered.

"And keep walking." That was Lacy. "I want you out of there in ten minutes or less."

"Will do," Jake breathed, his palms clammy now that he was deep in the heart of Poindexter RE, Inc.

According to Marlee, more Cambodia girls were being brought into the country tomorrow. If he couldn't pull off this Hail Mary pass today, every single one of them was in serious trouble. The reminder of all they'd have to endure sat like a heavy stone in his gut.

Jake kept walking. The security guard was correct about not being able to miss Poindexter's office. Expansive plate glass windows lined a large portion of the south wall near the rear exit door, right before the hall expanded into a reception area. Glittering chandeliers hung beneath a mirrored ceiling. Strategically placed greenery and leather couches proclaimed cozy sitting while several big screen wall-mounted televisions played listing after listing of million-dollar real estate properties along the East Coast, as far south as Florida. Life-sized photos of Poindexter Real Estate agents with smiling customers adorned the rest of the wall space. All a prospective buyer had to do was walk through the open doors and straight into the spider's trap.

"I'm in the reception area," Jake murmured. "I see Poindexter's office."

Who could miss the tinted glass wall between his office and the reception area?

"Don't hang up," Lacy barked. "It helps to hear what's happening on your end."

"And that's why you invested in me," he proclaimed loud enough for the receptionist to take notice. "Hold, please."

Trim and young, she gave him a dazzling smile right out of a toothpaste commercial. "Why hello there. What can I do for you?" Her bright blue eyes raked him over. She wrinkled her nose at him, coming on strong.

Jake shook off his doubt, imagined he once more wore his USMC *Teflon* coating. Extending his hand, he repeated his cover. "Bernie Rothschild at your service, ma'am. I've come to pay Rafe my respects for one-upping me in the real estate market and..." He dropped his brows as if he had top-secret intel to share. "If you want to know the truth, I'm hoping to catch him in a good mood. I've got an offer he'll want in on for sure. Is he in?"

"Damn, you're good at this, bro," Jamaal whispered.

Miss Blonde-and-Flirty's eyes lit up. "An offer?" She scrunched her shoulders as if they shared a secret. "We like offers around here, but..." Tap, tap went her fingertips on her telephone. "Let me check with his secretary. Annette will know if Mr. Poindexter is receiving visitors."

Jake gave her what once was his best come-on-down grin. It used to work. Sure enough, while she waited for her call to go through, she slid a business card across the desk. "Ah, Annette? There's a Mr. Rothschild here to speak with Mr. Poindexter. Is he...? Oh, I see. Yes, of course. Ah-huh, sure. Yes, ma'am."

The phone went back into its cradle with a decided 'thunk', and those flirty blues were all business. "I'm sorry, but Mr. Poindexter is out of the office. May I take a number where he can reach you?"

Jake slid the dark glasses down his nose, baring his black eyes. Women loved a wounded man. It triggered their nurturing natures—or something. "Listen, Miss" —he glanced at the card— "Constance Garritty. Connie, huh? That's my mother's name. What a coincidence."

"Is not," Jamaal hissed.

Jake pressed the phone against his cheek to muffle his buddy's big mouth. "Listen, Connie. I've come a long ways to clue my old friend in on the deal of a lifetime. If he's going to be out of the office the rest of the day, I'll leave, but this deal expires when the stock market closes." He waggled his brows, hinting at insider trading. "Mind if I hang around for an hour or two, just in case he shows in the nick of time?"

Her brows dipped into a cute little, worried V. "You poor thing!" she gushed. "What happened? Who hit you?"

Glad you asked. Jake rolled those black and blues, wincing because his nose really did hurt. "Damn. I forgot about them. You won't believe it, but a stingray clobbered me two days ago while my buddy and I were diving off the reef. It's the funniest story."

"That buddy'd better been me."

Jake darn near rolled his eyes again. *Hello, Jamaal. This story is F-I-C-T-I-O-N!*

"The Great Barrier Reef?" Now he had Miss Garritty hooked. "In Australia? I've always wanted to go there. What's it like?" Her elbows slipped to the top of her desk as her chin dipped to rest on her clasped hands.

Jake fingered her business card. "Why don't you find out for yourself? I'm going to Bora Bora next month. You wouldn't be interested in a business trip, would you? Is this a good number to reach you?"

Miss Garritty bounced out of her chair as if she'd been stung by a hornet. Reaching for the card, she scribbled on the back of it. "There. That's a better number for me. It's my personal cell and I always answer it. Call me. Any time. I can be out of here tomorrow if you need me."

He let his lips curl into what he hoped was a genuine smile, then folded his glasses and tucked them into his shirt pocket to show that he trusted her enough to reveal his true self. "Count on it. Now..." Jake glanced around the sitting area. "Where do you want me to sit while I wait?"

Around the desk she came with a grin on her face and a definite swish to her hips. "Let's put you in Mr. Poindexter's office, shall we? He won't mind, and if Annette does..." Connie's nose twitched. "That's too bad, isn't it? You're a friend of Mr. Poindexter, and friends get special perks around here, I don't care what she thinks."

Jamaal snickered. "Special perks. Get it?"

Clenching his phone to his thigh now, Jake slipped his glasses out of his pocket and reinstated them on his nose as he followed Connie into a lavish suite. Lucky for him. A dark-haired woman had just entered Poindexter's office through a side door. Talk about the evil eye, this woman had two of them.

"I thought I told you no," she challenged Connie as the door clapped shut behind her.

Poor Miss Garritty wilted on-site. "I… I…"

"Annette! How nice to meet you." Jake shifted automatically into the gregarious side of himself that he hadn't been in years. "Blame me, not Miss Garritty for this intrusion." He didn't dare refer to her as Connie, not as sharp as Annette's tongue was. "I'm afraid I never take no for an answer, so I might've steamrolled your associate here."

Up went Annette's nose. "Miss Plunkett to you and she's a secretary, not an associate."

All righty then. Miss Pain-in-the-Ass Plunkett it was. "So listen, I've got a once-in-a-lifetime offer for Rafe. You wouldn't want to tell him he missed it because of a little scheduling problem, would you?" He extended his right hand, going for broke.

Miss Plunkett's painted on brows arched nearly as high as the snarl on her upper lip, which Jake was pretty certain had been recently plumped with Botox. A lot of it.

Her nose wrinkled in that *ewww-so-disgusted* kind of way that uppity women had when forced to shake hands with a man of a lower station in life. "I don't know when he'll be back," she bit out as poor Connie slinked out the way she'd come in.

Come on, Weylin. Pour on the charm. You used to do this kind of stuff for a living.

"Lucky for me, I've got time." Jake took the nearest high-back leather chair. His ass sank into the plush, blood-red cushion. "But as I was telling your receptionist, only until the stock market bell rings. Then…" He flicked an invisible piece of lint off his knee. "It's sayonara for your dumb-assed boss."

She scanned the reception area beyond Poindexter's office where a young couple with *potential buyer* written all over their faces had just entered Connie's office. Two male agents trolled along behind them. "Fine. Stay," she snapped.

Jake jumped to his feet to grab the plate glass door for her, watching the transformation. The two agents stepped aside and closer to Poindexter's office to make room for Miss Plunkett. Annette's deep red lips curled into a smile. Her eyes brightened, and this was easier than Jake expected. Out the door she went, shouting over Connie, "Good morning! What may I show you today?"

One of the male agents tilted into his buddy's shoulder and whispered, "Shit, I hate her guts."

"She's sleeping with Poindexter, you know," the other muttered conspiratorially. "I've seen them together, the bitch."

"She's not the first. She won't be the last."

"No, but she's the worst. He's giving her all the corporate accounts and—"

Jake closed Poindexter's door, shutting the drama out and himself in. It turned out he wasn't in a spider's web at all. This was more like a shark tank, and those two young kids with stars in their eyes had just chummed the water, creating a feeding frenzy and the perfect distraction. Things were looking up. Rafe's employees wanted sales and each other's blood. Jake was in their way. Good deal.

"I'm in," he told his two accomplices over the phone. "One guard at the desk in the foyer. Three agents in the reception area outside Poindexter's office. A dozen or so civilians coming and going." *And one poor receptionist who needs to find another job.*

"Copy that," Jamaal and Lacy replied simultaneously.

Jake set the backpack beside the door for a quick getaway. "Remember how we thought someone might spoil our plans and contact him to tell him he has a visitor? It doesn't look like anyone cares."

"That might buy you a few more minutes, but once he gets to Bolling, he's not going to sit around and wait when Lacy doesn't show," Jamaal advised. "With one call, his security will be all over your ass. You'll be caught red-handed. It won't be pretty."

"Copy that," Jake whispered. "Listen guys. I need both hands to get this search done. I'll call right back."

"Copy that," Jamaal replied.

"Be safe," Lacy murmured and Jake nearly buckled. The last thing she needed was another death on her hands, and if this op went sideways? He shook his head at all the ways this day could end, none of them good.

"You know I will," he promised. Instead of pressing end call, he only pocketed his phone.

Rafe knew how to decorate. His office was more polished glass and wood than Jake had seen in a long time. An expensive looking carved desk dominated the room. A smaller table with matching wooden chairs sat off to the other side of the expansive room. A person could play baseball in there, but there was no time to waste gawking.

With one eye on the goings on in the reception area, Jake took a quick look behind the large mural of an ocean behind Rafe's desk. No wall safe. Moving to the three closet doors on the wall behind the conference table, he discovered that one was a walk-in closet, but the other two doors led to a full-sized bathroom and a smaller meeting room. Damn. They all needed to be searched.

He processed them quickly, checking for air vent covers that might be loose, hidden wall panels, or anything suspicious. Nothing. Returning to the main office, his heart kicked up a few beats. The outer office was now clear of agents and customers. Even Connie was nowhere in sight, but where would Rafe keep a deep dark secret? Definitely not too far from his fingertips. The information had to be here somewhere.

So find it.

The desk? Jake pulled the center pencil drawer all the way out. Sliding his hand inside, his fingertips traced the underside of the desktop. Nothing. All the drawers opened easily, and he performed the same search on them all. Still nothing. The more he searched, the tighter his nerves stretched. Nothing in the place was locked or suspicious. The clock kept ticking and the odds were against him. Rafe might already be on his way back, but Jake had found zero. Zilch. Nada. He stood and stretched his back, worried he'd risked Jamaal and Lacy for nothing.

Damn. It has to be here. Dr. Presley said it was. She died passing her intel to Lacy.

Panic started an annoying tap, tap, tap at the back of his neck. Icy fingers trailed down his spine. Zack always told him not to let the little things rattle him and to think. *Settle down. Take it easy. Steady and smooth. Deep breath. Exhale slowly. Take your best shot. Don't get mad. Get even.*

Jake gulped. *I can do this. For all those little girls, I have to do this.*

He dropped to the floor to check the underside of the desk, his ears straining to hear anything but the silence of this deadly predator's man cave. The carpet was thick and plush. He wouldn't be able to hear footsteps on the other side of the desk if he was caught. *So hurry!*

I am! He rolled to his back for a better view. The desk rested on four ornately carved footings, but there was no hidden safe secured to the bottom of it. No envelopes taped anywhere. No hidden compartment. Shit. Nothing.

He caught sight of the cordless screwdriver setting in a charger below the pencil drawer then. Why'd Rafe need that? Didn't he have a maintenance crew? Or was he just the kind of a guy who liked to handle his own small repairs? Yeah, right. Jake removed the tool from its charger. Designed with a pivot handle, the thing fit snug in his hand. Curious.

Chapter Twenty

"Jake! Get out of there right now!" Lacy hissed, her head low and her left hand over her mouth so as not to disturb the other Starbuck's customers.

"He's not hearing us," Jamaal said. "Keep trying. Call him one more time."

She and Jamaal had heard everything, all the bumps, shuffles, and other odd noises as Jake searched Rafe's office, but they needed him to pick up. The SUV was back. A uniformed guard ran out to open the driver's door, and out stepped the man in the black trench coat. Poindexter.

"Shit," she muttered. It was Rafe all right. He stood there for a moment scanning the streets, but all he could see was the street from where he stood, not her. She ducked anyway to keep out of sight. Her sixth sense tingled, but she didn't think he'd seen her. He couldn't see all the way across the street and into the window with those mean squinty eyes, could he?

"Please pick up, Jake," she whisper-growled as she dialed again. "Damn it, talk to me."

Poindexter stalked into the rear of his building and disappeared from view.

"I'm going in," she told Jamaal. "Maybe I can—"

"No, you ain't." Jamaal slapped his hands together, still on the curb across the street and acting the part of sentinel, trying to keep warm while he watched. "Jake's got time. He's smart. Give him a minute."

She swallowed hard. "I know he's smart, but he's outnumbered. The Rabbit and Ferret never left. Now Rafe's back. Jake's screwed." This was the worst thing that could happen, him inside facing who knew what, and her outside, helplessly waiting.

Jamaal glanced over his shoulder just as two men in business suits exited through the front doors. Lacy listened and watched, her heart climbing up her throat. *Not you too.*

"You can't make me leave. I ain't doing nuthin'," Jamaal muttered in a deep Southern drawl to the men. "Jes' waitin' for some kind soul to throw a couple crumbs my way, so's I kin get back home to Macon, Georgia."

Lacy couldn't make out what the men were saying when Jamaal shuffled away from them. He made it two steps before they tackled him. He threw an elbow, but they had him down on the ground before he knew what hit him. One held him by the neck while the other punched, and Jamaal was out for the count. Lacy stood. The enemy had the upper hand. They were all screwed.

"Jake," she demanded one last time. "Jake. Can you hear me?"

There was no time left. Shaking like a leaf and mad as hell, she tugged her cap down low and pushed her chair away from the corner table. Jake needed her help. Now Jamaal. She was going in.

Deep breath. Settle down. Take it easy. As long as Zack kept talking in his head, Jake kept his cool. He replaced the screwdriver in its charger and pushed off the floor, adrenaline pumping right along with frustration. He'd been in Poindexter's office too long, but there was nothing to be done but start over, so he did.

Back into the bathroom he went where an equally ornate wooden bathroom cabinet held a fancy bowl-shaped crystal sink and several drawers. The drawers revealed the same lack of anything useful other than hand soap and paper towels, so Jake crouched to one knee and opened the doors beneath the sink. Great. Cleaning supplies and a toilet plunger. Nothing mysterious about them.

He dropped to one knee and peered beneath the cabinet. The place looked spotless. The drain pipe, too. He reached one hand in to examine the underside of the top. Jackpot. A single, three-inch diameter metal tube was secured to the bottom right side of the cabinet top by two metal clamps, both screwed to the underside of the top. But time was running out. One of Poindexter's agents had to have called him by now. He was coming. Jake could feel it in his bones and his clammy fingers.

Retrieving the cordless screwdriver, he made quick work of removing the clamps. Carefully, he lowered the metal tube. It was nothing more than an aluminum pipe capped on both ends, but it was heavy. The caps unscrewed easily. He tilted the pipe and—

Shit. Jakes heart sank. There was no secret list in this damned tube, only gold coins. Had to be solid gold by the weight of them. So, Poindexter was a gold hoarder. Who cared? It was an odd place to hide it though. Jake crouched to view the rest of the cabinet. Four more metal tubes were attached to the bottom side of the wooden top. *Shit. Probably more coins. Not what I'm looking for.*

His heart pounded loud and clear to get out of there. He'd found nothing. He was just a petty burglar at this point and this was a B&E, pure and simple. But gold coins? What could Poindexter be up to that he needed a stash of gold in his office?

Hurriedly Jake reattached the clamps and restored the metal pipe to its hiding place. He strode back to Poindexter's desk to replace the screwdriver, intent on leaving before he got caught. He'd failed. He pulled his cell up out of his pants pocket to advise Lacy and Jamaal that he was going out. Lifting the phone to his ear, he heard loud voices in the hallway. The carpet might be thick, but the walls, not so much.

"Listen guys," he muttered to Lacy and Jamaal. "I came up with nothing. Get out of sight. I'll meet up with you—"

Of all the damned crazy things, the wooden part of the desk he'd leaned his palm onto had just shifted. It slid smoothly to the side, revealing a hidden compartment. Jake hung up on Lacy and Jamaal before he gave them a chance to answer, and he began snapping photos of the first sheet of paper. A list of foreign names with photos of dark-skinned Cambodian girls. The second sheet of paper was another list just like the first. And so on. He photographed five pieces of documentation in all. From his quick scan, the papers documented the sales and transportation of twenty Cambodian girls with a written guarantee from some guy named Prentiss.

Thrilled and scared to death at the same time, he texted the images to Lacy and Jamaal's phones. A stack of passports lay beneath the papers, bound tight with a rubber band. Hurriedly, he removed the elastic and opened several of the passports to the page with the girls' photographs. His heart hurt for those babies.

A plain brown envelope lay beneath the passports. He re-secured them with the rubber band before he lifted the brown envelope. It wasn't sealed and no address adorned the front. Sliding his finger beneath the flap, he tipped the single sheet of photographic paper out, and *'holy shit'* fell with it.

The shock of seeing that particular grinning face in this particular eight-by-eleven photograph stopped his heart. This was no arrogant state governor or sex-addict in the senate. This was Sterling Waterman, one of the most influential men in the United States, the billionaire who made presidents. On his knees. Naked. Raping an innocent girl from Cambodia.

Jake's stomach roiled at the savagery he saw displayed on the glossy photo. Now he knew what Poindexter was really after. Rafe wanted the highest office in the land. He wanted to be president, and with this incriminating shot of Waterman, the most prestigious, powerful job in the world was within his reach.

The oddest calm filled Jake. He might not be the expert sniper that his friend Zack was. Hell, he might not even be half the man he used to be, but the time had come to put the mad dog, Rafael Poindexter, down, once and for all. He, Jake Weylin, could save every last one of those poor, frightened girls.

Composing a quick text to Lacy and Jamaal, Jake attached the pictures he'd just taken, including the one of

Waterman. No doubt they'd make Lacy sick to her stomach, but she needed to protect the evidence. Just to be sure he had all bases covered, Jake blind-copied Zack Lennox as well. The attachments might shock him, but he'd get the message, and like always, Zack would help.

Jake restored everything to their previous locations. Taking one step from the desk, he activated the secret compartment, and Poindexter's ugly secret was hidden once more.

Jake had everything he needed. Except time.

Poindexter's office door handle was already turning.

Chapter Twenty-One

Lacy's incoming pinged. Tapping the handy dandy blue icon on her cell, she brought up a text message from Jake with 5 separate .jpg attachments.

Whew. About time. She stopped on the sidewalk just outside the Starbuck's exit. Her heart stopped pounding out of control. If he was texting, he was safe. She dialed and gave him one last chance. "You'd better pick up this time and talk to me," she muttered into her phone, her eyes on the dangerous predicaments Jake and Jamaal were in instead of where she was going. She turned and ran smack into a very hard male chest.

"Sorry," she muttered, aggravated this guy had been standing so close and that he hadn't gotten out of her way. The moron. He'd almost made her drop her one and only link with Jake. The guy didn't even have a cup of coffee in his hand. She glanced up to give him hell for not minding his own business. Damn, but he was a tall guy. And big. Broad shoulders blocked her view of the door.

Her eyeballs kept scrolling upward and her chin kept lifting. Over a black polo shirt beneath a leather jacket. On up and over an Adam's apple in a thick neck. Then a scruff of a beard, and finally, into the blackest pair of mean brown eyes she'd seen in a long time.

Whoever this guy thought he was, he had the nerve to glare down at her. His head was bare, except for more scruff. The hostility radiating off him stopped her cold, and if her instincts were right, he was ex-military down to his boots.

"Do you mind?" she asked. *I don't have time for this. Move it or lose it.*

"What are you doing here?" he asked as his gloved hand clenched down hard on her forearm. "You're coming with me."

"No, I'm not. Let me go," Lacy growled, jerking her elbow away from the behemoth. Whoever this jerk was, he palmed the door behind her and had her on the sidewalk almost before she could stow her phone in her pocket. Dragging her away from Starbucks, he headed in the opposite direction of Poindexter's building. For every single step he took, she had to take three just to keep up. Like she had a choice the way he was dragging her.

Not once did he give her a chance to ask questions or explain. *Who does this to a woman in broad daylight anyway?* Only a rapist or a perv.

"I said no!" She screamed as she jerked away from him again, but he just kept walking and dragging, like he had a right. *The ass!*

"Let me go!" she shrieked, leaning backward to counterbalance his pull. No such luck. All she succeeded in doing was scraping her soles on the sidewalk while he dragged her forward. He wasn't hurting her, just scared the daylights out of her.

The guy was all power and too damned much nerve! When he ducked around the corner of the Starbucks, she went limp to the ground. He slowed down for all of the two seconds it took him to lift her up by one arm and drape her over his shoulder like a ragdoll. She came back to life, kicking, punching and screaming. He growled, but not once did his massive paw move from the cheeks of her ass where he held her in place.

The last straw! Now she was scared. She screamed one last ear-piercing demand for help. Where the hell was everyone. Didn't anyone care?

Too late! He swung her off his shoulder and dragged her up into his face until they were nose to nose. Those black mean eyes skewered her into silence. She froze. Holy shit, this guy was wicked strong. His breath smelled like cinnamon.

"Listen," he hissed. "I don't have time for this. I'm trying to save your life. I've got two men in trouble, maybe three. Don't force me to fuckin' knock you out cold."

She gulped so loud even she could hear it. "Let me go," she pleaded, instantly mad at herself for sounding weak. A damned tear rolled down her cheek. She didn't mean that either, but the brute choking the life out of her collar saw it. His demeanor softened. He set her back to her feet, but he still held her tight enough she couldn't escape.

"You've got no business being here. Why are you watching Rafael Poindexter this morning? Why today? Tell me." He gave her a gentle shake.

Lacy wilted. This guy made three of her. All the worst things that could happen to a defenseless woman ran through her mind. Too bad she wasn't defenseless. She jerked her knee up and—bingo. Just like that, Mr. Big Shot let her go. Down he went, knees to the pavement and the most awful groan roaring out of his mouth. *How's it feel, tough guy?*

He rolled to his side and into a fetal curl, his eyes squeezed tight and his palms over what used to be his family jewels. Well, they were purple family jewels now. Maybe black, blue AND purple.

"You're not so tough now, are you?" she hissed, her fist clenched to knock him down again if he even thought for one second that he was brave enough to get back up.

"Lacy," he gasped.

She stopped dead in her tracks. "What'd you just call me?"

He squinted up at her out of one eye, one really dark brown eye that shimmered like it might have a tear in it. "Lacy Wright. Shit. I'm Zack Lennox, Jake's friend. He called me earlier."

"Oh, my hell!" she squealed. "You're Jake's friend, and I just kicked you in the—I'm sorry! Let me help you up. Oh, I'm so sorry!"

He shook his head. "No. It's all right. I should've—"

"Yes. You should have told me who you were before you grabbed me. I might be small but I'm no pansy-assed soldier." She offered her hand to pull him to his feet. "But I really am sorry. Are you okay?"

That one dark eye squinted up at her like he thought there was no way she could help him get to his feet. She latched hold of his elbow to prove him wrong. He might be a big guy, but she'd helped bigger and scarier. If she could get Jamaal up two flights of stairs and into her apartment, she could surely get this Zack guy to his knees. Maybe.

Ah, the poor guy. He winced, but he accepted the offer and let her help him. Male pride kicked in about then and he shrugged her off and stood all by himself, maybe not as straight as usual, but he was on his feet.

"I am so sorry," she explained, "but you scared me. I couldn't just let you drag me away and rape me and burn my body now, could I?"

He shot her a quizzical look. "No, it's my fault. I had to get you out of Starbucks before Poindexter's men got you, too."

"Where's Jake?" she asked, her need to apologize forgotten. "Do you know?"

"We suspect Poindexter's got him two floors down," Zack muttered, his hands to his knees and still breathing heavy. "If he's still alive."

"Still alive? What's going on?"

Zack took a deep breath and blew it out very slowly before he answered. "I've been watching some jerk named Manny Prentiss for eleven days now. Rafe Poindexter's name keeps popping up. I wanted to know why."

"Prentiss is the pig who's selling girls from Cambodia to Rafe," Lacy declared. "That's why. They're both into something called the virgin trade."

Zack looked at her closely. "Do you know that for a fact?"

She nodded excitedly, sticking her burner phone in his face. At that precise moment, it pinged with another text. "Yes. I have all the evidence we need to put him and Poindexter away for life. And Jake's alive. He just sent me another text. See."

Zack clamped his palm over his chest pocket and lifted his own vibrating cell phone out. "Looks like Jake's a busy guy," he said when he looked at the notification. "He just sent me a text, too."

He nodded his chin toward a black SUV, the same SUV she'd seen parked outside her apartment only a day earlier. "Let's get out of sight."

"You're the one who's been following me," she said, not asked. "That was you at my parking stall yesterday, wasn't it?"

"Not exactly," Zack answered slowly as he moved stiffly to the SUV. "Get in. I'll explain." He opened the passenger door and offered a small flourish for her to enter.

"I really am sorry," she murmured as she brushed past his bruised ego on her way inside.

"Yeah, yeah," he muttered as he shut the door.

Chapter Twenty-Two

"Lacy? Jamaal?" Jake whispered into the burner phone he was now holding close to his lips so as not to be heard. Poindexter was back all right. So were Rocky Rabbit and Ferret Face. He'd forgotten their real names, like it mattered anyway.

Neither Jamaal nor Lacy answered. All he got was static. Not good.

He was holed up in Poindexter's coat closet, standing on his toes just inside the door. If Poindexter had been smart enough to look to the right when he'd jerked it open, he'd have seen Jake sucking in his gut and trying to make himself invisible in the one-foot corner of the closet. But Poindexter hadn't done anything more than to reach inside for a wooden hanger to hang his trench coat on. He'd shut the closet door not realizing he'd already found the intruder he was reaming the Rabbit and Ferret's butts for losing. The intruder's backpack, too.

"You guys make me sick. You bust up one stupid black guy who can't tell me shit cuz you hit him so hard. Where is he? He gonna live?"

"In the basement with the rest of 'em," Rocky Rabbit mumbled. "It's all Leo's fault. He's the one that hit 'em."

"He'll live," Ferret Face, aka Leo, declared over Rocky Rabbit's finger pointing accusation. "Gawd, I just gave him one little tap to his chin. The guy's big, but he must be a lightweight."

Poindexter kept ranting. "I'll tell you what. That piece of shit nurse is sitting out there watching us right this very minute. Mark my words. If one of you doesn't catch up with her and slit her throat by six tonight, I'm putting a contract on the two of you. I'm calling Manny. He'll clean up this mess."

"No, Boss," the Ferret rasped. "We'll find her."

"See that you do. Now get out and send Annette in."

The door opened and closed. Rocky Rabbit and Ferret Face must've left. By the sounds of it, Poindexter was shuffling papers. He let out a deep sigh. "Good. At least she didn't get this. I'm safe."

Jake allowed himself to breathe. He'd been extra careful to not disturb the paperwork in the secret compartment of the desk any more than he'd needed to. He'd replaced the metal pipe beneath the vanity in the bathroom. The only thing that could ruin everything was the damned cordless screwdriver still clutched in his hand. There hadn't been enough time to put it back under the desk.

He swallowed hard past the dry patch in his throat. At least he'd gotten the last text off to Lacy. With Jamaal caught, she now had everything to go to the police and bring Poindexter down.

Poindexter had grown quiet. Too quiet. Jake cocked his head to listen. There was no way to know where Poindexter was in his office or what he was doing, but Jake knew what he'd be doing if he were Poindexter. He'd be covering his tracks and double-checking everything that mattered, his gold stash, his secret compartment, hell, everything. He'd also be pounding the shit out of Jamaal for information. He'd be dissecting every last call and text on Jamaal's cell phone if he'd still had it on him when he was taken down. And Poindexter would be looking for his damned screwdriver.

Relax. Zack's calm tutelage came back to him. *It aint over 'till it's over.*

Well, it sure as hell feels like it's over. Any minute now, Poindexter would open his closet door and the proverbial jig would be up. Jake wedged himself in nice and tight. Let Poindexter come. Jake had a weapon. The screwdriver wasn't much, but it was something. If he got in the first hit....

His gaze drifted through the dark to the backpack at his feet. He'd stand half a chance of winning if he had Lacy's nine-millimeter Ruger in his hand instead of a Black and Decker with a pivoting handle grip. Slowly, he sank to his knees without making a sound. He'd left the zipper on the backpack halfway open in case he needed the gun in a hurry. Keeping his ears trained to the room outside the closet, he set the B&D down on the carpeted floor while he slid his other hand into the backpack. The second his fingers touched cold steel, he calmed.

"Manny. Rafe," Poindexter's curt voice declared from the direction of his desk.

Jake pulled the loaded pistol to his chest.

"We got trouble. Yes. You know what to do. Did I say I couldn't take delivery? Hell, no. Tomorrow night, ten p.m. as planned. Right."

Someone knocked at the door, but Jake couldn't tell for sure if the door opened or not.

"Of course. Same fee as the last time, but I need you to do her today. She's been a pain in my ass for too damned long, and Clayton and Shunck ain't getting it done fast enough."

Rage filled Jake's heart. Poindexter had just put out a hit on Lacy.

"Double the fee? You bet. It'd be worth every penny to be rid of the redheaded bitch." A pause. "Yeah, I'll need another dozen girls next month. Keep 'em coming." He snickered. "Make that a dozen and a half. I know a guy who likes 'em young. The tighter the better."

Jake straightened in the closet, the time for hiding over. He just didn't expect that Poindexter would pull the closet door opened at the exact same moment and stick the business end of a rifle in his chest. Damn. Where had that thing come from?

Old battle-axe herself, Miss Annette Plunkett peered over Poindexter's shoulder. "Told you he had to be in here somewhere. I would've noticed if he'd left."

Poindexter cocked the rifle. "Two down. One to go."

"You'll never get Lacy," Jake declared as Poindexter's lady friend relieved him of Lacy's pistol.

Plunkett chambered a round in the Ruger and pointed it at his head. She closed one scary hazel eye. "Hmm. Nine mil. I might just need a little more target practice, Rafe honey."

Poindexter nodded toward his door. "I can arrange that. Move it, Weylin."

Chapter Twenty-Three

"Oh, my hell," Lacy exclaimed at the final picture Jake had sent. Zack got the same attachments. They were awful. Instantly he was on his cell and forwarding it to some guy named Boss. He wanted everything on Lacy's phone that Jake had sent earlier, so Lacy handed her phone over without hesitation.

Now that she knew who he was, Zack wasn't scary at all, more of a teddy bear than the rapist she'd mistaken him for. He was still wicked big, though. Damn. His thighs rippled beneath his pants. Her thighs weren't nearly as large or as firm as even one of his upper arms.

His head and face was bristled and scruffy, his brows dark but not bushy. Now that she had a chance to look at him while he and Boss growled back and forth at each other, he was growing on her. Not white but not black, his dark tanned skin belied a mixed heritage that made him light bronze and sexy as hell. Or it could've been the uniform. The black T-shirt stretched like it wanted off his massive chest, and those brown and green cammies housed some outstanding man-ware, as in bulging calves, thickly muscled thighs, and a nice taut ass. Yeah, she'd looked.

He answered Boss with respect, but not servitude. Whoever this Boss guy was, she got the impression Zack trusted him as much as Jake trusted Zack. *Interesting. Could that Boss man be the infamous Alex Stewart that Jake mentioned?*

Zack and Boss tossed a lot of military-speak back and forth, too. Words like deck, bulkhead, aft, and the ever-present *'Aye-aye'* punctuated their conversation regularly, but never *'sir'*. Again, interesting.

By the sound of it, Zack and Boss were discussing an immediate attack on Poindexter's lair. Better yet, they were both Marines, her favorite kind of guys.

But Lacy couldn't hold still to save her life. Her heart pounded with the need to get to Jake. She'd texted him while Zack chatted with Boss, but to no avail. Why wasn't he answering?

When Zack ended the call, he turned his body to face hers in the front seat. "You reach him yet?"

"No. Nothing."

Without another word, Zack placed another call. "Mother? Need you to track a burner phone for me. Understood, but I can send you the number, all of the calls that were made today, and the serial number. Will that help?" With a big sigh, he hung up. "No way to locate Jake or to know if his phone is still in that building. All she can do is triangulate, but that's no help. We already know where he is."

"We just don't know if he's alive," Lacy finished the thought, her eyes fixed to Poindexter's building. "Your mother works for you?"

Zack rolled his eyes. "Oh hell, no. My mom's a sweetheart with a bit of an Irish brogue. That Mother" —he nodded toward the cell phone in his hand— "is something else entirely. She's our lead techie. I'll introduce you when this is done."

Lacy looked past him to the building. "It's my fault. I should've been the one to go inside. Poindexter wants me, not Jake."

Zack's big hand covered hers on the console where she'd rested it. "And the Jake I know would've never allowed you to go in there alone," he said. "So tell me all you know."

She spilled every last thing she knew about the videos on Marlee's thumb drive, the fire at Lamont's Pool Hall, and the fact that Jake and Jamaal had been beaten up. Zack explained that yes, he had been staking out her place, but only because she'd taken Jamaal home with her, and where Jamaal went, Jake was sure to follow.

"So why did you follow Jake?"

Zack sighed. "He's my friend. I keep track of him. Sometimes he needs a hot meal and a hand up. It's the least I can do."

"So you followed him because you're his friend?"

He lifted one big shoulder. "Why not. It's almost Christmas and that's what friends do. You wouldn't happen to have that thumb drive on you, would you?" The man had the most gorgeous sexy eyes. The dark fringe of thick lashes around them pulled her into trusting him with her life. After all, Jake trusted him, though probably not because Zack had sexy eyes.

She pulled Marlee's USB drive out of her jeans pocket and placed it in the palm of his hand. "I didn't want to leave it in my apartment. You know, in case Rafe decided to torch it while I was gone."

"You don't have to worry about that. My boss put a couple men in Anacostia to watch your place," he said as his hand closed around hers and the USB. "How was Jake the last time you saw him?"

"Good," she said, but she thought *damned good*. His last kiss still burned on her lips. That was all it took to push her over the edge. She sucked in her bottom lip, but tears spilled out of her eyes anyway. "You have to help him, Zack. You're his friend, and he needs you, and—" Her heart dropped to the floor mat. There were no words big enough that could adequately describe the rugged man she'd fallen in love with.

"Hey, there." Zack's warm hand on her shoulder snapped her out of it. Kind of. "I'm sorry if I'm out of line, but you wouldn't happen to be pregnant, would you?"

"Oh, no. Not me. No way." That she knew for sure. "No way. We've known each other three years, but we've only just… I mean there's no way… I mean…" Lacy snapped her rambling mouth shut. She hadn't even thought of using protection when she and Jake had sex because, well, it had been a long time since she'd had sex, and yeah, she should have taken precautions, but everything happened so fast and—

She gulped one of her extra noisy gulps. They'd only been together once. How could Zack tell if a woman was preggo this soon? Any fool knew it took once to make a baby, one steamy, incredible time with the man who'd touched her soul with the blink of his gray eyes. She'd been swept off her feet. Carried away. Yeah. All those things. But seriously? Zack could tell?

He had the tenderest glint in his eye. "I'm no expert, but you have the same glow my wife had when she was expecting our last little girl. Just saying. I knew right away with Mei. My mother says it's the Irish in me."

Could it be possible? "Maybe," Lacy admitted, quietly confessing to this handsome man she'd barely met that she and Jake were more than friends, that she might be easy and loose and—

A big old tear dropped out of her eye and splattered onto the back of Zack's hand. Damn it. She was emotional, and now he knew it, too.

His phone vibrated. "Lennox. Yes, Boss. Understood." He turned to Lacy and moved his hand to her shoulder. "My boss is inside Poindexter's with the FBI and SWAT."

"He's inside? Already?" she asked, her gaze drawn back to the quiet looking building across the street. "But how? I don't see anyone. There's no smoke and I haven't heard any shooting." Who was this Boss guy anyway?

"Because they went in the back way. We've been working this undercover sting for months, Lacy. You and Jake showed up in the middle of it. That's why I'm here with you. I had to take you out of the picture, so Alex could go in after Poindexter. Once we have him, we'll move onto Prentiss."

"And Jake?" she asked, fearing the worst.

Zack's dark eyes stabbed her. "Alex said he wasn't there. Somehow Poindexter, Shunck, Clayton, and Plunkett got away."

"Jamaal?" she asked.

Zack blew out a big sigh. "Not sure about him, but my boss found your Dr. Anderson and a couple other ladies."

She didn't have to ask, Lacy could tell by the stark shadow on Zack's face. They were all dead, and now Poindexter had Jake and Jamaal. The SUV was suddenly too small. Too crowded. She couldn't breathe. The last thing she felt was Zack's rumbling voice swelling around her in the dark. "It's okay, Lacy. I've got you now."

But it wasn't okay. Nothing would ever be okay again.

The whole world tipped and Lacy fell out of it.

Chapter Twenty-Four

At least Lacy's safe. Jake hoped.

He stumbled, vaguely aware where he was being herded. Whoever the ass was behind him with the gun barrel in his back, kept pushing faster than Jake could walk. It wasn't easy walking with a plastic bag over his head. It had to be Rocky Rabbit back there doing the prodding. He always was a cruel bastard.

Ferret Face hadn't spoken lately, not since he'd been dumb enough to show Poindexter what he'd found on Jamaal's burner phone—enough evidence to put the real estate mogul away for the rest of his perverted, unnatural life. Poindexter freaked and swore, then slammed his fist into Ferret Face's, umm, face. That was when the black plastic bag went over Jake's head.

He lost track of Ferret Face because breathing became a little more important than worrying about a lowlife. But Jesus, Plunkett was a cold-hearted bitch. She'd plastered the bag against his mouth and nose long enough to make him believe she was going to kill him right then and there in Poindexter's office. With his hands tied behind his back, all he could do was twist and kick while she'd suffocated him. For fun. When she'd lifted the plastic, he'd been pumped full of adrenaline and spitting fear, but not so badly that he couldn't hear her laughing.

"My, my, but you're a big boy when you're aroused," she'd purred as her stinking fingernails had raked over Jake's crotch like she owned him.

"Not yet!" Poindexter bellowed. "Shit, Annette, I need him alive."

Well, yeah, Jake felt needed all right, kind of like how fish guts on the end of a line were needed for baiting alligators or sharks. *Please, God. Keep Lacy safe.*

"I thought you called Manny to take care of Wright," Plunkett snarked.

"You think I trust anyone to do their job anymore?" Poindexter bit out.

Besides their predilection for cruelty, Poindexter and Plunkett spoke in a language Jake didn't completely understand as he stumbled along. Words like chest harness and carabiners usually had more to do with mountain climbing than real estate ventures. He kept going. Their curious lingo wasn't the only puzzle of the day.

Where was Poindexter taking him, and how did he get from the halls of Poindexter's building into what sounded like a tunnel in a cave? Wherever they were headed, it was underground, and he was walking downhill. The smell of damp stone wafted into his face along with a chilled draft, and it was okay. He'd lived in darker and danker places, but still. There were plenty of tunnels on the south side of the Potomac that runaway slaves had created before and during the Civil War. Was he in one of them now, or was this somewhere else?

He needed to focus so his mind didn't slip away to the tunnels in Afghanistan. Above all, he needed to keep his bearings as much as his wits, but the air in the tunnel turned colder and damper. Finally, Rocky Rabbit plunked a heavy hand on Jake's left shoulder, which was good. His feet had hit concrete again, or at least smooth stone. Wherever he was, he could hear gulls screeching and he could sense wide-open space up ahead of him. His nostrils flared at what smelled like snow. He was outside? That couldn't be good.

"This is the end of the line for you," Rocky Rabbit mumbled.

Someone pulled the plastic bag off Jake's head, and he was hit with a slap of cold air and an extreme case of vertigo. No damned wonder. The toes of his dress shoes were nearly over the edge of a cliff that dropped a good twenty feet to the Potomac, most of it straight down. Bushes lined the bank, but damn, he could've fallen over the edge. One more inch or another shove from Rocky Rabbit and—

Jake took a full step backward and ran into the business end of Rocky Rabbit's rifle.

"You ain't going nowhere," the bully growled. "Stay where you are."

No shit, but what the hell? Leaning most of his weight backward, Jake peered over the edge. A slab of rusted metal sheeting lay vertical to the riverbank just below him. It had been there awhile, judging by the tendrils of Virginia Creeper vines grown over the rusty edges and the long orange rust stains that streaked the earth between it and the lapping Potomac. Shivers rolled over his shoulders and down his back. His fancy pinstripe jacket had been stripped from him when everything went south back in Poindexter's office. A man in nothing but a cotton dress shirt and dress slacks wouldn't last long in this weather.

Poindexter came to stand beside him and dropped a bag at his feet. "Ah, fresh air," he said, his chest stuck out and inhaling a deep breath. He offered a thin smile that didn't meet his black eyes. "You thought you and that little girlfriend of yours were pretty smart, didn't you?"

Jake looked the man in the eye. He guessed Poindexter was of English ancestry. He had the look of an aristocrat, the bearing of nobility in all the photos Jake had seen of him. His immaculately trimmed hair was always precisely combed, his suits most likely in the thousand-dollar range. Not today. Up close he looked more like the spawn of Satan. The wind coming up the riverbank whipped at his hair. No light reflected from his eyes, not even with the gray light of a winter day at high noon. His complexion declared a serious case of acne at some time in his past life. His nose was crooked. The man radiated cold better than Mother Nature.

"Where is she?" Jake asked.

Poindexter lifted his left shoulder with indifference. "You mean Lacy Wright? It doesn't matter where she is today. It only matters where she'll be tomorrow, and what she'll see when she closes her eyes every night for the rest of her life. You know how it is. Some images tend to stick in our heads. I'll bet you saw plenty of guys get blown apart when you were over in Iraq or Iran or wherever you were." He leaned closer, his voice gravelly and deep. "Tell me, Weylin. Does that bloody, gory picture in your head ever go away? Don't you still wake up covered with sweat and screaming because of all the guys you lost over there?"

Poindexter seemed to be waiting for an answer, but Jake closed his eyes and took in a deep lungful of the winter air.

Poindexter had already given him what he needed to hear. The rat bastard didn't know where Lacy was.

A wave of warm calm swept over Jake. He had no doubt that whatever happened next would scar Lacy. But scars were one thing. Death was another. He was thankful to the core of his worthless soul that Lacy wasn't there, that she'd been spared. She might hurt for a while after he died, but she was tough. She'd find a way to endure, and hell, maybe she'd paint him on one of her canvasses. Maybe he'd get to feel her sweet breath on his face one more time after all.

The notion of her soul reaching out to him after he died soothed Jake in a way he'd not expected. Lacy would remember him. He hadn't gone through all he'd gone through in vain. She would love him long after he was gone because he'd mattered to her. Maybe she'd get her oils and brushes out and they'd have a good long chat together before she painted him—home.

That profoundly special word brought another level of calm to the edge of the precipice. Somehow in the circuitous ways of destiny and fate, he'd been meant to be with Lacy, if only once. Lacy was his home, his comfort at the end of a tough, hard life. She'd opened up her apartment, but more, she'd opened up her heart. She could paint him home all she wanted, but he'd never leave because she was his home.

He stiffened his spine and took another deep breath for the task ahead, the task of dying without her. Even that brought a measure 1f peace because now he knew. Lacy wasn't here on the edge of life with him. She was safe. She would live.

"You see, Weylin," Poindexter said as he looped the rope through a metal carabiner, his voice almost conversational.

"I'm a very ambitious man. Do you know what accolades come after my name when I'm offered speaking engagements at college graduations and business conferences? They introduce me as the entrepreneur of the year. They say I'm driven and bound for success in everything I do. Even after all these years, they say I'll go far."

Plunkett busied herself by being a tramp. She trailed the tip of her tongue over the top of Jake's ear while Poindexter watched. Jake turned away from the treacherous woman. Connie really needed to do some serious job hunting.

"Stop playing," Poindexter snapped as he jerked the rope in his hand, dropped it, and proceeded to do the same with another section of the nylon coil and another carabiner. "They call me fearless and ambitious, Weylin. I'll bet you didn't know I own more high-end real estate property than any other person in the entire United States, did you? Hell, probably in the entire North and South American continents, and do you know why?"

Jake remained silent. Nothing good ever came from arguing with a fool.

"I'll tell you why." Poindexter stepped up to Jake with a switchblade in his hand. With one twist of his wrist, he flicked it open. "Because I'm a better man than everyone else, that's why." He reached around to Jake's back and cut the ties that bound his wrists, brought the wicked blade into sight again, and with another twist of his wrist, snapped it closed.

Rocky Rabbit grabbed Jake's arms then, straining his shoulder sockets until he had no choice but to lean over the edge. Gravel and dirt clods fell to the rusted slab of metal below. The damned thing had to be several inches thick. How it came to be there was one of those details a dying man wondered about, but didn't care about at the same time.

Cold-Hearted Bitch had taken position on the opposite side of him. And there he was, standing on the edge of insanity with a psycho to his left, one to his right, and a freaking moron on his six. He contemplated jumping. Breaking his neck in the fall might be an easier way to die.

Jake could've sworn he heard his buddy's words drift on the wind. *It ain't over 'till it's over.*

Not sure what your idea of over is, Zack, but this sure feels over to me.

"So I'm making you a one time good deal." Poindexter chuckled in his demented, twisted way. He tossed one of the ropes to Rocky Rabbit. "I'm going to let you live."

Rocky Rabbit jerked Jake backward and made quick work of wrapping the rope around his wrists, only this time in front instead of behind his back. And then Jake understood how bad it would get before it was over. His surroundings jolted into clarity. He saw the sunken dock below in the cold gray Potomac clearly. He was standing at the edge of an abandoned shipyard. A heavy-duty engine hoist stood behind him just beside the cave entrance, its boom extended over the edge. The damned thing was as rusty as the iron below. Mounted to the boom was a chain and hook. He debated jumping again.

Rocky Rabbit's left lip lifted into a sneer. "Want you to look pretty for your lady friend," he muttered as he grabbed hold of the hook and pulled it down. Poindexter and the cold-hearted bitch held Jake between them while Rocky Rabbit secured the hook beneath the bindings and worked the hoist lever. Inch by inch he lifted Jake until he was nearly off his feet.

Then the fun began. Cold-hearted Bitch stepped forward with her idea of a knife—a box cutter blade. "I hate to waste a good man," she said while she pressed the lever at the side of the cutter, pushing the razor into view. She pulled his shirt out of his pants and stretched it tight, creating a taut surface between them. Very slowly, her blade bit through the buttons on his shirt. "But I've already got a good man. What would I do with two?"

With Jake's chest now exposed, she took another step forward. The damned bitch winked at him like she was all hot and bothered, and this was all in fun. She lifted the razor to his throat.

Jake tilted his chin upward and stared at the gray clouds overhead, hoping she'd nick his carotid and he'd bleed out quickly. But no. She started at the hollow of his throat and cut one single slice down the centerline of his chest over his belly to his belt. He shuddered with the fiery pain, hissing against the words that sprang to his tongue. She hadn't cut him deeply enough to go through the muscle, just enough to part the skin and make him bleed. Shaking from the assault, he gritted his teeth and shook it off. He wouldn't give her the pleasure of uttering one word.

With his hands bound over his head, Rocky Rabbit shoved Jake backward off the cliff and Jake prepared for the worst. The terror of being suspended over thin air almost made him scream, but he chose to bite his lip and stare his murderers down instead.

That damned Zack had something to say about freezing to death, too. *Deep breath. Exhale slowly. Don't get mad. Get even.*

Shut the fuck up, Zack! You get even. You aren't the one hanging over a river and about to die, are you?

The wind caught him. His body swayed like a side of beef hung in the butcher's freezer. Poindexter had the oddest smile on his face. Cold-hearted Bitch lifted her fingers to her lips and blew Jake a kiss. He spat to his right, so there was no doubt what he thought of her.

Rocky Rabbit cranked the lever that lowered the hoist's boom. Inch by shivering inch, Jake dropped below their line of sight. Poindexter disappeared momentarily, but only long enough to return with a long wooden pole. He grinned from his higher position on the bank, stuck the end of the pole between Jake's arms, but only enough to turn him one hundred eighty degrees until he faced the river.

"Smile pretty," Rocky Rabbit cackled.

"Shit," Jake growled under his breath. He was lowered until he was directly in front of the rusted slab of iron. Inch by inch, his body was cranked backward. Shivers raked him at the frozen touch of skin on metal. One more crank and he came to rest, spread out on his deathbed.

"Die well, Jake Weylin," Poindexter called from high overhead. "It has been a pleasure matching wits with you, but as you can see, I always win."

Jake didn't bother to look up. His heart turned to Lacy. This would hurt her more than it would him. He shivered. The Potomac in December was a damned cold place to die, but it would be quick. Even the slice down his belly didn't hurt anymore. Maybe it was shock setting in. Maybe he was just numb like he'd been since he'd left the Corps. Who knew? He sure as hell didn't.

"You're a lucky man," Poindexter called over the edge.

Jesus H. Christ, why don't you just leave?

"You will be glad to know that I'm on my way to place an anonymous call to all the newspapers on the East Coast. I'll be sure to tell them where to look for you. I'm sad to say you'll be dead by the time they get here, but rest easy. You know how they are, Jake. They'll print every last picture of what they find, and they'll bring the television crews with them to take more pictures of your dead body."

Bits of dirt and gravel rained down on Jake as Poindexter monologued. "Birds and rats may already be feasting on you by the time they arrive, Jake. After all, animals like things that bleed, and you are bleeding, true? They'll be here before I fly off in my private helicopter. But think about this while you hang there and bleed to death." More gravel rained over Jake. "What's the last thing your precious Lacy Wright will see every night for the rest of her life? What will she dream of?

The bastard laughed. "You might have outed me to the world, but I'm not finished yet, Weylin. You are."

Chapter Twenty-Five

Lacy came to outside the open passenger door of his SUV with the mighty Zack on his knees, his palm on her forehead like he was checking for a fever. A buttery soft leather jacket was pulled up to her chin over Jake's denim jacket. But her cap was missing.

A section of her hair floated like wisps of cedar vapor in front of her eyes, and she was cold, a shivering kind of cold that went all the way to her toes. Two jackets weren't enough. Her palms went instantly to her biceps to rub warmth back into her body.

"Why am I so cold?" she asked, blinking up into liquid brown eyes. Damn it. If Zack had been dressed in any kind of military uniform, she'd really be in trouble. The guy was a walking babe magnet. Tall, dark, and handsome only skimmed the surface. His pecs didn't fit inside that too tight black shirt he had on. It was stretched nice and tight. Something about the guy made her heart skip a few beats. She would know. The damned thing was running a mile a minute and skipping, too. But Zack wasn't Jake, was he? He might be here, but she wanted the man who owned that crazy heart in her chest.

"There you are," Zack said kindly when he noticed she'd opened her eyes. He danced in and out of focus while he spoke into the cell phone tucked into the crook of his neck.

"Right. She's coming around now, but I need an ambulance. We're at—"

"No, you don't," she growled groggily, waving at one of his three faces. She swallowed past the dry lump in her throat. "No ambulance. Give me a break, Lennox. Didn't your wife ever faint?"

"Yes, when she was one month pregnant, but that's not why you passed out."

Oh, for hell's sake. Not that again. Lacy elbowed herself upright, holding tightly to his wrist for support and to keep her balance. "I'm not pregnant. It's just been a long week, and I'm tired. Come on. Let's go get Jake and Jamaal."

The damned SUV at Zack's backstop kept moving, only it was going side-to-side, not forward and backward like a vehicle on wheels should. Didn't matter. A little dizzy spell didn't equate to a ride in an ambulance. Her heart thudded louder, talking to her in a not so romantic way. She clutched her chest, more determined than ever to get on her feet and to stop the drum inside her ribcage.

"No," he said firmly, angling his wrist out of her grasp to press her shoulder back into the seat. Pocketing his phone, Zack ran his other hand down her cheek to her neck. "Lie still."

She closed her eyes and did as he requested. Damn. Her whole body was one giant pulse, and the normally sedate organ in her ribcage felt like the hooves of a hundred racehorses were tap dancing all over it. Maybe Zack wasn't that hot after all. Maybe he was right.

"Have you felt like this before?" he asked, his eyes intent on the gold watch at his wrist. He was taking her pulse. She stilled and let him.

"Like what? Like I'm, I don't know, ready to blow apart?"

"Have you had panic attacks before?"

"No, and I'm not having one now."

"Ever had a heart attack?"

"No," she gulped. "Well, maybe. I kind of had a heart problem once. That's the only reason, umm, he let me go."

"Who let you go, Lacy?"

"Him," she whispered. "Dr. Death." *The guy who said all those volts of electricity wouldn't hurt. It will soon be over. It's for your own good. That guy.*

Zack tucked his jacket more firmly around her. "Get comfortable. You're not going anywhere. I don't know who Dr. Death is, but your pulse is sky high. Whatever's going on, you're not fit for duty right now. I'm calling the game. You're grounded."

"No, I'm not, and you're not... calling anything. I'm going in... and I'm... finding Jake if... it's the last thing I do." Damn, it was hard to breathe.

"Lacy. You're ill. Stay down and let my boss locate him. He's already on scene, remember?"

"Where's my... hat, damn it?" she asked when the breeze blew her hair into her face for the last time. She'd had enough. Pushing off the seat, she set both boots to the SUV floor despite the big jock in her way. Lacy squared her shoulders and shot him her best USMC stare down. "Jake doesn't have all day. Are you coming... with me or not?"

Zack rolled his eyes, but said, "Yes, ma'am, I am," as he reached one long arm behind her and lifted her winter hat from the back of her seat. He handed it to her and offered a reluctant hand up. Lacy took a deep breath and pushed out of the SUV. She wasn't sure why she'd passed out, and she didn't care. Whatever was happening to her heart had something to do with whatever was going on in that building across the street. Jake was in trouble. How could she get comfortable while that was going on?

Zack offered one little nod, closed the door behind her, and hit the remote key lock on his key fob, which she'd just noticed he'd been holding in his right hand all along. Clever guy. He knew she wouldn't go easy into an ambulance. She did notice his left hand still cupped her elbow though. Good. She didn't need to face plant now that she was on her feet and moving.

The big guy was carrying. She returned his leather jacket so Zack could conceal the hardware on his hip. Besides, Jake's jacket was good enough for her. It smelled like him.

"Alex is still inside with the FBI. I'll radio him and let him know we're coming in." Zack's voice did have a baritone dipped in honey kind of tone. She shot him a quick glance out of the corner of her eye while she stuffed her hair back undercover. Was he related to Jake? They looked nothing alike, but Jake had that same mellow timbre to his voice that hinted of inner strength. That hidden strength that he didn't know he still possessed.

Her heart thudded, stealing her breath. The dizziness swelled up around her once more, a sneaky black shadow that made it hard to keep walking. But she did. Jake needed her help and she meant to get to him.

Chapter Twenty-Six

"Again!" Jake ground out. He'd already flipped his body over and faced the rusted slab. By now his face and chest were covered with blood and orange rust, maybe some ice. Oddly, the frosty metal had numbed the memento left by the Cold-hearted Bitch. He couldn't feel the slice on his torso any more. His slacks were thin protection at best and soaked. His socks too. He'd kicked the dress shoes off because he needed tread and their soles, wet or dry, were too slippery to gain traction on the metal.

Wet socks gripped the pitted surface better, and the slab slanted just enough that he could climb. Inch-by-inch he'd crept upward, and he'd gotten close enough that his fingertips touched the bottom curve of the hook. All he needed was another inch or two, and he'd be home free. The hook was solid enough. One good five-fingered grip, and he could pull himself up high enough to lift the rope over the hook.

Jake had a plan. Once free of that hook, he didn't mind falling even if he landed in the river. He could run the shore to keep warm. He could survive this war. Poindexter wasn't any different than any of the other assholes roaming the world for power and fortune.

But like the last hundred times, his feet slipped just when his fingers grazed the frozen hook.

"No, no, no!" he growled, willing his hands and fingers, his knuckles and joints, to stretch enough to make up the difference. He just needed an inch! "Shit!"

Down he went, jolting his shoulder sockets when he hit the end of the rope yet one more time.

Typical for December, it started to snow. Nothing of blizzard proportions, just enough to coat anyone dumb enough to be outside in the blustery weather. Jake shook the flakes out of his hair and spit, intent on surprising Poindexter by surviving. But icy rain came with the snow, turning the metal slab into a frozen slip and slide. His socks failed in their most important mission.

Zack's comforting voice in Jake's head had grown silent when he needed it most. Jake was running on empty. Shivering had become the only thing he could do well. Shivering and thinking about Lacy. She deserved better. She always would deserve better than him, but damn, he loved her, and the only legacy he'd leave her now would be a gruesome picture of his dead corpse.

Like hell. Marines. Do. Not. Quit. They kept trying until they dropped dead.

Lifting his weary face from the metal wall, with knees bent between him and the damned frozen iron, he braced his body to do his will one last time. But it had grown colder and now the wind kicked up. His knees complained as they ground against pitted weathered metal on their way upward. No doubt they were bleeding too. Well, so what? Skin and muscle could heal later.

Jake climbed for all he was worth. Slowly. Cautiously. Balancing his weight against the metal, he crept upward on his knees, keeping his center of gravity close to the iron. This was a better plan. *Don't use your feet, just crawl. Keep the rope tight, then pull yourself up. You can do it this time. You're a winner. It's just a few feet. Go, Jake. Go.*

Slushy snow pelted his back. Ice water trickled out of his hair and down between his shoulder blades. It could freeze for all he cared.

You're almost there. Focus. Hang on. No slack. Just muscle. Just will power. Just—

"Son-of-a-bitch!!" He hit the same slippery spot every time and dropped flat to his belly. Why wasn't the whole damned slab pitted? Wasn't that how rust worked? He needed traction, not an ice skating rink!

"I'm coming, Lacy," he told the metal wall once again at the end of his bleeding nose, shivering so damned hard his forehead bumped the unforgiving iron. "Don't give up on me. I promise. I'm coming."

But that last drop took a different kind of toll on Jake. Numbness crept up from his freezing feet and down his already numbed hands and arms. He looked skyward, resting his chin on the iron. Every muscle and bone ached from the extreme pull-ups he'd demanded of his body. To no avail. God, he hurt.

"Lacy," he said to the flakes swirling around him on the bitter December breeze. "Keep painting your heart out, baby. Keep strong. I'm coming."

A gust of winter's bite blasted the side of his face, but he smiled anyway. Lacy had already proved everyone wrong. Her stupid doctor. Her misguided parents. Even him. Lacy was stronger than she knew. She would survive, if only because she already had.

The shivers ceased. Jake hung as still as death while he contemplated a different strategy. There had to be a way off this hook. He just hadn't thought of it yet. Licking his lips, he fought to keep them from freezing while he brainstormed. His cheeks felt stiff, like maybe Jack Frost had already painted icy feathers and paisley swirls on them. For all he knew, he might be decorated like the windowpanes in his grandfather's unheated attic outside Little Rock, Arkansas.

"Grandpa," he whispered, "I miss you and Grandma. I miss sleeping in your granary and picking up chicken eggs every morning." *I miss everything.*

Jake had worked his grandfather Elias's farm the summer before he'd shipped off to join the Corps. Why that memory surfaced, he didn't know, but thinking of Elias and Jane Weylin and their farm in the country, brought a momentary wave of warmth to his chilly predicament. "I should've told you I'm home, but... I'm broken, Grandpa. Least I was. Couldn't decide where I was some days; if I was back there or over here, and I didn't want you to see me like that. But I'm better now. Except I'm dying. Maybe."

There was no visit or apparition of the silvery-haired gent who raised chickens and battled notorious red foxes in the thick hardwood forests around his one-acre farm. No message from the grave, either, but Jake knew it then. He had to check in with his folks and his grandparents once he got out of this mess. They needed to know where he was, and what he'd been doing since he'd come home. They'd always loved him; he knew damned well they did. It was time to man up and reconnect. He breathed another shivering puff. "I promise I'll be a better son and grandson. A better man."

Only the whine of the wind rippling over the sheer metal wall replied. No brainstorm and no brilliant other options presented themselves.

His mind wandered, and he was okay with that. It might as well wander. He wasn't going anywhere. Funny. By the time he got out of here—if he got out of here—he'd be a freaking work of art, all covered in frost flowers and feather frost like he'd seen in the dead of winter once in the extreme north of Canada. All of those decorations might ease the sight of Lacy seeing him dead. It might even make her smile to know that Mother Nature had painted him first.

"Uncle Jake?" LiLi's honey-sweet voice drifted through the flakes of white. "Uncle Jake!"

"Huh?" he mumbled. How could Zack's little girl be out here in the storm? "Wh… where you at?"

"Uncle Jake!" she squealed as she barreled into him and wrapped her arms around him. "Let's go inside. I'm cold."

"M-m-me too," he sputtered, damned thankful for the warmth of her tiny body. His chin dropped to the top of her head. The silly girl hugged him tight like he was someone worth hugging, but when she lifted her face, it wasn't LiLi's dark brown, almond shaped eyes peering up at him. It was Fantine, come to him in her bedraggled, bareheaded disgrace.

"We are the same," she cried. "Both born for greater things, now reduced to grovel for our souls."

I'm not groveling.

She whined like the wind, her breath as cold on his lips. "Kiss me then, and let us die together."

Uh-uh. Never. He twisted his mouth away from the ill-fated wraith as much as his stiff neck allowed. The only woman he was dying with or for was Lacy. "Why are you here?" he had to ask. The big ugly guy with the black robes and scythe he'd expected, not this pale ghost. "Why didn't you seek out Jean Valjean sooner?" *Why weren't you smarter than me?*

"Jake! Jake!" He opened his eyes as one ghost transformed into another, this one with vivid green eyes. "I love you, Jake," it whispered.

"L-lacy. S-s-sorry," he hissed, wishing she wasn't there. No woman ought to witness her man's death, not like this. He tried to swallow, but snowmen couldn't do what humans could. The saliva wouldn't come. A hard lump caught in his throat, burning him with the only hot spot on his entire body. He licked his lips instead, no longer sure of who or what he was. Man or frozen beast.

"Don't die on me, Jake. You are my heart," Lacy said, her fingers as cold as ice where they cupped his chin. She pressed cold lips to his mouth and kissed him with frozen vapor instead of sweet warm breath.

He closed his eyes to relish the apparition. Maybe she was real. Maybe she wasn't. He didn't know any more. "Hang onto me," he said, his voice filled with angst at what was to come. "Don't let go. I'll save you." *Please don't let this be an illusion.*

"You've already saved me," she breathed, easing away from him and his icy slab. Like a ghost, Lacy slipped out of and beyond his reach. His lovely dream evaporated over the choppy, gray Potomac.

Damn it, she wasn't real either. The only thing Jake could do was hunker into his icy pyre and cry. One. Frozen. Tear.

Chapter Twenty-Seven

Lacy strode forth with a little less enthusiasm than she would've liked. By the time the heavy glass entry door at Poindexter RE opened at her arrival, she felt shaky and weak. Zack might be right. She wasn't fit for duty, but since when did that stop a Marine? Not today.

The hefty armed man at the entry sported a bright yellow FBI SWAT across his navy blue jacket. He put out a hand to hold them back, but Zack flashed a badge out of his inside jacket pocket. Instantly, the man nodded once and allowed them inside. The place looked empty except for a row of professionally dressed men and women on fold-up chairs with more FBI agents taking notes and asking questions. Those must be the agents who worked for Rafe.

"He's down here," Zack said as he pressed a hand to Lacy's lower back and ushered her past a bank of elevator doors. The hallway was clear until they came to Poindexter's office where another army of FBI had taken up residence. One man in a tan linen business suit was face down on the floor, his hands cuffed behind his back.

Zack didn't slow down to enter. Instead they walked past the office, turned a right corner at the end of the hall and immediately opened the door to a stairwell. Three flights down they came to an exit door, but by then Lacy was in trouble. Black spots danced in and out of her vision, threatening to knock her down if she couldn't keep up. If not for Zack's steady hand at her elbow, she would have fallen more than once. He seemed to understand that her need to find Jake was more important than her health.

"Copy that," he said softly.

She looked over her shoulder at that unexpected comment. Oh. Zack was wired. He had an earpiece. He must have been relaying information all along.

"Who… who are you talking to?" she asked breathlessly, her heart on definite overload. The air had grown increasingly thick as they'd descended. Lacy didn't care. She had to find Jake. Then she could breathe again.

"My boss," Zack answered, his hand on the doorknob, but not turning it to let her pass. "I want you to think twice before we take one more step. You won't like what you'll see, so don't look. Focus on the guy standing in the tunnel at your far left. Go straight to him. I'm right behind you."

He opened the door ,only it wasn't the normal hall or an underground parking garage she'd expected. It was more like the tunnel in a mineshaft. The concrete pad she stepped onto butted against a stone floor and dirt walls. Wooden pillars braced an earthen ceiling. Electrical wires lined the floor of the corridor and portable lights were stationed every fifty feet or so.

"What is this place?" she asked.

"Tunnels. Poindexter's idea of a getaway. It's not on any city schematics and it wasn't here when the building was built. Keep moving."

But the smell. The sickeningly sweet odor of decay on the draft hit her nostrils. She looked at the angry guy in the tunnel to her left. Instead of wearing a helmet like the other guys, he wore a baseball cap with bright yellow USMC screaming his allegiance to the Corps. That—helped.

Lacy took a step in his direction. The man stood in the earthen corridor, his body angled to the right, urging her forward with sharp, impatient flicks of his hand. Zack's fingers at her shoulder kept her moving, but now she knew where her friends from the clinic were. Poindexter had murdered them. Right here. The only reason he'd brought them here was crystal clear. He must have tortured some of them, maybe all of them, first.

Oh God, oh God, oh God. This can't be happening in America. But it had. Lacy swallowed hard as her poor heart kicked up another notch, closing her airway. Every bit of her wanted to run from the bodies tossed in a pile in the dark at her right.

Zack's gentle palm at her shoulder kept her moving. "Don't look," he reminded her.

How could she not? "Is Jamaal—"

"We won't know until the FBI's finished processing the scene." Zack answered. "Keep walking."

"How many?"

"Six."

She couldn't reach the man in the baseball cap soon enough. Five of those bodies were her friends from the clinic. Jamaal might make six. *Oh God, oh God, oh God.*

"Miss Wright." The man in the USMC cap nodded an acknowledgment before he bit her head off. "Why the hell are you down here?"

Great. Another damned Marine.

"Alex, this is Lacy Wright," Zack interrupted. "Lacy, my boss, Alex Stewart. He's in charge of this op."

Him? Not the FBI? Lacy stopped trying to understand this incredibly dangerous op she and Jake had stumbled into like a couple idiots out to save the world. How did a civilian contractor merit control over the FBI?

Alex held out a hand to her, and she took it, rather her knees buckled and she nearly fell into him. He steadied her with an arm around her waist and crouched to see past her hair that had fallen over her face. "Are you okay?" he asked more gently, his other hand to her shoulder.

"I'm fine," she whispered, and extended her hand for a hearty handshake to prove it. Too bad it shook like a leaf.

"No, she's not," Zack spoke up from her six. "She should be in a hospital, but she insisted."

Alex offered a perfunctory shake, but he didn't look happy to see her.

"Where is he?" she asked before this Alex guy had the chance to chew on her some more.

"We haven't found Poindexter yet. The FBI has search and rescue dogs in two of the three tunnels we've located," Alex answered, pointing toward a lighted tunnel farther down the corridor to his right. "I was twenty feet into the third tunnel when you decided to play hero and join us," he snapped.

Damn, the man was abrasive.

"I meant Jake. USMC Sergeant Jake Weylin, damn you," she snapped back. She'd learned early. Meet a bully head on and he backed off. Sometimes. "I don't give a shit about Poindexter. Where are my friends?"

Alex glared over her head at Zack, but he didn't argue. "Get her a damned helmet."

Zack reached around her, a safety helmet already in his hand. He was the efficient one, and already had two, the other for himself. Seemed he thought he was going along with her. She strapped the helmet on, her fingers trembling and her legs about to give up again. She'd never felt so weak. What was happening to her body?

Hopefully, Alex didn't notice. How could he? He'd already turned his back on her and Zack, and stalked toward the third tunnel. The man was built more like Jake instead of husky like Zack, only he was in much better condition. Not as gaunt. Not as twitchy. He stood erect and one hundred percent in charge. Power seemed to shimmer around him like a fiery halo of *'fuck with me and you'll die'*.

Either that or she was seeing things that weren't there, and she was on the verge of passing out. The way her body was acting, it could've been either.

The bulk beneath Alex's lightweight, dark-colored jacket didn't escape her notice. He was carrying, two if she guessed right. One beneath each arm. He shot her a scant glance over his shoulder. "Keep up."

She intended to. Zack's boss led her to the edge of a cliff where the FBI's best dogs had converged. This tunnel ended on an outcropping of stone at the edge of the Potomac River. An engine hoist stood anchored to a concrete slab with its heavy metal chain dangling over the edge.

"Sorry ma'am," one of the FBI agents told her. "Jake Weylin isn't here now, but he was. These dogs would know. They followed his scent to this point."

"What scent?" she asked. "How could they?"

He waved an evidence bag with Jake's suit jacket and dress shoes. "These dogs know what they're doing. If he isn't here, he either walked or flew away."

She choked back a scream. The evidence was clear. The Bureau's finest canine officers tracked Jake through to this narrow ledge, where a hoist had been left to freeze and rust in the weather.

When Alex pulled the chain up, along with it came bloodied nylon bindings that further validated what the dogs found. Jake had been bound and dropped over the side. Judging by the copious amounts of blood on the thick piece of metal below, he'd struggled desperately to free himself.

His shoes had been located in the shallows below. They'd not floated away because they couldn't. The river's shoreline was nearly frozen, thick with slush and ice. So where was he? Where was his body? She needed to see it before she'd believe he was gone.

"These ropes look like he worked himself free, ma'am. Look. They're worn through," the same agent said. "He probably rubbed them against the hook until they broke, then dropped to the shore. That was the last location the dogs picked up his scent. Looks like he didn't walk away, though. I'm sure sorry. He might have been hypothermic at that point and went straight into the river. People do that. They get confused, and once he got wet—"

"No," she whimpered. "Not Jake. He's not dead. He can't be."

Zack waited patiently at her side, but even he was having a hard time dealing with the sad discovery. He stared at the icy river, his jaw clenched as tight as his fists. Alex hadn't said a word yet, just stood on the ledge, his hands on his hips and studying the murder scene. His hard gaze was barely visible beneath the snow covered brim of his hat.

"The snow's obliterated all the evidence," Zack growled, "and that son-of-a-bitch Poindexter will get away with this."

Alex nodded. "Maybe."

An FBI agent bagged the bindings that had held Jake while other canine officers patrolled the shore. Lacy couldn't—wouldn't—believe that the man she'd given her heart to was gone so quickly. They'd just had a Starbuck's coffee with Jamaal. They'd had a good plan to bring Poindexter down. It almost worked. Only now...

Lacy dropped to her knees, her palms in the dirty snow. Her heart no longer pounded as loudly nor as fast. The cadence had slowed. But if Jake were gone, she didn't want it to beat at all. She couldn't bear it. "Jake," she said quietly to the wind whirling around her. "Please talk to me."

Alex dropped with her, one knee in the cold snow. "You shouldn't be here," he said gently as his hand and arm slid around her waist.

"I can't leave," she breathed. "I have to find him."

Zack stood at her other side in silent solemnity.

"Help me," she begged. "Zack. Alex. Please h-help me find him." She choked, her cheeks raw from tears and freezing wind. Her chest heaved. Alex pulled her against his side. He was big and solid and warm, but her body was cold and her heart was fading fast. And she wanted it to.

That was why it pounded so fiercely before. It was linked with Jake's heart. It made perfect crazy sense. If he truly was gone—if he was dead—hers would stop beating any moment now. It had to. That was how love worked. *You gave all of your heart to the man you loved. Every last beat.*

"Mother," Alex said quietly, but Lacy didn't lift her head to know he was talking to the same woman Zack had called before. "Call everyone. Tell them to meet me at Poindexter's building in Foggy Bottom. We've got a crime scene. I'll run it by the FBI. No. They're standing right here. I'll take care of it." He paused. "Right. Get Mark and Harley on a Coast Guard cruiser in five. We've got a man to find."

Lacy choked. He said *man*. Not *body*.

She felt him pocket his phone, but his arm didn't move from her waist.

"My team is in transit," he said quietly. "I know the odds look bleak, but I want you to listen up, Miss Wright. I own two of the best tracking dogs on the East Coast, and every last one of my men and women are hands down the best in the business. Zack will take you home, but this thing isn't over. Don't you dare give up until I tell you to, you got that?"

She choked out a semi-hysterical chuckle. Man, the man was arrogant. Did he honestly believe he could fight Mother Nature? Did he dare offer hope when there was none to be had? Did he dare make her believe? God, she wanted to.

But even she could see the logic in what the FBI had found. If the dogs hadn't detected Jake's scent anywhere on the shoreline except for the point directly below the metal slab, then he'd most likely walked into the river, and a body would be damned hard to find in this weather. Hypothermia was a silent killer.

A strangled sob sneaked up her throat as she made eye contact with the man at her side.

Crystal blue eyes caught her breath. Alex wasn't kidding. Arrogant or not, he believed every word he'd just told her.

She hiccupped. "My heart hurts," she said softly, like he could fix that, too.

Those sad blue eyes misted over. Alex lifted her fingers and covered them with his other hand. "I know it does, Lacy. Hearts get broken when we give them away. That's just the way we're made. Let Zack take you home. Get warm. Jake will need you when we find him."

She wanted to believe.

"I promise. I'll call you when we find him." He kept saying *when*, not *if*.

"Okay," she whispered. "Call me. Promise?"

Alex sent her one curt nod while Zack cupped her elbow and helped her back to her feet. Together they made their way out of the tunnel and back to his SUV. He opened the passenger door for her, got her situated, and started the engine while he brushed the snow off the windows. By the time he was belted in, the vehicle was warm. The heated seat didn't hurt, but she shivered anyway as he drove her home. Traffic was light because of the snow.

Before long, she stood in front of her apartment door unlocking it. Zack didn't ask if he could stay. He just came in behind her, locked all the door locks, took a quick look around the place, and opened her refrigerator like he belonged there. "I make a mean homemade chicken noodle soup," he muttered as he began pulling supplies out. Carrots. Potatoes. "And I mean homemade right down to the egg noodles. Why don't you go take a hot shower? By the time you're warm, the soup will be done, and maybe Alex will have found something."

Wordlessly, Lacy went into her bedroom to do what Zack suggested. Shrugging out of Jake's sodden jacket, she hung it over her chair back to dry, then pulled a dry pair of running pants and a T-shirt from her closet. That stopped her in her tracks. Just this morning, she and Jake had made the sweetest love in that empty bed of hers. The oil she'd painted of him still faced the corner. It wasn't even dry yet. She turned it around.

The painting hadn't seemed like much this morning, but somehow it captured then what was happening now. She'd meant it to express Jake's unique strength, the picture a close up of a snowflake, its crystal Titanium White beauty caught against the cold of a Chromatic Black sky. The single flake almost sparkled around the tiny Alizarin Crimson heart beating at its center. It was Jake. Just this morning. When his heart pumped blood. When he still breathed.

But now....

The odds of finding Jake alive in the Potomac were slim at best, and infinitely worse in this weather. Lacy sank to her knees beside her bed. Doubt and fear scraped the thinnest veneer of hope off her. How could Alex be right? Had he truly called that Mother person to get his team out on the Potomac in the middle of a snowstorm, or had he simply pretended a hoax to pacify her? Was he as crazy as she was?

Lacy crawled onto the bed and sank her face into the pillow Jake had rested on only hours earlier. Rolling onto her back, she pressed the pillow against her face and breathed all that was left of him into her broken heart. His scent lingered and she needed every last atom of him, every last epithelial. A cavernous hole had opened inside of her like a monster, eating her heart from the inside out. She screamed into her pillow.

And screamed.

And screamed.

Chapter Twenty-Eight

When she finally came out of her room, her apartment felt like a morgue. The phone refused to ring. Zack's wife had to be the most spoiled woman on earth. A man who could and would cook was rare, but a man who cooked from scratch? One in a million.

"Tell me what happened to Jake in Sector 18," Lacy asked as she sipped at her bowl of soup, but only to make Zack happy. He'd worked hard. Someone needed to pretend they appreciated it.

"You probably saw it on the news over here," he said quietly, his bowl untouched. "'*Jihadist Dies at Camp Eggers Front Gate*' or some bullshit headline like that."

She wasn't so immersed in gloom that she couldn't detect his sarcasm. "You don't like the press."

"No, ma'am, I do not. The headline should've said '*Two More Heroes Gave All.*'"

Lacy agreed. The press corps of the world had yet to realize who protected their right to free speech. In her protection detail, she'd seen firsthand how important the sensational side of their business was. The reporters she'd been assigned to guard thought they were the celebrities instead of the real stars in front of the camera, the guys who'd put their lives on the line or died. They sure as hell didn't do it for the by-line. A good reporter was few and far between.

"So what happened? Were you there?"

"No." He stretched his legs, as tired from sitting as she was. "There is no Sector 18. It's one of those nicknames we gave jobs we didn't like. You're Marine issue. You know how it is. Sector 18 was anything Army related, in this case, Camp Eggers in Kabul. A couple of Jake's guys took out a radical bomber at the front gate. The asshat thought he could drive through with a shitload of explosives. Jake was there when it happened, standing only a few feet away. He's had Sector 18 mixed up with Anacostia since he got home. Once in a while, he grants himself leave and visits my place over in Maryland, but he never stays long. He's still on duty."

"He was on alert the whole time he was here." Lacy's gaze strayed to the position Jake had assumed on the floor. He'd had a good view of the entire apartment except her bedroom behind him. "So tell me about him. What was he like before?"

"One helluva hell-raiser," Zack said proudly. "We served in Iraq together. You know how it is. You make friends with every deployment, but some leave an impression. Jake's one of those. The first time I met him, he'd just dragged in off a three-week remote. Couldn't say where he'd been, but the man wanted a drink, and I knew a guy…" Zack's big shoulders lifted. "We were both different people back then."

Lacy knew the story. Despite rules against drinking while deployed to that part of the world, booze wasn't hard to come by—if you knew a guy.

A big smile wrinkled Zack's forehead. "He ever tell you where he's from?"

"Not yet."

"A little town west of Little Rock, Arkansas. His folks own a small dairy herd there and his grandparents raise chickens." Zack held up four fingers. "He's got three sisters and one brother. Don't think he's talked to any of them since he's been back."

Lacy let Zack talk.

"His Granddad's a bible-thumping preacher who makes his own moonshine. You'd like him. I met Jim once. A better man hasn't been born yet, 'less it's Jake."

"He asked me to paint one of his friends home. Emile, I think he said her name was."

Zack's lashes lowered. "Emily, but she spelled it Emile. Guess she figured if everyone thought she was a guy on paper, she'd get the same treatment as the rest of her squad. Jake always claimed she was a pain in the ass, always trying to prove herself bigger and badder. Always calling him Sarge."

"But he cared for her?"

"Yeah. That was what pushed him over the edge, seeing her die like she did. He thought he could handle it. Like a dumbass, he ignored the signs and took another tour in Iraq. That was where he lost his shit. They sent him home, but he never made it past a week in Walter Reed. Women shouldn't be in combat, damn it," Zack growled.

"We're not all cheerleaders sitting on the sidelines, you know," Lacy said softly. "We bring our own brand of courage to the fight, and we fight like hell."

He blew out a heavy sigh. "I get that, Lacy. Honest to God, I do. You're smart. Hell, women are better snipers than a lot of guys I worked with, but it doesn't change a man's gut instinct to protect you women. Shit. You'd have to be one damned butched-up, tobacco-spitting female before I'd let anyone hurt you. I don't care if it's not politically correct, it's the way we're made."

She had to smile. As tough as she'd been in the Corps, there was still a part of her that wanted a man to hold the door and watch out for her. To protect her. She also wanted him to know she could and would take care of herself, and that he'd better not disrespect her even though he could throw her over his shoulder like a sack of potatoes. But that night her car blew up, when Jake had her cornered, ready to die for her? So. Damned. Hot.

"How long have you known Jake?" Zack had a way of looking through her, like he had an instinct for crazy people or something.

Her lukewarm broth suddenly needed more cooling down, so she blew on it instead of meeting those dark chocolate eyes. "That's debatable. He's been watching over me for a couple years, maybe longer. I'd see him on the corner in the morning on my way to work. He never waved, just watched me drive by. At first he spooked me, you know, because he was always there. Watching. Staring. Guess he couldn't figure out why a mixed-up white woman moved into his Sector 18." She tipped the bowl up to her mouth and finished it off to make Zack happy.

"You didn't move into his territory," he said resting his palm on his knee. "Sector 18 only runs from Eighteenth Street west to Good Hope, and north to the river."

Damn. So Jake had gone out of his comfort zone to keep watch over her? Lacy's gaze hit her bowl again, only the broth was gone. She couldn't very well blow on an empty bowl, could she? Now she'd have to explain.

"The first time Jake actually talked to me was the day we met, the time he'd brought Jamaal in for stitches. I think I embarrassed him. He got this funny look on his face, kind of like he'd been caught doing something he shouldn't."

Zack offered a dark chuckle. "That's my boy. Women scare the hell out of Jake. So why are you here?"

It was funny how in the darkest night the smallest word means everything. A word like *scare*—not *scared*. "I'm hiding from my parents," she admitted honestly.

"Your father is Allen Wright."

She looked up at that quietly spoken truth. Zack already knew exactly who she was. Daughter of a wealthy banker. *Local female war hero goes wacko.* Yeah. There'd been a headline that day, too.

"Yes, he is. I had a meltdown when I got home. They took an extreme measure. I bailed. Been living here ever since. They think I'm crazy." *Maybe I am. Please don't tell anyone you found me.* "But I think I'm going to be okay." *Or I was...*

"You're not any crazier than the rest of us. You did a damned hard job for a thankless nation, and like a lot of soldiers and Marines, you came home to zilch. You're entitled to scream at the world any time you want. If screaming's your thing, let the whole damned world hear you loud and clear. You are a Marine, aren't you? Let 'er rip."

"Do you? Scream?" *Go crazy?*

He shrugged a shoulder. "No. I lift. Workout. Started hitting the weights when I was in Iraq. Too much down time between skirmishes. You know how it is. Lifting gave me a way to burn out the stress before it got the best of me."

"Did your parents, umm, did they understand?"

Zack met her gaze evenly. "Yes, they both did. My dad served in the Corps like I did. He and my mom still live in Florida, but he's from Jamaica. He'd signed up to become a Marine before he became an American citizen, and that's where I learned to salute the flag. At MCBQ."

Marine Corps Base Quantico.

"So you followed in your dad's footsteps?"

He sent her a sharp affirmative. "Yes, ma'am. It was all I ever wanted to be, just like my dad."

Talking with Zack felt good. He didn't give her any crap, just accepted who she was, and he was Jake's friend. A breath eased out of her. A lot of stress went with it. "I paint," she told him.

His brows lifted. "Cool. You'll have to show me your work sometime."

"I did one of Jake this morning. Would you like to see it?"

"I'd like that very much," he said somberly, and there was the deal. Zack felt as badly as she did about not finding Jake. He wanted to be out there searching, not stuck nursing her, and she knew it.

"You don't have to stay here. You can leave. I'll be okay."

His left top lip quirked in a gentle smile. "Don't go pulling that bullshit on me. Jake finally did something smart. There is no way I'm leaving the pretty lady he fell in love with, not on a crappy night like this. I'm fine. Go get your painting. Let's see what you've got."

By the time she was finished, Lacy showed him all of her works, not just the snowflake heart.

"My hell," he said with definite awe in his voice. "You need to let the world see these. They're unbelievable."

She shook her head adamantly. "No. Never. They're private. I won't betray my buddies. Besides, the world doesn't care."

"But these guys' and gals' families do. Hold a private showing, Lacy. Let them see their sons and daughters, husbands and wives, their moms and dads, one more time. It would mean everything to know someone cared enough to paint them home. God, help the world remember them. Their service."

Oh, that. Lacy gulped one of her extra noisy gulps. Zack made a good point. Maybe Terry's mother in Oklahoma wanted the pink rose her daughter had left behind for her. Maybe it would help to know that Terry's last thought was of her mom and family. *Maybe others do care.*

"I wouldn't know where to begin," she murmured. "I just paint. I don't know the business side of being an artist."

"Let me take care of that." Zack almost sounded hopeful. "I know a lady who knows a few people in the right places. The day ever comes you're ready, you just—"

His cell phone vibrated on his belt holster, and Lacy stopped breathing. His face hardened and his words told the rest of the story. "Sorry. The Coast Guard called the search off until the storm clears out. Zero visibility. They can't work in this weather."

Her heart dropped. "So nobody's looking for Jake?"

He shook his head and—enough! Lacy jumped off the couch and ran. She couldn't get to Jake's pillow fast enough.

Chapter Twenty-Nine

Lacy hid in her bedroom, unable to stop crying. Zack was one of the kindest guys but she wanted Jake. Only Jake! His pillow was wet, and she was losing the scent of him because she couldn't stop the torrent pouring out of her eyes. She raged against the evil man who'd hurt Jake as much as the Coast Guard who'd failed to find him. Yes, the weather was bad, but wasn't that their job? Their specialty? Weren't they the mighty protectors of the Potomac?

Damn, damn, damn!

Lacy's heart and soul hurt. Rationality got lost between her out of control rage and her soul-numbing grief. The hole in her heart took everything good out of her. She'd become one of those bombed airliners whose passengers were sucked out and tossed to the universe while it went down in a ball of flames. Black flames. Hopeless black flames. At Christmas! The time for peace on earth and all that other bullshit.

Damn, damn, damn!

Zack thumped on her bedroom door, but she debated answering. She'd turned inward, back to the demented woman she really was. He needed to leave her alone. "Go away," she told him and the rest of the world. *Leave me alone. Please just leave me alone!*

Another louder thump hit her door, and she caved. Gulping past the lump of mixed-up emotions in her throat, she rolled off the mattress and padded to the door with her hair in her face. Zack didn't deserve what she'd deteriorated into.

Combing all ten fingers through her mane, she pushed it out of her eyes and mostly back where it belonged. She wiped the tears off her cheeks and then wiped her hands on her pants. Zack needed to go home to his wife and kids, so she could cry and scream however and wherever, as long as she wanted. And she wanted.

Stifling another hiccupping sob, she pulled her door open. But it wasn't Zack leaning on her bedroom door with his forehead pressed wearily to his wrist. It was a very wet and very tired looking black man. "Jamaal?" she asked, not believing her eyes. "What the—"

"I got away from them bastards, Lace. It weren't easy, but then I got him. I got Jake," he gasped. "Damned near got us both killed getting here, but I got him."

"Jake?" she shrieked.

Alex stood drenched right behind Jamaal. "Get your coat," he ordered hoarsely. "We've got someone you need to see. Step on it."

She flew, snagging Jake's denim jacket off the back of her couch. Shuffling into a pair of flip-flops on her way out the door, she was ready to run.

Alex stopped her. "Real shoes, damn it. It's December."

She would've argued, but he was right. She wasn't thinking clearly, not one bit. Tossing the beachwear, she pushed her feet into her worn clinic slip-ons. "Where is he?"

"Downstairs," Jamaal answered. "I almost made it back when this guy here 'bout ran over the top of me."

"Dumbass," Alex growled and waved his hand at them to follow him down the stairwell. "You should've gone straight to the authorities. Hell, you probably passed a dozen Coasties on your way here. They would have helped get him to a hospital."

"Doubt that," Jamaal muttered. "They'd have put him in jail. Poindexter's still on the loose, you know. He would've killed us both if—"

"Poindexter's in son-of-a-bitchin' custody," Alex growled. "Two of my guys caught up with him. He never made it to his helo pad."

Lacy listened as much as she could to the information flying back and forth, but her heart was pounding out of control once more, making it hard to think, and these were big guys she was running down the stairs with. Fast big guys who could run. She couldn't keep up. Nonetheless, Alex stopped at the ground floor door and held it for her to exit first.

"Paramedics haven't left yet," he said even as he shot another dark look at Jamaal. "Climb in. They won't wait."

A blue uniformed medic waved her to the rear gate of the ambulance. "Over here, ma'am. You need to hurry."

She climbed onboard, and there he was. Jake. Her heart pinched at the sight of him, gray, lifeless, and glassy-eyed, but—*thank God! He's alive. Isn't he?*

Lacy looked closer. They'd stripped him bare and wrapped him in heated blankets. His eyes were open, black and sunken, but he didn't move. Didn't even shiver. She wasn't sure he was breathing. "Is he…?"

When the medic crouching over Jake didn't meet her eyes or answer her unfinished question, Lacy's heart sank. This was no happy reunion. They were just going through the motions, giving her time to say goodbye.

"Don't even think it," Alex barked behind her. "He isn't dead. These guys aren't qualified to declare time of death, are you?"

The grim professional at Jake's side didn't speak, just pinched his lips in a tight line like he had something to say, but didn't dare.

"You'll take extra good care of my man there, won't you?" Zack asked pointedly. "Because that guy's a decorated war hero, and he deserves every last lifesaving measure you fellows have up your sleeves."

The medic looked up from his array of tools and supplies at the implied threat. "What do you think I'm doing?" he bit out. "Back off. Let me do my job."

Zack mellowed and took a step back. "Yes, sir. Meet you there, Lacy," he said before he closed the door, locking her inside with Jake.

"Friends of yours?" the medic whom Zack scolded, asked.

She didn't get a chance to answer. A terse female voice came over the radio snapped to his collar. He passed Jake's stats to the woman on the other end of the line while she barked medical terms Lacy didn't understand back to him. Only one term stood out from the others. Her worst fear. Hypothermic.

Slowly the ambulance pulled away from the curb, but the EMT kept working on Jake. "Someone cut him up pretty good," he muttered as he slid a stethoscope beneath the blanket to the center of Jake's chest. "He's lost a lot of blood. Just so you know, I've already given him one unit of O negative. We've packed him with heat packs, but ma'am…" His gentle dark eyes pierced straight to her gut. "I don't want to get your hopes up. Cardiac dysrhythmia is the real threat here, not his wound and not his temp."

"Are you telling me his heart stopped?" she asked quietly as the vehicle rolled quickly over the Pennsylvania Avenue Bridge and into D.C. proper. "Is he dead? Is that why his eyes are open?"

"No, ma'am. I'm telling you that ventricular fibrillation is the number one killer of all hypothermic victims. His buddy back there might've thought he was helping by dragging this guy home, but that's the worst thing he could've done. He should've left him on the frozen ground and gone for help. Guys who've been in the river when it's this cold shouldn't be moved, especially not carried over someone's back like he was. The heart can only take so much. And his eyes are open because he's in a coma."

"His name is Jake," Lacy whispered. She lifted Jake's icy hand from beneath the blanket and encapsulated it within hers. "This is USMC Sergeant Jake Weylin. He's one of the best men alive, and that man who carried him is Corporal Jamaal McCune. You need to know that a good Marine never leaves his buddy behind." She hated that her voice rapped up with every word, but these men were heroes. The world needed to fucking know that!

The medic blew out a patient sigh. "I get that, ma'am. I was Army. I saw my fair share. Let's just hope his buddy didn't kill this Marine tonight by saving his life."

Chapter Thirty

He drifted on waves. Warm waves. Bright waves. Noisy waves. Maybe floated was a better word. Though why he was in the middle of the ocean on a bobbing raft escaped him. How he got there didn't matter. Only the fifty-pound weight on his chest. Breathing was damned difficult. Thinking was harder. Instinct told him he'd be safe as long as he stayed on the raft. He was dying maybe, but warmer than he had been. Not a bad way for a man to go.

A gentle hand skated over his forehead and raked through his hair. It lingered at the side of his face, holding him. Cupping him with something that felt a lot like loving him. *Lacy cut my hair,* he wanted to tell that person, so they'd know someone had cared about him once upon a time. Instead, he let the darkness win. He drifted away.

At last he opened his eyes to quietly beeping monitors. Wires. Tubes. A godawful cannula stuck in his nose. *Where's my raft?* He wasn't bobbing any more. A ceiling came into view overhead. A shimmery ceiling.

I'm sick, he quickly deduced. *Not adrift. Not dying. Not yet.*

He saw her before he heard her. Lacy came out of nowhere as silent as a Christmas angel, like she'd been standing post and watching for this precise moment. Tender green eyes peered down at him from above. She rested one soft hand on his arm, the other to the side of his face.

Lacy looked a thousand times prettier than an angel, but she was crying. Wordlessly, she laid her head on his chest, wetting the thin material of his hospital gown with warm tears. He breathed the fragrance of her hair back into his soul. There was nothing better than knowing she'd survived; that she was the only person with him. That the first thing he laid his eyes on wasn't Jamaal like he had every other day the last few years.

Drapes of red hair rolled over her shoulders, falling on his arms and neck like silk, draping him in silence. The very private place it created was filled with only him and only her. He fingered the strands that brushed over his fingers. She trembled in the way of all good women, and he could feel her breathing deep breaths the same as he was, as if they both needed each other's air to live. There wasn't anything better.

My Lacy.

Jake could barely lift his right hand to the side of her head to hold her against him. To never let her go. His heart swelled with love, but damn, he had no strength. Darkness tugged at him. "Lacy," he growled, not wanting to go. Not yet.

She lifted the blanket and climbed into bed, pushing her long legs alongside his and covering them both with the blanket. The woman he adored was completely dressed, but nothing felt better than her warm body snuggled close to his. Still she didn't speak, but snuggled under his arm like she'd always belonged there.

He lowered his face into her hair and drew in a deep breath of—oxygen. *Damned cannula.* Lacy took the hint.

Lifting the thing off his mouth, she traded it for a small kiss. It wasn't a barnburner like her other kisses, but it warmed him better than any blanket.

"Love you," he muttered thickly.

She didn't answer, just replaced the mask and melted her body against his with one hand over his heart. He was pretty certain she was crying again, and he wanted to comfort her, but his mind lost its focus. Floating was over-rated. This felt more like falling.

The darkness took him.

"How is he?" Zack asked quietly as he entered Jake's very nice private hospital room and made himself as comfortable as he could on one of the regularly sized plastic molded guest chairs. For a big guy like Zack, that had to be a tight squeeze.

"Better," Lacy replied. She'd grown fond of this gentle warrior who kept faithful guard over his friend and her. Zack reminded her of Jake in a lot of ways. He'd always been somewhere in the background, taking care of his buddy—and now her.

The FBI confirmed that Rafe Poindexter and his men had murdered all of the clinic's night shift personnel. The cruel deaths of her friends, Roxy, Jeanette, Carol, and Bonnie, even the unlikeable Dr. Anderson made Lacy sad. She'd never cared for the man's abrupt bedside manner, but no one deserved what Poindexter had done.

And that sixth person? Sapphire Dawn, a sixteen-year-old runaway who'd ended up a hooker in Foggy Bottom's dark back alleys. No one knew yet how she came to be in that basement or why she'd been murdered. The FBI was still sorting through a wealth of DNA evidence taken off her body, but that little girl had a mother and a father somewhere, and Lacy wanted to meet them. She wanted to paint poor Sapphire Dawn home. Every little girl and boy deserved one last chance.

While Jake slept the first days after being rescued, Zack made sure she took care of her heart problem. Turns out all that shock treatment she'd been given by Dr. Death had either caused heart damage or further exaggerated an existing condition. She didn't know which, just knew the medication she was on now resolved the problem, and those scary palpitations were gone. Plus she now had a no kidding *cardiologist* who actually cared about his patients.

The afternoon after she was properly diagnosed and treated, Zack had brought his pretty wife, Mei, and their three daughters to visit their Uncle Jake. It was Christmas day, and it was all Lacy could do to not cry when sweet LiLi climbed onto the bed and gave Jake a big sloppy hug.

"I love you, Uncle Jake," she told the sleeping man in no uncertain terms while tears dripped off her nose and ran down his neck. She pulled a wad of green tissue paper out of her coat pocket and tucked it into the palm of his limp hand. "You were supposed to come visit me cuz I got you a Christmas present, see?" Her lower lip quivered. "You'll like it. I did chores for Daddy and saved my money and bought it just for you."

Lacy had to wipe her face. Kids. Damn. They hit below the belt.

Zack and his family weren't the only visitors. Before the day was done, Alex had stopped by with his wife, Kelsey. Some big bruiser named Mark dropped off a picnic basket of snacks, so she'd have something to munch on besides hospital food while she waited at Jake's bedside. Then a bunch of other agents from The TEAM shuffled in with a piping hot Starbucks for her and a flower arrangement for Jake that declared, *'Get well, buddy!'*

Everything made her cry, but them calling a guy they barely knew 'buddy' did her in. She wrote their names down so she could tell him who all stopped by when he finally woke. Taylor, Gabe, and Maverick. On Christmas evening, Rory and Ember.

Last of all, Jamaal had stopped by with a plush teddy bear he'd gotten from who knew where. He hadn't stayed long because he'd started bawling and Lacy understood. A man could only lose so much, and Jamaal knew how close he'd come to losing everyone important to him that day. She'd told him to go back to her apartment where he'd been staying, then she'd hugged him and that started another teary downpour that ended with Jamaal blubbering how much he loved Jake and her. Poor Jamaal.

The few times she'd run home to change or bathe, she hadn't run into him, but her tiny place was always spotless and the refrigerator filled, so she knew he'd been there. Once Jake recovered, they might need to move into a bigger place.

A lot had happened in the short time since Jake had been rescued. Zack hit the headlines when he planted a fist into the belligerent face of one Mr. Manny Prentiss, whom the FBI, along with Zack's assist, had been caught red-handed with his pitiful human cargo from Cambodia. During the arrest,

Prentiss pulled a gun, but Zack disagreed with him, and—
BLAM. His fist came up and Prentiss went down. Lacy cut the
newspaper article out and taped it by Jake's bed where he
could see it the moment he opened his eyes.

"His hearing any better?" Zack asked, pulling her out of
her reverie.

"He keeps talking. Sometimes he grumbles in his sleep,
but of course I can't tell him that he's deaf. He hasn't woken
up long enough for conversation yet."

"Could be a lot worse. Alex been by?"

"Yes, a lot of other people too. I kept a list so I could
remember all their names."

"He leave anything for Jake?"

Lacy nodded toward one of the flower arrangements on
the counter. "The brown and yellow flowers. Why?"

"Oh, nothing." Zack shot her a cute smile like he knew
something she didn't.

"Will you stop teasing and tell me," she hissed.

"Alex should be the one to tell you, but…" Zack leaned
forward. "He's hiring Jake if Jake's willing."

"No. Really?"

"Sure. Jake's the kind of guy Alex respects. He's no
quitter, and the dumb-butt went into hell with nothing more
than a fancy suit and a nine mil he never intended to use."

Zack certainly knew his friend. "Do you think Jake will
accept the job offer?"

"Probably not," Zack admitted. "Guess we'll know when
he wakes up. How's your heart?"

She smiled. "As good as his. Thanks for making me see a
doctor. I do feel better."

Zack winked, the big flirt. "Don't you think it's bizarre that you'd never had a heart problem until Jake was in trouble?"

"What's bizarre is that his heart survived despite him nearly freezing to death. That's how most hypothermic victims die." Lacy reached for Jake's hand, needing to touch him, hoping he'd open those dark grays and offer that serious crooked smile of his.

"What's even more bizarre is that the two of you had life threatening heart problems at the exact same time. Hell, Lacy. You were as gray as he was by the time Alex and Jamaal showed up at your front door. Either of you could've died that night."

"I was gray?" She hadn't known that.

"Yes, you were. Maybe it's true. Maybe two hearts combine once they finally hook up with the right one. Maybe that combination kept you both going when you should have died."

Lacy stilled. Zack's words rang true. The real problem that day had nothing to do the erratic electrical impulses of her battered heart. Jake had been scary close to dying, yet somehow their hearts had reached for each other across time and space. Cried for each other. Found each other. Maybe even strengthened each other. Definitely saved each other.

She shivered and it had nothing to do with being cold. "Maybe," she said at last. If there was one thing the last few days had taught her it was that anything was possible during Christmas, the season of the heart.

"And another thing. Why did you decide to paint Jake's heart in the middle of a snowflake instead of something else?" Zack asked. "It was as if you had a premonition of his death, Lacy. In doing that, in putting that one little drop of red paint in the middle of all that frost, I think somehow you also captured his future. You painted a single speck of life in a frozen wasteland. You painted him home just like you've done with your other pieces."

Tears filled her eyes, and Zack needed to shut up. He was too damned insightful for a man with bulging muscles all the way to his toes. She didn't know why the inspiration had hit her to place a heartbeat in the middle of frozen death. She just had. After making the kind of love she and Jake had made, it just felt right that morning, to sit there close to the man she loved and paint the gift of a heart for him.

"I love him," she admitted quietly. "He is my heart." *Every last beat of it.*

Zack sat so close that he bumped her with his brawny bicep. Lacy didn't have to look at him to know he was emotional. That was why she liked Zack. He was another tough guy with a marshmallow heart.

"How did Jamaal get away from Poindexter's men?" she asked to change the subject.

"Said he faked being knocked out once they dragged him down to the basement and left him for dead." Everyone else being Lacy's friends from the clinic. "Said he'd never been so scared in his life, so he ran like hell. Least he was smart enough to stick close by. That alone saved Jake's life."

True. Jamaal was the unlikeliest of heroes, and God, she loved him for watching over his buddy like he had. "They're two lost souls," she told Zack.

His head bobbed. "They are, but those tunnels," he murmured. "Back in the day, Foggy Bottom was a breeding ground for gang activity. Irish. German. Black. You name it.

The neighborhood was full of bootleggers and prostitution. Used to be known as *'Round Tops'*, named after one of the worst gangs. Poindexter must've tapped into one of those underground alleys. God knows there were plenty of them."

Lacy swallowed hard, the memory of Rafe's tunnel and the smells in it were hard to forget.

Zack kicked a long leg out. "Jake better wake up pretty soon. I'm damned tired of looking at his ugly face while he gets his beauty sleep."

Lacy smiled, her fingers intertwined with Jake's and her heart beating with his. She wasn't tired of looking at Jake, but, yeah. He'd better wake up soon. She needed to kiss the stuffing out of him.

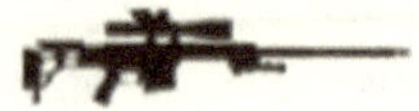

Finally. Jake Weylin opened his eyes. The weight on his chest had lifted, the oxygen cannula was gone, and someone had hold of his left hand. *Oh. Lacy.* She'd fallen asleep in the chair next to his bed with her arm outstretched and her fingers wrapped around his. He tightened his hold. *Sweet.*

Her green eyes lit up at that telling squeeze, and he was pretty sure she'd said something. Her lips moved, but he couldn't hear a thing. "Eh?' he had to ask, his throat raw and thick with congestion. "What happened?"

Up she came until she was kneeling on the edge of his bed. She braced her palms to the sides of his face and answered with a teary kiss that would've melted his socks off if he'd had any on. Some kind of magical energy shot straight through his tired-as-hell body to his bare toes. He cupped the back of her skull so he could get a better hold on her. Tubes and wires came with his arm, but it didn't slow him down. He wanted more of that mouth of hers.

She cocked her head for easier access. So much warmth came with her touch as she deepened the kiss, pushing her tongue between his lips and sparking feelings no dead man had a right to own. Lacy Wright was making a meal of him, and she was the perfect desert. The only thing that could make this moment better would be if they were both naked.

For some crazy wonderful reason, his eyes brimmed with tears. She had to stop. This was too much, too soon, and, oh, what the hell. No, it wasn't. Not really. He got it now. He might not ever deserve her, but Lacy Wright was his to love and to hold for time and all eternity.

He asked again, "What happened?"

Lacytouched her fingertips to her lips and pressed them to his chest. Jake might not have heard the words, but his heart leapt up to catch that homerun "I love you" like a rookie on second base. He pressed his lips to her forehead and let his tears mingle with hers.

The divine strains of George Frideric Handel's chorus welled up from inside of him while Lacy's love washed over him, baptizing him again and again. The war was finally done.

Alle-freaking-luia!

Chapter Thirty-One

"Uncle Jake!" LiLi and Song squealed together at Zack's front door. "You came! You came!"

Jake nodded to the excited youngsters. His hearing had returned once the congestion in his head cleared, but his bout with pneumonia had left him weak and tired most of the time. He couldn't complain, though. Not with Lacy at his side.

"Did you like my present?" LiLi asked, her big brown eyes full of excitement.

"I do," he said, lifting the chain around his neck out from under his shirt so she could see he meant what he said. The cute little gal had given him a Saint Christopher medal, the patron saint of weary travelers, to help him find his way home the next time he got lost. Damned insightful for a child to give an adult, especially him.

LiLi was smart like that and incredibly perceptive for a child her age, but she was still a little girl. She scrunched her shoulders and asked, "Do you have a present for me?"

"Of course I do. Me and Lacy brought presents for all you kids."

"My goodness, let Uncle Jake and Aunt Lacy get inside the house," Mei scolded the kids away—for half a second.

Suddenly surrounded by a bevy of little ones with radar ears, Jake closed the door behind him and sank to his knees in the foyer. The moment overwhelmed. All those little hands and tender voices reached deep into his emotions, pulling out forgotten feelings. Panic raised its obnoxious head, but this time something else came with it: Inner strength and some old jarhead named Sergeant Jake Weylin, who apparently had more work to do before he processed out of Jake's head. It was a good thing, too, having your old self at your six. Some folks might call him crazy, but that was the last thing Jake was. Healing was a better word. Happy sounded good, too. Best of all, he was in love.

He and Lacy handed out extra-large peppermint candy canes with small fuzzy stuffed pink bears for the little girls, gold teddy bears for the boys. But for LiLi, he had a special gift. If she wanted to be an astronaut, he intended to deliver. He'd bought her a telescope for stargazing and had to duck back to the Lennox's front porch where he'd left it.

Mei rolled her eyes. "You shouldn't have."

"Oh yes, he should've." Zack angled through the crowd and wrapped his arm around Jake's shoulders in a one-armed, guy-kind of sideways hug. "Now I don't have to buy her one. It's about damned time you got here. What kept you so long?"

"Yeah, well…" Jake didn't know what else to say. No way was he telling Zack what he and Lacy had been doing with and to each other since he'd gotten out of the hospital. It seemed the more he made love with her, the faster he'd gotten his strength back. She'd become that needle in his arm, only the addiction she'd brought with her wasn't at all like what he'd seen addicts on the streets go through. If anything, the moment he pressed his lips to hers, he was transported to another—him. A better him. He could feel again. Better yet, he wanted to.

How a woman could anchor him, yet at the same time set him free, he didn't claim to understand, but Lacy did just that. She didn't seem to mind all the sex they'd been sharing, either. A smile tweaked his lips just thinking about how they'd blessed every flat surface in her tiny apartment. A few vertical surfaces too.

Jake stuck out his hand, but Zack being Zack slapped it away and pulled him into one of those brotherly hugs, his arm around Jake's neck and his mouth to Jake's ear. "You son-of-a-bitch. I meant what I said. My house is yours."

Zack wanted Jake and Lacy out of Anacostia, and Jake understood why, but as tough a neighborhood as it was, Anacostia, specifically, Lacy's apartment, was good enough for now. Living indoors in clean quarters was a big enough change.

Jake hung on for a second longer than he should have because, well, Zack was the only one who'd come looking for him after Kabul, and he'd never stopped watching out for him, not even when Jake tried to get lost. Even after he married Mei, Zack had always reached out and reeled Jake back in for a home cooked meal or two, a new jacket, and maybe a pair of boots. Zack had never left him behind, and that was saying a lot—a helluva lot—considering Jake was down on his luck and living on the streets of hardcore Anacostia.

"Thanks, brother," Jake said as he ended the man hug. "You've done enough."

Zack tilted back from his waist, his grip still tight on Jake's biceps. "There's no such thing as enough when you're family." His eyes lit with that Lennox signature smile.

"There's only *'get your butt to the table before the ham's gone'*, now move it. You too, Lacy."

Zack pulled her in for a hug. "I swear, you get prettier every day. How goes the art show?"

Up went her brows and her pretty green eyes nearly popped out of her head. "Oh Zack, where do I begin? It's a lot more work than I expected, but I've got orders and letters coming in from parents and wives of service members all over the world. It breaks my heart every day, but…" She reached for him again, her arms around his thick neck. "You were right. People do care."

His brow lifted in that dangerous, teasing way he had. "You get in touch with your folks yet? Your mom?"

Lacy let go with an extra noisy gulp. "Not yet, but that's my New Year's resolution. I'm going to."

Zack grinned. "That gives you three hundred and sixty-five days to make good on it. Don't let her down." He turned on Jake then. "I hear you're going west?"

How the man knew about Jake's travel plans was a surprise, but not a shock. Zack was a covert operator after all. "February," Jake announced his upcoming trip home to visit Arkansas. "I told them I'd be out next month."

"Your folks will be glad to see you. Your Granddad too."

Zack always claimed his greatest power came from his family. Jake meant to prove his buddy right. As he stepped away with Mei, Jake steered Lacy into the festivities. It might be January first for the rest of the world, but it was still Christmas at the Lennox house.

Instead of grabbing a plate of the banquet spread on the extra-long table in the dining room, Jake ducked inside the Lennox's spacious living room with Lacy on his arm. Damn.

Zack had a big house, but the place was full of people. Too many people. Lots of beefy guys. He recognized the ex-military stamp on their faces. It looked like Alex Stewart's entire team was here, their wives and children too. Mark Houston, he knew. Harley Mortimer and Rory Dennison, too. Taylor Armstrong. Gabe Cartwright. Maverick Carson. But all those kids...

They were everywhere, and they filled the house with squeals and laughter and a creeping sense of *I've-got-to-get-out-of-here*. Jake halted before he got too far from Zack's front door. Maybe this wasn't a smart idea.

"You good?" Lacy knew him too well. Heck, she'd probably turn tail and run with him if he decided to, but that little cutie-pie Song had run up to him, and now she had hold of his pinkie finger.

The little tyke determinedly tugged him into the heart of the boisterous Lennox extended family. "Come on, Unca Jake. You is walking too slow," she grumbled.

"I am, huh?" He blew out a deep breath. "Well then..." Another deep breath. "Let's do this." Summoning his inner jarhead to the party, he swung Song up to his shoulder and the three of them marched on in. "Where do you want to sit, Princess?"

Song clapped her hands and squealed, "I is a Pwincess! Over there, Unca Jake. I wanna sit by the Chwissmas twee!"

"Coming through," he declared loudly and proudly. The tree had to be twenty feet tall. He looked up to where a star or an angel should've been. Instead a shiny red heart sparkled. Zack never did do things like everyone else. "What's that, Song?" he asked as he pointed up top.

Zack's sweet little baby tipped her cheek to Jake's cheek and whispered. "It's a heart, siwwee."

Lacy snorted. He peered at this adorable kid. "Did you just call me silly?"

"Ah-huh," she answered as her little arms came around his head. Song grunted as she squeezed him tight. "You is siwwee and I is Song. Merry Chwissmas, Unca Jake."

Man, what's a guy supposed to do after a Christmas hug and a wish like that? He swung her into his arms and set her gently to the floor before he wimped out and had to trade in his man card one more time. "Merry Christmas, Song. Go find your sisters. Scoot."

"Merry Christmas, Lacy. Junior Agent," Alex said as he lifted his wine glass in a toast from one of many comfortable loveseats scattered around the edge of the room.

"Same to you, sir," Jake answered, his head clearer now that he was officially inside the room. Alex's job offer was still a little overwhelming. Accompanying Harley and Mark to places unknown for a contract with the World Health Organization didn't sound difficult, but he also knew how those simple sounding operations could turn to hell in a hurry.

Alex rolled his steely blue eyes, shaking his head. "You want to try that again, *Junior Agent*?"

Did the noise in the house just drop a few decibels? Crap, even the kids were suddenly silent. Jake nodded at his new boss even as that creepy sensation prickled up the back of his neck, certain that all eyes were fixed on him. He looked to Zack who had the shittiest smirk on his face. Oh yeah. The funny story about Mark calling Alex 'sir' came back to Jake. Alex worked for a living. He hated being called '*sir*'—with a passion. *Shit, I haven't set foot in his office yet, and I already blew it.*

Damned if that cocky son-of-a-bitch, Sergeant Jake Weylin, didn't show up unexpectedly. He was fast becoming a regular in Jake and Lacy's life. "Did I just call you 'sir'? Me? Did I do that?" he challenged Alex, back-pedaling like only a Marine knew how. "I'm sure I said 'Boss'. Didn't I?" Jake played to the crowded room. "What'd you guys hear? Did I say 'sir' or —?"

"Boss!" every last male in the room shouted. "You said 'Boss', and 'Oorah!'"

The women giggled and the boisterous men outright laughed, while Jake faced the other man he respected as much as Zack. He'd heard stories how Alex had refused to give up the search even after the Coast Guard called it quits the night Jake had supposedly walked into the river. Alex was one of those rare leaders who actually led his men into battle instead of pushing them from a safe distance behind the lines. Zack never had a bad thing to say about the man.

At the moment, Alex had a pretty dark-haired woman beside him and a glass of red wine in his hand. "Well said, Jake. Well said. Zack might be right after all. This is my wife, Kelsey. Kelsey, Junior Agent Jake Weylin and his girlfriend, Lacy Wright."

"Hi, Jake." Kelsey offered a pretty smile as she toasted him with her nearly full goblet. "I've been waiting to meet you, and I already know Lacy."

"Evening, ma'am," Jake replied, hoping that word of respect was acceptable.

Lacy waved back at Kelsey. "Hi, Kelsey. We weren't expecting so many people."

"Neither were we," Alex said in the same humorless, deadpan tone, his sharp blue eyes scanning and quartering the crowd, no doubt looking for trouble before it started. "Guess that's what families do. They just keep getting bigger and funnier. Why don't you sit your ass down?" He shot Jake a sideways glance that would've looked disdainful if a half-smile hadn't twitched his lip.

"Yessssss…" *Whew.* "Boss." That damned USMC sergeant under his skin had very nearly called Alex the 'S' word again. Note to self: *Don't do that!*

He and Lacy took a seat against the wall nearest to, and nearly behind the tree. Old habits died hard, but this was a safe place in more ways than one. Not only could he see straight up the hallway to the front door, but no one would step on his legs and fingers back here.

Jake scanned the filled-to-overflowing room. The only ones who didn't fit the military mode were the kids and a grizzled old man in the rocking chair with somebody's baby on his lap. Wait a minute. Was that Marty snuggling that baby? The old drunk who'd found that little Chinese orphan in the dumpster behind the now defunct IGA store in Anacostia, the same one Jamaal and Jake used to sleep in? By hell, it was. *Good old Marty.* It was his act of kindness for a tiny one as lost as he was that had provided the clues needed to end the selling and buying of Chinese orphans in the D.C. area.

Jake sent him a hearty, "Hey, Marty. Whatcha doing?"

Up came Marty's gray head with a grin of recognition. "I'm rocking my baby. Least, I'm rocking somebody's baby."

"That'd be mine." Connor Maher raised a hand from the loveseat where he snuggled with another TEAM agent, his wife Izza. "You got her to burp yet?"

Marty shook his head, his brows pinched. "No, she s'posed to?"

Izza's dark eyes sparkled. "I don't want her back until you get one out of her. Better be a big one."

That seemed to please Marty. He settled back in the rocker, patting that little one's back like a proud grandpa instead of a recovering alcoholic. In minutes, Zack came by with a couple brewskis and two plates of heavy hors d'oeuvres for Jake and Lacy. Ham. German potato salad. Crackers and cheese sticks. Stuff like that. Mei followed with silverware and napkins. LiLi set up a folding TV tray next to Lacy to hold their drinks while they ate.

Jake rolled the pinch out of his neck and shot a quick glance at Zack's boss, now his boss. You'd never know Alex Stewart was a self-made millionaire, not the way he sat there with one arm flopped over his wife's shoulder while he sipped at his wine. Everyone was dressed casually in jeans and T-shirts or sweatshirts. Alex too. He looked more like some local frat boy with that blue sweatshirt he was wearing, his absolute allegiance to the Corps declared in the bright yellow USMC logo across his chest.

But his face told another story. The man wore scars along his jaw like a badge. He'd be a boss to be reckoned with, and for the first time since deployment ended, Jake looked forward to the challenge.

Kelsey chatted with Libby Houston at her other side while Libby's husband, Mark, held one of their three little girls on his knee, bouncing the baby enough to keep her giggling and grinning. The two couples looked like a damned pair of bookends. Happy bookends.

Chapter Thirty-Two

Son of a gun, my life has changed. Jake wouldn't have it any other way.

While he'd spent the first few days of recovery sleeping, Zack had made certain that the AMA, the American Medical Association, got wind and evidence of Dr. Death's extreme method for treating hysteria, hyper-vigilance, and PTSD. It seemed Lacy's parents weren't the only ones duped into paying thousands for false claims of a fast cure for Post-Traumatic Stress. The man actually was board-certified, but the greedy bastard had preyed on families of returning soldiers. Had a glamorous clinic and everything. Not any more. The last Jake heard, the AMA had closed Dr. Death's clinic down pending a thorough investigation and possible charges. Jake would've taken it one step farther, but murder was against the law.

Poindexter was still making headlines, along with Rocky Rabbit, Ferret Face, and bloodthirsty Miss Annette Plunkett, who turned out to be Poindexter's mistress from hell. She'd flipped on Poindexter faster than he could turn state's evidence on his long-time buddy, Manny Prentiss. It didn't take her long to rat out everyone Poindexter had blackmailed on his way up the corporate ladder. Plunkett knew where every last girl was, and she made certain the press knew, too.

The gossip rags blew up with Kelly Poindexter's much publicized and televised declaration of divorce. She'd become a favorite on all the feel-good talk shows, investigative reports, and the like. The kingdom Poindexter had sold his soul for now resided in the hands of Homeland Security, Interpol, and a star-studded divorce lawyer from Hollywood.

The California Attorney General vowed Poindexter would never see the outside of the federal prison he was headed to, and his ex-wife vowed he'd never see his daughter—if he lived long enough to ask for parole or visiting privileges. Not likely. The man had too many enemies in the system who wanted him to disappear, and some were powerful enough to make it happen. *Stupid, stupid man.*

As far as all those poor little girls from Cambodia? Zack and Alex already knew exactly what those kids needed. They'd had a run in with another human trafficking ring, this one out of China, not too long ago. As quickly as the State Department and Immigration processed the girls, they were placed in better, safer hands. Some went willingly back home to relatives in Cambodia. Some went into the witness protection program. Some went into trustworthy foster care.

Then there was Lacy's art show. Her big debut was coming up quickly, and Jake wouldn't miss it. Alex's wife had talked Lacy into a private showing at a torpedo factory over in Alexandria, though what Navy torpedoes had to do with art was still a mystery to Jake. It seemed Kelsey was on some society board, and knew people in all the right places. Once she'd seen Lacy's work, she offered to set up the private showing for the families of the soldiers Lacy had painted.

Kelsey and Lacy had been planning the event for days now. Because it was scheduled for the week of Valentine's Day, they'd decided to call it *The Gallery of Soldier's Hearts*. Lacy was a bundle of nerves, but she'd be okay. The woman was a genius in disguise.

Jake's painting, the one of snowflakes on a backdrop of black was the centerpiece of the show. It wasn't going anywhere but back to her apartment. She'd painted it within hours of their very first time making love, and the damned thing spoke straight to his soul. It was her perfect red heart—not his—in the middle of that beautiful masterpiece of ice crystals.

The minute she'd given herself to him, he'd changed. A man couldn't receive and accept that kind of a gift and not want to be better. She'd done that. Jake knew he might be crazier than a loon to believe like he did, but it was the gift of her heart that had kept him alive that treacherous night. Jamaal might have carried him, but it was Lacy's love that kept him breathing.

"Hey, Jake. You-hoo. Earth to Jake." Harley called from the floor in front of the Christmas tree where he'd been entertaining Zack's littlest girl, MiKi.

Jake jerked out of his mental wanderings and set his empty plate on the table with Lacy's. "Yeah, Harley. What's up?"

"You seen Jamaal's interview yet?" Harley asked while cute little MiKi played with his hair, his lips, and ears. The more she tweaked, the funnier faces Harley made until she was giggling herself sick. Little Song draped herself over his back watching and giggling, too. It was a lovely sound on a lovely day.

"Someone interviewed Jamaal?" *That oughta be good.*

"Oh, yes, you've got to see it," Ember said from where she sat on her husband, Rory's lap. Half the team seemed to prefer the floor to the love seats, but damn, those two kids did a lot of kissing and necking. Of course, Jake had his arm around Lacy, too. He was one to talk. "Do you have a tablet? I'll show you."

"As a matter of fact, I do." Harley pulled up a mini-tablet from the floor beside him, flipped it open, and with a few deft taps of his index finger brought up the interview. "Here you go," he said as he handed the device over. "Watch this."

Jake leaned into Lacy so she could watch too, and suddenly, LiLi was hanging over his back, MiKi crawled over to join him while Song squirmed under his arm and took possession of his lap.

As usual, YouTube video brought up a commercial. "Oh here," LiLi said, her fingertips working the screen like she knew precisely what to do. "You don't want to watch that stuff. It's so annoying."

One of the major networks logo flashed on screen and, lo and behold. It was Jamaal, all right. He looked indifferent answering the reporter's questions with a play-by-play of how he'd found his buddy, Jake Weylin, on the bank of the Potomac back in December. He didn't look any happier when he explained how he'd hacked the nylon ropes with a pocketknife because that was all he had on him. Neither did he look the reporter in the eye.

"What's wrong with him?" Lacy asked. "Do you think he has stage fright?"

"Maybe," Jake answered. *I sure as hell would.*

Jamaal's head dropped as he described how his best friend was talking out of his head when he'd found him because Jake was damned near 'froze to death' by then. He described how dead Jake looked and how scared he'd been that he'd arrived too late to save his brother. Jake had icicles hanging off his chin and eyebrows. Finally, Jamaal told the reporter how Jake didn't weigh a thing when Jamaal laid him over his shoulder and began the long trek back to Lacy's apartment in Anacostia.

Jake stared. He had no idea all his buddy had gone through to save his life. Jamaal hadn't wanted to talk about it. Apparently, he did now.

"But how did you keep him warm?" the reporter asked. "That had to be a long walk."

Jamaal's big brown eyes brimmed. He brushed a big hand over his face, still not making eye contact. "It's like this. Jake Weylin's my brother, man. I put my coat over him, and I figured as long as I kept trying to save him, my coat would keep him warm enough. And I prayed. I prayed so damned hard, there weren't no way he was gonna die. God just don't work like that."

The reporter leaned into Jamaal. "Excuse me, but that's impossible, Mr. McCune. It's more than a dozen miles from that riverbank to Anacostia, and the weather was frigid. The roads were closed and sections of the Potomac were frozen. It had to have taken you a long time to walk that far. Your friend should have been dead by then"

Jake rolled his neck at the uppity tone to that reporter's voice. Was he there? No. Did he have a clue what a good man could do under real pressure? Abso-fuckin'-lutely not.

"I hate reporters," Lacy muttered. "You're here, so it *is* possible and it *was* a miracle."

"Ain't nothing impossible," Jamaal muttered, finally looking the reporter in the eye. "'Sides, I ain't stupid. I didn't hafta walk far, only down to the river cuz I stole a boat." Jamaal's head bobbed as he got his swagger on. "That's what I did. Once I got Jake down from that slab of iron he was stuck on, it didn't take no time gettin' him onto the river. I just fired that outboard up and away we went. Only problem I had was staying clear of the Coast Guard. Damned guys were everywhere."

"But they were looking for *you*." The reporter shook his head as if Jamaal was an idiot. "They could've helped."

Jamaal shrugged. "Now how was I s'posed to know that? Poindexter tried to kill us. For all I knew, he could've been blackmailing someone in the Coast Guard, too. Only ones I trusted that night were Jake and Miss Lacy, and Jake was dying. 'Sides, I just told you—I stole a boat. I was a wanted man."

The reporter sank back in his chair. "What you are, Mr. McCune, is one lucky and very amazing man. Without a doubt, you did the impossible that night."

"I know." Jamaal's USMC swagger showed up right on time. "But my buddy's the real hero, not me. I just run interference for him and Miss Lacy. I knows how to cook now, too."

The video clip ended and MiKi squealed, "Play it again!"

Song bounced up and down on Jake's lap, clapping her pudgy hands.

"I like Jamaal," LiLi said wistfully in his ear. "He's like you, Uncle Jake. He's one of the good guys, isn't he?"

"He is," Jake said humbly. Jamaal was one of best.

It was good to know that he was doing well. Old man Lamont Adams had given Jamaal a job helping rebuild the pool hall, and he'd promised Jamaal the bartender job when the hall was finished. The first thing Jamaal had done when he got that job was move out of Lacy's apartment and into Lamont's home where he helped take care of Mrs. Adams. It was a win-win. Mr. Adams gave him free room and board and something every honest man in the world craved, a paycheck at the end of every week and his pride back.

Alex lifted his glass. The room stilled. "You need a drink in your hand, Jake," he said. Funny how it sounded more like an order instead of a suggestion.

Zack shoved another long neck brewski at Jake, one for Lacy, too. She gulped one of her extra noisy gulps like she always did when she was getting emotional.

"To Sergeant Jake Weylin," Alex said, his glass raised high.

Everyone in the room lifted a glass or bottle to Jake while he sat there on the floor, fingering his icy cold longneck. Zack's little girls had rejoined Harley, so Jake pulled Lacy in close, feeling awkward and put on the spot. "I didn't do anything but nearly get myself killed."

"You did, too. You got the smoking gun," Lacy whispered. "It was all you, Jake. You brought Rafe Poindexter down, and you saved all of those little girls from Cambodia. Look at the people in this room. They're not the press. They're your friends, and they know a real hero when they see one. They care about you."

Now it was his turn to gulp. He was no hero. Jake looked to Alex. Something about the guy commanded. He still had his glass raised, but those damned blue lasers pierced across the room and straight to Jake's guilty soul. "Work starts at eight," Alex said without blinking. "Be there."

Once more "Yes, sir," came automatically out of Jake's mouth. *Damn. I have got to stop pissing off my new boss or I'll be doing KP.*

Alex downed his drink, but just as quickly, Harley raised another toast. "To good friends and fast women!"

"Harley!" a redhead with two little boys at her side scolded from the leather couch. "The children." Her brows lifted as if she expected better from him. Had to be his spitfire wife, Judy. Good on her for calling her husband out for that lame toast. Everyone laughed, but still.

Harley winked at his woman, sticking his chin right back at her. "I know, darlin'. I was just seeing if you were awake."

"I am now." Was there a challenge in her tone?

Grinning like a fool, Harley raised his glass again. "In the words of a famous snowman, whom we all know and love, have a *'holy jolly Christmas'*, folks. Live long and never forget" —he winked at Jake— "there's angels amongst us, people. They show up when you least expect them. Some of 'em are big and black, and some of 'em got red hair." He tossed a sexy wink at his wife. "Cheers." Harley downed his drink and stuck his empty glass out to one of the little boys. "More, Georgie."

I'm no angel, Jake thought, but damned if Lacy's butt didn't scoot in closer to his. "Here, here," she said quietly.

He brushed a kiss to her temple. Now that he had time to notice, those boys of Harley's were identical twins. "Here you go, Daddy," Georgie said as he delivered a can of A&W's finest. "Want me to pour it for you?"

Harley's bows lifted as his hand settled over the already open—and dripping—can in his eager youngster's hands. "Not unless Mom's got a towel close by. Thanks, son. Now step back while I pour the bubbles."

Georgie's twin scrambled to his dad's knee as the liquid refreshment glugged out of its can. "Kin I stick my finger in it?"

"No, it's my turn," Georgie argued, his wiggly body inching alongside his dad.

Harley settled the feud when he handed the can to Georgie and the glass to the other. "Be nice, boys. It's Little Alex's turn."

"There's something I have to tell you, Jake," Lacy murmured, her fingers choking the stem of her wine glass. "As soon as we get home."

Jake cocked his head, lowering it enough to block the sudden scowl on his face. She wasn't looking at him. "Anything wrong?"

She shook her head, but damn. Were those tears in her eyes? "No. Everything's perfect. There's just something I've been meaning to say."

His heart stuttered. Did she already know? "There's something I've been meaning to tell you too," he muttered into the side of her head. Lacy's hair smelled of peppermint and snow. He inhaled deeply, held her scent as long as he could, then released it slowly. He had nothing to worry about, nothing in the big wide world. This was Lacy after all.

"To my buddy, Jake Weylin," Zack said heartily, interrupting Jake and Lacy's private moment. "Best damned friend a man could ask for."

Bottles and glasses clinked. Jake bumped bottles with Lacy and Zack, but when he turned to Lacy, he paused. Those soft green eyes of hers were filled up with liquid love, and he wasn't in the middle of Zack's living room anymore. He wasn't in the company of snipers, either. The world would always have its Sector 18s, but God willing, it would also have people like Lacy who knew how to reach the lost ghosts of war and paint them home. Or at least paint the heart back into them. Just like she'd done with him.

"I love you so much, Jake Weylin," she whispered, one of those crystals tears perched at the edge of her lower eyelid. "You saved me and I saved you, and that's the way it's supposed to be, damn it."

Jake loved it when Lacy got her dander up. He bumped his forehead to hers in the best Christmas toast ever. "I know."

Chapter Thirty-Three

The gathering at Zack's home was perfect, but Lacy couldn't wait to get back to her little apartment. There was one more gift to be given, and she wanted to be alone with her man when she showed it to him.

But Jake had relaxed as the pleasant afternoon drifted into evening and then night, so she bided her time. To the squeals of delight from all the children in the house, Zack and Mei pushed back a set of panels at the far end of their expansive family room to reveal a closet full of sleeping bags, pillows, and blankets. Apparently, this Christmas-after-New-Year's party was a slumber party for the youngsters.

LiLi took over, which seemed appropriate since she was taller and the oldest of the tribe, also the bossiest. But she got things done in her domineering way. She handed the sleeping supplies out in quick order and told the younger children where to put theirs so her daddy could tell a story. "Hurry up. We hafta be in our beds and we hafta be extra quiet."

Baby MiKi pursed her lips and spit out a bubbly "Shhhhh" as if she'd done this before while Song dove into her sleeping bag lickety-split, the cutie.

Brand new pajamas appeared courtesy of Alex and Kelsey, and the best part of the day commenced watching all those big guys with their large hands and callused fingers change their kids' play clothes for sleep clothes. What a circus.

Most knew what to do, but Harley's and Judy's little ones ran for their lives, squealing and whooping it up. Harley's chasing after them didn't lessen the racket, but Lacy couldn't miss the enjoyment on Harley's face or the amused smile on his wife's face. Judy didn't look angry. If anything, she looked—smitten.

Lacy also kept a close eye on Alex. For as tough as he sounded, the man was as gentle as a lamb with his little girl, Lexie. Kelsey looked on while the toddler squirmed, but over and over, Alex patiently laid Lexie back to the floor where he sat cross-legged, until he had her out of her jeans and Christmas sweater.

Training diapers, huh. Pull-ups? Interesting. Lacy took note of the tenderness on his rugged face as he cared for his daughter. By the time Lexie was changed and dressed, she'd forgotten about the party behind her. When he lifted her to her pajama-footed toes and said, "There you go. Now scoot," she dove headlong into his arms and squealed, "I wuv you, Daddy! Mostest of all!"

If that didn't bring a tear to Lacy's eye, nothing could. Apparently it worked on Alex too. He swiped a hand over his face as he took his place beside Kelsey. Those two. There was something between them that set them apart from everyone else. It might've been the way Kelsey melted into his side, her fingers fluttering on his chest and a warm glow in her brown eyes. Maybe it was the way he pulled her in like he needed her, or the way he closed his eyes when he kissed her forehead. It could've been nothing more than the soft smile on her pretty face when his lips touched her skin. Whatever *it* was, Lacy wanted it.

Finally, Little Alex and Georgie were in their pajamas and the restless natives settled for the night. Lacy and Jake had since moved to one of the loveseats facing the tree. The fire in the fireplace crackled with real logs instead of gas, a nice touch that had kept Rory busy since he seemed to be in charge of it.

At last, Zack dragged a wooden stool to the wide stone hearth. He hooked his boot heels on the lowest rung, folded his arms over his chest, and—

"Wait. Don't we get out treats now?" intelligent and wise LiLi asked, blinking those big brown eyes at her father.

"Oops," Mei yipped. "I forgot."

"You stay put, I'll get them," Hunter Christian said, one foot in the kitchen already. He and his wife Meredith had shown up late in the afternoon with their son, Courtney, but what a handsome pair. Clean cut and shaved, Hunter was a walking piece of damned hot eye candy, while Meredith still looked like she'd rather be in bed sound asleep.

"Morning sickness still bothering you?" Libby Houston called out.

"I've never thrown up so much in my life, not even with my first," Meredith said, nodding. "I'm glad Hunter's getting the treats. I don't think I can handle looking at food."

Courtney was already tucked in the sleeping bag he'd dragged alongside Rory and Ember's son, Tyler, but oh my heck. What were Zack and Mei thinking to invite all these children for a sleepover? It wasn't Christmas and Santa Claus wasn't coming. What was going on?

"Ahem," Zack cleared his throat as he eyed the children while Uncle Hunter passed popcorn balls and juice boxes. "Are we ready?"

"Yes, Uncle Zack," the smiling tribe replied in unison as if they'd done this before.

"Okay then. This is a story about true love," Zack began quietly, his hands on his knees and making careful eye contact with each of the kids.

The little boys set to grumbling while a collective "Aww…" came from the girls.

Zack lifted an eyebrow. "What does it take for true love to start and to grow?" The rapport he had with these kids was sweet to watch.

A tiny blonde girl who looked more like an elfin princess than a human child waved her hand. "I know. I know!"

"Suzette?" Zack prompted.

"A princess and a prince!" she belted out. That must be Gabe Cartwright's little one. With those mahogany curls, she looked just like him.

A red-haired boy of maybe three frowned at Suzette, his lips pursed. "Doesn't always hafta be a prince. My Daddy loves my Mommy, and he's no prince. He's just a regular dad."

The adults in the room chuckled while Lacy lost track of whose child was whose, until Tess Hart muttered, "You tell 'em Charlie." *Okay. Charlie belongs to Lee and Tess Hart. God help me remember all these faces and names.*

"But what does it truly take?" Zack asked as his fist thumped his chest. "Down deep. What does it really take for a man and woman to be happy together?"

Lacy smiled. He'd already given the answer away. These little ones just had to think for a moment.

Damned if Jake didn't unfold his long legs and stand to attention beside her. "I know what it takes," he said, his back stiff and his eyes on Zack. All those little faces turned expectantly upward to Jake.

"What are you doing?" Lacy asked. "Sit down. This story's for the little—"

"True love takes true love," Jake said loudly and proudly, and, *oh, my gosh.* He turned and dropped to one knee. Lacy blinked and blinked again. Someone giggled, and she was pretty sure it wasn't her. "Jake Weylin?" she asked, her heart fluttering as if a million butterflies had just taken wing inside its chambers.

"Lacy Wright," he said as he tugged something out of his back pocket. "Will you marry me?" he asked, not a bit of doubt in his strong, masculine voice.

Oh, wow. Oh, Wow. A… a diamond ring.

"M-m-me?" she asked, stuttering enough for the both of them. Oddly, she couldn't come up woth any moisture in her throat when she needed it most, but her eyes had plenty.

"Yes, you, you, you," he said as he nodded. "You're my heart and soul, Lacy. I want you to be the rest of my life, too."

"Are you sure?" she asked, thinking of all those paintings in her closet.

It seemed the room held its breath. Not Jake. "Never been surer," he said without missing a beat.

"Yes," she managed before she choked on the emotions in her heart. "Oh, yes, Jake Weylin. I'll marry you."

Without a single tremor, he placed the ring on her left ring finger. It fit. Perfectly.

A sweet "Awww…" came from the little girls, a few of the older girls, too.

"See, what'd I tell you?" cute little Charlie stage-whispered. "It just takes a smart man and a smarter woman to fall in love."

Lacy sputtered at that. Oh, the stories Charlie's mom must have told him.

"You may kiss your future bride," Zack intoned like a minister.

"Yes, I may," Jake growled as he leaned in and blessed Lacy with a moist, warm, but chaste, kiss.

She couldn't let him go after that, just pressed her forehead to his. His lips pressed another kiss to her nose. "Like the man said, it just takes a man and a smarter woman."

Chapter Thirty-Four

The goodbyes took longer than the hellos, but when it came time to leave Zack and Mei's, Jake was on top of the world. His lady said yes! He was walking on air. He couldn't feel the cold snap in the evening air, and the accumulated snow on Lacy's brand new Toyota, the one he'd bought with his bonus for joining The TEAM, didn't bother him one bit.

He looked up at the leaden overcast sky, which blanketed most of the eastern seaboard, and his heart lifted to heaven with thanks for second chances. All the operatic voices in his hard head had gone silent. Even sweet Fantine hadn't spoken a word since the day he'd nearly died on the edge of the Potomac. What more could a man ask for?

"Do you want me to drive?"

Jake looked down at the woman in his arms, for the first time seeing his reflection in her green eyes. Lacy was the same as him. They'd endured the same kinds of inner battles; she just hadn't buried her heart so deep that it couldn't breathe. He got it now, the whole two becoming one thing between a man and his wife. It made its two separate parts better and stronger. Braver.

"Tonight, yes, but tomorrow, I'm getting my license back. You don't need to be driving me everywhere I'm supposed to go."

"Like to work? I don't mind."

"Yes. Like to work." He winked and opened the driver's side door for her. "Alexandria isn't exactly on the way to the Good Samaritan. Speaking of which, when will it re-open?"

Lacy took her place behind the steering wheel. "Possibly the end of January. One of the doctors over at Holy Cross is taking over until there's a permanent replacement for Marlee, and quite a few nurses in the area volunteered to keep it running. We don't always need a physician on staff, but sometimes..." She took a deep breath. "Did I tell you how much I love this new car smell?"

Jake grinned as he ran around the car and let himself in. "It was nice to be able to shop for you for a change. Where do you want to get married?"

She cast a look to the loving home at her left. "At Zack's."

That put a grin on Jake's face. "Good idea. Do you want me to ask him or would you rather?"

"I think we should both ask him and Mei, but not tonight. They've got their hands full with... how many kids are sleeping over?"

"A hundred?"

A chuckle bubbled out of her throat. "It seemed like a hundred, didn't it? So, umm, kids. We've never talked about that. How many do you see us having? None? Two? Six, like Libby and Mark are trying for?"

That deserved an eye roll. What was Mark thinking? "Not six," Jake replied firmly, his fingertips tapping a beat on his knees. That was half a dozen and too close to a hundred.

Despite having had a good day at his buddy's home, he was smart enough to know he still needed help. He hadn't broached the idea of counseling with Lacy yet, but Harley knew a good group near Mount Vernon that he'd used back when he was struggling with PTSD. Jake wanted to check them out. Drugs and anti-depressants with all their side effects were a definite no-go, but the Malinois pup Harley had also offered up might be the perfect solution. The little guy was pure black, the offspring of proven service dogs, and sharp as a blade.

Hmmm. Blade. That'd be a good name. "Can I get a dog?" blurted out of his big mouth before he gave it license to speak.

"So you'd rather have a dog than kids?" There was something different about Lacy tonight.

"Oh no, I just..." His fingers stabbed through his hair as Lacy started the car, maneuvered out of their parking place, and began the drive back to Anacostia. "We could start with one kid and go from there," he suggested.

That got him a funny giggle out of his sexy driver. "That's the way it usually starts, Jake. One egg. One sperm. One infant that looks like either you or me. It was funny that every time I turned around today, you had a little one sitting on your lap. Song seemed to think you were her personal chair, and who was that little boy sitting on your shoulders when I was helping Mei in the kitchen?"

Oh, him. "That was Taylor and Gracie's little guy, umm, Peter, I think his name is."

"He looked mighty comfortable." Lacy gave Jake a sideways glance. Those pretty green eyes were up to something, but he still hadn't a clue. "You're good with kids, I can tell. You seemed to attract them like magnets."

And it was time to change the subject. "So what's the secret you couldn't tell me at Zack's?"

Streetlights on the bridge across the Potomac cast a muted yellow glow through the windshield. "You'll see."

"You do know I'm going to molest you in all the best ways tonight, don't you?" he teased, his fingers itching to unravel her.

"That's the plan."

"So this is the surprise?" Jake asked, his eyes wide at the latest painting in Lacy's hands. He'd made himself comfortable on the couch, his boots off, and his long legs taking up most of the cushions, his stocking feet crossed at the ankles. Lacy stood at her open bedroom door, but he sounded disappointed.

She peered around the canvas, canting the painting from side to side, "What did you think I meant?" Her heart thumped a little faster than normal. "Don't you like it?" *Look closer, Jake. Come on. You can do it.*

"It's different than the others. It's not... bloody." Cocking his head to a sharp right angle, he looked totally flummoxed, his eyes narrowed, and those adorable—yes, adorable— brows pinched together.

"I know, right?" It was hard not to laugh out loud. This guy didn't get hints very well. "But this right here is Marlee. She loved the sunlight streaming through our windows every morning, so we agreed. I painted sunflowers and shadows, also known as cadmium yellow and black."

"You really do talk to them, don't you?"

Her head bobbed. "I knew her longer than everyone else I've painted, so yes. This one was easy and now..." Lacy released a sigh and the worry she'd been holding onto along with it. There wasn't anything she could do at this point. Either Jake would fall in love with it or not. That would be up to him. Now... if he'd only notice the real surprise hidden between her fingertips and the canvas frame. She tilted the picture one more time and asked, "Can you see what I've hidden right in front of you?"

That brought him up on his knees and like a lithe jungle cat, he crawled to her end of the couch, his shoulder blades jutting under his shirt, and she nearly set the canvas aside and jumped his bones right then. That all male body was headed her way and he'd tripped every early warning indicator in hers.

His brows furrowed. His lips pinched. Oh, this guy! How could he not see what she wanted him to see? "Look closer," she suggested, shifting to the left so the right side of the canvas frame was directly in his line of sight.

But—argh! His nose followed her painting, his laser sharp eyes center stage and not on her fingertips at the edge. "See what?" he asked, his nose wrinkled now as he scrutinized the starburst design closer. "Did you paint a puzzle I'm not seeing, an image hidden in the shadows? Or am I just that—"

"You're not stupid, Jake." She cut him off before he could voice that false conclusion. Hyper-vigilance did not equate to compromised intellect, and he needed to stop cutting himself down. *But you are a little dense sometimes...*

Finally! Jake plucked the real surprise out from under her fingertips. "What's this?"

Please be happy. Please don't be mad.

The sharp eyes of a sniper landed on her, and Lacy froze. "A pee stick? Are we pregnant?"

A tsunami of relief coursed through her at the word he'd chosen. *We.* Not *you.* She set the canvas aside, and jumped into his arms. "We are," she announced, her body thrumming at the momentous news she'd just revealed. "Isn't that great?"

"No." Jake's hands were saying all the right things. He held her close, but his mouth was another story. "I would like to have exercised a little more forethought. That's a big decision and..." His fingers combed over his head, his signature tell when he was nervous or stressed. "We're pregnant?"

Her mouth fell open and her lips went dry. "You don't want it?"

"No," he said again, his eyes wide and his chest heaving. He shook his head and her world fell out from under her.

Lacy twisted away from him and shoved to her feet. How could he be the man of her dreams one moment and such an ass the next?

"I should have taken better care..." he murmured, his voice as distant as his gaze, "of you. I should've thought to use protection instead of going down on you like some animal. You deserved... God, Lacy, you deserve better."

"Better than what? This baby?" she snapped, her Irish up. "Better than the man I love in my bed every night with me? Better than the father of my child in my—in *our* lives?" The temperature in her dinky apartment soared, and suddenly she was sweating and fed up with the entire male gender.

"Lacy, stop!" he barked.

She stopped all right, but her heart was broken, and now, she was drenched in sweat, and tears, damn him. This was Jake's fault. He'd done this to her. No one respected a female Marine who bawled her eyes out when the going got tough. She crossed her arms over her tender breasts and told Jake in no uncertain terms, "I'm keeping it."

He launched to his feet and she found herself pressed against a solid male chest that still smelled like the home she craved, damn him. "Of course we're keeping it," he growled. "I just wished I'd put your needs before mine instead of thinking only of myself when we made it, ah, him. Or her. Guess it could be a girl."

That sounded different than what she'd thought she'd heard a moment ago. Lacy eased back to peer up at Jake, her fingertips fluttering at his collarbones. "Zack knew when he ran into me at Starbucks. He said I glowed like his wife did when she was pregnant."

The bug-eyed comical look wrinkling Jake's face made her smile. "That soon? But we'd only made love—"

"Once. I know. I guess you're really good at doing what you did to me," she offered slyly. "So you're not mad about the baby?"

His entire face wrinkled then. His head shook. "Oh, hell no. It's our baby, Lacy. Yours and mine. Why would I be mad about that?" He scooped her off her feet and into her—ahem, *their* bedroom they went. Jake set her down gently, her back at her headboard and knelt at her side. "Our baby," he murmured, his tone filled with wonder this time. "I like the sound of that."

And I'm falling in love with you all over again. Warmth blossomed in Lacy's chest as his skillful fingers slid under her shirt to her bare tummy. Palming the flatness of it with his big rough hand, the biggest smile broke over his face like the sunrise on Christmas morning. "I'm a father," he told her in a reverent hush. "What do you want? A boy or a girl?"

Lacy answered him true. "You, Jake. I want you."

Chapter Thirty-Five

And baby, I want you. Jake fell into Lacy's arms and straight into love. A baby! They were having a baby, and why that made him hard as a spike, he didn't quite understand. Jake only knew he had to get her out of her pants, so he could sink into the luscious body trembling beneath his fingertips.

The man in him peeled her clothes off with incredible speed, while the lover in him anointed her lips and mouth, her chin and her cheeks with kisses he couldn't hold back. *She's mine,* he thought. *All mine.*

As much as they'd already made love, knowing that it was his seed growing in her belly juiced him up like nothing else. He couldn't kiss his wife-to-be hard enough or deep enough. Certainly not long enough.

After all they'd been through on their different paths, after all they'd suffered, they were finally safe and sound in each other's arms. Knowing he was where he was meant to be, pumped a man up was what it did. Jake needed her scent all over him and his all over her—now—before he went up in flames.

His fingers and hands knew what to do, and before long, her hips started bucking, and she started moaning and… "God, I love the sounds you make, Lacy."

A needy whine lifted from her throat. "Then you know what I want."

Oh, yes, he did. Leaning over her like a grunt pounding out pushups for a drill sergeant, he eased inside her slick fiery core, and like a match to a trail of gasoline, they went up in flames together. Sex with Lacy was as close to heaven as he'd ever been, and with her long legs wrapped around him and her heels digging into his ass—paradise beckoned just a throbbing heartbeat away.

He gave all and she returned the favor, meeting him every inch and thrust of the way until... her fingernails pierced his shoulder muscles. That sweet strong feminine muscle inside her gripped him like a determined hand in a glove and she...

"Come for me, Lacy," he whispered. "Come all over me."

She screamed as she obeyed, "Jake! Jake!"

A man loved to hear his name on his woman's lips, especially when she was sweaty and gripped with passion. That was all it took to tip him over the edge into breath-stealing sweet surrender. Lacy had never screamed before. *What the neighbors must think, but who cares?*

Jake came to rest with his heart pounding in his throat and his face in the crook of her neck, the scent of her sexy hair in his nose. This was the fragrance of paradise to a man used to waking up in a cold abandoned basement surrounded by all the rank odors of the homeless and damp concrete left too long in the dark.

"Stay here. I'll be right back." He said as he rolled off his woman and made a mad dash to the bathroom for a warm cloth to clean her beautiful self. Back in their bedroom, he eased her knees apart and took special care wiping the folds where a baby would soon make its entrance into the world. "This is the best Christmas present ever," he whispered. "In nine months, we're going to be parents."

"And then we'll start using birth control," she whispered, her eyes big and black, her attention one hundred percent on him.

"But what if we want more?"

Up on her elbows now, and still spread like a feast before him, she asked, "Do you want more children, Jake? Would you like a big family?"

"Yeah, I do." He nodded, extraordinarily emotional for the tiny life his war-hardened body had helped create. What a miracle it was that a man like him had enough of the *right stuff* left in him to still do good. To be good. "This little girl or boy we're bringing into the world is our Christmas gift to each other, Lacy. Think about it. Why wouldn't we want more?"

Something shimmered in her pretty green eyes. "I know he'll be smart like you."

It was all Jake could do to not cry with Lacy. He pulled her against his chest, her head tucked under his chin so she couldn't see what a blubbering mess he was about to turn into. Smart was the last thing he was, but teachable? Willing to learn? Eager to try again? Oh, hell yeah. Better yet, he was ready to live. "Thank you for painting me," he told the woman he loved with his whole heart and soul.

"I painted *us*," she whispered, and Jake had to agree. It was true. It had taken years to get here, but USMC Sergeant Jake Weylin was finally—*home*.

The End

Excerpt From *GABE*

In the Company of Snipers, Book 8

©2015 by Irish Winters

Pop! Pop! Bang!

Backfire? Gunfire? Could've been, either.

Junior Agent Gabe Cartwright jerked his gaze to the exit gate of the underground garage. He'd just parked his Land Rover in its assigned stall. With his revoked driver's license, he shouldn't have been driving, but he was. Barely had his feet on the ground.

His boss, Alex Stewart, lingered at the gate in a black SUV. Always in a hurry, the speed demon should've stomped on the accelerator and roared off into traffic by now.

Damn. Was that gunfire?

Gabe couldn't get to his boss fast enough, then couldn't believe his eyes. Alex sat slumped forward in his seatbelt, his forehead tilted down and his mouth open in shock. Three crimson bull's-eyes blossomed dead center of his white dress shirt.

"No! No! No!" Gabe jerked the door handle. Locked. His palms hit the window. "Boss!"

Alex didn't move. The damned engine still idled.

This can't be happening. Not here in America. Not to Alex.

Gabe grabbed his cell phone and stabbed 911, his heart roaring in his ears. He barked address and details to the dispatch operator, then his teammates two stories up. "Shooting. Parking garage. Alex. Get down here now!"

Where the hell had those shots come from? The busy traffic on the street looked normal. The office building across the way, too. No glint of a scope. No shadowy figure skulking away. It was just another sunny day in Alexandria, Virginia. *Like hell.*

No time to waste. Gabe braced the sole of his boot to the windshield and pushed it inward far enough to loosen the window seal, then jerked the entire sheet of safety glass out.

"I'm... shot?" Alex gasped.

Yes, damn it. Only Alex would be surprised at that. And still talking. *Had to be in shock.*

Leaning over the dashboard, Gabe shoved the shifter into park and unlocked the doors.

"Gabe?"

"Yeah, I heard you, Boss. Help's coming. You're gonna be okay."

Please. Don't let him die. Not Alex! Not my boss!

He didn't need CPR. He was still conscious, still huffing shallow breath. A sheen of sweat glistened on his upper lip. There just wasn't enough blood. He had to be hemorrhaging internally. *To death.*

"Kelsey," Alex whispered, his eyes glazed and his voice fading. "Tell... Kelsey..."

"No, Boss. You get to tell her yourself. Promise."

Lies. All lies.

Alex didn't curse. Not even once. He closed his eyes with a soft sigh, barely breathing.

Just that fast Gabe was inside the vehicle with him, releasing his seatbelt, easing him out of the SUV and onto the concrete. He locked his hands together and commenced first-aid, applying hard pressure to stop the bleeding.

Alex would not die. *Not today.*

The men and women of The TEAM tumbled out from the stairwell. Gabe heard the rumble of boots on concrete, but offered not one second of precious time to acknowledge them. All ex-military, they knew what the hell to do.

"Is he still breathing?" Harley asked, shoulder to shoulder with Gabe on the cold garage floor.

"Yeah. Three shots. Professional hit. Came out of nowhere." Gabe kept the pressure up. *Not Alex. I'm not losing another friend. Not again.*

Mark knelt at his other side with a fistful of sterile packing. He covered Gabe's hands with it, and together they applied enough pressure to make a grown man cry.

Alex never even groaned.

What kind of man survives three mortal wounds? Superman, maybe. Ironman. Alex was close to invincible, but the harsh reality of ballistics sucked.

Sirens shrieked. Maybe two. The paramedics barked orders for everyone to step back. They took over first-aid and had Alex off the ground and on the gurney in no time.

Gabe sucked in a lungful of stale concrete air. Damn. Could this be Alex's lucky day? Could he bully Death as he'd bullied everyone and everything else?

God, I hope so.

The medics loaded the ambulance, the clock ticking. Gabe stepped forward, going with his boss every step of the way.

"No riders." The driver secured the tailgate, his palm in Gabe's face.

"But I—"

"Follow in your own vehicle. We need to move."

They didn't waste time. Sirens blared away as quickly as they'd come.

Every team member scrambled to his or her vehicle. Gabe found himself pulled into Junior Agent Zack Lennox's family van. "Come on. He'll need Kelsey."

"You're not going after the boss?

"No, Gabe. We're not. We're going to take him his reason to live."

Good thinking. Gabe climbed into the van, wiping the blood off his fingers, needing the sticky stuff to stick somewhere else. Anywhere else.

"Did anyone call her?"

Zack only growled. Obviously not. This kind of news had to be delivered in person. With tender care. He aimed the van toward the elementary school where Kelsey taught.

Gabe pushed a fist to his sternum as if that could stop the drum roll in his chest, the creeping suffocation of an imminent panic attack. Triggers. It was all about managing his response to the triggers that initiated that claustrophobic sensation of the world closing in.

Not now. Keep it together. Breathe in. Breathe out.

By the time Zack roared into the school's loading zone and hit the school ground running, Gabe had it under control. He followed. Maybe Zack knew how to break this kind of news?

Yeah, right. Words always failed. How do you begin to tell a woman her husband had been mortally shot? How do you to tell her he may already be dead? That it could be too late?

Gabe flat out didn't want to know. K.I.A. notifications sucked.

The morning kindergarten class must've barely begun. Kelsey looked up, smiling from the two-foot high table where she sat surrounded by her teaching assistant and maybe a dozen adoring five-year-olds. "Zack? Gabe? Why are you—? What's wrong?"

"Alex needs you," Zack replied calmly, his hand outstretched to take hers, his fingers urging her forward. "Come on, Kels. We've got to go. Now."

The light left her eyes. She already knew. With barely any words of instruction to her assistant, she left the quiet morning behind and hurried with Zack and Gabe out the door and into the van.

"How is he?" she asked, her chin up, Zack's van already ten miles over the speed limit to get her to the hospital in time.

"Not sure," he replied evenly, squeezing her hand on the console between them.

"He's been shot before, you know," she offered quietly. *Hopefully.*

"Yes. He has," Zack agreed.

Sitting behind her in the van, Gabe kept his mouth shut. Kelsey needed to believe her fierce warrior husband could survive this time because he'd survived others. Too bad life didn't work that way. A man only had a certain number of chances before the bullet with his name caught up with him. The odds always decreased. Any dumb jarhead knew that.

Gabe glanced at his watch, needing to run instead of sitting on his ass. The trip took too damned long!

Finally at the emergency room, he joined his somber teammates with poor Kelsey sandwiched between him and Zack. As if that could stall the inevitable. As if anyone could protect her tender heart from what lay around the tiled corners.

She'd clutched Gabe's hand when he'd helped her out of the car. She hadn't let go. He couldn't bear to.

Junior Agent Izza Maher wiped her face when she looked up and saw them. Ember Dennison turned away. Their husbands, Connor and Rory, stood tall and silent.

Newbies, Taylor Armstrong and Maverick Carson were ashen. The office IT genius, Mother, bowed her head, her shoulders trembling.

Harley was nowhere to be seen.

Damn. We're too late.

That everyone was there should've been Kelsey's first clue as to how bad things were. Instead, like the lady of grace she was, she offered small talk to her too quiet friends. "Mark. Connor. My goodness. You're all here. Hi, Rory. Taylor. Any word yet?"

She made it sound as if this was simply another pickle Alex had gotten himself into. As if this too was all in a day's work for a covert operator. But Gabe caught the tightened grip of her fingers. She needed a lifeline. Someone to hold onto. He let it be him.

"The doctor's waiting," Mark said, his voice tight. "Come with me."

Kelsey nodded.

Gabe steeled his heart as they followed Mark beyond the waiting room, his whole being screaming, *'Hit rewind. Replay. STOP!'*

The corridors seemed to narrow with every step. Mark pressed the metal push pad to activate the wide emergency room doors. Once beyond, doctors and nurses in light blue scrubs hurried through the corridors as if Death didn't stalk right along with them.

At last, another door. Not just a curtained-off examination room, though. More like one of those family counseling rooms with solid walls. In case of crying. Cursing. Screaming.

A doctor had barely exited. "Mrs. Stewart?" he asked gently.

Kelsey's hand lifted out of Gabe's to her lips. "Yes?"

"I'm so sorry." The doctor reopened the door, ushering her into the room where Harley stood somber and still over a sheet-draped body. Bloody packing splattered the floor. The stifling drift of alcohol and antiseptics filled the air.

"No," she whispered. "Please, no."

Gabe didn't need to hear the words. He could read, and Harley's bleak, teary face was an open book with an ungodly ending.

Hell had come to The TEAM.

Alex Stewart was dead.

It took a while to figure it out. The first clue? Gabe Cartwright, leaning over him, both clenched hands pressed to

his chest, crushing the hell out of him, as if his life depended on it. The kid had crystal-green eyes, a fierce shade he hadn't noticed before. Full of life. Just as full of rage. Disbelief maybe?

The second clue? Softhearted Harley crying big, sloppy tears. The guy never should've been a soldier. Never should've been a sniper. Too much heart. Just wasn't mean enough.

But the third? Mark turned away with a too somber face and a tight lip, his jaw clenched, the way a warrior shuts down when he's seen too much. Gone too far. Can't bear any more.

Plus, he had stopped cursing. Even the unseen gentlemen who'd fired the killing shots had received no more than a mild rebuke, which was rare coming from a man with a formidable vocabulary of curses. The passion that had stoked his life only minutes before dissipated in the bright blurred light of—wherever he was. "Oh," became his strongest oath, somehow sufficient, maybe even a little bit over the top. Just—oh.

The fog in his head made everything surreal—the siren, the lights. The dark. The cold.

Air filled him with weightlessness until he was no longer bound to Earth by anger, bone, or muscle—a rare sensation for a man who'd once carried the weight of a few too many kills. Regret for never having been a better man. For all the wrongs he'd not been able to set right.

For Sara.

For Abby.

And now—Kelsey.

A brilliant light enveloped him from every side, blinding him to the strict methodology and logic that had ruled his life.

Things like means, motive, and opportunity paled to mist and vapor.

Think.

But he couldn't. The light shone so purely he could barely focus. Numbing darkness followed. Then came the cold. Time drifted in this new place. This new dimension of—where am I?

He struggled to remember anything, but nothing came to him.

That was... then.

This was... now.

A man can't decipher nothingness.

But. Oh. Wait. This was weird. He floated over a casket while a collage of shadows marched by. The guy in the casket looked like—me? It couldn't be, could it? He slapped his heavy right palm to his chest for verification. That was what real men did. They proved they could keep on keeping on. But his hand hit nothing. No flesh. No bone.

The casket morphed into shadows, then people come to say—goodbye? To who?

Me?

How odd to see them, but not be able to shake a friendly hand, or tell an old Marine's lie. Friends. Governors. Congressmen. Faithful Marines. Soldiers. Airmen. Sailors. Sad and somber, they came and went.

He shifted through the dimension of here and now, pulled toward a somber group lingering beyond the coffin. He should've known right then and there. Something was dreadfully amiss, but nothing mattered because he'd caught a glimpse of her—the woman who'd saved his soul and breathed new life into his heart.

Kelsey. My Kelsey.

Her eyes searched for him. The hungering love of dewy brown riveted his heart to hers across time and space. She truly looked for him. More than once, he thought for sure she'd seen him.

He reached for her. God, he tried, but his fingers clutched nothing. They passed through her like shadows. She looked away, a tissue to her nose, a depth of sadness in her eyes. The kind of sorrow he used to be able to shield her from.

He would've cried if he could've cried. She'd always had that effect on him. She'd made him feel when others could not. She'd helped him remember the man he truly was. She made him want to live again. Even now.

Another man pulled her into a gentle hug of condolence. He whispered into her ear, like a knight of old swearing undying fealty to the queen of his fallen king. "I'm here for you, ma'am. Any time. Any day. You let me know what you need, I'll make it happen."

No. No. No! That's my job!

Who was he? Who did those startling green eyes belong to? Zack? Maybe Gabe? Maybe not.

Everything blurred, pulling him from the lovely, sad scene. He hurried to commit the exquisite details of Kelsey's face to memory. This might be his last chance to see her in this—this wherever he was.

Time ran out.

Her smile faded.

He couldn't breathe, the loss of his beloved more than a man could endure. His hand clutched the ragged hole where his heart used to be. Air no longer mattered. He had no reason to breathe. No more reason to live.

Realization dawned slowly. He'd just witnessed a funeral.
His funeral.
His widow.
Her tears.
He, Alexander Bradley Stewart, toughest dog in the fight, was nothing but a shadow. A memory.
A ghost.

Can it be true? Alex Stewart is dead? Murdered?

While The TEAM struggles to deal with the blow they never saw coming, former USMC scout sniper, Gabe Cartwright is assigned to protect Alex's widow, Kelsey. Already haunted by the fear that he let his boss die, he vows to protect her with his life. Nothing and no one will get in his way—until bossy Nurse Sullivan arrives to care for Kelsey. Sullivan is anti-gun, anti-dog, and seemingly anti-the whole male gender. The last damned thing he needs...

It's her way or the highway.

Shelby Sullivan is an admitted control freak. She loves her new client, Kelsey Stewart, and intends to help her in any way possible, but has no use for Kelsey's bodyguards. Not even the semi-charming Agent Cartwright will interfere with the perfect performance of her duties—until Shelby disregards his protective measures and leads Death straight back to Kelsey. It seems Gabe isn't the only one who's haunted…

Purchase Gabe by clicking HERE
http://amzn.to/2vx5l8U to find out what's really going on
with Alex, Kelsey, and The TEAM.

Thank you for reading Jake's story!

Want to know what happens the day Jake and Lacy bring their baby home?
Turn the page for a bonus Company of Snipers short story called *"Painting Home."*

If you enjoyed this book, be sure to check out the rest of the guys and gals of *In the Company of Snipers* on Amazon.com.

Other Irish Winters' books:

King of Hearts, Deuces Wild Series, #1
Joker Joker, Deuces Wild Series, #2
Smoke, Hearts and Ashes Series, #1
Ash, Hearts and Ashes Series, #2

These ebooks are also available on Barnes and Noble, iTunes, and Kobo.

Coming soon!

Seth, In the Company of Snipers, #17
One-Eyed Jack, Deuces Wild Series, #3

YOU ARE THE KEY TO THIS BOOK'S SUCCESS!

Please tell other readers why you liked Jake and Lacy's story by leaving an honest review at the retail site where you purchased it.
Recommend it to your friends. Lend it.
Most of all, enjoy it!

The best way to keep up with my new releases, giveaways, and actionable intel is to sign up for my spam-free newsletter at IrishWinters.com.

Painting Home

A *Company of Snipers* Short Story

Tired out from the short drive home from the hospital, Lacy sank into the plush leather of her very own easy chair with her firstborn son. She had it all. A handsome new husband who doted on her hand and foot, a darling baby boy with lots of dark, curly hair like his dad, and her first home in the 'burbs. So why was her heart pounding to beat the band again?

It made no sense. For the first time since she and Jake had moved into the charming fixer-upper in Alexandria, Virginia, it creeped her out. Seriously. They'd spent months house hunting until this particular one called to the both of them. Yet now, it felt—haunted. Lacy knew ghosts, and she couldn't shake the unsettling sensation at the back of her neck that someone was looking over her shoulder this morning. Watching. Waiting.

At first glance, the house was nothing more than a brick box, a perfect starter home, if you didn't mind investing weeks of sweat labor and tons of elbow grease. Unfortunately, the most recent tenant hadn't cared for it properly, which got them evicted. But man. The interior was a disaster with holes punched through the sheetrock walls, deeply soiled and matted carpets that should have been burned instead of hauled to the dump, and an odor that led them to stacks of garbage bags in the basement.

The outside was no better. Weeds had overtaken the flowerbeds beside the concrete front porch. Not to be outdone, the died-and-gone-to-goat-head-hell lawn boasted nothing but the promise of a lot of hard work in Jake and Lacy's future. The frayed blue tarp that had dangled dangling by nylon ties off the carport had truly been the icing on the cake. The place had absolutely no curb appeal, and nothing going for it. They really should have run from the money-sucking-pit. But then...

They bought the place. Something about it had cried out for rescue to Lacy that day. All it needed was a little—make that a lot—of TLC, and she'd felt certain that it could be turned into a home again. It had been once. She could feel honest vibes from the poor place. It had potential.

Further investigation proved her right. Once upon a time, someone had done a bang-up job remodeling the interior of the place. Walls had been moved where two of the three bedrooms had been converted into a master suite, complete with a walk-in closet. How cool was that? The lavishly tiled, adjoining bathroom with the sunken tub also testified of someone with definite carpentry skills in the house's past.

Jake was the one who'd said it first, when they'd stopped at the curb. "This is it."

Lacy had agreed wholeheartedly—then. But now? Now she had a baby to feed and a jittery case of nerves. Motherhood seemed a daunting task for the Marine she was at heart, and bringing her brand new baby home turned out to be the pinnacle of stress.

She hadn't been around many babies growing up. Had no sisters or brothers. No cousins, nieces, or nephews. Give her an artist's palette, her camera, or an M16 any day. Those things she understood, but the infant who now relied on her for every second of his care, his future, and his next meal? Just too much!

"Found it," Jake called from the baby's room. He'd left Raymond Elias, so named after Lacy's and Jake's paternal grandfathers, in the twitchy fingers of his exhausted mother like she knew what she was doing simply because she'd given birth. The funny guy.

Lacy forced a confident smile as Jake strolled into the living room with the powder blue baby blanket Kelsey Stewart had made. He'd positioned her chair near the living room picture window. Now shuttered with hunter-green shutters that offset the crisp red of their freshly power-washed brick home, the spotless windows let in the lovely view of her re-sodded front lawn. Lacy wished she could enjoy it.

He'd been extra busy while she was in the hospital. Her home now boasted new paint throughout, a sprinkling system to tend both front and back lawns, and matching hunter green trim along the eaves and windows. He'd divested the piles of garbage and junk in the basement and attic.

A crew was due early Monday morning to enclose the carport, turning it into a garage, complete with a garage door opener. How cool was that? To a girl who'd been living in a cramped tiny apartment and parking in an uncovered, assigned parking stall for the past couple years, this place felt like a mansion. She had a full-sized kitchen for heaven's sake. A sunken tub that, now sanitized and sparkling clean, she loved to lounge in.

Baby Ray curled his entire hand around Lacy's pinkie finger, and that went a long way to calming her, so why was she still on edge? Maybe because her perfect little home had also once boasted a high-end security alarm system, and the leftover frazzled magnetic tapes on every window declared a scary need to keep someone out. The frayed wires from security cameras dangling under the eaves warned of unscrupulous neighbors. Or stalkers. Or worse.

"What's wrong?" Jake asked as he covered her and Baby Ray with the blanket. "Did the trip home wear you out? Can I get you something to drink? Are you hungry?"

Ah, she loved him so hard. "I'm fine. Just crabby."

He dropped to his knee at her side and reached one hand to the nape of her neck. Drawing her forward, he kissed her forehead. "Not crabby. Just tired. Want me to take him off your hands while you catch a few winks? I can do that, you know."

Closing her eyes, Lacy pulled the spicy scent of her man into her soul. He'd brought so many things with him into their marriage, but the smell of him was her number one favorite. She craved it now, the strength of him, the intimacy of his touch, and his steady foresight. Tears blurred her vision at the ways he'd changed right before her eyes. The scruffy vagrant he'd once been was gone, replaced by a fiercely protective, clean-shaven male who—most days—seemed ready to fight the world again.

Lacy squeezed her eyes to stave off the flood of tears that came at the thought of how much she loved this guy and what she wouldn't do for him. Hormones! Who knew they ruled the world like they did? Her breasts ached like two bags of milk about to burst, and her heart hurt because she should be better than this, not falling apart like some sniveling woman who couldn't take care of a little seven pound infant. Her baby!

Jake looked past her to the front walk. "Don't look now, but Alex and Kelsey are here. Damn. Gabe and Shelby, too." He pushed to his feet. "We've got company."

"Oh, great," Lacy said, not feeling up for visitors. Why couldn't everyone leave her alone?

"Enter," Jake announced proudly from the new steel security door he'd installed all by himself just days ago. The man couldn't seem to do enough with their home. "Mi casa es su casa."

He loved saying that. Lacy brushed her tangled hair behind her ears, determined to look more energetic than she felt, but really. Didn't these people know a new mother needed rest? They should've come tomorrow. Maybe next week. At the very least, they should've called.

Kelsey stepped over the threshold first, her eyes wide and bright as she scanned the hall to her left. Chocolate fudge tangles curled over her shoulders. Dressed in jeans and a soft pink blouse, she smiled, but a shadow shifted across her pretty face. She schooled it quickly, but what was that about anyway? Could she smell the lingering scent of garbage? Lacy doubted it, but suddenly, her feminine territorial radar was on full alert.

Alex entered second, his hand at the small of Kelsey's back. Like his wife, he'd dressed casually. Jeans. Gray polo shirt. Boots. Blue eyed, dark-haired, and the most intense man Lacy had every met, his razor sharp gaze zeroed straight to the backdoor Jake had recently painted a clean, crisp white. If Lacy didn't know better, she'd swear Alex had been in this home before the way his eyes quartered the house from left to right, rear to back. Interesting.

Gabe and Shelby ducked through the front door together, his arm around her shoulders. Like Alex and Kelsey, they wore jeans. Shelby's were black, Gabe's faded blue and torn at both knees. Shelby was one of those tiny women who looked almost pixyish, not that Lacy would ever tell her that. Her blond hair cascaded in fluffy curls over a tiny white t-shirt that stretched tight over her breasts but barely covered her tummy.

Gabe on the other hand, towered over her like a bodyguard. His t-shirt declared allegiance to some hotrod club, *Cruisin' Nova Knights*. Lacy couldn't help but shiver as their gazes settled to the junction in the hall that separated her cozy but small living room from the newly restored kitchen. The sensation of being watched prickled up her spine again. What the heck?

"Wow," Kelsey said breathlessly, her nose wrinkled. "Fresh paint. You guys have been busy."

"That would be Jake," Lacy said. "I've been too busy being pregnant to paint."

Jake grinned in his humble way, a bright red flush creeping into his cheeks. His hands went deep into his jeans pockets. "What can I say? A man likes to work on his castle, and I can't seem to do enough around here. I knew Lacy'd be worn out when she got home with the baby and all, and…" His voice trailed away as their visitors' gaze drifted elsewhere. "What's up, Boss?"

He'd picked up on the same strange vibes resonating from the Stewarts and Cartwrights that Lacy detected. A chill whispered over the fine hairs at the back of her neck. Someone else *was* here, damn it. Unseen and silent maybe, but she could feel—him! *Aha. I have a male ghost in my house, but who could it be? Why now? Why today?*

Alex turned on Jake then, his palm still protectively at his wife's back. "Do you know what you've done?"

"I do," Jake declared, his shoulders squared as if ready to fight, and Lacy felt that way too. She didn't care who these folks thought they were. They had no right showing up unannounced and acting so proprietary. "I bought a home for my wife and my son," Jake said.

Kelsey stepped between the men, blinking, her big brown eyes shimmering. "Yes, and it'll be the perfect home for your little family, Jake," she soothed. "We wanted to help with the renovations, but Alex and I have been in Oregon a couple weeks. My sister's husband hurt his back, so Alex helped bring in the hay for him. Congratulations on becoming a first time homeowner and a Dad! What did you decide to name your son?"

Lacy cocked her head, trying to figure out what was truly going on. Kelsey had said the right words, but there was something left unspoken in her eyes. Whatever this off-balance, creepy sensation climbing up Lacy's spine was, she'd sort it out later. "Come meet Raymond Elias," she said proudly. "Raymond after my grandpa, and Elias after Jake's grand—"

With a startled cry, Kelsey turned into Alex, her hands on his chest. "Raymond. Did you hear that? They named him Raymond."

Alex just stared like he owned the place, damn it. These people were bugging the shit out of Lacy with everything they weren't saying. "What?" she asked point blank. "You all know something about this house, don't you? Spit it out."

Shelby's head bobbed and Gabe opened his mouth to say something, but Alex beat him to it. "This cracker box used to belong to me," he bit out, his gaze down the hall to the master bedroom and his jaw clenched tight.

"It was our *home*," Kelsey corrected softly. "We lived here for years before—"

"Before I killed a man in it," Gabe ended, his usually soft green eyes narrowed and hard.

"Shit," Jake hissed. He couldn't get back to Lacy's side fast enough. "Here? You sure about that?" The world felt better the moment he settled one hand to her shoulder, but why was he rattled while she seemed calm?

Alex nodded, his eyes grim. "Right here in this room. Ever hear of Ron Fallon? *Chaos Now*?"

Lacy shook her head, but those names jostled something loose in Jake's mind. He remembered reading about the treacherous VPOTUS somewhere, maybe at Zach's house or a newstand. He'd been living on the streets then. "Weren't they involved with Vice President Winston's treason a couple years back? We all heard about the helo going down on the White House lawn that night. That was you who took him out, wasn't it?"

Alex neither confirmed nor denied, but Gabe spoke up. "There were a lot of people involved in that mess. Mark Houston. Zack Lennox. Me, Kelsey and Shelby, but yeah, Winston was behind *Chaos Now*. He masterminded Ron Fallon's scheme to bring the District to its knees with a dirty bomb. He had big plans for this country that didn't work out like he'd planned." His gaze shifted to Alex. "I can't tell you all Alex went through, but Fallon followed Shelby and me back here the same night Winston died in that crash."

"He shot Gabe," Shelby said. "Right in this room, but then Gabe killed him, and I... and I..."

You fell apart, Jake thought. Shelby suffered from a case of PTSD comparable to what some of the guys coming back from the sandbox endured. Jake didn't know what triggered it, but that explained Gabe being overly protective where his wife was concerned. Even now he had one arm circling her waist and her waif-like body aligned with his. Normally an easygoing guy, he didn't look too happy being back at his ground zero.

"It's okay, Shelby. You don't have to remember if you don't want to," Lacy said quietly. "Want to meet my baby boy?"

"Yes, please." Shelby blew out a shaky breath and took a seat in the corner of the couch nearest Lacy. Visibly shaken, the poor woman was wound as tight as if that shooting had just taken place.

Lacy must've picked up on that vibe. She shifted Baby Ray into Shelby's outstretched hands, and, with a sigh, Shelby tossed her blonde hair back over her shoulder and tucked the little guy's head into her neck to snuggle him. The little guy moaned and instantly, motherly instinct kicked in and her body began to sway. "He's so small," she told Lacy as she tilted forward and backward, the same way Jake found himself doing when he held his little man.

"I know, right?" Lacy grinned, her first real smile since she'd been home. "I'm so afraid I'll hurt him when I feed him. He's so tiny."

"He's tougher than he looks," Alex cut in gruffly, and in that instant, it seemed even the rafters in the house took a deep breath, sighed, and relaxed along with Shelby.

Kelsey joined her on the couch, cooing over the new arrival. Jake closed in on Gabe and Alex in the hall, wanting all the details. To find out now that he'd bought not only his boss's old place but a prior crime scene was disconcerting at the least. Weren't there laws requiring real estate agents to conceal that kind of horrific information to prospective buyers?

"Where's Suzette?" Lacy asked after Gabe and Shelby's daughter.

"She's with my mom and dad," Shelby said as she licked her lips. "I didn't want to bring her here. She doesn't need to hear how her daddy nearly died. It still gives me nightmares."

"Can I get you folks a drink?" Jake offered, finally remembering his manners. "Coffee? Beer? Lemonade?" He ended up bringing beer for Alex and Gabe, lemonade for the ladies.

Gabe took a thirsty pull on his long neck and explained, "I woke up alone that night and went looking for Shelby. By then, the president was safe, and the bomb was disarmed. We should've been home free, but Fallon was here. He had his hands on her, and God, I've never been so scared in my life."

Alex dragged his fingers through his dark hair and down the back of his neck. "Fallon was running for his life. Somehow he suspected I was working with the FBI, and he wanted revenge. Zack already had Kelsey stashed at another location, but damn it to hell. I thought I'd arrived too late again."

Jake nodded as more details came back to him about that horrendous few weeks in The TEAM's history. Under orders from President Adams, the FBI had *'shot'* Alex in his own parking garage. They made everyone believe that the number one sniper on the East Coast had been assassinated, when he'd really gone—albeit involuntarily—deep undercover to serve his president. That cleverly planned tactic had to have been a time of pure hell for Kelsey, but the ruse fooled VP Winston into believing that Alex was sick unto death of the politics running rampant in America, and that he wanted change badly enough to betray his wife, his president, and his team.

Winston fell for it. Alex infiltrated the conspiracy of *Chaos Now*. Days after the nation was once again secure, President Adams showed up at TEAM headquarters in Alexandria, Virginia, and explained the plot to the men and women Alex had inadvertently betrayed.

Shelby's head came up from snuggling Baby Ray. "It was awful. Gabe almost died. I nearly lost him."

He tapped his upper chest. "Fallon missed my heart, though I was sure I was seeing ghosts for a minute there. Turned out to be Alex. Damned glad to see you that night, Boss."

Alex grunted. "Son-of-a-bitchin' bastard."

That made Jake smile. Alex was one bad-assed man's man, born to lead and die in the process. A hard but fair taskmaster, he expected perfection from his men and women, but mostly, from himself. Knowing he'd arrived in the nick of time to save Gabe's life that night cast a different light on Fallon's death. Yes, a fatality had happened in Jake's new home, but what a testament to honor and valor. To courage and loyalty. There weren't enough leaders like Alex in the world.

"So what's the deal with Raymond?" Jake had to ask. He hadn't missed the way Kelsey had gone pale and leaned into Alex at the mention of Jake's son's given name.

"Ah, that." Again, Alex raked a hand through his hair, and Jake noticed the silver at his temples. Alex had to be in his late thirties, too young to be showing the wear and tear of his chosen profession. "Kelsey? Would you mind? You're better at telling that story than I am."

Her face brightened. "Sure. I love talking about my boys."

Gabe plopped cross-legged on the floor opposite Shelby while Kelsey told how she'd lost her two small sons to her murderous first husband before she'd met Alex. As hard as that was to hear, she continued through her unexpected love affair with the grouchy owner of this little home. "I was a mess back then, and what'd he do? He whisked me out here to the East Coast and he saved my life is what he did."

Still standing in the hall doorway, Alex looked out the kitchen window at time or two instead of adding to the tale. But God, what these two people had suffered on their way to happily-ever-after. Not only had Kelsey's ex killed her two baby boys, but the rat bastard had nearly killed her and Alex at a later date, too.

"For a while, we were happy here," Kelsey insisted, her eyes warm and her tone wistful. Jake believed her.

"Not me," Alex grumped, his gaze still out the back window. "I wanted to buy her the moon, but the damned woman wouldn't move."

She giggled. This pretty abused woman who'd survived more than her share of crap—giggled!—like a happy little girl. "Oh, Alex, you know I couldn't leave this place. It was your home, and the first time I'd been happy in a long time. You gave me that. How could I have left it behind?"

He turned and winked then. And there it was again—the invisible bond between one hard-assed warrior and his queen, reminding Jake of his feelings for Lacy. A smile crept over his mouth, curving his lips. He chanced a glance in her direction, and there she was. His queen. Smiling at him as if she'd read his mind.

"So..." Kelsey drew in a deep breath. "How do I describe Raymond...?" Another sigh. "I guess you could say he was a lost little boy who got tangled up with a bitter older woman."

"Ethel Durrant. Kelsey's ex mother-in-law," Alex bit out. "The bitch. Another close call." The man couldn't seem to speak without swearing.

"Yes, but Alex," Kelsey said. "You saved me that time."

"Like hell I did." He snorted. "You ended Ethel before I got there with Harley and Judy. You showed the whole damned world how much better than her you were."

Kelsey's shoulders lifted, her eyes shimmering under Alex's praise. "But I still lost him."

"You never stood a chance, honey," Alex replied, his voice gone soft and kind. "Acromegaly ended Raymond long before you met him. He was already living on borrowed time."

"But I didn't know that then. All I knew was he was my second chance to make up for losing my sons, and I failed him."

"You made him happy," Alex said, a definite hint of tenderness in his gruff voice. "Probably for the first time in his life, he had someone who really cared for him, and that person was you."

She nodded, her eyes brimming. "Yes. I did. I still do."

Jake watched the way these two talked, not tearing each other apart as much as building each other up. They loved each other and it showed.

"What's acromegaly?" Lacy asked.

"A dysfunction of the pituitary gland," Kelsey explained. "Raymond was a very big man with the mind of a very little boy. The first time I saw him, he scared the daylights out of me. I thought he was a giant, but he was so sweet, it was impossible not to fall in love with him."

"Seven feet, three inches tall and built like a damned brick shithouse," Alex said. "Four hundred pounds. Oversized head. Protruding forehead with one thick, black unibrow that made him look like Frankenstein's monster."

"Poor Raymond had a bad heart and other health problems due to his disproportionate size," Kelsey added.

"Kelsey collects strays," Alex grumbled like that explained everything.

Her lashes fell to the slender fingers she was wringing on her lap. "Yes, I'm afraid I do, but I'd do it all again. Raymond needed someone to love him. Ethel used food to entice him to kidnap me. He was so hungry from living on the streets, and she knew just how to trap him. She had him dig a hole, a grave really, for me out west in the Shenandoah Forest. I was supposed to die there, and she meant for no one to find me. She did it to torture Alex, because she blamed him for her son's death, which wasn't true. Harley ended Nick, but that's another story. Poor Raymond never understood how twisted she was. He wasn't made that way. He only cared about the hamburgers she'd bought his soul with."

Kelsey wiped one slender finger under her eye. "One day she left him alone, and he let me go. We ran away together, but we got lost. The last day in the Shenandoah, she caught up with us, and she nearly killed me. But I knew that if I died, if I let her win, she'd kill Raymond, so I... so I..." She swallowed hard. "I defended myself, but it was too much for Raymond. He died there under the trees and I miss him."

"We can stop by our family plot on our way home if you'd like," Alex said.

So tough guy Alex had buried a stranger in his family plot? Jake didn't miss the desperate plea hidden within his boss's words. Like any man who loved his wife, Alex would do anything to make her smile.

Kelsey nodded. "I'd like that, Alex, but Jake? Lacy? Don't you find it strange that you bought Alex's old house and—?"

"Your old house," Alex cut in.

Now it was her turn to wink. "Yes, my *home*," she corrected before she turned back to Jake. "You also named your baby, Raymond. That isn't a trendy, popular name, and to be honest, it surprised me to hear it again, especially here." Her fingertips fluttered over her heart.

"Tell me about him," Lacy said.

Jake recognized the command in her voice and the light in her eyes. The ghosts she painted home always brought it shimmering to the surface like a sympathetic echo lifted up from her soul. A glow really, it radiated in all of her paintings as if she gave part of herself away to each ghost she enabled to go home.

"I have a picture if you'd like to see him." Kelsey reached for the cell phone in her pocket. Thumbing it to life, she handed it over. "There. That's my Raymond."

Jake ducked closer to Lacy, needing to see the lost boy Kelsey had befriended and loved. It was a photo of an artist's rendering, a pencil sketch. But whoa! Alex was right. This was no boy, but an adult male with the bulky body of a monster. A gentle smile graced his crooked face but those brows...

"He has blue eyes," Lacy said brightly, as if that were a good thing. Of course, she'd noticed that, not the monster-at-first-glance. And she'd spoken wisely. In the present tense. *Has.* Not *had.*

"It's no wonder he scared you," Jake said. *Imagine running into that guy in the dark.*

Alex finally joined Kelsey, his arm stretched behind her back on the couch, his other hand cupping her knee. "He scared everyone, poor kid."

Jake bonded with Alex in that instant. They had something in common. They both needed to touch the women who'd saved—yes, saved—them. Alex might be the supreme alpha at war and at work, but he was right when he'd said Kelsey collected strays. Apparently, Lacy did, too.

Lacy traced her fingertips over the sketched shaggy head of the man-child that Kelsey still loved. This was the presence she'd felt in her new home, the one watching and waiting. She was sure of it. That evil Fallon guy Gabe that killed wasn't the one who needed to go home. It was this lost soul who, apparently, still loved Kelsey like a little boy loved his mother. Raymond hadn't been watching Lacy as much as waiting for his mom to come save him again. And here she was.

"Would you like me to paint him home for you?" Lacy asked Kelsey.

"No, I'm good," she said, shaking her head, not that Lacy believed her. "I've made my peace with what happened with Raymond and my boys. It's okay. Save your talent for people who really need it."

"I'm sorry. I should have asked that differently. I meant to say: May I paint Raymond home for him?" Lacy offered quietly. "I think this is more about Raymond and what *he* needs, not what you need. What if he hasn't made his peace with what happened in the Shenandoah, with leaving you? What if he's been waiting for you to come rescue him again? To show him the way?"

"He never had the chance to tell you goodbye," Alex told his wife. "That had to be as hard on him as it was for you."

"I know but…" Kelsey's lips pinched as her eyes flooded. "Oh, God, I don't know if I can go through it again."

"Sure you can, honey. You'd do anything for your boys, wouldn't you?" Alex knew the way to his wife's heart.

Her lashes fell even as her head bobbed. "Yes, please," she whispered, swiping her cheeks again. "Since the day Zack told me about your incredible paintings, I've thought about Raymond. He must've had a mother and father, maybe brothers and sisters. I might never know their names, but he does. Besides me, someone had to have loved him once upon a time. I'm sure he'd like to be with them again."

Lacy swallowed one of her noisy gulps. This was an opportunity of healing like no other. "I can paint him now if you have the time."

She didn't need to hear an answer. *'Yes'* glimmered in Kelsey's soft brown eyes. This woman still loved Raymond as if he'd been her biological child. What a rare find she was in this crazy, selfish world.

Without being asked, Jake scrambled to his feet, ran down the hall to their bedroom, and returned with Lacy's easel under his arm, her case of oil paints, and a fresh canvas. "You want me to set up here or in the kitchen?"

She could've kissed him. "I think the light in the kitchen's better this time of day. Do you mind?"

"Not if it makes you happy."

With Baby Ray sound asleep and still snuggled with his new Aunt Shelby and Uncle Gabe, Lacy began another journey home for a lost soul. She closed her eyes and breathed in the scents of linseed and oils, the lingering turpentine she cleaned her brushes with, the smells of a thousand possibilities on the untouched, waiting-to-bemapped canvas. "This one's for you, Raymond," she whispered, sure he was listening.

Kelsey sat at one end of the table, while Lacy took the middle. Jake and Alex had stepped out on the back step, a concrete block that led to a cracked sidewalk into what would be a new garage by the end of the week. Lacy lost track of their deep voices as an image crystallized front and center in her mind. Drawing in a deep breath through her nostrils, she caught the scent of pine needles, sunshine, and wind.

"It happened in the spring?" she asked Kelsey to be sure.

Kelsey's head bobbed. "Yes. Springtime in the Shenandoah."

That was all Lacy needed to know. The painting flowed through her like water out of a faucet. She began with a wash of blues and yellow for sunshine and sky. Next came the almond outline of two deeply set, indigo blue eyes, shadowed by a thick fringe of black lashes. Not cat eyes. Not Asian eyes. More the childish eyes of innocent wonder.

She painted an overlay of green pine tips and boughs, the fresh new growth of spring, the kind where every pine tip glistened with beads of dew as if those eyes were peering through them. Adding a sprinkle of baby green pinecones in one corner, she placed a yellow star in the other. Kelsey watched as silently as that other person in the room, the one Lacy could almost feel peering over her shoulder.

"He's here, you know. Raymond. I didn't feel his presence until I came home today with Baby Ray, and I can't help but wonder if he knew you were coming to visit."

"He's here?" Kelsey asked.

Lacy nodded as she added—of all things—a squared off chunk of chocolate cake dripping with fudge frosting in another corner. Odd, but that was the impression that came to her.

"Oh," Kelsey whimpered when Lacy ended the frosting of that very out of place image with a flourish, almost as if she'd just frosted a real piece of cake. "He is here. He's really here."

Lacy nodded, never more sure that Raymond's spirit lingered as close to this side of the veil as he could get. The air was thick with his presence. Lacy could almost picture him with his arms wrapped around his earthly Mom.

"Hug yourself," Lacy told Kelsey. "Do it now. Wrap your arms around yourself and close your eyes. Picture him hugging you. He's here, and he wants you to know it."

Tears dripped over Kelsey's cheek and ran down her chin to her neck as she complied. "Those are his eyes," she murmured. "I'd know them anywhere. One day we were tired, hungry, and covered with bug bites. We were both on our backs looking up at the trees and he said… he said… *'The sky is blue and the trees are big and you...'*" She could barely go on, but she squeaked, "'*...and you is my bestest friend in the whole world.*'"

This was the hardest ghost Lacy had ever painted home, more so because his *Mom* was right here helping him like she'd done before. Suddenly, Alex knelt beside Kelsey, tugging her into his arms. "You were his only friend, honey. Believe me. He knows you love him."

Lacy's eyes watered at the tenderness in this tough guy's voice.

Kelsey sobbed. "But I told him I'd make him a great big hamburger and chocolate cake when we got home. He loved hamburgers. My poor boy. I never got the chance..."

"Don't cry." Alex pressed his mouth to her temple. "Let him go, Kelsey. Please. You've got to let him go."

Lacy's lips pinched. She tried not to look at the intimate scene unfolding at her kitchen table, but she couldn't make her eyes not see the beauty this *painting home* had created. Her heart grew tenderer by the second. It seemed as if all Kelsey's lost boys were suddenly here, reaching for their Mom to comfort her. The kitchen felt full, almost crowded.

It took no time at all to add a border of little boy handprints, one small, one a little larger, and every third print man-sized. With every stroke of her brush, Lacy filled Raymond's homecoming with love from him to Kelsey and from her to him. But the hardest was yet to come. There was a downside to painting people home. They left.

Lacy didn't understand how her crazy gift worked, but now she worried. Did Kelsey feel the presence of her sons surrounding her now? And if she did, could she handle Raymond and her sons leaving her again? Lacy wasn't sure that she could. This gentle smiling giant's presence was a nice addition to her little home. He certainly filled it up.

"I may have to keep this picture for myself," she murmured. "Raymond's been watching over me and Baby Ray all morning. I kind of like having him around."

Jake shifted his hands from his pockets to her shoulders. "Say what?"

She looked up at him standing behind her. "That's right. This guy's been hanging around our house this morning. Didn't you feel someone watching us?" She set to outlining the blue eyes of an angel and the shadow of each individual pinecone scale. She highlighted each and every needle, adding depth here and definition there, hopping between charcoal grays and bright yellows to bring Kelsey's beloved man-child to life.

Jake ran a hand over the back of his neck. "Now that you mention it, yeah. I thought it was just, you know. Crazy."

"You're not crazy," Alex growled.

"Yeah, I am," Jake asserted unabashedly. "It's the only way to survive in this world, Boss. Be a little crazy."

"Then I'm certifiable," Kelsey said, finally letting go of her biceps and taking a deep breath. "So are you, Alex. You still dream of Abby and Sara. I know you do."

There was another story Lacy wanted to know. "May I paint someone home for you, Alex Stewart?" she had the nerve to ask.

"No," whipped out of his mouth as quick as lightning. "I'm good."

No, you're not, but that's what guys like you always say, and believe me, it's okay. Whoever Sara and Abby are, the day will come you ask me to paint them home. I can wait. She finished Raymond's painting, willing to work until her baby needed her or until Gabe and Shelby got tired of babysitting him.

At last the piece was done. Her shoulders ached as Lacy settled back in her chair, calmer now. Still kneeling with Kelsey, Alex reached for his back pocket. "What's your going rate?"

"I don't charge for works of love," Lacy said. "It ruins the gift."

Alex stopped cold. His chin dropped, and it seemed he found the new linoleum floor interesting—until Lacy saw him blink. The muscles in his cheek clenched. This was as hard on him as it was on Kelsey. "With your talent, you should be living in a mansion, not here in this... this..."

"Cracker box?" Lacy chided him as gently as she could. "I'm happy here, Alex. This is my home now and I'll take good care of it."

"You're as bad as my wife," he bit out.

"Thank you," Lacy replied. She understood. Really, she did. Alex was a battle-hardened jarhead who'd done well transitioning out of the Corps. He'd started his own business and he made good money. He paid his men and women well, but her mission in life was different now. She wasn't in the business of painting war heroes home for the wealth or the fame.

These paintings, as bizarre as some of them were, were merely gifts of her heart. Besides, what could she possibly have charged all those poor moms and dads for the priceless gift of being reunited with their sons and daughters one last time? This was Lacy's way paying it forward, the least she could do.

"Look, honey," Kelsey told him. "Lacy caught the boys' handprints just like you did. Remember?"

His head came up then. He ran a quick hand over his faced. Sniffed. Then nodded. "Thank you," ground out of him. "Thank you for..." He cleared his throat. Coughed. Finally looked Lacy in the eye. "Everything."

"You're welcome," she replied, pretending not to notice the raw emotions raging within the windows to his soul. Some things were just hard, damn it, and a warrior shouldn't have to defend or explain his tears to anyone, not even to her.

Setting the canvas back from the edge of the table where it wouldn't get bumped, she leaned into Jake. "I hope this helps Raymond find peace," she told Kelsey, "but you need to know that ghosts usually leave once I paint them home. One minute, they're there; the next they're… whoosh. Gone."

"As they should be," Kelsey said with a drawn out sigh. "It's time for him to move on. I've made my piece with what happened long ago, but it's nice to know Raymond wanted to say goodbye to me, too." She dabbed her eyes, took another deep breath, then said, "Let's go home, Alex. The dogs need a run before bedtime. So do I."

He lifted to his feet and pulled her into his side. "You sure I can't pay you?" he asked Lacy, his hand at his rear pocket again. "I'd feel better if I could."

Somehow, she doubted Alex would ever feel better. He had an entire squadron of ghosts around him, but none of them looked like a Sara or an Abby. Whoever those two women were, they were already home. Like Raymond with Kelsey, Alex just hadn't let go of them yet. He hadn't moved on, but they had.

"No, sir, it's been my pleasure," Lacy told him firmly. "The painting will be ready after I apply a coat of varnish to protect it against ultraviolet rays and dirt. Pollution. Stuff like that. I'll deliver it then." *I'll have painted your Sara and Abby home by then, too. When I give you that picture, you'll see. It really does work.*

"We'll pick it up," Alex corrected. Man, he was persistent. Wasn't he in for a surprise?

"Okay," Lacy acquiesced. "I'd love that. Next Sunday. Just tell me when."

"Thank you," Kelsey said, her eyes dry and her chin up. "I think you're right. I don't sense Raymond as much as I did for a moment there. He's finally at peace. I can feel it. So am I."

"That's how it works," Jake declared as he tugged Lacy against his side. "She paints 'em home, and they're happy to go."

Gabe and Shelby strolled into the kitchen, both sleepy-eyed. "We, umm, fell asleep," he admitted sheepishly as he delivered a squirming and wide-awake infant into Jake's hands. "Sorry. What'd we miss?"

"Raymond's gone home," Lacy said simply.

"Damn, and we missed it?" Gabe asked, raking a hand through his thick, mahogany hair. "Can you do it again? I mean for someone else?"

Lacy narrowed her eyes, striving to see past the boyish good looks of one of Alex's best snipers. "I'd love to paint someone home for you, Gabe."

"It's not for me, it's for a guy I know. It's for..." He shook his head. "Man, he'll be freakin' pissed at me, but—"

"Maverick," Jake said what Gabe didn't seem able to say. "It's for Maverick, isn't it? You want Lacy to paint his brother home."

Gabe nodded. "Yeah. Maverick. I think this might help, only, crap, he'll beat the shit out of me if he finds out I put you up to this."

"Then don't tell him," Lacy declared. "I painted a hundred warriors home before I ever gave a single painting to their families, Gabe, and to be honest, I didn't start doing this for their parents or anyone they'd left behind. I did it for them, for the ghosts. They talked to me, and I just listened. Why don't you bring Maverick and China over for a beer sometime? Let me take care of the rest.

"That's an ambush," Alex growled. "Not fair."

"Not really," Kelsey said, one hand on her touchy husband's forearm as she looped her other arm around his waist. "Think of it as an intervention on Maverick's brother's behalf. Darrell's like Raymond, Alex. He wants to go home, and deep down, Maverick wants that, too. He just doesn't know it."

"Darrell, huh?" Lacy asked as an image of Batman and Robin, stick horses, and little boys with cowboy hats raced through her mind. "I really like that name."

Jake strolled up the dark hallway. The deal was that after Lacy fed Baby Ray during the night, Jake got burp duty, because, well, she had equipment Jake didn't have for the feeding part of this new adventure. But burp time was Daddy time. Just a man and his son, the way it should be.

With Baby Ray tucked into his arm like a football, they roamed the hallway, circled once through the living room, then headed out the back door into a humid August night. Stars glittered down from an inky black sky and the moon shed silvery light on the white vinyl fencing Jake had installed around the backyard. Crickets chirped and some neighbor's dog barked a block away. Which reminded Jake...

He now knew a kennel for Alex's dogs, Whisper and Smoke, had once stood in the corner of hisbackyard. The previous owner had torn it out and replaced it with—nothing. Whoever they were, they must've loved dirt because before

Jake had this backyard re-sodded, there'd been nothing but ruts, weeds, and dust.

The disgust on Alex's face when he'd heard how much work, time, and money had gone into restoring this little *cracker box*, as he'd called it, was heartwarming. He'd gotten uncharacteristically chatty for a minute there. Talked about fighting a wisteria vine that choked the wooden swing he'd built for Kelsey every spring. Told Jake an oak tree had once stood guard over the dog kennel, and how it shaded the entire yard when the afternoon sun got high in summer. Shared a couple stories about that empty space in the basement where his woodworking shop once turned out toys for tots at Christmas. Told Jake how Kelsey couldn't handle a sheet of sandpaper, much less a nine-millimeter pistol when he'd first met her.

"Poor thing was scared of guns back then," he'd said. "You ever need a hand installing a security system or building a doghouse, you let me know."

Somehow that sounded like an order. Jake agreed, but that was the moment Alex left him standing on his back porch alone. Apparently the guy had radar when it came to his wife. He was back inside the house before Jake knew what happened. But it was okay. All that guy-chat had opened Jake's eyes to the real Alex. He wasn't so different than other married men. Everything he did, he did for Kelsey, his country, or the people on his team.

Baby Ray squirmed so Jake snuggled him against his chest, humming low and soft, but nothing operatic. Not any more. That day was in his compulsive past where it belonged.

"Wanna swing, little guy?" he asked as he dropped his butt to the new cedar swing he'd bought Lacy, but hadn't had the chance to show her yet. Oddly, he'd placed it at precisely where the swing Alex had made for Kelsey had once stood. Talk about weird. Tiny green sprouts were breaking through the cracks in the concrete. Apparently that wisteria vine was making a comeback.

Weirder still, Jake looked forward to fighting the pesky vine almost as much as he looked forward to mowing his lawn and raking his leaves from the sugar maple soon to be planted by the kennel he still needed to build. This tiny house needed a couple diligent trees standing guard over it, maybe an English walnut or two in the front yard. what was more, Jake looked forward to shoveling snow off his front walk in the winter, and coming into the bright, warm heart of his home after a hard day's work, hugging his wife and his little boy. Mostly of—*coming*—with that unexpected angel sleeping in his bed. *God, life is good.*

Easing Baby Ray upright to his shoulder, Jake cupped his son's head extra carefully. Sure enough, the little guy let out a man-sized burp to be proud of. "Way to go," Jake praised. "Wanna do it again?"

Easing two fingers up the little guy's spine, he coaxed another wiggle and a smaller burp out. Nothing extraordinary but still. "That's my boy," Jake said, his heart filled with pride for the child in his arms. "Wait till I tell Mom what a good job you did."

Baby Ray settled his cheek into the crook of Jake's neck and let out a tiny sigh of contentment. And there they sat, father and son rocking in *their* backyard, surrounded by *their* fence, and living in *their* very own—*home*. The word meant everything to Jake now that he'd finally gotten his head straight. Well, mostly straight.

He didn't time warp like he once did because he knew how to anchor himself to reality now, as in Lacy, and that went a long way to solving most of his other issues. He'd gotten the counseling he'd needed, and he'd reunited with his family. Mom and Dad both cried like babies when he'd shown up in Little Rock with a pregnant wife, but Grandpa Elias damned near crushed the life out of him, he'd hugged Jake so hard. Hugged him like he wasn't a former Marine but that hard-headed ten-year-old kid who needed to remember who was boss again, and just who loved him best. The old coot made Jake cry. Even now.

He ran a quick finger under his eye, not ashamed of his tears. "Thing is, Baby Ray, tears need to come out else they'll mess up your head," he whispered. "They weren't meant for storage, no sir. They're a gift to wash out the heart, so you cry all you want. 'Course, not in front of the other guys and not when Mom's sleeping, okay? She needs her rest right now, but you just give me the word, and we'll come out for another swing if you need to let loose. Don't ever be ashamed to have a heart, son. That's what makes this country great, men and women with hearts like your grandpas' hearts. Like your Mom's."

Baby Ray offered a tiny sigh of agreement, and that was enough for Jake. He stretched his long legs and rocked that wooden swing, loving the quiet creak of complaint between the chain and the S-hook overhead. *Might need a drop of oil for that.* Loving the stars in the sky and the woman tucked in his bed. Loving just about everything at the moment. Life couldn't get more perfect than this.

Oh, wait. Yes, it could get maybe just a teensy bit more perfect. Jake rubbed his lips over Baby Ray's downy head and drew in the powdery scent of his firstborn. Pressing a fatherly kiss to his boy's dark hair, he whispered the first of many father and son conspiracies. "Don't tell Mommy yet, but Harley's giving us a puppy. His name's Blade and you're gonna love him."

The End

About the Author

Irish Winters is an award winning, Amazon best-selling author who, when she isn't writing, dabbles in poetry, grandchildren, and rarely (as in extremely rarely) the kitchen. More prone to be outdoors than in, she grew up the quintessential tomboy on a dairy farm in rural Wisconsin, spent her teenage years in the Pacific Northwest, but calls the Wasatch Mountains of Northern Utah, home. For now.

She believes in making every day count for something, and follows the wise admonition of her mother to, "Look out the window and see something!"

Connect with Irish online:
On Facebook: https://www.facebook.com/author.irishwinters
On Twitter: https://twitter.com/irishwinters1
Or at www. IrishWinters.com